Stars
In Our Window

Stars
In Our Window
An American Family In Wartime

A Novel By
F. Mark Granato

F. Mark Granato
fmgranato@aol.com
Fmarkgranato.com
www.facebook.com at Author F. Mark Granato

Stars
In Our Window

An American Family In Wartime

A Novel by

F. Mark Granato

Also by F. Mark Granato

Titanic: The Final Voyage

Beneath His Wings:
The Plot to Murder Lindbergh

Of Winds and Rage

Finding David

The Barn Find

Out of Reach:
The Day Hartford Hospital Burned

UNLEASHED

This Boy

This story is dedicated to my wife,
whose boundless love of family, home and life
are reflected in every word of this book—
stories handed down through the years
that are now cherished memories.

We'll Meet Again

Let's say goodbye with a smile, dear
Just for a while, dear, we must part
Don't let this parting upset you
I'll not forget you, sweetheart

We'll meet again
Don't know where
Don't know when
But I know we'll meet again
Some sunny day

Keep smiling through
Just like you always do
'Till the blue skies chase
Those dark clouds far away

And I will just say hello
To the folks that you know
Tell them you won't be long
They'll be happy to know
That, as I saw you go
You were singing this song

We'll meet again
Don't know where
Don't know when
But I know we'll meet again
Some sunny day

Recorded by: Benny Goodman, 1942
Written by: © Hughie Charles and Ross Parker

Authors Note

Journalist Tom Brokaw called those Americans who grew up during the Depression and then faced the horrors of global war, the "Greatest Generation." Only history will prove his assertion, but there is no doubt of the "greatness" of the generation that lived for so many years with so little — and then accepted the need to give so much.

This is the story of one small-town family among millions in America who fought two wars from 1942 to the end of 1945: one on the battlefields of North Africa, Europe and in the Pacific, the other on the home front. They gave up their boys to the harsh realities of war while at the same time sacrificing the few luxuries of life that the poor and middle class could afford. A set of tires, a gallon of gas, a pair of nylons, a stick of butter or a pound of meat. The list of rationed commodities was thorough beyond logic at times, but was largely adhered to without question or supervision. Anything that was required to defeat the enemy and support our boys in uniform was embraced in a spirit of patriotism America had perhaps never seen before and may never experience again.

It is also the story of how Americans came to embrace a new sociological order — at least for a time. Jobs occupied by men, vacated as they left for war, were filled by women. Whites worked side by side with blacks in occupations that had once been completely segregated. Churches of all denominations were filled with people praying for the common dreams of peace, the safety of loved ones, or the souls of those lost.

And it is the story of an entire nation that lived in terror and anxiety for four long years, and whose people shed a trillion tears. People like the Hughes' of Wethersfield, Connecticut, one of the millions who hung Blue Star Banners in their windows.

F. Mark Granato
January 17, 2018

One
~~~ ℘ ~~~

July 4th, 2001

The night air dripped with stifling humidity that had been building since daybreak in central Connecticut, and it seemed as if a blanket of steaming heat had stalled over my small hometown of Wethersfield. It had been a bright, cloudless summer day with a golden morning sun that broke searing hot at dawn and never cooled.

But despite the relentless temperature the evening sky was filled with the traditional celebration demanded by the Fourth of July: the pageantry of brilliantly colored fireworks shooting across the heavens, the bursts, crackles, pops and whistles of neighborhood firecrackers, and in my backyard, gales of laughter.

To my delight, the source of the latter was the 88-year-old guest of honor of our July Fourth party, my adored Aunt Catherine who was just warming up, regaling generations of her extended family with decades of family lore.

Since early afternoon, screams of happy play had filled the backyard as my two boys and a dozen or so cousins spent hours in the pool, oblivious to their skin reddening under the scorching sun. And even after stuffing themselves with hot dogs smothered in mustard, potato salad, watermelon, ice cream and gallons of iced lemonade, they cannonballed right back into the water, as happy and carefree as kids on summer school break had every right to be.

It had been the perfect family gathering on this Independence Day, one long overdue. Most of my cousins and I had buried parents over the last several years and our gatherings since had been joyless, somber affairs. Now, of my father's 12 siblings — seven brothers and five sisters — only two of my aunts remained and only one was healthy enough to join us today with the children and grandchildren of one of Wethersfield's oldest and certainly largest families, the Hughes'.

Chilled beer and conversation flowed with ease all afternoon and into the night. Most of the chat was about childhood memories of grand family gatherings with our parents, aunts and uncles and cousins and how we had played and schooled together. Some of them had been my best friends growing up, and still were.

I was quietly pleased to see that everyone had spontaneously spent some time with my elderly aunt, who for reasons never explained to any of us was known as "Ka." She was the third child born of the 13 Hughes' but had outlasted all but her sister Beverly, the youngest of the brood. But even at nearly 88 years, Ka still had the spark of a wildcat in her eyes and a slightly wicked grin that told you she was always up for a night of dancing on the town if only a handsome beau would ask. She always seemed to have a smile on her face and affection in her heart, but I knew there was a touch of sorrow in her too, having buried two husbands she had loved dearly.

But it was her dyed, silver-blue hair, always perfectly coiffured, and brightly painted manicured nails that gave away a hint of the high-spirited personality still burning within her soul. And after a glass of wine or two her stories of growing up in a small house shared by 15 people on a farm on nearby Highland Street confirmed she had been no angel on her life's journey to senior citizenship.

I had always delighted in listening to her reveal long held family secrets and mysteries, most of all those that had to do with my father, her little brother, whom Catherine had particularly adored. Nearly ten years had separated them at birth, a whole decade at a time when the world was simple yet exploding with change.

The 13 children had suffered the devastating loss of their beloved mother, Catherine Scanlon Hughes after a long illness on Christmas Eve in 1933 when my father was just a boy of nine. Although her mother's death was a shattering blow, at 19, Catherine found the strength to become the family's matriarch. She had once shared with me that the worst memory of her life was the sight of her brothers and sisters all crowding around her mother's deathbed, each frantic to touch her as she faded. They wept and clutched each other in anguish while their father sat quietly in the corner of the bedroom he had shared with his wife, his head buried in his hands, completely overwhelmed by grief.

Intuitively, Catherine had realized the young brood would need a loving hand to tend to their needs and a strong shoulder for her broken-hearted father

3

who'd taken to drink. Now, in her later years she was looked upon as the family's grand dame. Some of my favorite holiday memories included her joining us for Christmas or Thanksgiving dinner, her brother, my beloved father, beaming at her presence.

Shy, but delightfully mirthful and very much like Aunt Ka, Richard "Speck" Hughes had passed nearly 25 years before, succumbing to cancer at just 57 years old. I had loved him so dearly and never did come to terms with his loss, often longing to sit with him again; there was so much of his life that I knew practically nothing about. And now as I approached my own mid life, knowing more about his history became somewhat urgent. In fact, knowing more about all of my uncles and aunts who had passed was becoming an itch I couldn't scratch. I knew my closest cousins shared the same curiosity, but like me had lost the opportunity to ask the source. I had learned, as they had, that conversations with cemetery gravestones were tearfully one sided and questions hung in the air unanswered.

I could tell that Aunt Ka was reveling in the doting attention her nephews and nieces of all generations were giving her, but especially the little ones who naturally gravitated to her gentle smile and soft touch. I knew that within her memories lay the answers to so many of our questions. Would there ever be an opportunity to probe those recollections again? The simple reality was that at 88 years of age, every day was a gift. I shuddered at the thought of losing her, and selfishly, all she knew.

I wandered into the kitchen under the pretext of making some more iced tea but stopped and stared out the window at her sitting on the patio. In the background, the kids were lighting off a frightening array of fireworks that my husband had driven all the

4

way to Massachusetts to buy just for the occasion. Abruptly, a Roman Candle burst well above Ka's silver-blue coiffure, and the shower of red, green, yellow, blue and gold sparklers glowed on her face. The embers slowly died and drifted as minute particles of ash to the ground. The metaphor was not lost on me.

Impulse struck. I had to ask her.

Now.

I ran to my bedroom, a sudden idea coming to mind. It was just the thing to get her thinking — and most preciously — talking about her siblings, my father included. I opened the drawer to my nightstand and found the envelope that was never far from my heart. I could already feel my eyes getting wet at the thought of the contents.

I stopped in the kitchen and grabbed a handful of little cordial classes and a bottle of Limoncello that had been in the freezer all day and rejoined the party.

I set the bottle and glasses down on the patio table next to Ka and pulled up a chair to sit closer to her. She looked up at me, surprised but obviously delighted.

"For me?" she laughed. "But it's not even my birthday!"

"No, I just wanted to tell you how happy I am that you came today, Aunt Ka," I said, "and I wanted to show you something I found recently in a box of old letters belonging to my father."

"Oh, Bobbie," she said, bringing one of her thin hands to her chest, knowing that whatever I had for her would be emotional for both of us. I poured shots of the sweet lemon-laced liquor into the glasses and saved the last two for us. I handed one to her then showed her the envelope.

5

Her eyes went to it and immediately I noticed a tremor in her hand. She recognized it, even despite the awkward scribbling on the yellowed paper.

"That's a letter to me from Speck, from your Dad," she said without hesitation. "How did you..."

"I found it upstairs in a box of my father's 'treasures.'" I responded. "I don't know why he had it, but it was with his war diary and a few other letters he had written or received. I've spent hours poring over them but it's all a bit confusing..."

"They were confusing times, Bobbie, I can tell you. I wish your Aunt Bobbie, and Dot and Flossie and..." she stopped. It was hard to say all their names without being overwhelmed by sadness. "They could put all the pieces together for you."

"Do you remember this letter, Ka? "I asked. "He wrote it to you, I think it was after the war, but I can't be sure."

She studied it for a moment, squinting at my father's awful left-handed cursive, and then a smile came to her face. I looked around. My sister and her husband and some of my cousins had gathered closer. They could smell a story telling session brewing.

"Why... this is just your father writing to tell us he was nearly home after his long trip from Hawaii," she said upon reading the contents, "the last place he was stationed during the war."

"Hawaii?" I blurted out in surprise.

"Oh, yes, he was at Wheeler Field after it was rebuilt after the Japanese bombed it during the attack on Pearl Harbor. That's where he was going to be shipped out to the..." She suddenly stopped and looked out over the backyard, smiling at the little ones playing in the shallow end of the pool. "Where they were all headed. To Japan. For the final battle."

6

"To Japan?" I repeated in confusion. "What do you mean, all of them?"

I noticed a tear on her cheek. I had touched a nerve somehow.

"It was a scary time, Bobbie, let me tell you."

"When Ka, when are you talking about? There's no date on the envelope."

"That letter was probably written in late 1945, after the war. But the scary times all began on December 7, 1941... when the bombs fell and the world changed... and they didn't end until late 1945," she answered me.

I stared at her, wanting more.

"We held our breath every day waiting for all of them," she said. "Your father and your Uncles Jim, John, Phil, Peachy, Jigs and Dot's husband, Ed... every day we waited with dread for a car to pull up in front of the house or for a telegram.

"It was like walking on glass for four years."

She abruptly lifted the Limoncello to her lips, toasted silently, and downed it in a single swallow. I noticed her eyes had become watery.

She sighed, as if thinking about something, then suddenly asked the strangest question.

"Do any of you know what my favorite holiday is?" she asked. "What day do you think was most important to my brothers and sisters — your moms and dads and uncles and aunts?"

"Christmas!" my 19-year-old college student son Jack piped in, not unexpectedly. I sometimes thought he still believed in Santa Claus because he loved Christmas so much.

"Thanksgiving!" his younger brother Jay shouted almost simultaneously.

"No, not Christmas or Thanksgiving, boys... believe me you couldn't guess in a million years. Because

7

it was a secret all 13 of us shared and kept to ourselves." She said it mischievously but then paused and thought for a moment. "You know, it was actually 14, because there was my father too. Pa." She turned to me. "He was your grandfather, Bobbie, I don't know if you remember him. You were just a little girl when he died. He knew the secret, too." The sparkle in her eye had never been brighter.

"I remember him, Ka," I said. "He was tall and had a moustache and raised boxer puppies. My father used to bring me to visit with him all the time and he'd let me into the pen, where he always seemed to have a litter of puppies, so I could play with them." The memory was so clear I was startled by it.

"So what holiday is it?" Jack asked, determined to know what could possibly outrank Christmas.

Aunt Ka laughed aloud.

"You're asking me to break a sacred covenant," she said, smiling.

There was complete silence and then a dozen voices demanded that she fess up.

It was my turn to laugh. She was having a good time at our expense.

"Well, all right, if you insist," she responded, handing me her cordial glass to be refilled. "I suppose there's no one left to give me hell about it." Just as quickly she covered her mouth.

"I'm so sorry," she apologized. "The young ones shouldn't hear such language."

"You're forgiven, Aunt Ka. Now spill the beans," I demanded, handing her a fresh Limoncello.

"There's a long story that goes along with it," she said.

"We've got no place to be, Aunt Ka," my sister Kathy responded. "The night is young."

8

"And the bottle is still half full," I laughed.

"Ok," Catherine said, preparing to reveal her secret.

You could have heard a pin drop. Even the Cicada's were cooperating.

"My favorite holiday is what my brothers and sisters called… 'The Telegram Day.'"

The Cicada's took over again.

"The what?" my youngest son Jay asked.

"Yes, 'The Telegram Day.' April 3, 1945. Believe me if you want. It's what we called it. It was to commemorate the most important day in all our lives."

"You mean you put it right up there with Christmas and Thanksgiving… even the Fourth of July?" Jack probed.

"Oh, it was much more important to us than any of those days. So much more…" she responded distantly.

She took a sip of the liquor, then downed the rest of the glass. Her eyes closed and I could tell that her mind had wandered off to another time, another place.

"Tell us, Aunt Catherine," I asked. "Please? It would mean so much… to all of us."

She sighed.

"It's not easy to tell. We were very afraid. All of us," she admitted. Another tear rolled down her wrinkled face. I gave her a hanky.

She looked at the glass in her hand.

"One more for the road?" she smiled at me.

Catherine began as I poured.

"Well, it all began on a Sunday…" She hesitated, then stopped, beginning anew.

"No, that's not right, it began much earlier than that," she reconsidered. "You see, there were so many of us, we took care of each other."

She shook her head.

9

"It was even more than that. We cared about each other, too. And that's what made that Sunday so important.

"Actually, so terrifying."

She paused again, this time taking only a small sip of her drink, and then began.

"The day was so beautiful. Cold, but clear. Most of the family was in the living room after Sunday dinner listening to a football game. I think it was the Brooklyn Dodgers and the New York Giants…"

Jack interrupted her again. "Aunt Ka, the Dodgers were a Brooklyn baseball team," he said, more than a little confident of his baseball trivia.

Her eyes swung defiantly to his.

"In 1941 there was a Brooklyn Dodgers baseball team and a Brooklyn Dodgers football team," she responded confidently. "Look it up, college boy. I believe the Dodgers beat the New York Giants that day."

"But…" Jack began.

"But nothing," she smiled at him. " Can I go on now?" I was reassured. There was nothing wrong with her memory

"Sorry, Aunt Ka," Jack laughed. "Please do."

She sipped from her glass again," and sighed in satisfaction.

"As I was saying… it was a Sunday afternoon, we were listening to the game when there was a news bulletin… about 2:30, I think…"

10

Two

~~~ ⚭ ~~~

December 7th, 1941

It wasn't the sudden hammering of anti-aircraft shells punching black holes in the azure blue, early morning Oahu sky, or even the shockingly shrill call to "Battle Stations" screeching from stem to stern that awoke him in his bunk. Nor was it the angry howl of enemy bombers diving from thousands of feet above, a noise that grew into a terrifying scream just before they released deadly, armor-piercing bombs into his ship. That wasn't the uproar that roused him from the comfort of sleep aboard the gently rocking floating goliath at its berth in Pearl Harbor. Those were the sounds he would hear in a few moments — acts of war that would send him on a desperate, unwinnable race from the steel bowels of the battleship *USS Arizona* to his gun station and the cool sea breeze that blew across its bow.

11

No. What woke 26-year-old Ensign Monty Whitehead Jr. was something far less ominous.

It was the sound of the 21 members of the ship's band, sharply arranged in two rows on the fantail to play the National Anthem as it did every morning at exactly 0800 hours, abruptly dropping their polished brass instruments to the deck. Below, those sailors still stirring in their bunks listened in confusion to the clatter and then the pounding steps of men rushing forward toward the bow.

Of the 1,500 men aboard the Arizona, only a few knew that in the event of an attack the band members were assigned to pass ammunition from the ship's magazine to the number one main gun turret several decks above. Whitehead was one. He leapt from his bunk, slipped into his untied shoes and raced toward his own battle station with the confidence that only a real attack would prompt the musicians to abandon their precious horns. Adrenalin pumped through the veins of the Naval Academy graduate who had not yet tasted battle.

An instant later, even as Whitehead raced through the ship and frantically climbed steel ladders to the main deck, the calm Sunday morning peace was shattered by a message reverberating from the ships' loudspeakers at 0758 hours: "Air raid, Pearl Harbor. This is not a drill."

He heard the first blasts of anti-aircraft fire from a ship some distance away. Quickly, more guns from more ships were blasting away at the sky suddenly full of enemy bombers, torpedo planes and fighters who had taken aim at the US Navy's Pacific Fleet in Oahu, Hawaii. Nearly every vessel of the Pacific Fleet — 97 in all — was berthed at Pearl on this morning. Only the Fleet's three mighty aircraft carriers were at sea. Below

12

decks, Whitehead could not be aware that the crimson red Rising Sun painted on the wings of the attacking airplanes meant the enemy was the Japanese.

Then came the sound of bombs and torpedoes exploding all over the harbor, many having found their targets in the first wave of the attack. Whitehead and hundreds of other sailors now rushing to their battle stations were suddenly rocked as a 1,760-pound bomb pierced through the *Arizona*'s stern. It was the first of four direct hits the 39,000-ton battleship would receive before it could fire any of its eight, 25 caliber five-inch guns in self-defense.

At 0806 hours, the fourth bomb, dropped by pilot Tadashi Kusumi from a high-altitude "Kate" bomber off the Japanese aircraft carrier *Kaga*, released his deadly load from low altitude and pulled up over the *Arizona* at the last second. He turned his head in the cramped cockpit of his aircraft and watched the bomb strike the battleship between the starboard turrets of its number one and number two guns. Kusumi was disappointed when only a minor explosion occurred.

But seven seconds later, still climbing for altitude to escape the reaches of anti-aircraft fire, the young Japanese pilot's bomber was rocked by a concussive wave rising from a massive explosion beneath him. The bomb had hit home after all.

The huge converted artillery shell that Kusumi dropped on the defenseless *Arizona* had penetrated the ship's armored deck near its ammunition magazines. It took several seconds for the initial explosion to spark black powder stored in the magazine. But then, in a fraction of an instant, 180,000 gallons of aviation fuel ignited and 500 tons of gunpowder and more than a million pounds of munitions detonated, combining to create a cataclysmic rush of energy that blew out the

13

sides of the bow and crushed the internal structure of the forward end of the ship. The forward gun turrets, conning tower, foremast and funnel collapsed into the void created by the explosion and tore the great steel ship in two.

Inside, those sailors who weren't instantly incinerated by the explosion were drowned as the ship self destructed, or burned to death by fires that burned for two days.

Ensign Monty Whitehead, continuing his desperate climb towards the light above felt the shock of the fourth bomb as it hit the forward deck. In the split second he had to comprehend that he was about to die, before his eyes flashed a vision of his parents waiting at the door for him at their small house on Clearfield Drive in the tiny New England town of Wethersfield, Connecticut, his hometown. Then the stairs beneath his feet gave way and an all-consuming fireball was upon him.

In the very first moments of WWII, Ensign Whitehead became one of its first casualties.

And the town of Wethersfield had earned its first Gold Star.

*   *   *

The slightly built young man waved a golf club back and forth high over his head to attract his younger brother's attention. Despite the frigid December air he wore only a sleeveless brown argyle sweater over a well-worn blue flannel shirt. A cigarette dangled from his lips and the tobacco smoke and condensation coming from his breath in the cold mixed into a cloud that formed around his head. From a distance, he appeared to be headless to his brother who laughed out loud at the lunatic waving at him.

"Hey, Jiggs, watch this..." 20-year-old Speck yelled to his sibling as he carefully lined up a well-used, wooden-shaft wedge with a yellowed golf ball at his feet. It was one they had fished out of the ponds that dotted the golf course that neighbored their fathers' seven-room farmhouse on Highland Street. The brothers spent their summers after work harvesting the errant shots of duffers into the water holes of the Wethersfield Country Club. The golfers bought the balls back from the boys. For Speck, the couple of hours of effort each afternoon after his shift at Capitol City Machine Company, where he worked as a machine repairman, put a few bucks in his pocket and gas in his 1932 Chevy.

Speck waved the cloud of fog away, ditching the cigarette with a practiced flick of his thumb and forefinger.

"Ok, listen," he yelled to his brother. "Two bits... over the barn and on to the fairway." He nodded at the target in their back yard, more than 75 yards away.

"Bullshit," Jiggs mumbled under his breath, knowing his brother was a lefty and the club he held was right-handed. Speck ignored him and looked up at the old barn several times, gauging the distance. Then, with an effortless motion that suggested he played a lot of golf, the thin young man expertly swung through the ball, lofting it well over the roof of the sagging barn and dropped it precisely on to the 16th fairway of the golf course. He laughed and shook his head as he patted down the slight divot he'd made with the head of his club. It was just too easy for him.

"No way," Jiggs yelled in disbelief. The ball had travelled a good 100 yards from their front lawn despite

15

the fact that his brother had hit it cross-handed and nearly never played the game.

"Hey, you should see what I could do with the right club!" Speck kidded his hotheaded younger brother who'd just lost the quarter bet. He might have been thin, but he was a scrappy kid, a lot tougher than his shy smile revealed. Jiggs on the other hand was going to be a moose when he grew into manhood.

"C'mon," Jiggs hollered. "Let's go get the ball and see if you can drive the pond on 16. Double or nothing," he dared.

The five years that separated the two brothers from birth was nearly a lifetime. Their personalities were as different as different could be, yet they were the closest of all their siblings. Speck, a handsome, soft-spoken young man with wavy hair didn't say much unless he thought it needed saying. Jiggs was the exact opposite, prone to using his fists first and asking questions later. He was a bit on the loud, wild side and his outsized body made him fearless. Being the youngest brother of the 13 Hughes kids didn't require him to spend much time worrying about defending his siblings, no matter the issue. But whenever there was a confrontation involving any of them, you could depend on Jiggs to be standing at the ready with fists clenched.

"Nah," Speck answered him.

"Chicken?" Jiggs tried to antagonize him.

"No, you chump. Because I don't want to get all sweaty," Speck yelled back. "I gotta pick up Elvira later when she gets off work at Lincoln Dairy."

A few orphaned leaves hung limply from the mostly stripped branches of the giant Elm tree in the front yard of the house. Winter was near and the greyness of the afternoon light was a perfect backdrop for fallen, dried leaves that were darting through the air as Jiggs slowly walked back to his brother on the windy Sunday afternoon. In another month there'd be hard snow pack on the ground and there wouldn't be much use for golf clubs. So the two brothers were sucking up as much of the outdoors before the typically harsh New England weather arrived within the next couple of weeks.

"Elvira," Jiggs said, intentionally pronouncing the name with a long "I". "Geez, Speck, you sure are sweet on that Italian beauty. I'm surprised her father even let you in her house. The 'wops' don't like anybody but their own kind…"

"Knock it off, Jiggs," Speck shot back without hesitation, atypically sharp in his response. "She's no wop, and yah, I like her. Her parents like me too, if you can believe it."

Jiggs was smart enough to back off. "Well, good luck with that, nothing personal brother…"

Speck threw the golf ball at his younger brother from close range and it bounced off the boy's barrel chest. They both laughed.

"Hey, man, I said I was sorry, " Jiggs repeated. "The hell with this, I'm cold. Let's go see if there's any more of Ka's pumpkin pie left. That was good, I already had two slices."

Yah," Speck answered sarcastically, "you look like you need it."

Before Jiggs could defend himself, the front screen door of the house suddenly swung open with their brother Phil on the end of it. Even from a distance they could tell it was Phil because of the thick horned-rim glasses he wore. He'd suffered from poor vision since he was a young child. The glasses had earned him the nickname "Doc" in the schoolyard. It stuck.

17

"Hey, you two, c'mon in here, quick, there's something you better hear," Phil hollered out to them. There was urgency in his voice.

"Bad?" Jiggs asked, a frown drawing his heavy eyebrows low over his eyes. It was a look that he naturally assumed when there was trouble.

"Yah..." Phil answered, "real bad."

Jiggs dropped the golf ball and the two brothers raced to the house. Speck would one day remember it as the last few steps of his boyhood.

Inside, the family was gathered around the big Westinghouse radio that sat on a table near the fireplace in the living room. They had been listening to the Brooklyn Dodgers game against the New York Giants after the family Sunday dinner. A news bulletin had abruptly interrupted the coverage of the game.

Speck scanned the packed room, barely large enough to absorb the family. It was normal for everyone to be home on Sunday afternoon for dinner, but unusual for the whole family to be packed around the radio. The girls would typically be chatting in the kitchen while their brothers and husbands listened to a ball game.

"What's going on?" Speck asked in alarm. No one answered. The crowded room was thick with cigarette smoke.

"Just listen. They'll broadcast it again in a minute, I'm sure," Jim said, fiddling with the radio dials.

"Broadcast what?" Jiggs asked. "What's happened?"

"Shh," his sister Dot hushed him. "Listen."

Dot, the oldest of the girls at 31 was holding the arm of her husband Ed Ames and clutching a handkerchief. She was looking into Ed's eyes for some reassurance, but he had little to offer. Their eight-year old son Skip was staring at his father too, his own eyes

18

wide with confusion. Big brother Jim, 32 and a 6'5"
giant of a man nicknamed "Bull", impatiently fiddled
with the radio, trying to tune in NBC for more news. His
siblings were in various states of agitation.

Henry, 30, held his wife Lee's hand in silence as
he listened to the news.

Ray, a year younger, huddled with his wife Rita
and their four-year old son, Garret, who sat quietly on
his father's lap, sensing his worry. Phil, 19, stood next to
Georgia, his bride of a year. His hand rested on her
shoulder and she held it. Their infant son Phillip Jr. was
sound asleep on his mother's lap, oblivious to the
tension in the room.

Catherine, a striking brunette at 28, walked back
and forth from the living room to the kitchen finishing
up the dinner dishes with her year younger sister Flossie.
Married less than a year to her husband Eric Anderson,
Catherine was more interested in watching his reaction
than listening to the news. She knew what he was
thinking and her heart was already breaking.

Flossie stood leaning against the kitchen door
casing, absent-mindedly rubbing a terry cloth towel over
a dinner plate. Her wide eyes moved furtively back and
forth between her husband Alphonse and their year old
son, Jimmy, who was sleeping on his shoulder, and her
brother Jim, still fussing with the radio.

"Again, we interrupt this program to bring you
an urgent bulletin just coming into our newsrooms this
minute," the radio announcer barked. "Our NBC
affiliate KGU radio in Honolulu, Hawaii is reporting that
the Japanese have attacked the United States Naval and
Air facilities at Pearl Harbor. In fact we have just now
established a direct line with a reporter in Honolulu with
live coverage of the attack."

"Geez," Jiggs muttered, his eyes wide.

"I know a boy who's stationed at Pearl Harbor," Flossie mumbled out loud. "He was in my high school class. Now he's in the Navy, on some big battleship I think." No one gave her any attention until she added a thought.

"He's so young. I hope he's safe."

Suddenly the words being reported over the radio became personal for the Hughes family.

A moment of silence was followed by seconds of excruciating static. Jim impatiently reached for the tuning knob but his younger brothers John and Peachy simultaneously yelled for him to stop.

"Jesus, Jim, you'll twist the knob off," Peachy admonished him with a nervous laugh, trying to ease the tension in the room. He was only weeks away from his 22nd birthday, and up until this moment, the only worry in his life was his golf handicap.

"Yah, Bull. Peachy's right. It's gonna be the same whichever direction you turn that dial. Be patient," John chimed in, drawing from the cigarette hanging from his lips. On the outside, John, the smallest and perhaps gentlest of the brothers, appeared calm as he listened to the news. Inside, the young man who would celebrate his 23rd birthday the next day was filled with dread.

Suddenly, the high-pitched voice of a reporter, his words filled with the excitement of the moment, burst through the static.

"*1,2,3,4... hello NBC, hello, New York?*" the reporter asked for confirmation that he had a line.

"*Yes, this is New York, Honolulu, go on,*" NBC in New York responded.

"*This is KGU Radio in Honolulu, Hawaii,*" the reporter began. "*I am speaking from the roof of the Advertiser Publishing Company Building. We have witnessed this*

20

morning in the distant view a brief full battle of Pearl Harbor and the severe bombing of Pearl Harbor by enemy planes, undoubtedly Japanese. The city of Honolulu has also been attacked and considerable damage done. This battle has been going on for nearly three hours. One of the bombs was dropped within 50 feet of KGU tower. It is no joke. It is a real war. The public of Honolulu has been advised to keep in their homes and away from the Army and Navy. There has been serious fighting going on in the air and in the sea. The heavy shooting seems to be..." The signal was temporarily lost. "*...a little interruption. We cannot estimate just how much damage has been done, but it has been a very severe attack. The Navy and Army appear now to have the air and the sea under control.*"

The living room was filled with gasps as the Hughes family listened to the shocking news. Jim continued to fiddle with the radio, looking for updates. The scene was being repeated all over Wethersfield; in fact, all over the country Americans sat and listened mostly in stunned silence. It was a moment they would all remember: the instant their lives changed.

"Somebody better wake up Pa, he's going to be upset at having missed this," blond, petite 17-year-old Bobbie said nervously. Beverly, pretty and innocent and the youngest of the family at 13, was sitting on the arm of the easy chair occupied by Henry Thomas Hughes, patriarch of the huge clan. She gently squeezed the hand of the widowed father of 13 children who'd been dead asleep since shortly after Sunday dinner. In his other hand was a half-empty glass of whiskey, resting precariously in his lap. It was not an unusual way for Henry Sr. to spend his Sunday afternoons.

He had always had a penchant for drink, but since the death of his cherished wife Catherine eight years before it had become his constant companion. At 52 years of age, Henry looked to be a much older man,

21

gaunt and grey, much of his spirit gone. By day he was a deputy sheriff who served court papers and complaints to town residents and businesses, a job he disliked and that only deepened his depression. He was also Captain of the Wethersfield Volunteer Fire Department's Company #2, a responsibility he had once relished. But he planned to retire from the department soon, his zest for the excitement of the fire service also greatly diminished. And never far from his mind was the accident...

"Pa, Pa, wake up. Something important is happening," Beverly said fretfully. "I think we're in a war." Hughes awoke with a start, the word "war" catching his ear.

"We interrupt this broadcast to bring you this important bulletin," a radio announcer for the Mutual Broadcasting Company blared. "Flash. Washington. The White House announces Japanese attack on Pearl Harbor. Stay tuned for further developments."

"Damn it," Jim cursed at the radio. "They just keep repeating the same thing. Gimme some details, for crying out loud," he muttered. " The entire Pacific Fleet is anchored at Pearl Harbor. There's no telling what kind of damage the Japanese did." He lit another cigarette and glared at the radio, willing it to tell him more.

Speck and Jiggs sat quietly on the floor near the fireplace. The warmth from the burning logs did little to take the anxious chill out of the air. Speck looked around again. The girls were really getting worked up. He looked at his watch. He figured his girlfriend Elvira would be all over him with worry when he picked her up from work in an hour.

Jim, a car salesman, had been paying close attention to the growing hostilities in Europe and the chess game Washington seemed to be playing with the Japanese throughout 1941. He was certain that the United States was going to get dragged into the war in Europe, eventually forced to come to the aid of Great Britain. It was a wonder Roosevelt had kept America out of the Nazi-Germany led hostilities to this point, he thought. Fully two years had passed since Hitler had treacherously invaded Poland to spark World War II, but thus far, the U.S. was only sending supplies and munitions to their European allies in England and France. This new development with the Japanese meant the country was going to get dragged into war on two fronts. And he knew that spelled trouble for him, and his brothers.

He looked around the room at each of them and quickly analyzed their situation. Right now, the Selective Service would only draft men between the age of 21 and 36. But he figured that would soon change; there had already been considerable debate about lowering the draft age to 18. For the moment, Phil was too young, but even if they did drop the age requirement, being married and having a baby might save him, at least for a while. Certainly his job wouldn't help him. He worked at Royal Typewriter as a machine operator. Ray and Henry Jr. both had kids too, but worked at Finn Manufacturing in Hartford producing military equipment. They stood a good chance of escaping the draft. John was a machinist at Sikorsky Aircraft in Stratford; that might give him a pass. But he knew his younger brother. There'd be no way John would stay home if any of his brothers served. The rest of them? Jiggs wouldn't be old enough to enlist for quite a while, no matter what the Selective Service decided, but the minute he was, there'd be no holding him back if war was still waging. For himself, Speck, Peachy and John, he figured their futures were predictable. He doubted any one of them would be home for Christmas next year. How long would it be after that, he wondered.

Jim sighed. It wasn't as if he would be leaving much excitement behind. He was bored. His day job was selling Plymouths at the Walter Meals dealership in East Harford. He was certain that was about to change. Then he felt a sudden cold on the back of his neck as the next obvious question hit him. He looked at the faces of his brothers.

There were eight of them. Three of them were certain to get called up if the bloody thing lasted more than a year. Maybe four. Five if it lasted long enough for Jiggs to become eligible. Six, if the need existed to draft men with dependents. In that case Phil would go, too. Then there were his two brother-in-laws. At least one would be drafted, maybe both.

What were the odds they'd all make it home?

The girls, or at least his older sisters, were way ahead of him in their fears and doubts. Dot, Flossie and Catherine were in tears, fearing the worst. Eric "Andy" Anderson, Catherine's husband of less than a year, stared quietly out the bay window facing Highland Street, sucking on his pipe. At 32, he was already wise enough to avoid his wife's anxious stare.

Phil, sitting on the arm of a chair next to Ray, removed his heavy glasses and rubbed his eyes. They were always red and fatigued. He wondered if the weakness would keep him out of the military, but also whether he'd want to be kept out. Given the chance to join up, he figured he'd go with his brothers.

The radio crackled on, but with little new information reporters were filling the airwaves with speculation. It would be days before the full tragedy of Pearl Harbor became known, but less then 24 hours for the President to declare that the United States was at war with Japan. For that matter, war would also be affirmed against Germany, as within days, Hitler would inexplicably declare war on America on the heels of the Japanese attack.

"Well, that's that, boys," Jim addressed his brothers. "Sure as hell, Roosevelt will declare war, probably as soon as tomorrow. You can bet he's going to use this excuse to bail out England, and France, too. So that means war on two oceans. They're gonna need a helluva lot of soldiers and sailors. Quickly."

No one responded, absorbing Jim's words. It was hard to argue his logic.

"Some of you guys may have options. The way I see it John, Phil, Ray and Henry might be able to dodge this thing. At least for a while. But me, Peachy and Speck... hell, the three of us might as well drive in to Hartford tomorrow and get in line at the Selective Service Office." He looked over at his younger brother John. "But I suspect you'll probably want to come along, too, John." His younger brother only smiled and nodded his head.

"It's only going to be a matter of who we sign with: Army, Marines, Navy, the Air Corps...what'll it be?" Jim concluded.

"Oh my God," Dot said out loud, and began to cry. It was the first time someone had actually said what they all were thinking.

Henry T. Hughes shifted uneasily in his chair, slowly emerging from the haze of alcohol. 'War', he thought uneasily. The word was so simple to say, so tragic to live. He remembered another conversation a long time ago that was painfully familiar. He closed his eyes and saw the face of his lovely Catherine on that morning in May 1915.

25

The flimsy newsprint tore in the angry clench of the tall, lanky man who gripped the edges of the Hartford Times with calloused hands and shook his head in seething frustration. He could barely contain himself.

Nearly the entire front page of the newspaper he held was filled with news of the sinking of the 44,000-ton British passenger steamship, the RMS Lusitania, a day before. The unarmed Cunard luxury liner had been sunk by the single torpedo of a German U-boat in the Irish Channel fired without so much as a warning and within sight of the safety of Queenstown. The great ship foundered in less than 18 minutes only seven miles from shore off the Old Head of Kinsale Lighthouse, dragging into the depths with her nearly 1,200 passengers, including 128 Americans. The world was aghast at the viciousness of the attack and condemnation for the barbaric act was universal.

The only other story on page one was a renewed cry for a US military draft by some members of congress concerned about America's readiness should the country become embroiled in the rapidly expanding European war.

"It's a bloody sin, I tell you," Henry Thomas Hughes said to his wife Catherine, already mother to three children in only their fourth year of marriage. Another was well on the way as she stirred the breakfast porridge for her growing brood. She absentmindedly held her other hand against her swollen belly, as if to guard the baby in her womb against the heat of the cast iron stove. She was only 24, a beautiful young woman with long brown hair and lovely blue eyes. She looked older. Her husband was hungry to grow their family but she was already tired from the strain of raising their children.

"Now what sin would that be, Mr. Hughes?" she asked, feigning interest above the din of their children crowded around a small kitchen table in the three family apartment on Zion Street in Hartford, all jabbering at the same time. Catherine had little time for idle chat.

"Here it is, my wee one's," she said cheerfully to them, carefully spooning portions into wooden bowls that her husband, a carpenter, had turned on a lathe himself.

"Blessed Mary, you'd think we were starving them," she laughed as the two oldest attacked their bowls with wooden spoons. She poured molasses over the porridge to sweeten it.

"I'll get to you in a minute, my darling Henry," she said to the youngest, tousling the wisp of hair atop his head as he sat in a wooden high chair also made by his father. Nearly every stick of furniture in the small apartment was handmade by Henry Thomas Hughes.

"It's a sin the bloody German's get away with it, I tell you Mrs. Hughes," Henry replied, oblivious to Catherine's efforts to feed their children. He didn't look away from the newspaper. "Yes, indeed, I tell you, if I was a younger man…"

With that, she turned to him, wiping her hands nervously on her apron. She'd been hearing such nonsense talk from other fearful mothers she met when she took the children to the park every afternoon. They're all the same, she thought to herself: more bravado than brains. What were they thinking? But she was careful to say her peace in the respectful tone of a loving wife.

"Speaking' of sins, Mr. Hughes," she chided him with just the slightest irritation in her voice, "it is just short of sin to think about leaving your children behind to fight someone else's war. Wouldn't you think now?"

Jim's booming voice stirred his father back to the present. The big man was pointing his fingers at his younger brothers.

"I'm telling ya, we go in to the Army recruiter in Hartford tomorrow morning together and enlist right away. Chances are they'll put us in the same outfit. Let's not wait for the draft to pick us off one by one.

27

Army infantry, that's the only way to go..." he argued to his brothers.

The rest of them weren't so sure, and those with wives knew they'd better measure their words.

"Hell, Jim, I dunno," Peachy responded. "Why don't we wait a bit..."

"Ah, I've no patience for waiting..." Jim interrupted his brother and waved him off in disgust. His anger was clouding his thinking.

"I have to agree," Henry Jr. started, but his father suddenly raised a hand, stopping him in mid sentence. When Henry Thomas Hughes spoke, they all listened.

"You know, Jim, a long time ago..." he began, the sound of his wife's voice ringing in his ears, "I heard such talk from a lot of young men who couldn't wait to go off to war." He took a sip from the whiskey in his glass. There was silence in the room.

"Every one of them saw some kind of romance in the idea of war," he continued. "I was ready to leave your mother and four of you... at least three of you were still in diapers. I was so filled with the need for vengeance and the idea of going off to fight that I was ready to turn my back on all of you. It was some kind of ego thing, I think, that made me and a lot of other men my age blind to the right choice."

"You didn't join up, Pop..." Phil said.

Henry let out a deep breath.

"No, I didn't."

He slowly scanned their faces, knowing they were all filled with different emotions.

"That's not to say I wouldn't have... if I needed to. If my country called," he added.

"I'm glad you didn't go and fight," Bobbie said, wiping tears off her cheeks with her fingertips.

28

"You can thank your blessed mother for making me see what the right choice was, Bobbie," he sighed. "She was always the one to see the right way. I was needed here. Not in France."

"But Pop, some of us don't have commitments like you did," Jim said softly, a bit confused by his father's message.

"I understand how you feel, Jim. And even with my responsibilities here I still live in regret for not being with those boys in the trenches. Some of them were my friends." He hesitated. "A bunch of them didn't come home."

He took a long pull from his glass, fighting back tears of his own. The memories were hard. He waited a moment to compose himself.

"This is all I'm going to say for the time being," Henry responded. Every eye in the room was on him as he spoke.

"Wait. Be patient. Don't be running off to enlist thinking it will make you a hero. If you must go at some point, I'll be the last man to get in your way. But don't jump the gun. Let's see what happens next. There will be plenty of time for making a decision..." he paused. "When heads are cooler and the right choice is clear."

No one spoke for several minutes. The radio crackled on with the same news until Dot asked her big brother to turn it off.

"There'll be nothing new for a while, Jim," she pleaded, sobbing as she spoke. All the girls were weeping, with the exception of Flossie. She remained in the doorway drying the same dish, lost in thought.

"I guess you're right, Dot," Jim responded and reached over to turn the Westinghouse off. He was resigned to waiting for more news that would ultimately

29

decide his future as well as what it would bring for his brothers.

The family gathering gradually broke up and the oldest left for their apartments in Wethersfield or Hartford. Speck, Jiggs, John, Peachy, Bobbie and Beverly still lived in the small farmhouse with their father. Henry had fallen back to sleep and the boys tuned the radio to the game again before wandering off in separate directions, each deep in thought. The girls went to the small bedroom they shared to do homework. The house was unusually quiet.

Henry dozed, but he was restless with anxiety. Catherine's image flittered across his eyes again, just out of reach. He remembered how cross she had been with him so many years ago when he had talked of going to war.

His young wife's voice had wavered as she finished, anger on the tip of her tongue at the thought of her husband leaving them to fight the Germans in France. Her long brown hair was already graying from the task of raising a growing family. But more children would follow since their marriage had been consecrated in the Roman Catholic Church. The Catholic's encouraged large families, although it did little to support them beyond spiritual guidance.

Henry was a diligent worker, a carpenter and cabinet maker whose hands could make wood sing, and that's what kept his family out of the breadlines well known to many of their neighbors. The well to do in Hartford's West End, which was sprinkled with their mansions high on hills overlooking the state's Capital city, kept him steadily employed and provided a paycheck that allowed them to live comfortably, though hardly care free.

The growing Hughes family lived in the Frog Hollow section of the city, so named after the marsh-like conditions in parts of that neighborhood, amidst a sea of Irish immigrants who mainly worked in the factories that lined both sides of Capitol Avenue. The factories depended on the Park River, which ran through Frog Hollow as a source of waterpower. It was a lovely part of the city of Hartford, with its three and six family houses in rows on streets lined with great Elm trees. Most Irishmen thought it was as close to heaven on earth as he'd ever have the right to be.

Henry had met Catherine by chance in Pope Park some five years before, when she had come to visit cousins in Hartford. She lived in Wethersfield, an adjoining town of fields and farms, most notable for its tree-lined Cove off the Connecticut River that served as a bustling place of commerce for the greater Hartford area.

Catherine Scanlon had just celebrated her 18th birthday and was strolling in the Park one spring Sunday afternoon when Henry literally almost bowled her over. Out of nowhere, he had crashed hard at her feet after being tackled during a neighborhood Irish football match. He quickly gathered himself and kicked the heavy ball back into play, then turned to mutter an apology to the girl. But when he suddenly caught sight of her long, wavy brown hair drawn up in a bun that emphasized her beautiful face, he promptly stopped in his tracks to gaze at her. Henry was so taken with the girl that he simply forgot about the game and began walking with her, oblivious to his chum's taunts. All he could hear was the sound of his own heart thumping in his chest as he searched for something to say.

"Fair lady, the boys'll think I've gone knackers, they will," he said to her, the first thing he could think of. "But a walk with you is much more inviting, even if they threw in a pint for winning."

"Well, then," she replied, not sure of what to make of the good-looking and muscular young man who couldn't seem to take his eyes off her, "I suppose if I'm worth more than a pint I should be flattered, Mr…" She hesitated.

31

"Hughes. Henry Hughes," he quickly answered. "Henry Thomas Hughes to be exact. The 'Thomas' is for my old Da, you see. And you would be?"

Her eyes were twinkling from the unexpected attention. He really was quite handsome, she thought.

"Catherine. Catherine Leon Scanlon. The 'Leon' being my mother's maiden name."

"It is a pleasure to be meeting you, Miss Scanlon... actually, I mean... that is..." he stammered, suddenly flustered and a bit queasy. He brushed his thick, black hair back off his forehead and swallowed hard. "What I mean to say is that I've never laid eyes on a more beautiful lass in all my life, Catherine Leon Scanlon."

She laughed aloud and began to stroll again, wondering if he would really leave his football. Without so much as a glance behind him he followed and reached for her hand. She didn't pull away. They were married less than a year later in a simple ceremony in Sacred Heart Church in the oldest section of Wethersfield before returning to Frog Hollow where they would live, but only after he was able to convince her quite skeptical parents, four brothers and three sisters that he was worthy of her hand, a near Herculean challenge. They moved into a small flat on Zion Street and within a month Catherine was pregnant with their first child.

"But Catherine, so many of the lads will join up at President Wilson's first call to arms," Henry had argued defiantly, despite the chaos of his pregnant wife feeding three hungry children staring him right in the face. There was honor at stake, and he was a proud man.

"When the call comes, Henry. When," she snapped back defiantly. "There's only talk of a draft now. And your friends will be offered the reward of citizenship if they volunteer and survive. What will the Army offer you, Mr. Hughes? You are already a citizen of the United States. Perhaps a missing limb or a wheelchair, or a pine box filled

32

with your pieces and a few ribbons and metals left for me to bury?" She began to weep.

As if on cue, the unhappiness of their mother set all three of the children to crying and the growing boy in her belly to kick his displeasure. Henry shook his head, folded the newspaper and laid it on the table. He rose and went to her, wrapping his arms around the apron she wore.

He held her close enough to feel the baby in her womb, kicking. The combination of the tears of his wife and children and the protests of his yet unnamed son, all who depended on him to make good decisions, brought him to his senses. He breathed in the sweet smell of Catherine's hair before speaking.

"Sometimes, a man's urge to fight is more powerful than what his brain is telling him is the right thing to do," he whispered in her ear then gently kissed her on the neck.

"Henry," she admonished him. "The children..."

"The children should be hearing this directly from their Da, even if they don't understand a word he's saying. There'll be no going off to war for me," he said. " How could I ever leave those that I love so much? Even the wee one who's acquaintance I've yet to make..." He patted Catherine's belly.

His wife playfully hugged him then pushed him away. She dried her eyes with the hem of her apron.

"Now off with you, go to work," she said. "You'll be late."

"Yes," he sighed. Henry went around the table and kissed the forehead of each of his children, then gave Catherine a peck on the cheek and was out the door.

He remembered walking down the street and suddenly being overcome by the urge to look over his shoulder. He turned and found his instincts were right. She was staring at him from the front door as he walked away. He blew her a kiss and she waved.

"Catherine..." he called, as Bobbie shook him awake, interrupting the dream. The image of his now long passed wife quickly evaporated from his eyes.

"Pa, Pa... wake up, please, Pa," Bobbie said as she shook his arm. Her eyes were red from crying.

"I'm afraid, Pa. All the boys are going to go off to war. What will we do?" she asked her father.

Groggily, he reached for her, pulling his young daughter's head to his shoulder, kissing her blonde hair.

"There isn't much we can do, sweetheart, except to wait and see what will become of this mess," he answered her.

She wept as he held her.

Henry searched for something to say to comfort her. It came to him.

"Perhaps our sheer numbers will act in our favor, Bobbie," he said.

She pulled back and looked into his eyes, puzzled.

"What do you mean, Pa?" Bobbie asked.

"Well, 14 Hughes' should be able to say enough prayers to get the Lord's attention, wouldn't you think?"

A smile slowly came to her face.

"Yes, Pa," she laughed. "In fact, I'm going to have Speck drop me off at the church on his way to pick up Elvira," she said, the sound of relief in her young voice.

"We need to begin right away."

Henry sighed, knowing in his heavy heart that fate would ultimately deal with the Hughes family. God had little to do with war, he knew, remembering all the good Catholic boys he had seen come home in military coffins some 20 years before. Some had never come home at all, their bodies buried in cemeteries on French soil. But there was no sense in sharing his doubt with his daughter, or any of his children for that matter.

"Yes, Bobbie, the sooner we pray, the better," he said.

Reassured, Bobbie jumped up and called for her brother. "Speck?" she yelled. "I need a ride to church, ok?"

Henry watched his daughter leave the room, her face full of hope. Then he closed his eyes again.

"Oh, Catherine... my love... put in a good word for your boys, my darling," he prayed, then fitfully dozed off again.

Three

~~~ ❧ ~~~

Ka's voice dropped off as she finished the story, the years, the tears and the sweet but potent liquor all combining to tire her. She sat silently for a moment, oblivious to the dozens of eyes staring at her, all eager to hear more. The backyard was silent as her family waited, only the sound of fireworks disturbing what was an enthralling moment for the offspring of her 12 brothers and sisters who were hungry for history.

"It's getting late," she innocently said, "I should be going..."

The instantaneous chorus of protests startled the old woman who hadn't realized her audience's appetite for her story. A smile came to her thin lips.

"Well, my, isn't that surprising," she said, genuinely taken aback. "Why would you all be so interested in the silly memories of an old lady?" she asked.

"Are you joking, Ka?" I asked her, reaching out to touch her hand. "There's not a one of us here who knows what happened to all of you back in those awful years."

"Or why Christmas isn't your favorite holiday," Jack said, genuinely puzzled.

"You still believe in Santa Clause, don't you Jack?" his younger brother teased him, cautiously backing away from his reach.

Voices around the table hushed him because there were a number of little ones within earshot who still did believe in Santa.

"Oh, sorry," Jay said, grimacing. Ka laughed at him. She'd always had a soft spot for the blond haired boy who was the spitting image of her brother Speck, my father.

I had to get her attention again.

"And you're the only one who can tell us, Ka, the only one who can share with us what it was like back then for all of you. It must have been so heartbreaking."

She swung her face back to me and stared into my eyes for a moment, remembering. Then she brought a hand to her lips, as if wanting to keep the words inside.

"Heartbreaking?" she asked. "I don't think that's the right word, Bobbie. We were all so confused I don't know what we felt. Sad perhaps. Mostly confused. You see, we were all so close... and most of us still hadn't gotten over my mother's death yet."

Even the sound of firecrackers couldn't penetrate the silence around the table.

"When Ma died, our little world on Highland Street shattered into a million pieces," she continued. "But it pulled us all together, too... we learned to care for each other more than ever before. We found comfort in each other. Then suddenly, this great big,

37

earthshaking thing called war just crushed that little bit of happiness we were trying to hold on to. I thought Pa was finally going to go crazy after struggling so many years without his Catherine... the thought of his boys going off to war..."

She stopped and took her glasses off, then wiped a tear from her eyes. I'd had no idea this journey I'd started her on would be so painful. Then again, none of us ever knew what had happened.

"Aunt Ka, there's no need to go on, I understand," I said to her, trying not to give away my disappointment. I changed the subject. "C'mon, I've got cupcakes, ice cream and watermelon for everyone. Jack and Jay give me a hand, will you?"

I pushed away from the table but Ka reached for my hand.

"No, Bobbie," she said, smiling. "There's plenty of time for that. You all need to hear this. It just dawned on me how important it is for you to know what that time in our lives meant to me and my brothers and sisters. What it meant to our family...and I guess, just how much it shaped them as your mothers and fathers and aunts and uncles..."

I beamed and heard whispered approval all around the table.

"Thank you, Ka," I said. "You have no idea what this means to all of us."

"Ya," said Jack. "And I need to know what holiday could possibly be more important than Christmas!" Laughter erupted, breaking the tension. Several of Jack's cousins dragged him to the edge of the pool and threw him into the water to rousing cheers.

Catherine leaned her head back and laughed out loud.

"I think I need one more of those delicious little drinks, Bobbie," she said, back in form. I poured another round. This one was for sipping and listening.

"Well, my sister Bobbie went off to church that night... and every day for the next four years... maybe more," she said, continuing. "We all did a lot of praying, but particularly on the next day." She paused again, but no one interrupted.

Ka looked up at the stars and let out a sigh before going on.

"That's when President Roosevelt got on the radio and gave his 'Day of infamy' speech, which pretty much confirmed what we all suspected."

She slowly lifted the glass of Limoncello to her lips and took a sip.

"Yup," she continued.

"The world had gone stark raving mad and even a little town like Wethersfield was going to share in the insanity."

Four

~~~ ‿ ~~~

December 8th, 1941

There were few Americans who slept soundly that night, the omens of war impossible to escape even behind closed eyes. War in itself was not new to them. Indeed, surviving veterans of Gettysburg and Appomattox, San Juan Hill and the Battle of Belleau Woods on the Marne River in France were still honored each year across the nation. It was not only the shock of the surprise attack by the Japanese that unnerved the country, it was also the realization that by the end of the day, war would be a reality on nearly every continent on earth.

But most of all, it was the uncertainty. For the first time in its history, an enemy whose cunning and brutality the likes of which it had never experienced before had directly attacked the United States. Since the air raid at Pearl Harbor, radio reports had filled the airwaves with stories of desperate attempts to rescue sailors hopelessly trapped in burning and sinking naval vessels.

These were not the rules of war Americans knew. The country's naiveté was almost as disturbing to accept as the villainy of the Japanese act.

And what exactly would shifting America to a war footing involve? What sacrifices would be necessary? There were too many unanswered questions for even the most optimistic to stave off that night.

But the most horrific recognition of all was the as yet unstated but obvious requirement that America's sweethearts, sons, husbands and fathers would be called to arms. Throughout the long, restless night across the nation, a universal terror emerged: how many would be called, and how many would fall?

Henry Hughes paced his living room while his family slept that night. Fueled by whiskey and anxiety, his mind raced with worry at the prospect of this new threat to them. They had faced so many together.

First, there had never been enough money to provide for them all, despite Henry's willingness to take on any job he could find. The Depression of 1929 had all but wiped out his small carpentry business, but fatefully he'd already had what seemed like the good fortune to be elected town constable a short time before the country plunged into economic chaos. Being a well respected man in Wethersfield, he won the election handily and the work of serving court papers, few that there were in the small town, provided a bit of extra money to help with the insatiable demands of providing for such a large family.

The crash of October 1929 completely changed the character of the job however, and with his business in ruins he was forced to accept his fate of serving what quickly became mountains of court papers to people in his own community who were down on their luck. Evictions, foreclosures, seizure of properties — these were the responsibilities that put food on his family's table. He hated himself for it. After all, those he served were his neighbors, too. The job racked him with guilt.

Volunteering for the town's fire department helped him to temper his guilt and his dedication to the department was exemplary. But even that source of pride was tinged with regret. Just after being elected Constable, on a cold, icy night in January 1928 while racing to a fire call, Hughes had accidently struck and killed the Captain of Company #2 on Griswold Road. J. Stanley Welles, a close personal friend, died of a fractured skull after being hit by Hughes' car when the lights of an oncoming fire truck blinded him. Welles, a prominent citizen of the town who also served as Chairman of the Board of Education, died at Hartford Hospital, where he had been rushed by Henry and other firemen.

An inconsolable Henry T. Hughes was charged with criminal negligence in the accident, but the charges were later dropped. Welles' prominence in the community resulted in the accident receiving front-page coverage in the Hartford Courant. Nonetheless, Hughes steeled himself to the tragedy and served as a pallbearer at his friend's funeral. For weeks after however, he all but hid in his barn to avoid being seen by even by his wife and children and drank heavily to assuage his guilt.

Ironically, it was his fellow firefighters who rescued him from his anguish. Just two months after the accident, the great respect they felt for the man resulted in the election of Henry Hughes as the next captain of Fire Company #2. While he was moved immensely by

42

the honor, it did little to relieve his sorrow and regret over the accident that had taken his friend's life. The event still haunted him and would all the days of his life.

And then, even as he continued to struggle with providing for his family, the ugly nature of his job and relentless guilt, his lovely Catherine suddenly became ill.

By age 38, the light of his eyes had borne him 13 children, a family of which he was immensely proud. But doctors warned the couple that any further pregnancies would pose enormous risk to Catherine's health, as her body was simply worn out by the stress of having so many children so close together.

After her daughter Beverly was born in May of 1928, Catherine had suffered hemorrhages that weakened her severely. It took her months to recover and resume the heavy load of mothering so many and she never did fully recuperate. She was constantly weary despite the help and attention foisted on her by her sons and daughters and the husband who adored her. In early August 1933, doctors discovered that her constant fatigue was the result of severe anemia and that she was suffering from a blood disorder that was preventing the production of red blood cells. They urged her to remain at Hartford Hospital for intensive treatment but she refused, preferring to be near her family at home on Highland Street. Henry took a job as a janitor at the Colonel John Chester Elementary School, working nights to pay for the doctor bills that Catherine fretted about.

For nearly five agonizing months, Henry and his children watched as she slipped away from them, finally succumbing as they crowded around her bed and held her on the night before Christmas.

The devastated children almost lost their father as well. The death of his wife was nearly more than

Henry could bear and he retired to his barn once more to be alone with his grief and to drown it with alcohol. It was his oldest son Jim and Catherine who finally pulled him out of his stupor by reminding him of the promise he had made to his wife on her deathbed.

"I will hold this family together, no matter what," he had pledged to her in their final private moments.

Somehow he had kept that promise, despite stumbling through his days filled with sorrow. He went back to work and even held onto his night job to keep busy. He tried to fill the spare moments of his life, when he was most susceptible to regret and drink, at the firehouse. But a bottle of whiskey was never far from his hand.

All through the long and terrible night after the attack on Pearl Harbor, Henry reflected on all the challenges life had thrown at he and his family. They had survived through their collective stubbornness and care for each other. But now, as the lonely hours passed, his courage wavered. He wasn't sure he could summon the strength to face the terrifying possibilities of this new threat, one that could crush his promise to Catherine.

Henry pondered the realities of December 8, 1941 as he stared out the picture window and watched the morning sun begin to crest. Worst of all was the recognition that there was nothing he could do to alter the destiny that awaited his sons and the family left behind.

He shook his head in frustration at the conclusion. In war there was no bargaining, only fate. Some lived, some died, some were scarred. The pain was unevenly shared, but all, the soldiers who fought and those who loved them waiting anxiously at home, suffered. From the moment a young, naïve Japanese pilot had released that first bomb over Pearl Harbor, there no longer existed any place on earth free of fear and pain. The only question was the degree of magnitude.

Finally, in abject defeat, he came to the only conclusion possible: what will be, will be. A vision of Catherine's loving eyes came to him as he wept.

When Bobbie arose soon after to make breakfast for him, she found her father sitting in his chair, gazing out the window, tears streaming down his face. Wordlessly, she climbed into his lap, hugged him and cried too.

All the Hughes family but those who were working gathered at Pa's that afternoon as President Franklin D. Roosevelt addressed a solemn joint session of the U.S. Congress.

At exactly 12:30 p.m., Roosevelt's determined voice echoed from millions of radios across America. What the President had to say was not a surprise, but frightening nonetheless.

Bobbie and Beverly sat with their father, his long arms embracing each of them. Jim had come home from work just to hear the speech. Speck had snuck out of the Country Club where he caddied when he wasn't working at a gas station in town as a mechanic. There weren't many golfers today, he'd told Pa.

"*Mr. Vice President, Mr. Speaker, members of the Senate and the House of Representatives,*" Roosevelt began, the hushed members of Congress packed into the Capitol hanging on every word.

"*Yesterday, December 7th, 1941 — a date which will live in infamy — the United States of America was suddenly and deliberately attacked by naval and air forces of the Empire of Japan.*" Catherine, who had come in the front door just as Roosevelt began his speech, gasped at the finality of

45

his words. It was if hearing the President say it made the attack a reality rather than just a very bad nightmare.

"Oh, dear God," she whispered.

"The attack yesterday on the Hawaiian Islands has caused severe damage to American naval and military forces," the President continued. *"I regret to tell you that very many American lives have been lost. In addition, American ships have been reported torpedoed on the high seas between San Francisco and Honolulu."*

Bobbie whimpered and buried her face in her fathers arm. "Pa, I'm so afraid," she said. But the President's address became even more ominous.

"Yesterday the Japanese Government also launched an attack against Malaya." Roosevelt shifted his tone to a staccato beat, emphasizing the obviously long and well-planned nature of the attacks.

"Last night Japanese forces attacked Hong Kong. Last night Japanese forces attacked Guam. Last night Japanese forces attacked the Philippine Islands. Last night the Japanese attacked Wake Island. And this morning the Japanese attacked Midway Island," the President continued. This was all new news to most radio listeners who had not yet understood the comprehensiveness of the Japanese planning and attack.

Jim shook his head, astonished. He looked over at his father. Henry's eyes were closed, but not from drink. He was absorbing every word Roosevelt uttered, assessing the magnitude of his words. His son's lives depended on what Roosevelt planned.

"Japan has therefore undertaken a surprise offensive extending throughout the Pacific area. The facts of yesterday and today speak for themselves. The people of the United States have already formed their opinions and well understand the implications to the very life and safety of our nation.

"As Commander-in-Chief of the Army and Navy I have directed that all measures be taken for our defense, that always will our whole nation remember the character of the onslaught against us." The solemn silence of the Capital was broken for the first time by a standing ovation at the President's remarks.

"No matter how long it may take us to overcome this premeditated invasion, the American people, in their righteous might, will win through to absolute victory."

The Capital rotunda was once again filled with the applause and a roar of approval from Congress.

"I believe that I interpret the will of the Congress and of the people when I assert that we will not only defend ourselves to the uttermost but will make it very certain that this form of treachery shall never again endanger us.

"Hostilities exist. There is no blinking at the fact that our people, our territory and our interests are in grave danger."

The President concluded his brief but powerful remarks, his voice rising with emotion.

"With confidence in our armed forces, with the unbounding determination of our people, we will gain the inevitable triumph.

"So help us God."

And then came the words that all Americans knew would be said, but wanted desperately not to hear.

"I ask that the Congress declare that since the unprovoked and dastardly attack by Japan on Sunday, December 7th, 1941, a state of war has existed between the United States and the Japanese Empire."

A thundering, prolonged applause echoed from the Capital Rotunda as Congress stood in near perfect bipartisan unity to support the President's call to war. The noise came through the radio as a sort of growl, fitting for a country that was fighting mad. Jim got up and turned the volume down. Like everyone else in the room, he found Roosevelt's words invigorating, but certainly not worth celebrating.

He glanced over at his father and saw lines of worry etching the tired man's face. He was obviously troubled by what he'd just heard. The oldest son wondered what it must be like for him to contemplate his boys going off to war.

As the ovation at the Capital continued unabated, Jim suddenly recalled being a little boy and Pa hoisting him up on his shoulders at a victory parade held in Hartford for the returning vets of the first war in Europe. It was more than two decades before but he could almost touch the images flashing before his eyes. The blaring sound of a brass band victoriously trumpeting "You're A Grand Old Flag" emerged from long ago and for a moment he felt the marching cadence of the Color Guard on the pavement as it passed by. They were much older men who proudly hoisted brilliantly colored satin flags. A couple of them had real rifles resting on their shoulders with polished bayonets that glimmered in the afternoon sun. They all seemed to be having a good time, he remembered. But not everyone was as happy. Most of the soldiers walking by wore somber faces and seemed disinterested in all the commotion.

He was startled as the rest of the memory came rushing back at him. Some of Pa's Irish friends who had gone to fight had come back missing an arm or a leg or were severely scarred. The wounded soldiers straggled by — some using crutches, some pushed in wheelchairs, others lying on hospital gurneys. They had frightened him. Since he didn't understand what war was, they weren't heroes to him, just broken men whose sad faces were scary. He remembered some of them being drunk.

But most of all he recalled the tears falling from his father's eyes.

Little Jim Hughes learned that day that there was nothing glamorous or romantic about war. As the memory faded, it struck him that in the entire Hughes family only he and Pa knew anything about war, and even that was limited to what others had suffered.

But now, after a long sleepless night, he had come to a decision, one he knew would disappoint his father. He had never run away from a fight in his whole life and he wasn't about to start now. Before the end of tomorrow, he was going to enlist.

Henry Hughes finally opened his eyes and stared at the ceiling, hugging his daughters closer. Speck shook his head in disgust and lit a cigarette. The idea of going to war didn't worry him; he just wasn't the type to get excited by rhetoric. He knew Roosevelt's call to arms left him with a very difficult decision. But he too had already made up his mind.

"There'll be hell to pay with Elvira tonight," he mumbled.

The only girl Speck had ever cared for had pleaded with him the night before not to act impulsively after the Japanese attack earlier in the day. He hadn't even had the time to greet her before she jumped into his car at Lincoln Dairy and wrapped her arms around him. She was already weeping.

"Please, Speck, please..." she cried into his shoulder. "You're just a boy! You can't leave me to go off and fight a war! Oh my God, what will I do without you?"

"Vera," the soft-spoken young man responded to the girl in his arms. "Hold your horses. C'mon. I'm not going anywhere... yet."

At 17, Elvira Pignone was a senior at Buckley High School in Hartford's South End and lived with her parents on Linnmoore Street. She'd met Speck as a freshman, soon after she had taken an after school job at the ice cream bar. He was a junior about to drop out of Wethersfield High where his lifelong battle with book studies was nearing an end. He wanted to be a mechanic, having been born with a natural aptitude for tools and anything connected with a nut and bolt. Speck was a fine student but just couldn't justify spending hours poring over history and math books when he could be wrenching a car at a local gas station and helping Pa with feeding an oversized family. He was only waiting for Vera to graduate before asking her to marry him.

It was an unusual match for the times. His family was a Celtic blend of Irish and English blood, and her family hailed from Naples, Italy. Elvira immigrated to America as a very young child with two even younger siblings. Surprisingly, their potentially new families welcomed each.

John walked in the front door just as the Capital applause was fading.

"Did I miss anything?" he asked, a grin on his face.

"Not much, John," Speck answered his older brother. "Just that we're at war with Japan."

"Aw, shit."

Catherine broke down, finding nothing funny about John's humor. She got up from her chair and wrapped her arms around her little brother.

"I' can't believe this is happening," she said.

John patted her gently on the back, reassuring her.

50

"Ah, it'll be nothing, you watch," he said with more bravado. Inside, he wasn't so certain. "The Japs have no idea who they've picked a fight with. This will be over by next Christmas, you watch." He grinned at her to emphasize his confidence.

"What are you going to do, John?" Jim asked his brother directly. "And you Speck?"

Henry stared at his oldest son. Always to the point, that one, he thought to himself. He already knew how they would answer and there'd be no talking them out of it.

"Well," John answered. Thought a lot about this last night. I'm going to take the bus into the city tomorrow to the Selective Service Office." He looked at each of his brothers. "My car's in the shop. Don't suppose one of you would drive me?"

"Just so happens I'm heading that way myself," Jim replied.

"That so?" Speck drawled. "Now there's a coincidence. I might as well drive, need to gas up anyway."

Henry hugged the two girls still sitting by his side.

"What's it going to be, boys? Army, Navy..." Henry asked quietly. There was no sense starting an argument he couldn't win. But he would gladly go in their place if he could.

"Army," Jim answered without hesitation. "I'd just as soon keep my feet dry." John shook his head in agreement."

Speck thought for a moment.

"Not sure, but I want to talk to someone about the Army Air Corp," he said. "Figure I'm about the right size to be a pilot."

51

"Think you're going to need a high school diploma to fly, Speck," Jim said.

"Well, if I do, there's plenty of work for a mechanic in the Air Corps. Can't be much different than wrenching a car," he replied, unfazed. He stood up.

"Think I'll go and pick Vera up at school. Might as well get this over with."

Henry blinked hard but he wasn't surprised. As much as he missed Catherine, he was glad she would be spared from seeing her sons head off to war. He wondered how the others would decide.

He leaned down and kissed each of the girls on the top of the head then got up from the couch and went into the kitchen. They all listened to the familiar sound of the cabinet door with the squeaky hinge being opened as Pa took out a bottle of whiskey. Then they heard the back door slam shut as he stepped outside and walked to the barn.

The old man needed to be alone with Catherine for a while. They talked quite often in that barn.

Five

~~~ ૭ ~~~

"They waited in line for nearly 16 hours at the Selective Service Office the next day. There were thousands of young men who had made the same decision. Recruiting stations all over the country were mobbed with volunteers and had to stay open 24-hours a day to deal with the boys who wanted to join up. Everyone was behind Roosevelt. The anti-war people just sort of disappeared. And the Selective Service wasn't very picky about who joined up," Catherine recalled.

"If I remember, a man had to be at least five feet tall and no more than six and a half feet, weigh at least a hundred pounds or so, and have most of his teeth. He could wear glasses and had to be able to read and write, but couldn't have been convicted of a crime. Unfortunately, my brothers and my husband and Dot's all qualified.

53

"So by the end of the day, Jim and John had enlisted in the Army and Speck the Air Corps," my Aunt Catherine told her spellbound audience. "Peachy decided to wait a few months to help out the bank he was working for because they were shorthanded. But Bull was right, there'd be no flying for Speck, because once they saw that he was employed as a mechanic and hadn't finished high school, that was that. He was disappointed but Pa and the girls were happy that he'd probably spend the war on the ground fixing airplanes rather than being a pilot or part of an aircrew. But there was no telling where any of them were headed. We didn't know if it would be to the South Pacific to fight the Japanese or over to Europe to do battle with the Italians and Germans. You see, Hitler and Mussolini declared war on us just a couple of days later."

She paused and took a sip from her glass.

"Actually, it was months after they left for boot camp before we knew where any of them were going to be shipped."

"What about the rest of the boys, Ka? Did they all enlist right away?" my cousin Claudia asked. She was my Aunt Bobbie's daughter.

Ka thought for a minute before responding.

"As best I can recall, Peachy enlisted in the Army in the spring of 1942, Henry and Ray both got deferments because they were working in military factories and had young families, and Phil's young family pushed him way down on the draft list. He didn't go in until late '44 and was stationed at Fort Dix. Ed Ames got the call in the fall of '44, too, I think he was in the Army artillery somewhere. Pa made Jiggs wait until he graduated from high school and then he too got drafted in December of 1944." She laughed out loud. "They fought about it nearly every night at dinner," she

54

said. "Jiggs wanted to quit school and enlist even though he was too young. He begged Pa to let him fake his age and sign for him. But Pa just wouldn't have it. I still remember the hollering," she laughed, but only for a moment, as more memories came rushing back to her.

"Eventually, seven of them went in... all so far away... we never really knew if they were all safe, sometimes it would be weeks before we'd hear from some of them," she said. I watched as Ka began to wring her hands, remembering the strain of worry.

"Pa aged before our eyes," she recalled. "Of course, his whiskey didn't help. But it was the only way he could cope with them all gone. He spent a lot of time in the barn. One of us was always checking on him. Sometimes he'd be talking to himself — you might have thought he'd gone crazy. But we knew that he was talking to his Catherine, my mother."

A tear rolled down her cheek. I thought to stop the conversation and reached for her hand. But she held it up and waved me off. "I'm all right, Bobbie. It's just been so long."

She took another sip from her glass.

"That Christmas was one of the worst my family ever shared, even harder than after my mother died. You see, on Christmas Eve we got the news that a Wethersfield boy, Monty Whitehead Jr. had been one of those killed on the *USS Arizona* at Pearl Harbor. I'll never forget it. He lived on Clearfield Street, a little more than a mile a way. Pa knew his parents and he was a classmate of Flossie's. I remember Pa loading us all into his big touring car and we drove slowly by the Whitehead's house to see the Gold Star banner hanging in the window. The star had been blue. Then they changed it to gold, meaning he had been killed.

"What stars, Ka?" I asked.

55

"It was a tradition, I think going to back to WWI, that families would display an embroidered blue star on a banner in their front window for every son or daughter serving in the military. They were made out of cotton or wool and some women's groups used to sew them for free. If the soldier representing the blue star was killed, it would be sewn over in gold thread. Some banners had blue and gold stars, even red if a soldier was captured or missing. We had several that hung in Pa's front picture window during the war as the number of our family members in the service continued to grow.

"At the Whitehead's, it was like a parade. Hundreds of cars drove by their house for days. I guess it was the town trying to pay respects. It was so shocking, even numbing. But he was only the first of many boys from Wethersfield who would die fighting that awful war. In fact, it's so ironic, Monty was one of the first to die and another boy we knew, Bob Keeney was one of the last to die in the war." She waved her hand. "Keeney lived right up on Wolcott Hill Road. We went to high school together, same class and I knew his parents Bill and Emma because we all went to Sacred Heart Church together. Bob was lost when the *USS Indianapolis* was sunk in the South Pacific after..." her voice wavered. "Can you believe it?" she continued. "He was killed just days before the Japanese surrendered in August 1945 and it was months before we knew he had died. We were all dancing and hooting it up on VJ Day, not knowing..."

She shook her head.

"Young Bob's death took an awful toll on Bill, but especially on Emma. She lived the rest of her life doing everything she could to make sure people never forgot her son and the sacrifice he had made."

56

She was quiet, then. The memory had been powerful. But to my surprise, she pressed on.

"It was hard to find anything to laugh about in those days, but there were plenty of things to cry about. The news of Monty Whitehead's death just made it all so terribly real. The boys tried to act brave, but inside everyone was afraid. Jim, John and Speck left in mid February for boot camp, and I can remember having a big dinner at Pa's house the night before. It would have been horrible, but mercifully, all the boys could talk about was the fire at the Wethersfield Country Club a couple of days before."

No one said anything. My sister and a few of my cousins leaned forward in their chairs, their eyes wide.

"What fire?" Claudia asked.

"The one that burned the clubhouse to the ground, of course," Ka answered immediately.

When there was no response except for more puzzled looks, she suddenly realized we didn't know about the fire.

"You mean to tell me that you all never knew that Peachy, Speck and Jiggs were heroes — before they even left for the war?" she asked. She gave us another glimpse of that mischievous grin.

"Well I'll be."

We waited for her to go on.

"Oh, you'd like me to tell you about it?" she asked, feigning uncertainty.

At least a dozen people hollered 'Yes!' simultaneously. Ka just laughed.

"Well, just about a week before Speck was scheduled to leave, he, Peachy, Jiggs and I were sitting in the living room with Pa listening to the radio when Peachy jumped up from his chair all of a sudden and went to the window.

"'Damn,' he said, pressing his nose to the glass, 'The Country Club is on fire!' Lordy, I remember him saying that like it was yesterday. We all jumped up to look and sure enough, up on the hill we could see this orange glow in the air and flames getting higher and higher.

"The three of them were out the door before I could even slip my shoes on and they jumped into Peachy's car. We didn't have a phone back then, so Pa and I drove to Company 2 on Griswold Road to get the fire truck but some of the volunteer firemen had seen the same glow by then and the truck was just pulling out as we got there. They only had this old Republic fire engine at Company #2 but it was shined up like the dickens and I always got so excited to see it pull out of the firehouse," she laughed.

"Well, Peachy and the boys got there first and found the upper floor of the Clubhouse completely in flames. Apparently there was no way for them to go through the front door, but Speck ran around to the back entrance of the first floor and broke into the Pro Shop to where all the new clubs were displayed and the members stored their own clubs. The three of them grabbed something like 75 sets of golf clubs off the racks before the fire and smoke drove them out. They were real life heroes. The fire made the newspaper the next day, but the bigger story was how Peachy, Speck and Jiggs braved the flames to save the golf clubs. The boys spent a couple of days strutting around like roosters, I tell you..." She abruptly paused, the smile leaving her face. "But then it was back to getting ready to see Speck, John and Jim off.

"Seeing them leave at the train station a few days later was one of those things you just never forget. My God, the carrying on by my sisters and I was awful," she

58

said. "And your mother... Elvira," she added, looking into my eyes. "She was so upset. The poor girl was only a high school senior and her boyfriend was being shipped off to war. I don't think she believed it even at the train station."

The kids next door suddenly launched a barrage of bottle rockets that lit up the sky with flashes of color and tiny explosions. Ka looked up at the heavens, her glasses reflecting the sparkling lights.

"There were hundreds of young men taking the train that day to Fort Devens in Lancaster, Massachusetts. That was where all boys from New England were inducted into the military and then they got assignments to other Army bases all over the country.

"The train station was bedlam. But what I remember most is that despite all the noise the trains were making, you could still hear this huge sobbing sound and all kinds of commotion in the background. It was impossible to get away from people hugging and crying. Hundreds of boys... fathers, sons, brothers, boyfriends... some of them would never come back," she said, and looked out over the pool where some of the kids were still swimming. "So many young men."

She sighed deeply. "You'd have thought it was the end of the world." She looked up again as another tiny rocket exploded above her.

"In a way, I guess it was," she continued. "Elvira, her heart broken, wouldn't let go of Speck and Bobbie was nearly as hysterical. I think I cried as hard as they did and hugged my brother until he finally broke it off, he was getting all flustered. But he whispered in my ear, and I've never forgotten it, "Ka, you have to keep the family together until we get back. And I promise you we will all come home."

"Well, I tell you, that nearly did me in because in my heart I didn't believe him. But I had to. We all had to." I squeezed her hand again and she smiled.

"John and Jim just gave each of us a quick peck on the cheek, hugged Pa and walked away quickly," she said. "I think they were worried they would cry."

She wiped away another tear of her own.

"So the train pulled out and my three brothers all leaned out the window and waved to us as they went by. We stayed and waved at them until the train was out of sight. Then Ray and Henry helped Pa down the stairs to the car because he was so shaky. I remember having a hard time driving because I was crying so hard. God it was awful waving goodbye to them."

She brought her hand to her chin and I noticed her lips were trembling.

"You know, looking back, the only way Pa and the rest of us got through it was the letters."

She shook her head up and down, remembering.

"Letters?" I asked.

"Yes," she answered. "No doubt about it. It was the letters that kept us sane."

Six

~~~ ⁂ ~~~

February 1942

The three brothers spent four cold nights at Fort Devens sleeping on canvas cots in metal Quonset huts that had been hastily erected to house the immense build up of American men being inducted into the military. But their brief stay at the induction center allowed little time for griping about discomforts.

From the time an Army bugler sounded "Reveille" at dawn to rouse them from their sleep, some form of military readiness occupied every minute of each day. First, they spent hours filling out government forms to have their official Army records initiated. Extensive physical examinations, mental profiling, vaccinations for yellow fever, typhoid, smallpox and tetanus, and an inspection for venereal disease followed that.

Next they were administered "literacy" tests that evaluated their intelligence to a fourth grade level. That was followed by the *Army General Classification Test*, a 150-question multiple-choice exam that measured "trainability" or "usable intelligence" such as reasoning, basic arithmetic and mechanical aptitude. This test often determined what assignment the new soldier would be given. The top score was 160, but a score of 110 or better allowed a man to apply for Officer Candidate School.

"Cripes," Jim complained to his brothers after hours of testing, "I could have graduated from college without taking so many exams. Are we going to be soldiers or schoolboys?"

All three scored above 120, but only Jim elected to apply for OCS. An Army classification specialist interviewed each of them.

"I'm not interested in being a leader, " John said when informed he could apply for officer training. "I just want to do my time and get home. Just get me to where I need to do a job that will end this."

Speck was of a similar mindset, although a little more flexible.

"I'll have enough to do learning about aircraft mechanics," he reasoned. "Not sure I want the added duty of being an officer. Think I'll see how well I swim in the shallow end of the pond before jumping into the deep end."

Jim was pointed, as usual.

"I'd sure as hell rather give orders than take 'em. Especially where there are guns involved. I'd like to give OCS a shot. You never know, I might just like this military thing as a career. It wouldn't take much to top selling cars."

Then there was the long line to receive their first issue of Army clothing and personal items, from uniforms to helmets and shaving kits — more than 70 items in all including two pairs of leather boots. Everything was stuffed into two canvas duffel bags and tagged with the soldier's name. After a haircut that left no more than a quarter inch of stubble on their skulls, they were finally ready to get to the business of becoming soldiers. The next day, the three brothers received their training assignments.

Speck was to travel to Blythe Airfield in the small town of Blythe, California near Los Angeles for basic training, then take classes and receive field training in aircraft maintenance and repair. John was assigned to Camp Croft in Spartanburg, South Carolina for basic training as an infantryman. Jim was assigned to the 1st Infantry Division at Fort Benning where he would receive basic combat training and then attend Officer Candidate School.

The time had come for the three to say their goodbyes. They were well aware that it might be some time before they saw each other again… if at all.

"We gotta write to each other, agreed?" Speck demanded of his siblings. "No matter where we are or how long   this lasts, let's stay in touch."

They shook hands on it, slung their new Army issue duffel bags over their shoulders and set out for the trains that would take them to their first assignments. Each walked away with a heavy heart but didn't look back. Pa, the house full of family on Highland Street, the barn, the golf course, cars, girlfriends and all the life they knew before this day instantly faded into the background. Never before had each of them felt so alone.

In Wethersfield, the Highland Street mailbox was checked by one of the girls at least three times a day for a letter from the boys. And finally, a week after they had departed, the first of what would become hundreds of letters arrived to be shared with the entire family. The first was from Speck, who had drawn the short straw among the brothers to write home about their induction experience. Beverly squealed with delight when she saw the envelope and instantly recognized Speck's awkward, chicken-scratch cursive. She tore it open and read it before running into the house, calling for Pa.

February 15, 1942

Dear Gang,

Well, we are officially soldiers in Uncle Sam's Army and have the uniforms and shaved heads to prove it! Fort Devens was quite the experience, an absolute mad house with hundreds of guys taking tests, physicals, getting vaccinated and loaded up with uniforms and the rest of our gear. Then finally, after picking and poking at us for three days we got our assignments.

John is headed for Camp Croft in Spartanburg, South Carolina for basic combat training as an infantryman and Jim is on his way to Fort Benning near Columbus, Georgia for basic and — get this — he's applied for Officers Training School. If he makes it, he'll come out a second lieutenant. Don't exactly know what that means in terms of responsibilities but he'll be an officer in charge of some kind of unit. John and I both qualified for OCS but decided just to concentrate on the job at hand and really have no interest in a career in the military.

Me? I'm off to Blythe Field in a little town of the same name outside of Los Angeles for basic training and classroom and hands on instruction in aircraft maintenance and repair. I'll be working on everything from fighters to bombers. I'm pretty excited to get my hands dirty on something besides a Chevy or Ford.

I'll write more when I arrive. Right now, it's just spending long days on trains heading for the West Coast. John and Jim both promised to write often as long as this lasts.

Wish us luck. Miss you all like crazy. I'm already so homesick and lonely. Gotta write to Elvira now.
    Love ya,
    Speck

Over the next couple of days, every one of the Hughes clan had read the letter at least twice. Within a week, John and Jim had followed suit, reporting in about their new temporary homes down south.

Jim: *"I'm stationed in a barracks that overlooks the Chattahoochee River which runs right through Fort Benning. It's hot as hell here, I almost miss the snow back home! Basic training is brutal. I have sore muscles where I didn't know I had muscles. I'll be glad to see Officer Candidate School begin. Somehow the idea of sitting in a classroom is a lot more attractive than running ten mile forced marches in full gear. Hope you're all great. Don't worry about me. Never had so much to eat!"*

John was struggling with homesickness but gave the family something else to worry about.

"We drill and drill and march and march from dawn to lights out. Can't say I've ever been more tired. It's hot here, you constantly have to be on the lookout for snakes and the mosquitos are the size of small birds! Can't tell you how much I miss you all and Highland Street.

"But it just so happens I'll only be here for my eight weeks of infantry combat training. A couple of days ago, some Captain came into our barracks just before we were turning in and asked if any of us wanted to volunteer for the 'Airborne.' None of us knew what he was talking about. He said we'd get special 'elite' training for parachuting out of airplanes into combat situations ahead of major invasion forces. This guy said it was a real honor to be in a paratrooper unit, only the best guys made it. There wasn't much interest until someone asked if the pay was any different. The Captain says, "Sure. It's double what an infantryman makes. $100 a month instead

of $50. " Well, that's all I had to hear. 'Sign me up,' I hollered. So now, after my eight weeks of basic training at Camp Croft, I'm being transferred to Camp Taccoa, about ten miles from Taccoa, Georgia where I'll join the 101ˢᵗ Airborne Division and get jump training. Don't know what I'm getting myself into but the extra money is some incentive. Now that I've written to you guys you have an address to write to me. So let's get busy, hey? Miss all of you..."

"Dear God, what in hell is that boy thinking of," Pa complained to Phil after reading the letter. "He'll kill himself in training, for Christ's sakes. Just for money? It ain't worth it, I tell you."

"C'mon Pa, John's always been the one to try something new. I'll bet they have fancier uniforms. He'd like that. I'll give him credit, he's got guts. Bet he likes the idea of being able to send some extra money home to help out around here, too."

Phil paused, removed his glasses and rubbed his eyes. He was troubled. "This is hard, Pa. I know I have to worry about Georgia and little Phil, but staying behind..."

"What? Don't talk nonsense, boy," Henry snarled at his son. He was genuinely worried about John becoming a paratrooper, figuring he was just making the odds of his survival that much worse. But then he caught himself.

Henry reached out and touched Phil on the shoulder, worry still visible in his eyes. But he knew the boy was frustrated because he couldn't join his brothers and without saying it, that someone would think he was a coward.

"Phil, listen to me, please?" Henry said to his son. "I know how you feel. I struggled with the same frustration many years ago when I saw my friends marching off to France to fight. I wanted to join them in

66

the worst way, thought it was my duty. But your mother, God bless her soul, made me look at my responsibilities to her and our children. And she was right, hard as it was to swallow. You can't think that you're ducking your duty, in any way. You're not, son, believe me. You've got responsibilities here. You just can't up and leave that family of yours because of your pride. They need you."

"Hell, Pa... I worry about my brothers day and night. Staying home is driving me crazy," Phil admitted.

Henry shook his head in understanding.

"I know, Phil, I know. But if you think not going is driving you crazy, just think how full of worry you would be if you left Georgia and Phil behind. You wouldn't have a moment's peace. I hope you'll stay put here as long as you can, son. That draft will come calling for you eventually, I'm sure. And it will be a sad day in my life to say goodbye to another of my boys.

"For now, do your duty here."

But even as the Hughes boys were being readied to enter the war in either the Pacific or European conflict, back on the home front Americans were confronting their own form of training to prepare the country for the challenges. Signs of shifting to a wartime economy were almost immediate with rationing efforts ramping up as soon as January 1942.

Vast shortages of raw rubber and steel, desperately need to build up American requirements for new airplanes, tanks, ships, guns and ammunition, brought a halt to the production of new automobiles, household appliances and typewriters for the duration of the war. The purchase of bicycles, shoes and rubber footwear were severely curtailed, automobile tires were strictly rationed and gasoline was limited to three gallons per week per household. Pleasure driving was outlawed.

By late winter, rationing had spread to food stocks as well. Sugar, coffee and cigarettes were almost immediately rationed, and within a year, pickings were slim for processed foods, meats, cheese and canned fish and canned milk. Ration coupons that were issued to households on a monthly basis controlled the purchase of all limited goods. A substantial government-led propaganda campaign urged homeowners to provide for themselves with "Victory Gardens" and even provided cookbooks aimed at creating meals without the use of rationed goods.

"Keep the home fires burning" became more than a romantic idea. Severe shortages of fuel oil and kerosene, brought about by a concerted German U-boat campaign to sink fuel tankers and cargo ships off the Eastern Seaboard during the first six months of 1942 starved much of the country's need for heating and cooking fuels. It wasn't until the Coast Guard and Navy began fighting back with coordinated fury that the Nazi submarines were driven off the coast and convoys of ships resumed safe operations. In the first six months of the war however, the Germans sunk some 400 ships off the Atlantic coast, from the Outer Banks of North Carolina as far east as Maine, often within sight of shore and killed as many as 5,000 men.

College classrooms began to empty out as young men sacrificed their education in favor of enlisting. After the Selective Service lowered the age of registration to 18, high school seniors began to follow suit leaving in mid semester.

Cities and towns across the country were dark at night, as blackouts became the law. Air raid drills were common place everywhere and more than 10 million men and women volunteered for the Civil Defense Force, organizing homeland security.

March 20, 1942

Dear Speck,

I'm sitting here half listening to my teacher because I can't stop thinking about you. I hope your training is going well, but I can't help but tell you how lonesome I am without you. And it's so scary here. The houses and streets are all dark at night because of the blackouts and at least once a week we have to take shelter in the basement during air raid drills. The Civil Defense wardens are so strict here because of all the factories around us making parts and weapons for the war. A nice man who patrols our block at night looking for open shades and blinds that let light out in the darkness told me that they're afraid Hartford and all the surrounding towns are a target of the Germans because of the factories, like Pratt & Whitney and Fafnir Bearing.

I'm so terrified and it's worse because you're not here with me. But we all have to be brave and get through this. Listen to me complaining while you're so far away in California. I just pray you don't get shipped to a place where they're fighting in the Pacific. I don't think I could sleep at night.

Did I tell you that I'm going to get a job at Pratt & Whitney after I graduate? They're hiring women now because so many men have enlisted and at least it will help me believe I'm doing something that will get you home to me sooner.

Things are so different now. You just can't go to the grocers and buy whatever you want because rationing is strictly enforced. My father is already planning the 'Victory Garden' he's going to plant as soon as the warm weather comes. I swear it's going to take up our whole backyard on Linnmoore Street. He told me to say hello for him, you know he really likes you. He made a huge batch of wine right after

Christmas just before the sugar rationing began, so he'll have enough of his Muscatel to last until the end of the war.

It will be over soon, don't you think?

I have to go now before I get caught writing this letter. I'll stop by your father's tonight after work and say hello. He misses you and John and Jim terribly. I just heard that Peachy is being inducted next month. Highland Street is becoming awfully quiet.

Write soon, please?

Love you always,

Vera

Boys like Speck Hughes devoured the news from home that came in such letters, and taxed the abilities of the U.S. Postal service with a deluge of responses. But more often than not, military censors whose only job was to prevent the accidental leak of information that might abet the enemy's efforts heavily redacted soldier's letters. Some correspondence made little sense by the time the censors had finished drawing a thick black line through some word, phrase or comment deemed too sensitive to share. It only made the heartbreak of separation worse as families and girlfriends struggled to understand the situation of their loved ones. At times, especially as American troops began to go on the offensive, even their location could be held secret.

At the end of March, having completed basic training at Blythe Airfield with the Army Air Corp's 46th Bombardment Group, Speck was awaiting orders for his next assignment. Rumors were flying hot on the California desert base that his unit would be heading to Wheeler Field in Oahu, Hawaii. Frantic efforts were underway to repair Wheeler and the dozens of fighters and bombers that had been salvaged from the Pearl Harbor attack.

Unexpectedly, he and a dozen other mechanics were plucked from his unit and ordered to McClellan Field seven miles northeast of Sacramento. Their orders were without details but with immediate effect. The bewildered group flew out to McClellan with no idea of their assignments.

As the DC-3 flying them to McClellan dropped its nose to line up for final approach to the base, Speck was excited to see a large collection of new B-25 Bombers neatly parked outside huge hangers. He hadn't seen the aircraft up close yet and was intrigued to get a better look at the bomber's distinctive glass nose and vertical tailfins. It would end up that he'd get more than a look.

The DC-3 taxied closer to the B-25's and as the men climbed out, a jeep pulled up in front of them. In the passenger seat was an officer. Speck and the rest of the new arrivals dropped their duffel bags and stood at attention.

A balding, slightly built middle-aged man jumped spryly from the jeep and ordered the men to stand easy. He welcomed them to McClellan Field.

"Boys, he said, "I'm Lieutenant Colonel Jimmy Doolittle. I can't tell you much about this place having just arrived myself with my crews and this bunch of Mitchell B-25 bombers you see here. We'll be moving out again in a couple of days so I won't get the chance to get to know most of you."

Something was up, Speck figured, but was doubtful that he would learn all the details.

Doolittle walked over to one of the planes and rapped his knuckles on the fuselage. Across the side of the nose was painted the nickname its crew had given the aircraft: *Whiskey Pete.*

"This is one hell of an airplane, gentlemen," he announced with pride. "The best the Army has right

71

now. There's some new stuff in the pipeline that will spin your head when you see it, but for now, the B-25 is the bomber that's going to raise hell with the Japanese."

He paused, looking each man in the face as he continued.

"Now I can't tell you much more about why I'm here or what we're doing. I can only tell you that it's important, damned important. And I need your help over the next 48 hours to make some odd but necessary modifications to my 16 airplanes. I said 48 hours because that's all the time we have and you won't be seeing a bunk for at least that long." Doolittle paused, looking the men in the eye.

"You with me?" he asked them.

"Sir, yes sir," they barked in enthusiastic response. Doolittle muffled a laugh at the formality, something that wasn't high on his list of critical measures of a man's worth.

"You're probably wondering why you're here," he said affably. "Well, you've been selected as the best mechanics in your class and the closest to McClellan, to be completely honest. Like I said, we have no time to waste. "

A grin broke out on Speck's face. For a moment he forgot about how homesick he was. It was good to be needed after so many weeks of endless training and schooling without so much as the echo of a kind word. He liked this guy and would do his best over the next two days to give him what he needed.

"We start right away. We're going to break you up into small groups and you'll be working with the pilots of these aircraft who will oversee your work," he continued. "Specifically, on these 16 birds you're going to work on removing the lower gun turret..." He stopped, seeing all eyes upon him suddenly widen.

"Sorry guys, some of these things are going to seem a bit strange but they are necessary, trust me. Wish I could tell you more. Ok?"

"Sir, yes sir." Doolittle smiled again.

"You're also going to be installing de-icers and anti-icers, and welding steel blast plates on the fuselage around the upper gun turret. You're going to pull some radio equipment, the guns in the tail cone, replace the bombsight and install new auxiliary fuel tanks." He looked around at the faces of the men he was depending on. Their eyes were even wider.

"Yah, guys," he said, shaking his head in agreement, "a lot of work, even pulling a two day shift." Some of them were shaking their heads in doubt.

Someone spoke up.

"We can do it, sir," the guy standing next to Speck said loudly. He didn't hesitate.

"I agree," Speck said without hesitation. "Seems like we're wasting time talking about it."

Doolittle stared at the two boys.

"That's the spirit, guys. Like I said, this is important. You'll understand eventually. "

"I'll take your word for it, Colonel," Speck said, grinning again.

"Then let's get to it," Doolittle responded, returning the look.

From behind them, the pilots of each of Doolittle's B-25's moved in and introduced themselves. Then they were separated into teams and led off into the first hanger, where one of the airplanes had already been moved.

"Ok, guys, we have three hours per aircraft," the first pilot said. "We'll take a ten minute break after we finish each plane for a visit to the head and a smoke.

Leave your gear on the runway; it will be taken to your barracks assignments."

With a look of determination that he hoped was infectious, Doolittle released them.

"So, let's go."

Speck and two other mechanics climbed a ladder and began working on welding blast plates on the fuselage around *Whiskey Pete*'s upper turret. Welding equipment had already been laid out for them.

"I don't want to know why we're doing this," Ray James, a 22-year old boy from Missouri said to Speck quietly."

"Yah. Just glad I'm not going wherever these guys are."

Within an hour, the welding was completed and Speck's team moved to their next assignment, removing the rear turret guns. Speck looked over what was required and didn't see much of a problem, but he was puzzled. The goal was obvious: reduce weight. But Doolittle's team was giving up a lot of firepower to do it. He had a better idea and told the pilot so.

"That so..." *Whiskey Pete*'s pilot responded. "Wait here."

Speck suddenly felt the hair on the back of his neck stand up. He had forgotten his rank.

"Private Hughes?" he heard someone call his name from behind. He turned. It was Doolittle. "Front and center," he ordered.

"Yes, sir," Speck saluted.

"Relax, Private. What's your name?

"Richard Hughes. But for some reason my family chose to call me 'Speck," he replied, his voice a tad shaky.

"Speck," Doolittle repeated. "I like that. And I like your spunk, Private. Speak up," he commanded.

74

"Well, sir... I was just thinking... I mean, I'm guessing you're ditching those twin tail guns to get rid of some weight," he said. "Uh...I was just thinking that that rear end is going to look naked without those 50 caliber guns sticking out of the tail cone. It's going to make for an inviting target for some fighter pilot."

Doolittle's eyes narrowed.

"You're right about the weight, Speck. What do you propose?"

"Just that we don't give away our secret, Colonel. I think we need to make that fighter pilot see something that isn't really there. Let's mock up some fake guns. A broom handle painted black will do the trick. Probably take us 20 minutes to rig the whole thing up."

"A broom handle..." Doolittle repeated.

"Yes, sir," Speck answered, wondering if there were any rank lower than Private.

"Great idea, Sergeant, let's do it," Doolittle responded.

"Yes sir," Speck grinned, then stopped.

"You heard me right, Speck. Sergeant. We don't have time to sew on some new chevrons right now, but we'll get to it. Think we'll add a couple of 'rockers' to your shirtsleeve. Well, done, Sergeant Hughes." Doolittle saluted the young man. Speck responded accordingly, but was speechless. He wrote home about the incident two nights later when the work on Doolittle's B-25's had been completed.

April 2, 1942

Dear Gang,

Well, I've finally escaped that desert hellhole in Blythe and am now stationed at McClellan Airfield near Sacramento. The brass yanked me out of Blythe so fast I barely had time to pack. They took me and another 11 guys from my class – 'the

75

best' they said — and flew us to McClellan without telling us what our assignment was.

It just so happens that a flock of B-25 bombers were waiting for us at McClellan for some modifications and we were given 48 hours to get the job done. A Lieutenant Colonel named Doolittle told us it was a real important job but that was all he could share with us. I won't tell you about what we did, because the censors would just take it out anyway.

But it was a helluva long 48 hours I can tell you. And guess what? I took a risk in making a suggestion on something and Doolittle was so impressed he gave me a field promotion on the spot to Sergeant! So now I'm 'Sergeant Richard Hughes!' What do you think of that, Pa? Can't wait to share the news with John and Jim. By the way, have you heard from them? Tell them slackers to write to me.

Don't know how long I'm going to be here. Think I could be headed to the South Pacific pretty soon. You'll be the first to know (if I can tell you!).

The excitement around here was great and getting out of the desert suits me just fine. But I can't tell you how much I miss home and all of you. I hope you miss me, too. Keep those letters coming; they help me sleep at night. Hey, did Peachy get drafted? Haven't heard from him.

That's all for now, gotta go find my bunk and then I want to watch those B-25's fly out of here later tonight. Should be quite a sight.

Love you all,
'Sergeant' Speck Hughes

At 08:00 hours that night, he and most of the guys stationed at McClellan Field turned out to watch the parade of Doolittle's B-25 bomber's head out over the horizon, their destination unannounced. Speck was proud to have worked on the team that readied the aircraft for whatever mission they were on. He had to

76

share it with Vera that night before he finally collapsed into his bunk for the first time in nearly three days.

I tell you, Vera, my stomach was going flip flop watching those guys take off. You can't imagine the noise those planes made tearing down the runway. What power. It's hard to believe someone would attack us knowing we're capable of building such weapons. And I think we have the determination to knock the Japanese on their ass. Sort of wish I were with those guys, but don't worry, I won't revisit the issue of trying to become a member of a flight crew. I've learned a lot about aircraft mechanics, and I'm sure it will come in handy some day. Like I said, don't worry, a promise is a promise. In the meantime, I just do what they tell me to do. Hey, what do you think about your boyfriend being promoted to 'Sergeant?' Now there's something to tell the girls! I'll write tomorrow.

Forever yours,
Speck

Seven

~~~ ॐ ~~~

"Well, Speck's letter arrived in early April when things were looking very bleak," Catherine continued, showing no signs of fatigue. "We were at war but it didn't seem like we were doing much fighting. The headlines were full of news about Japanese advances and Hitler racing through Europe. Hearing from your father made us all feel pretty good and Pa smiled for the first time in months when he read about Speck becoming a Sergeant! " She beamed at me. I felt my eyes watering.

"But then, by God, it all made sense a few weeks later when we woke up to headlines that 'Doolittle's Raiders' had bombed Tokyo in retaliation for Pearl Harbor. I think it was around the middle of April. Why you would have thought we'd won the war with all the celebration and carrying on. And Speck had worked on the bombers that made the raid. It would be years before we knew the details. He was just as shocked. But boy, was he proud." Her smile was as wide as I imagined my father's was the minute he understood his role in one of the most memorable moments of the war he served in.

Then her face turned serious again.

"But it wasn't all good news. Jim and John were still busy with training, Bull at OCS at Fort Benning and little John at Camp Taccoa learning how to be a paratrooper. Pa was really worried about him. And then Peachy had to leave to be inducted at the end of the month and we all saw him off at the train station."

Another single tear rolled down her cheek.

"My God, saying goodbye to Speck, Jim and John was bad enough, but this was even worse. Peachy was my fourth brother to go off to war. The Blue Star Banner hanging in Pa's front window had four stars on it. Every time I saw it, I winced. It made me proud, but it hurt my heart at the same time.

"We weren't alone. Boys were pouring out of Wethersfield into the military. There were hundreds of families in Wethersfield displaying Blue Star banners. The terrifying part was wondering which of them would be the next to become Gold Stars — meaning their son had been killed," she said. "It was terrifying… truly terrifying."

"Where did Peachy go, Aunt Ka? The Army?" my sister Kathy asked.

"He enlisted and joined the Navy, Kathy," she said. "He was shipped off to the Naval Air Station in Jacksonville at the end of April. He was just a kid…"

Ka sighed. "With the exception of Jim, they were all just boys, barely young men. But my brothers were a lot more mature than kids their age today. They had to be. We had lived through the Depression, lost my mother… we didn't grow up in an easy time. The war was just the final blow…"

She reached for her little glass of Limoncello again and sipped at it.

"You know, Bobbie, this is really good. What's in it? It sure makes me talk," she laughed. "My sisters would have loved this stuff," she added, her eyes twinkling.

"They were a wild bunch, I can tell you. Loved to party. But the war made them all grow up. The only time we danced during the war years was when one of my brothers came home on leave. "

She thought for a moment about that and then burst out loud in laughter. "Oh my Lord, how we would party!"

The backyard was suddenly filled with laughter.

"Oh, dear, it's amazing that you can remember the good moments in all those bad times."

We sat in silence for a few moments, listening to the cacophony of fireworks exploding all over the town. It was quite a night and the heat hadn't let up yet. Several of the kids took advantage of Ka's breather to take a quick dip in the pool. My aunt watched them closely.

"I can see my brothers and sisters in them, they're such darling children, you all are so blessed," Ka said aloud. "I didn't have any children of my own, I guess that's one of the reasons why my family was so important to me."

She took another sip from her glass and resumed her story.

"Well, by the middle of 1942, the war in the Pacific against the Japanese was making all the headlines. There were huge battles… let me see now…if I remember there was the Battle of The Coral Sea,

Midway and Guadalcanal during that spring and summer. These were all places we had never heard of before. But the boys in the Navy got some more vengeance for Pearl Harbor with victories in all three battles, and prevented the Japanese from invading Hawaii or Alaska. It seemed the war in the Pacific was already turning in our favor and there was a lot of hope that it might end soon. We had no idea how bloody it would get. So many more boys would die..."

She shook her head at the memory. "Speck was in California and we were terrified that he would ship out to one of the islands where they were fighting."

"What was happening in Europe at that point, Ka?" my sister Kathy asked her. "It seems all the fighting was in the Pacific."

"Well the news was just terrible in Europe. We hadn't even begun to fight that war yet." She stopped and thought for a moment.

"Have any of you heard about a place called Dunkirk?"

Most of the adults nodded silently. It was a name most recognized, but few knew its story like Ka.

"They called Dunkirk a miracle. The Germans had nearly 400,000 British and French boys surrounded with their backs to the English Channel. They were about to be slaughtered. The news here was full of the desperate attempts to evacuate them. The miracle was that they managed to pull nearly 350,000 of those boys off the beach and back to England. What a story it was. But it just emphasized the power Hitler had. I tell you, there was celebration, but the Nazi's were even more terrifying to us after Dunkirk."

She let out a loud sigh.

"And there wasn't a single thing we could do about it at home. We just devoured the newspapers and

81

listened to the radio and waited for a letter from one of the boys. We worked in our Victory Gardens and canned vegetables and fruit all summer while Pa continued to work as a sheriff and spent his spare time in the barn making furniture to sell and trying to keep his big old Hupmobile running. It was a broken down touring car of some kind on its last legs. The boys had left their cars in the barn for safe keeping while they were gone, but Pa wouldn't think of using them. He thought it would be bad luck if he took one of their cars.

"Yup, it was an awfully lonely, quiet summer," she said, remembering. "But at least we knew where Jim, John, Speck and Peachy were. They were still stateside in training, and at least for the moment, safe." Then she was silent. Her eyes shut. I thought she had fallen asleep. But no, she was just catching her breath.

"But then the fall came." Her eyes flew open.

"And suddenly we wished it would get quiet again."

Eight

~~~ ∞ ~~~

August, 1942

Dear Pa,

I wanted to let you know that I finished in the upper quarter of my class at Officer Candidate School a couple of weeks ago and I am now a full-fledged 2nd lieutenant and a commissioned officer in Uncle Sam's 1ˢᵗ Infantry Division, known as the 'Big Red One.' These gold bars on my uniform lapels look pretty good. Make sure to tell 'Sergeant' Speck that I now outrank him!

I command a platoon of 40 men. They're good guys and I think they respect me. Every day we drill and run and spend time on the firing range. There's some urgency now, because we've been told to be ready to move out without much notice. Not sure what that means other than a move to another Army base for some reason, or maybe we're finally

83

headed overseas. Don't know, and I doubt I'll be able to tell you much if and when it happens.

Part of me wants to go to war, Pa. I'm sick of reading about Hitler and the Japs kicking our butt all over the place. It's time we got into this fight. I'm ready so don't be afraid for me. I'm no hero, Pa, but I promise I'll do my job and make you proud of me.

I can imagine things are hard at home with all this rationing I read about. On my end of things it's hard to complain. Our chow is great and there's plenty of it. I wish I could send you the leftovers.

Haven't heard from John, Speck or Peachy lately, but I'm sure they're well. That was really something about old Speck helping out Jimmy Doolittle's guys. You should be proud of him. I sure am. At least he had a hand in some payback for Pearl Harbor and all those guys who died.

Things must be getting pretty quiet around Highland Street with Peachy gone now. Hope he's enjoying Jacksonville. Probably hot as hell there but at least he's near the ocean.

I have to cut this letter short, Pa, my first sergeant just told me I've been summoned to an officer's meeting. Guess something's up. I'll write again when I can.

Be home before you know it, Pa. Count on it. Love to everyone.

Jim

2nd Lieutenant James Hughes licked the envelope to his letter closed and mailed it as he walked to the 1ˢᵗ Infantry Division's headquarters at Fort Benning. Inside the stifling briefing room were dozens of officers of the division, most sitting in silence in the company of a cigarette. Rumors had been flying for days that the *"Big Red One,"* the division's nickname coming from the distinctive shoulder patch on their uniforms, would be shipped overseas within days. It was almost

2100 hours. It was late for a briefing unless it was for something very unusual. He looked around the room and could see the tension on the faces of dozens of guys like himself who'd been well trained, but had never seen battle.

"That might be about to change," he thought to himself and lit up a smoke.

Presently, Major General Terry Allen, a decorated veteran of the First World War, entered the room. Every man present stood and snapped to attention. Allen motioned for them to sit.

"Gentleman," he began with a nod. "You've trained hard over these last months to make the *Big Red One* worthy of it's hard won reputation for distinguished service in defense of our great nation. I stand here tonight to tell you that all that training is about to be put to use in the coming weeks. While I can't share with you the details of our mission, I can tell you that we will be moving out tomorrow morning, our destination the New York Port of Embarkation. There we will be boarding ships bound for Gourock, Scotland. Upon arrival we will board a train to Tidworth Barracks in Wiltshire in the southwest end of England. In subsequent days, you can expect to lead your men in intensive amphibious landing training near Glasgow. That's the extent of what I can tell you for the moment.

"So, brief your men — only so far as we will be transferring to a New York location — and have them ready to go and assembled in full fatigues at 0600. After morning chow we will be boarding trains bound for the North River piers in Manhattan."

Allen looked around the room at the grim faces. There was little more that he could say. Only a handful of men in the room had seen combat. The majority had only the minimum training, OCS and their own wits to

85

guide them through what would be a test of their courage, intelligence and leadership. The General knew from experience that some of them would distinguish themselves in the worst situations imaginable, others would do what was asked and no more, and still others would be overcome by fear in the first moments of battle. Allen prayed that the men in this room would find the courage he was depending upon to lead an untested infantry to the first American victory of the war on European soil.

"Gentleman, it is an honor to serve with you. That is all. Dismissed." He walked off the stage without another word.

Hughes hurried back to his barracks and assembled his men, giving them the necessary instructions. They knew better than to ask questions.

He tossed and turned that night and got up several times to write another letter home. But each time he thought better of it. He'd write when he could tell his family something that might ease their worry. Instead he penned quick notes to Speck, John and Peachy, letting them know that he was about to leave Fort Benning for the New York Port of Embarkation. He wondered if the information would survive the censor's sharp eye.

Don't know exactly what will happen next, but I'm sure these 'butter bars' I'm wearing as a 2nd Lieutenant will mean I'll be one of the first to know.

I learned a lot in OCS, just hope that I'll step up for my guys when the time comes. I'm more afraid of failing them than I am of dying. This is the time when a man wonders how he'll react under fire. Will he stand and face it or turn and run? I think living with the knowledge that you are a coward would be worse than death. You know I've never run from a fight in my life; I'll let you know if my streak continues when

86

the time comes! If you're writing to any of the gang, please send my love. I may not be able to write for a while. God bless and protect you, brother.

   Jim

*   *   *

Some 200 miles northeast, John Hughes could only wish he was in his bunk at Camp Taccoa. A 101st Airborne trainee assigned to D Company, 2nd Battalion 506th Parachute Regiment, he had spent the early morning hours in a grueling 30-mile march with his unit in full combat gear to Clemson Agricultural College in South Carolina. There they spent several hours training on the military school's firing range before marching the 30 miles back to Camp Taccoa. Besides lacking a firing range, Camp Taccoa also had inadequate facilities for parachute training, its runways deemed to short for safe operation of their C-39 and C-47 jump planes. Soon the unit would move to Fort Benning for intensive jump training.

But for what Camp Taccoa lacked in facilities, it more than made up for in intensive conditioning, a training strategy that the Camp's commanding officer, Lt. Colonel Robert Sink employed to prepare his men for the long distances he knew they would be forced to march following combat deployment. Taccoa was famous for its daily run up and down Currahee Mountain, a brutal exercise memorialized by the cry of "Three miles up, three miles down" by the would be paratroopers. "Curahee" became the battle cry of the 506th, a Cherokee Indian word meaning, "Stand alone, together."

Dear Dot,

Being the oldest and all without Jim around, I figured I'd show you some respect and write directly to you! I know you'll shoulder the responsibility of sharing my letter with the gang.

You probably won't believe this, Dot, but I actually wish I could go back to the day when there were 15 of us living under one roof. I am that homesick and missing you all. I for sure don't know what I got myself into here with this parachute training, because we haven't done any parachute training yet! All we do is run and march from sunup to sundown and at least once a week, we march 60 miles round trip in full gear, half of it in the middle of the night just to fire off a few rounds at a college near here. Can you believe an Army training camp doesn't have it's own shooting range? So, all we do is conditioning. I swear to you, if they let me go home, I'll bet you I'm in good enough shape right now to run nonstop all the way to Highland Street. But that's only a dream. Eventually we're going to move on to Fort Benning, where Jim is now, for jump training. I hope he's still there. Be great to see him.

How are things at home? I hear rationing is difficult. I can't imagine you not being able to buy nylons and girlie stuff. But it's all for a great cause: keeping me fed and equipped (although for the life of me I don't know why I'd need nylons!).

Please give everyone my love. I really do miss you guys so much. And give Pa a giant hug for me. I'll bet he's lonely, too. If you get a chance, send me Peachy's address so I can write to him and complain about him playing golf everyday in Florida. Some guys have all the luck! Give my best to Ed, too. Hope the Draft Board lets that husband of yours stay home. Skippy needs his dad.

Love ya, sis, write back.
John

The reunion between brothers John and Jim at Fort Benning wasn't to be.

At 0600, 2nd Lieutenant James Hughes inspected his platoon and marched with them to the mess hall for their last meal at Fort Benning. The guys were quiet as they ate. There was good reason. Then the entire 1st Infantry Division — 15,125 young men — began loading on to trucks for the drive to Columbus where they would board trains to New York, a two-day trek. What would happen next was the question on the mind of the boys for every minute of each mile of track they traveled on that long, lonely trip.

The uneasy quiet aboard the cramped train made Jim edgy. Hardly anyone spoke for hours at a time, and only the endless, mind numbing repetition of the train's forged wheels churning for traction on the steel track filled the air. Jim wondered if he would ever forget the contradiction of feeling so lonely while being surrounded by so many people. A small ball of fear began growing in the pit of his stomach, but he pushed it down. He couldn't let his men see any signs of anxiety on his face. Sleep was almost impossible. Every time he closed his eyes he was jarred by the thought that no one in his family had the slightest idea where he was or where he was headed. He knew that his sudden, unexpected silence would be a heavy cross to bear, especially for his father.

On August 2, the 1st Infantry Division pulled into Manhattan at the North River piers and immediately began boarding the ship that would take the huge number of troops to Europe. At Pier 90, the ship that awaited its first cargo of American soldiers was an awesome sight to the nervous boys, most of who were already overwhelmed by their first ever glimpse of the skyscrapers of New York City.

89

When Jim Hughes stepped off the train, his jaw dropped at the sight of the ship that would take him to war. The vessel was the legendary *RMS Queen Mary*, the 1,019-foot long 81,000-ton floating steel juggernaut. It was the largest and fastest passenger liner ever to sail the unforgiving North Atlantic Ocean.

A product of the marriage of the Cunard and White Star Lines, the *RMS Queen Mary* waiting at Pier 90 was a far different vessel than had been launched in 1936. Gone were her distinctive pre-war livery colors of black and red hull, white superstructure and three distinctive Cunard Red funnels. The enormous vessel had been repainted with a drab, uniform coat of "Light Sea Gray" that the Royal Navy had selected to camouflage the ship against an open ocean horizon. The paint job earned the once resplendent ship an ominous nickname: "The Grey Ghost." But there was no doubt that the phantomlike appearance of the massive vessel and her extraordinary 30-knot top speed were her greatest defenses against German U-Boat commanders who were incentivized by Hitler to hunt down and sink the *RMS Queen Mary*. A million reichsmarks (about $250,000) and the coveted German Knight's Cross with Oak Leaf Clusters, equivalent to the US Medal of Honor awaited the U-Boat commander fortunate enough to discover the great steamship in the cross hairs of his torpedoes.

Also replaced were the legendary ship's luxurious accommodations for 2,119 passengers and 1,035 crew. Every square inch of the liner had been scrubbed of the accouterments of refinement and luxury — an ambience hardly necessary on a ship now designed to ferry between 8,500 and as many as 16,000 troops to war torn Europe.

The ship that once epitomized leisure and wealth was also refit with a new, decidedly less welcoming personality. Just weeks before at the Boston Naval Shipyards, the Grey Ghost was provided with military armaments that gave her the firepower nearly equivalent to a US Navy light cruiser. Finally, she was equipped with a copper wire degaussing coil wrapped around the perimeter of the ship's hull. When charged with electric current, the coil neutralized the Queen Mary's magnetic field, rendering it impervious to German magnetic mines that were a constant danger in the North Atlantic.

Like many of the men who were about to step aboard, one of the first things Hughes noticed about the ship was the pitiful number of lifeboats. If the ship were to go down, the loss of life would be staggering.

As he grabbed his bag from the train, a runner appeared and informed him that an officer's briefing was scheduled before mess call that night strictly intended to address the ship's safety, bunking requirements and assignments in the event of an enemy attack. The 2nd Lieutenant was relieved to know that he would at least be able to answer the questions that were evident in the eyes of every one of his men.

She may have been big, but to the more than 15,000 men who were about to sail on her, the *RMS Queen Mary* appeared to be the world's largest coffin.

Five long and anxiety-filled days later, the vessel docked in Gourock, Scotland, one of the few harbors in the British Isles deep enough to welcome the huge ship that was out of range of German bombers.

The voyage had been a tremendous success, Hughes thought, considering they had made it across the U-Boat infested North Atlantic without a Naval escort and in conditions that brought some men to the brink of madness. Sleeping in shifts on "standee bunks" in stifling heat and the inescapable stench of vomit from seasickness, sweat, cigarette smoke and diesel fuel, it was a wonder any of them could even stand. Claustrophobia and the constant threat of being torpedoed or attacked from the air played with their minds. It had been nearly ten days since any man in the 1st Infantry Division had slept a full night.

But they had made it.

As he stepped off the gangplank and onto Scottish soil, Jim Hughes had to fight off the urge to drop to his knees and say a prayer of thanks. He turned and looked at his men following him and knew he couldn't allow himself that luxury. Instead, he barked orders to bring his platoon to close order formation and led them off in the direction of the train station that would bring them to Tidworth Barracks.

Dear Jim,

It's been more than a week since your last letter. I know that everyone's been writing to you like crazy, but we haven't heard anything back. It's troubling. We all know that you're a thickheaded tough guy, but that you would write if you could. So I am assuming you aren't able to communicate with us, and probably won't even get this letter for some time.

Please know that you are always in our thoughts and prayers. We listen to the radio constantly to try to keep up with what's happening, but it really doesn't tell us much. Just know that we love you and want you home here with us again, safe and sound and bullying us around! We miss your fearsome spirit, but also know that it will serve you well wherever you may be now.

There's little to report from home. Peachy is terribly homesick, but he says his commanding officer in Jacksonville has caught on to the fact that he's such a good golfer. Ray, Henry and Phil still haven't been called by the Draft Board, which is good news. Spec made Sergeant, as you've probably heard after helping out Hap Arnold's crew on the famous raid on Tokyo. John says he's headed your way — to Fort Benning — for paratrooper training in the near future and hopes to catch up with you. Pa needs tires for the car and can't get them so he's thinking about having them retreaded, whatever that means. Me, I'm trying to feed a lot of hungry mouths, but it's not easy with the ration situation. Thank goodness for our Victory Garden. Bobbie, Beverly and I have been canning like crazy for the winter. I don't think we'd see a vegetable until next summer otherwise.

That's all from here. Remember, we're all praying for you. Be safe and wear your helmet.

Love from the whole gang, and never forget that we're all waiting for the day you'll come marching home to us.

Ka

P.S. Please, please write to us just as soon as you can.

Nine

~~~ ❦ ~~~

September, 1942

Henry Thomas Hughes, brooding over the absence of his sons, sat on the front steps of the house on Highland Street that he had built with his own hands and thought back to the circumstances that had brought his family to Wethersfield and a better life.

He and his beloved wife Catherine had made the courageous decision to move from their apartment on Zion Street, away from the comfort of family and friends, when it became clear that their growing family would soon outlive its welcome in the crowded neighborhood. It was their precocious six-year old daughter, Dot, who had innocently forced the decision they had been mulling over for months after she had gotten into an argument with their landlady.

"They're our flowers, too, Mrs. Murphy," Dot had informed the elderly woman who owned the tenement building in which the Hughes' lived. Mrs. Mary Murphy, a widow well into her years, short on patience and not particularly fond of children, had scolded the girl for picking a few chrysanthemums that grew along the front porch of the house.

"Well, young lady," Murphy replied pretentiously, "they are not your flowers, they are mine. I planted them with my own two hands and they are growing on the front lawn of the house I own.

"For heaven's sake," she continued, determined to discipline the girl. "You and your family are only renters," she added with ringing disdain. The tone of the crotchety old woman's response did little to dissuade the girl from her desire to pick the flowers for her mother.

"My Daddy pays rent for our apartment so some of those flowers should be ours," Dot argued.

"Your father pays for the roof over your head and the water in your faucet. He does not pay for the flowers. And I'm warning you again, do not pick them, young lady. Do you understand or do I need to bring this to the attention of your parents?"

"You can do whatever you like, Mrs. Murphy," Dot replied angrily. "I might just come back and pick them all if I feel like it," she said and stormed away.

Murphy's eyes widened at the brashness of the little girl. She bristled with anger.

"Well… just wait until your Da gets home from work, you little brat," the landlady called after her. "We'll see who has the last word about them flowers."

After a long day's work, Henry Hughes came home with the setting sun at his back to find a still quite peeved Mrs. Murphy waiting on the porch steps for him. She wasted no time in letting him know the full extent of his daughter's crime.

"Mrs. Murphy, my dear lady," Hughes implored. *"Why surely you can spare a few blossoms for a child to give to her mother?"* He spoke gently, trying to diffuse the situation.

"Absolutely not, Mr. Hughes!" Murphy replied indignantly. *"And if that daughter of yours so much as touches my flowers, there'll be a policeman at your door with a summons for destruction of private property. My brother-in-law happens to work for the Hartford Police Department so heed my words."*

"Indeed I shall, Mrs. Murphy," Hughes responded, holding his anger in check. *"Indeed I shall."*

At the dinner table, Henry made it quite clear to Dot and her five siblings that Mrs. Murphy's flowers were not to be disturbed.

"But Pa..." Dot appealed.

"There'll be no 'but's' Dorothy, am I clear?"

"Yes, Pa," the little girl responded but she was already planning her revenge.

From the other opposite end of the table, Catherine cleared her throat loudly to catch her husband's attention. He looked up from his plate and caught the look in her eye.

He nodded in understanding. *"Now Mrs. Hughes?"* he asked, making sure.

"Well I think it about as good a time as any, Mr. Hughes. It would seem that Mrs. Murphy has helped us to make our decision," Catherine replied and winked at her husband.

Henry smiled. Several months before, the couple had discovered a little piece of property for sale in nearby Wethersfield that with a bit of money, plenty of elbow grease and quite a few prayers, could be theirs. It was Catherine's dream: a seven-acre parcel of land with trees and fields and pastures where their growing family could thrive and escape the confines of the busy city and the cramped apartment, open the windows to find fresh, clean air and have room to run and roam just as she had as a child growing up in her native Ireland. They had fretted over the decision, worrying about money, Henry's proximity to work and the knowledge that life in the country would bring challenges to children who were already becoming street urchins. Mrs. Murphy's pettiness had pushed Catherine over the top.

"Now there'll be no need to go aggravating Mrs. Murphy anymore, Dorothy," he said to his headstrong daughter, "but this is a good opportunity to share with you some news that should make you feel much better about things. In fact, I think it will make you all smile."

The six little heads turned to their father.

"We are moving to the country. To a little town called Wethersfield where you can plant – and pick – all the flowers you desire. I am going to build our family a brand new house surrounded by seven acres of property with fields and pastures and trees. Why, it will be like living in the park!"

Jim, Dot, Ray, Catherine, Flossy and Henry either yelped their approval or clapped their hands, depending on how much they understood of what their father had said.

Dot was ecstatic, although not only because of the news.

"I'm going downstairs right after dinner and tell that mean Mrs. Murphy," Dot said, a wicked smile coming to her lips.

Henry rolled his eyes.

The next morning, Henry Hughes took the trolley to Wethersfield and met with the owner of the farm property. He gave the man a deposit of $100 on the seven-acre parcel of land on Highland Street, shook his hand and then spent several hours walking out a plan for a house and a barn. It would take him more than a year to accumulate enough wood and building materials – all of which had to be ferried to Wethersfield aboard the trolley that ran from the city – and clear a dozen trees before he could begin constructing the family home. He spent every spare minute working on the

97

house and he moved his family out of Hartford when it was
nearly completed just after the war ended. But it would be
many years before the Hughes would know the luxury of
plumbing again.

As the memory faded from his eyes, he sighed.
His heart had broken when he lost Catherine, and now
the specter of losing another of his loved ones haunted
him day and night. He looked over at the banner
hanging in his front window. It was white, bordered in
blood red and each of the four blue stars upon it
represented one of his sons serving somewhere in the
war effort. It was something to be proud of, people said
to him. He just shook his head, unable to respond that
the banner simply terrified him.

Henry shook off the thought and looked down
the road for signs of traffic. There were none. It was
quiet, he thought, unusually so for early September
when the light still extended well into the evening. But
now it was rare for a car to go by at this time of night
with gas rationing all but prohibiting any more than
necessary driving. And with Bobbie and Beverly at
church and Jiggs working at his job after school, he was
alone.

It occurred to him that he couldn't remember the
last time he had been by himself. He was amused to
realize that he hated the quiet. After so many years of
living in a house full of the noises of family life, the quiet
now was unnerving. Some might have found the chaos
unmanageable, perhaps even unlivable. But he and his
Catherine had cherished the cacophony naturally created
by the existence of 13 children under one roof. One tiny
roof, he thought, wondering how it was that they all had
managed to fit. But the music of that time was gone
now.

Gone too were the birthday celebrations, the Sunday dinners, the holidays that always brought them together, the crowd of family gathered around the Westinghouse in the living room. And gone away were four of his sons and a chunk of his soul with them. Perhaps a few more might have to leave. A vision of his wife flashed before his eyes, and he wished that she could be there so they could help each other through this time of uncertainty and anxiety.

The sound of a car in the distance distracted him. With a sigh of relief he realized that it was moving away from Highland Street.

Henry hated the sound of a car approaching his house now. When they did, he usually closed his eyes and grit his teeth until it had passed. His nightmare was to hear the car come to a halt, the sound of doors opening and closing and footsteps climbing the stairs to knock on the front door. He knew that if he opened it, a military officer and a priest would be there.

To tell him something was terribly wrong, but that he should be very proud.

His eyes began to water.

He lit a cigarette and reckoned that he could learn to live with the quiet. But he wondered if he could bear more of his children going off to war. A sudden chill raced down his spine. He shook off the thought of one or more of those blue stars suddenly turning gold.

He had to tell himself that it was just his mind imagining his worst fears. He could not allow himself to dwell on the unthinkable. His job as a father was not done yet. He still had a family to help through this obscene time, his sons and daughters who were struggling with the same nightmares.

Henry sluggishly stood up from the stairs and walked a few feet away from the house. He turned and faced it, slowly letting his eyes take it all in.   It once meant something, this little house. It was place that gave their family a footing. Somewhere where his children could always find love and safety. It was where he could protect them.

He wasn't so sure anymore.   But until he breathed his last, he would try.   After all, he had promised Catherine on her deathbed that he would be strong and finish the job they had begun together. He was not about to fail her, especially now, in this darkest of times.

No matter what happened.

Slowly, he shuffled back to the house and up the stairs.   For the fourth time that day, he stopped and checked the mailbox for a letter from one of the boys. It was empty.

He suddenly needed a drink, badly. He poured himself four fingers from the bottle of whiskey always present in the pantry and sat in his favorite chair in the living room. Then he stared out the front window and watched the sun slowly disappear over the horizon, trying to avert his eyes from the Blue Star Banner hanging there.

Alone, in the disturbing quiet.

Ten

~~~ ઝ ~~~

Fall, 1942

The good news about being stationed at the Jacksonville Naval Base in Florida was that you could play golf twelve months a year, Peachy Hughes thought to himself. The bad news was having the base commander, who was obsessed with the sport, find out you were a scratch player.

Before enlisting in the Navy, the 24-year old, fifth born son of Henry and Catherine Hughes had spent his youth playing the game every available minute. Like his brothers, he was a natural at the sport, but he was a cut above his siblings in ability. Living near the Wethersfield Country Club did offer some interesting opportunities. During the spring and summer, it wasn't unusual to find the Hughes brothers playing a few holes late at night. They would position their cars strategically

101

along the fairway and greens on the holes across Highland Street where the course was divided and play for hours using their headlights for illumination. But it was Peachy Hughes who gained a reputation as being the golfer to watch, the one who gripped a club with soft hands that let him feel the game.

Seaman Hughes had harbored ambitions of serving on a fighting ship in the Pacific. That goal was put on hold after he completed six brutal weeks of "Boot" camp at Naval Station Great Lakes near North Chicago with 100,000 newly drafted or enlisted sailors. To his great disappointment and in spite of his exemplary training record, instead of being assigned to a ship in the Pacific he found himself on a train to Jacksonville. Somehow his secret talent for the links had gotten out. On arrival, he was assigned to an administrative post assisting the base commander, the fiery Captain Roy Jenkins.

But playing golf was not the reason Hughes had enlisted in the Navy and he made it clear to his commanding officer he would transfer out of Jacksonville at first chance.

"Well..." his CO responded in a deep southern drawl, "I can't say that I don't admire your grit, boy," he said. "But the fact remains I hear tell you can hit a golf ball a mile and I do intend for Jacksonville Naval Air Base to smite all contenders to the honor of having the best god damned golf team in the Navy. Now... have I heard correctly, son?"

Peachy shuffled his feet and didn't respond.

"I say, boy," the CO raised his voice a notch. "If I do recall correctly, you are standing at attention in front of a superior and I have not mentioned the words, 'at ease.'"

"Yes, sir," Peachy responded, snapping back to attention.

"I'll repeat myself, boy, something I do not make a habit of doing. Am I correct in my understanding that you are one god damned good golfer?"

"Well, I... yes, sir... but that's not why..."

"Hell," the officer interrupted Hughes. "You're too dumb to know that's why you were born, son. To play golf for me on my team instead of scraping paint on a leaky destroyer in the frigging South China Sea. So I do foresee slim odds of you being transferred anywhere but to the bunk next to yours as long as you can swing a club. Do I make myself clear, boy?"

"Yes, sir, but I must protest this unreasonable..." Peachy began to respond.

"And I'll help you with that, son, it's only fair," the CO replied sarcastically. "Why, I'll personally provide you with the address of President Franklin D. Roosevelt hisself and you can write your protest to the god-damned Commander in Chief directly if you please. I imagine Mr. Roosevelt has nothing better to do than listen to the world's luckiest seaman complain about serving his country by playing golf."

"Lucky, sir?" Hughes said, shaking his head.

"Yes, lucky. You're a young man who's going to have a bright future because his commanding officer ordered him to play golf for the duration of the war instead of offering him up to fight the Japanese, who quite frankly couldn't give a tinker's damn about your ability to play golf and want nothing more than to shoot you right in your ungrateful Yankee ass. Do I make myself clear?"

Peachy Hughes couldn't thing of any way to respond. He was beginning to think Captain Jenkins was not only a redneck, but a bit unhinged. He was right on both counts.

"Now, unless you have some other pressing request to discuss with me that I will also deny, I suggest you let me get back to my own pressing business," Jenkins finished, reaching for his putter leaning against the wall behind his desk.

"Yes, sir," Peachy responded once again, completely disarmed by the absurd conversation.

That wasn't the end of it. Peachy protested vigorously at every opportunity, but his commanding officer wouldn't hear it. So in the months ahead, while he watched seaman after seaman ship out to various combat assignments, he begrudgingly carried out his staff work. And played stellar golf because he knew no other way.

October 3, 1942

Dear Pa and Gang,

Life is just grand here in Jacksonville, home of alligators, mosquitos the size of small airplanes, snakes of every color (most aren't very dangerous but who wants to find out?) spiders and more. But worst of all is the summer heat. Oh lord, the heat. I never thought I'd wish for snow again as long as I live. But what I wouldn't do for a family snowball fight!

The good news is boot camp is over and done with. The bad news is I'm in Jacksonville instead of being assigned to the Pacific Theater. The base CO got wind of the fact that I'm a pretty good golfer and he's determined that I will spend the entire war assigned as his assistant so I can play on his golf team. Every time my unit gets shipped out, he assigns me to another one. It's very disappointing. I didn't enlist to play golf. I keep putting in my papers for a transfer and he keeps rejecting them. So it looks like before I can get into the war, I'm going to have to win a battle here.

Has anyone heard from Jim? It's been weeks and I haven't had a word from him. He's not answering his letters. Let me know if you hear anything.

Well, that's all from Jacksonville. Got a match this afternoon. Hope I lose.

Wishing you all peace and happiness,
Peachy

*   *   *

On the same day Peachy's note finally made it into the hands of his brother Ray, the last family member to see it, 2nd Lieutenant James Hughes was fighting a losing battle to keep from retching over the side of a 36-foot long Higgins Boat in full view of his platoon of 40 men. It was November 8th, 1942. Jim's unit was among the more than 18,000 men of the 1st Infantry Division that were part of *"Operation Torch"* — the first Allied challenge to the Axis powers in occupied territory, the amphibious invasion of North Africa.

Hughes, commanding officer of Platoon B, Fox Company, 2nd Battalion, 16th Combat Team was part of the first wave of U.S. forces to begin the long-awaited effort to beat back Hitler's plan for domination of Europe, Africa and Russia. Although President Roosevelt had initially desired to open the land war against Hitler with simultaneous invasions of France and North Africa, U.S. and British military planners had rejected the plan for multiple battlefronts as too risky. Instead, the decision was made to focus first on French North Africa. Casablanca in Morocco, and the coastal cities of Oran and Algiers in Algeria were to be attacked by combined British-American forces.

105

The invasion plan took immense preparation and the 1st Infantry Division was to play a critical role. After dashing unescorted across the North Atlantic from New York to Scotland on board the Queen Mary, the *Big Red One* had arrived in Europe on August 7. The 15,000 man Division then made its way to Tidworth Barracks in England, followed by weeks of exhaustive training including intensive mock amphibious landings near Glasgow. On October 26, the Division departed England aboard 22 troop ships for the journey to the French African coast. On November 5th, Hughes and his platoon stood at the ship's rail as they passed through the Strait of Gibraltar, the entrance to the Mediterranean Sea bordered by the continents of Europe and Africa.

It was a place that few Americans could ever claimed to have set eyes upon. But the significance of the event was lost on most of the young troops. They knew that within days, perhaps even hours, they would be in the thick of combat. The 1st Infantry Division was to assault Oran, but more than 95 percent of its troops had no previous combat experience. The Algerian port city was to be the *Big Red One*'s trial by fire, a fact that weighed heavily on boys not yet old enough to vote.

Most of the men were preoccupied with checking and re-checking their gear and cleaning their guns, writing letters home that would be mailed after the invasion, playing craps under the nose of officers who looked the other way, or even praying. Sleep was hard to come by in the hot, cramped troop ships but it was their nerves that were really the culprit.

Jim Hughes contemplated writing to his own family on his last night of peace. He knew they were probably worried sick after not hearing a word from him for more than three months, and not knowing how they were faring further troubled him. But he fretted that his emotions would be transparent no matter what he said.

He knew that what he wrote might turn out to be his last words to them, and if that were the case, to say what he wanted to Pa and each of his siblings would bring out emotions in him they had rarely seen. They would read it as his goodbye letter to them, certainly not what he intended, but exactly what it might turn out to be. In a few hours, the odds of him living another day would diminish enormously.

He pondered the letter for nearly an hour, finally deciding to wait to write until his first chance after the landing in Oran. If he survived, he'd have plenty to say. If he didn't, better that Pa and his brothers and sisters held on to their memories of him and whatever sense a chaplain could make of his death.

Late on the evening of November 7th, after a full 24 hours of holding position several miles off shore, the 1st Infantry Division began mounting up. Hughes and his men climbed aboard a Higgins Boat and at 0057 hours they pushed off from the mother ship and aimed toward the shore, nearly four miles away.

As his landing craft approached the beach and the sound of enemy artillery began filling the air, Hughes sucked in a deep breath and wiped the salty Mediterranean Sea spray from his eyes with the sleeve of his damp jacket. He thought back to his first days at Fort Devens with his brothers John and Speck. It was only months ago but now it seemed like a lifetime.

Since then, his every waking moment had been about training, preparation, learning to lead and inspire, and finding the will to fight off homesickness and his own fears of combat. Now it was all behind him and the war he had been playing at was only moments away from becoming desperately real. He recalled his last words to his father:

"I'm no hero, Pa, but I promise I'll do my job and make you proud of me." Jim Hughes hoped he would live up to that promise, but at this moment his hands were trembling.

Hundreds of the wood and steel LCVP's (landing craft, vehicle and personnel) were pushing through the heavy but shallow surf at the coast of Arzew, east of the city of Oran, in northwest Algeria. The Higgins boat racing towards the Oran beach with Hughes' platoon was struggling to make headway against unanticipated sand bars at low tide. The constant impact with the ocean floor and resulting engine surge jerked the boat violently and caused even more anxiety for the frightened, inexperienced infantrymen aboard. Many silently prayed the boat would not break up under the stress. Luckily, resistance from the Vichy French, an unlikely enemy who had not yet joined the Allied effort, seemed to be light as they drew near shore. But Hughes knew that the closer the landing craft could get to the safety of the Oran beach, the better the odds were of his platoon surviving the opening minutes of their first battle together. The two .30 caliber machine guns mounted at the stern of the LCVP fired continually at six heavily fortified shore batteries defending the beach.

Hughes turned to his men, standing up in the lurching boat to give them one last order before they entered combat. Even over the roar of the Higgins boat's two diesel engines, exploding artillery and gunfire, they heard him clearly.

"Remember, there is no one tougher, no one more committed, no one more ready to fight than a soldier in the *Big Red One*," he said. "This is why we've been training like mad men, this is what the world has been

108

waiting for. Let's give everyone at home something to cheer about." A roar of approval rose up from the bowels of the cramped boat, despite the jitters of every man aboard.

Finally, the Higgins boat commander could find no more water beneath his landing craft although it was still more than 300 hundred yards from shore. Reluctantly he shouted the order to drop the boat's heavy steel ramp into the shallows. Hughes was incredulous. His men would have to wade more than three football fields in knee deep water weighed down by heavy backpacks, tools and weapons without cover. They were completely exposed to enemy fire.

But there was no choice. To remain in the false safety of the landing craft was a fool's choice.

"Go, go, go! Fast and low. Get to the beach!" Hughes hollered as machine gun fire ripped across the water and over their heads. Miraculously, every man escaped the boat. The thought crossed his mind that the poorly trained Vichy French firing at them were either lousy marksman or their hearts weren't in the battle. Both were probably true. But he wasn't about to wait around to see if their aim or attitude improved.

Following the last man out of the LCVP, Hughes lunged forward and began slogging through the surf. He moved as fast as his long legs would carry him, focusing on the sandy beach hundreds of feet ahead. With every step, he waited to be cut down and watched as men to his left and right fell face forward into the water. The French were finally finding their range. Panic swept over him as he continued to forge ahead, desperate to reach the shore. Images of his father and his brothers and sisters at home waiting for him flooded his vision. Then suddenly, his mother's voice rang in his ears.

"I love you James, you be a good boy at school today. Make me proud of you," her voice echoed in his head. It was what she said to him every morning as he left for school.

"I will ma, I will..." he answered aloud, then shook off the vision as he tripped over a body in the surf. He didn't recognize the man, but he was alive. Hughes grabbed a strap on the soldier's backpack and began to drag him towards the beach with him.

"Keep moving, keep moving!" he urged his men, some of whom were just making it out of the water and on to the beach.

"Don't stop, move forward, find cover," he barked. As the last word came out of his mouth, a bullet grazed his helmet, ripping it off his head and knocking him down. He fell to the water from the shock of the impact but immediately surfaced and got back on his feet. He snatched his helmet out of the surf and raced the final yards to shore still dragging his wounded comrade.

Finally, Hughes fell heavily to the sand next to one of his men, breathless. He had made it.

"Medic!" he screamed to get help for the man he had saved. He looked down at him.

"Hang in there buddy, you're going to make it..." he told the soldier. A medic suddenly appeared and dropped down beside the two.

"I got it from here, Lieutenant," he said calmly and pulled the man away from Hughes and further up the beach. Jim went to follow them then regained his focus. He had a job to do. Raising his head slightly from the safety of the sand, he took in the situation.

Hundreds of men were pinned down on the open beach by machine gun fire from concrete shore batteries above them. They needed to move and fast. He looked

110

around for his commanding officer, but couldn't spot him. There was no waiting.

"Combat Team 16, defilade behind the dunes 30 yards ahead. Move now, that is an order," he yelled, urging the frightened men to get to their feet and run to the cover of rising dunes and tufts of tall, coarse beach grass that would block the enemy's vision as they fired down on them. He jumped to his feet, taking hold of the man next to him by the shoulder.

"Move out!" he barked again and jumped to his feet, racing to the dunes. Hundreds of men followed his lead. Reaching the sand dunes, he burrowed under a large growth of sea grass and looked behind him. Dozens of men lay dead or severely wounded on the beach from where he had come. The water lapping at the shore was blood red. Corpses rocked face down in the bloody surf. Several LCVP's were stuck in the shallows, stuck on sandbars. All were in flames.

"Why the fuck did they drop us at low tide?" Hughes cursed to himself. It was a lesson he would carry back to mission planners when he was debriefed.

From the modest protection proffered by the dunes, Hughes directed a covering fire as several infantry men raced towards the shore battery that had caused so much carnage among the landing craft and had pinned the unit down on the beach. The deafening and deadly barrage of M-1 rifles, Thompson sub-machine guns and Browning Automatic Rifles firing at the small ports of the concrete bunker allowed the men to get close enough to set up a Bangalore torpedo, a weapon designed to blow a hole through heavy barbed wire. The bunker was buried in the lethal, razor sharp wire and would have to be cleared before troops could attempt to take the concrete encasement. Quickly, with practiced hands, three men put the Bangalore together

111

by joining five, five-foot long sections of pipe and set the charge and fuse.

"Fire in the hole," one of the men shouted moments later, a warning to take cover. Immediately a 40-pound charge of TNT shot through the 25-foot long Bangalore and a huge explosion followed. Sand and bits of wire rained down on the troops. When the shower of debris ended, it was clear they had successfully opened a ten-foot wide hole in the wire.

"Shoot and scoot," Hughes ordered the men of Combat Team 16 hunkered under the dunes with him. Immediately, another barrage of fire raked the bunker as several men from the Bangalore detail ran through the opening in the barbed wire. Enemy machine guns in the bunker returned fire at the smoke from where Hughes and his men had shot. But their rounds found nothing but sand as the remnants of Fox Company and Hughes' platoon had already dashed from their hiding places and were sprinting toward the bunker. Before they could reach it, several large explosions burst through the bunker, the result of hand grenades dropped through the gun ports by the Bangalore squad.

Hughes ran above the bunker, lifted the heavy steel entrance door to the concrete shelter and dropped another grenade inside. Vichy French dropped out of any opening in the bunker in an attempt to escape but were immediately shot by the large contingent of men now surrounding them. He turned and looked down the coast. Five other shore batteries housing 7.6-inch guns were under attack by members of Fox Company using the same tactic.

"Cease fire," Hughes ordered. "Save your ammunition. We'll need it." He sucked in a deep breath. "Next stop, Oran."

112

The 2nd Lieutenant, his own hands shaking, scanned the faces of the men around him. None of them were celebrating and most appeared to be in shock from the ordeal of the last 20 minutes. He saw grown men crying. Others hid their faces. But Arzew was secure and the path to Oran was clear. Hughes had his platoon radioman call in the success of the mission and relay the signal that the beach was clear so the invasion commanders could land the tanks and artillery of the 1st Armored Division.

"Grab a smoke, guys," Hughes ordered the men around him. "We move out in ten." He quietly gave his First Sergeant, a 22-year old kid from new Hampshire named Mike Pettig instructions to do a headcount of his own platoon and get the best assessment he could of casualties in Fox Company. He was all but certain his Platoon had taken some casualties and continued scanning the beach for familiar faces while he sucked on a Lucky Strike to calm his nerves. He said a short prayer in hope that the men under his command had escaped injury or worse. The thought occurred to him that he would have to write to the parents if...

Pettig was back in less than ten minutes, a grim look on his face. Hughes braced himself.

"We lost four men, Lieutenant. All in the water," Pettig said softly.

Hughes swallowed hard.

"Who..." he asked immediately, trying to hide his emotions.

"Aleksom, Brice, Gilberto and Walker," he responded, shaking his head. Three instantly. They just lost Gilberto on the beach. Head wound."

Jim Hughes, a mountain of a man who before today had been afraid of no one or nothing and rarely displayed any form of sentiment, stared at Pettig in silence.

The Sergeant wordlessly handed him four sets of dog tags that he had retrieved from the bodies of the members of Platoon B. He dropped his eyes to the pile of metal he had placed in Hughes' hand.

"At least 200, maybe more in Fox Company," Pettig said. He turned and began walking away, then stopped and faced the Lieutenant.

"What were they thinking of dumping us a mile from shore in four feet of water?" the Sergeant asked, his voice tight with rage. "The assholes didn't know it would be low tide?"

Jim Hughes didn't hear the pointed question. He was squeezing the dog tags in his hand, his face purple with anger. He made no attempt to hide the tear that rolled down his cheek.

"This war just got real," he said, his big hand shaking the dog tags in anger. He slowly reached up and placed them in his breast pocket, buttoning the flap to make sure they were secure.

"So help me God, I'm taking these with me to Berlin and I'm going to shove them right up Hitler's ass."

Pettig looked into the eyes of his commanding officer. His fury was contagious.

"Well then, I'm coming with you, sir."

The two men stood in silence for a moment, considering the long days ahead.

"Round 'em up. Time to kick the shit out of anyone in Oran who wasn't smart enough to run when he saw us coming."

By November 10, the battle for Oran was over and the Vichy French had surrendered. Combat Team 16 was pulled off the line for a brief rest. Jim Hughes hadn't slept in more than 48 hours but he refused to close his eyes until he had written his letters, including one to his father.

November 10, 1942

Dear Pa,

I'm sure the newspapers back home are telling you all about the invasion of North Africa. Well, as you probably suspected, that's where I am, in a city called Oran on the coast of Algeria. We have been training for this invasion for months. I hope you will understand why I wasn't allowed to write to you before this and how little I can say even now. I'll tell you all about it someday. But I'm writing this letter only to you; I'll send another to the family soon. There are some things I want to share with you alone.

When I left home, I thought I was a tough guy, a big man with a big mouth. I don't feel so big and tough anymore, and I can tell you for sure I don't have as much to say about every little thing now. I've learned a lot about being a man, Pa, that I know for certain.

When I jumped out of my LC into the surf near Oran with bullets spraying the water all around me, I felt fear like I never have before. It was not so much about being afraid of dying as it was of panicking, of being a coward. I had men looking to me for leadership and I was terrified I would let them down.

I think I did ok, Pa. I need you to know that.

But now I feel something else. I've been a hot head most of my life, as you know well. That fire in me burns hotter now than ever before. I feel a rage that I can hardly explain. Earlier tonight, I had to send letters to the parents of four young men in my platoon who were killed before their boots ever hit the beach. Not one of them was yet 20 years old.

Before they died, under my command, I arrogantly felt like this war was my ticket to becoming a hero. Like I said, I don't feel so tough now and being a hero is about the last thing on my mind. But losing those boys and having to tell their

115

parents that they died with honor has filled me with anger that keeps me fighting mad. That's a good thing, Pa. I will not succumb to despair. What is hardest now is recognizing that every second that passes until I am back with you in the living room on Highland Street is one I'll never get back.

But I will come home, Pa. And I'll be a real man you will have reason to be proud of.

Take care of yourself. We all need you.

Your loving son,

Jim

Eleven
~~~ ❧ ~~~

"I didn't see that letter from Jim, nor did any of my brothers and sisters for many years after he wrote it to Pa," Ka explained to us. "My father did a good job of keeping it to himself as my brother had asked."

By now there wasn't a seat left at the table and all but the youngest of the children were riveted on her every word. It was still hot as the dickens even as the Fourth of July celebration was winding down and the pops and bangs of neighborhood fireworks had begun to die off. I think even the cicada's had toned down their summer symphony out of respect for the old woman's story.

"A couple of days later, Jim wrote and asked me to tell everyone that he was fine and not to worry. He never mentioned how bad a time he had gone through, or how much danger he was in. We were all so elated that he was safe after not hearing from him for so long.

117

At the time we were so relieved to hear from him that we didn't find it odd he wasn't depressed about the whole thing. He actually sounded rather carefree. Looking back, that was rather strange for someone who'd gone though what he had. But then again, everything about the time was a bit unusual... right down to our butter, " she abruptly added, throwing her head back in laughter at the sudden memory.

"Butter?" someone asked with a giggle. "What was so funny about butter in 1942?"

"We didn't have any!" Ka laughed again. "With the rationing, we couldn't buy it. Instead the government produced this stuff called 'margarine' that was supposed to take the place of butter but was more like a lump of lard. It was horrible tasting and it looked even worse. There was some law that didn't allow the margarine to be sold the same color as butter, so it came all white. "

"Yuck," my brother Jeff reacted, the vision crossing his mind also registering in his stomach.

"Yuck is right," Ka responded. "Eventually, someone got the idea to include a little orange capsule when you bought the stuff at the grocers. You were supposed to soften up the stick of margarine and then mix in the orange contents of the capsule."

"Did that improve it?" I asked.

"Well," she chuckled again. "If you liked the taste of orange colored lard better than white lard you were in luck."

Laughter erupted around the table. Ka beamed.

"It wasn't so bad," she added. "We all had to do our part. Actually, the Victory Gardens were wonderful. I've never tasted such tasty vegetables since. So fresh. I guess the thought that we were doing something to help probably made them taste even better."

STARS IN OUR WINDOW

"What happened with Uncle Peachy?" my sister asked. "Did he win his private battle?"

Ka just shook her head and thought back for a moment before responding.

"You know, we all felt bad for Peachy. He had enlisted to fight for his country and it wasn't fair what happened to him. We could tell he was embarrassed, but there wasn't a blessed thing he could do about it." She hesitated again.

"But to tell you the truth..."

She stopped and sighed again, mulling over whether or not to go any further.

In typical fashion, she went for it.

"About a week after we got Peachy's letter about his predicament, our little town got its second taste of tragedy in that God awful war. This time it was one of my brother's own classmates. Bobby Brouder, a close friend of Peachy's in high school, was reported killed in action during the Guadalcanal battle. Pa knew his family well, they lived on Main Street. Bobby was on a destroyer, the *USS Little*, I think it was, that went down with all hands in September..." she paused trying to remember... "yes, it was September. That's all we ever knew. Just what the newspaper reported. His body was never found."

There was dead silence for a moment while everyone absorbed what she had said. In that moment, her story took on a whole new urgency. Just as it had for the Hughes family, I was sure, when they had gotten the news of Bobby Brouder's death 60 years before.

"We'd all been sympathetic to Peachy's situation, I can tell you Pa even talked about bringing it up with our congressman. But there's nothing like shock to shake some common sense into your head.

119

"You see, since Pearl Harbor, when we lost Monty Whitehead, the war had only separated us from people we knew and some we loved. But none of them had been hurt or killed. The whole thing became a bit abstract and I think we spent more time worrying about the rationing than what was happening in the war. Suddenly, Wethersfield had another Gold Star, another grieving mother and father, and it all became much more real.

"And very, very sad."

She folded her hands in her lap and stared at her empty Limoncello glass for a moment.

"If I have one more of these delicious little drinks will someone give me a lift home?" she asked with a devilish grin.

"I'll take you home myself," I answered her and poured another cordial glass of the sweet, but sneaky liquor.

"Grampa never did talk to that congressman, did he Ka?" Peachy's son Bill asked.

"Not that I know of, Billy," she answered softly. "I think we all played along with Peachy wanting him to think we were rooting for him to get assigned to a ship in the Pacific. But really... I know I prayed that his luck held out and he stayed right where he was, working on his short game. I think Pa and everyone else did, too."

There were smiles of understanding around the table. And then Ka opened her soul to us, and for the first time I understood what she had gone through all those years before.

"I found it ironic, even back then, when I heard men complain about not getting to fight. They were ashamed of that. I'll tell you, my brothers were all heroes to me — those who fought, those who were ready to fight and those who remained home because they

120

were needed here. None of them had to prove their courage to me by fighting the Japanese or the Germans. I hope Peachy... well, I hope they all knew that.

"But this was a time when there were very few men who didn't want to serve. There was a real spirit of support for the war back then. Everyone put their back into it, I think because it felt like we had been wronged. And, everything we had always taken for granted — our freedoms — were suddenly at risk. The Nazi's and the Japanese Empire had their eyes on the prize: us! So men wanted to go off and fight.

"Don't get me wrong," Ka was quick to add. "We hated the war. We lived in constant fear of bombings or an invasion even though they were very unlikely to happen. But most of all, we learned to live with hearts that were always on the verge of being broken. Perhaps 'shattered' is a better word. On any given day, at any moment, a car with a military officer and a priest might pull up in front of Pa's house..." she said, choking up at the memory.

"You know, I think every one of us slept with one eye open each night... waiting, always waiting."

The silence was painful as we each imagined what it must have been like to live in constant fear of losing a loved one. The parents around the table swallowed hard.

"So, you have to understand why they were all so intent upon going to war. For Jim, John, Speck and Peachy it was an easy decision. But Phil and Henry and Ray, Dot's husband Ed and even my own husband Andy felt tremendous pressure being home while their brothers and friends were at war, even though they were contributing in their own way with their jobs in the factories. And some of them had wives and children who needed them, so they couldn't just up and enlist.

"My Dad never really talked about it much, but I know he struggled with staying home even though he had two kids," Bob Hughes, Phil's youngest son said.

Ka shook her head in agreement.

"It might have been worst of all for Jiggs, who was just so full of anger and feared nothing. He wanted no part of school. All he wanted was a gun in his hands and an enemy to shoot at. Pa had his hands full with him. Like Peachy, Jiggs just would not accept 'no' for an answer."

"Now that sounds like my husband," my Aunt Joan said, widowed just the year before when my Uncle Jiggs had passed away.

Jimmy and Holly, her children, roared with laughter at the thought.

"I'm surprised that Uncle Jiggs didn't just enlist for the draft when he turned 16 in 1942," Claudia's brother Fred remarked. "Actually, I can't believe Pa was able to stop him."

"Well the only way Jiggs could have enlisted at 16 was if he dropped out of high school and Pa signed for him. And that wasn't going to happen. And by the time Jiggs turned 18 and could make his own decisions, Roosevelt had changed the draft law — I think it was at the very end of 1942 — so that men weren't able to volunteer even if they wanted to. The President was worried about having enough men to defend the homeland in the event of an invasion. So, after that, every man, even those who wanted to enlist had to wait for the draft board to call him. Jiggs couldn't join the military until 1944, two years later, and that was only after he pleaded with the draft board to take him. He wasn't an easy person to live with during those years, poor boy. He was so frustrated.

"And the letters from his brothers only made it worse."

Twelve

~~~ ço ~~~

December, 1942

Pfc. John Hughes, an airborne trainee assigned to D Company, 2nd Battalion 506th Parachute Regiment, flinched when the red light mounted on the cockpit bulkhead of the Douglas C-47 "Skytrain" he was crammed into with 19 other soldiers suddenly flashed to green.

The green light meant that Hughes' basic training was over except for finding the answer to one question: did he have the guts to jump out of an airplane flying 1,400 feet above the earth? It was a hard thing to ask of a boy who had just celebrated his 24th birthday.

Hughes had survived the brutal weeks of conditioning and psychological indoctrination at Camp Taccoa. He'd run a thousand miles up the Curahee Mountain and learned to be proud to sing "3 Miles up, 3

Miles down" when he and his fellow trainee's had mastered the physical challenge. They laughed about it now. And he'd learn to respect the Cherokee word "Curahee," meaning "Stand Alone" that had been adopted as the regiment's motto since that was the objective of the 506th when it was behind enemy lines: fighting alone to take strategic locations from the enemy ahead of the main invasion force.

Hughes had absorbed the best punches his Commanding Officer, Colonel Robert Sink could throw at him, including the regiment's 137-mile march to Atlanta upon completion of their training at Camp Toccoa. There the unit boarded trains to complete their journey to Fort Benning in Georgia for Airborne School. Sink ordered the march because he had read an article in Reader's Digest about a long distance marching record set by a Japanese infantry company. The 506th shattered it, with 544 men making the march in just over 75 hours.

The young man's body had become rock hard and he'd learned the basics of paratrooper combat. He had survived a half dozen mock parachute jumps from a 200-foot high tower and learned to properly fold and pack his own parachute. To the greatest degree possible, he was taught to take control of his own fate and reminded repeatedly of the meaning of "Stand alone." And finally, he'd accepted the difficulty — perhaps even the improbability — of surviving the battles ahead.

He and his fellow Curahees had sung their own version of the "Battle Hymn of the Republic" as they marched toward their waiting C-47 just that morning. The song was known as "Blood Upon The Risers" — referring to the strips of webbing joining the harness and rigging lines of a parachute — and it was the paratrooper's macabre way of laughing in the face of fate. They had to laugh or the fear they each held inside would rob them of the sharp edge to which they had been honed as fighting men.

> *"There was blood upon the risers*
> *there were brains upon the chute,*
> *his intestines were a-dangling from*
> *his paratroopers suit.*
>
> *He was a mess, they picked him up*
> *and poured him from his boots,*
> *he ain't gonna jump no more.*
>
> *Gory, gory what a hell of a way to die.*
> *Gory, gory what a hell of a way to die.*
> *Gory, gory what a hell of a way to die,*
> *he ain't gonna jump no more!"*

The grins on the faces of the marching men faded as they approached their assigned aircraft. And as it finally spend down the runway and nosed into the air, there was silence inside the packed transport. Finally it was time to see if all the training had paid off.

For all of them, this would be their first actual parachute jump. Each man would either win his jump wings in the next few minutes or wash out of paratrooper school. "You only get one chance," his instructors had repeated over and again.

"Freeze at the door when it's your turn to jump and you'll be on a train to the nearest infantry unit before you can say Curahee," the jumpmaster had told them as they boarded the C-47.

And now they were over the drop zone.

"Oh, shit," Hughes mumbled under his breath as he saw the green light come on. Time to find out the answer to the question.

He followed the jumpmaster's command to "Stand and hook up your static line" and shakily rose to his feet, struggling with both the awkward weight of the parachute pack strapped to his back and his nerves, and took his place among the 20 man "stick." Following the procedure that he had practiced repeatedly in simulated jumps, Hughes reached over his head and clipped a metal snap hook attached to the ripcord on his parachute to the static line running the length of the aircraft. The simple system would ensure that four seconds after he jumped his parachute would automatically be deployed. If his canopy unfurled and filled with air, he had nothing to do but enjoy the gentle ride to earth and prepare for a textbook landing. If not, if the lines to the canopy above him were tangled, he had a few seconds to attempt to untangle them. If he was unsuccessful, his last resort was the reserve chute strapped across his chest. If that didn't work...

He shook off the thought as the jumpmaster yelled the next command: "Go! Go! Go!" and the first man in the stick stepped to the open door of the C-47 — aptly named the "Gooney Bird" — and leapt. Hughes was seventh in line. He stepped forward as the first man jumped, moving his snap line ahead and again as each man ahead of him left the airplane. In less than five seconds he was at the door.

He looked down at the Georgia landscape. It was a hell of a long way down. As he launched his body out of the airplane he wondered if the extra $50 a month he'd be paid as a paratrooper was worth this insanity.

"Hell no!" he screamed into the roar of the wind as he fell, praying for the jolting shock that came with the opening of his parachute.

127

Four seconds. He counted them off as instructed despite the adrenaline rushing through his veins that threatened to burst his arteries.

"One thousand one, one thousand two, one thousand three," he gulped, "one thousand four."

December 12, 1942

Dear Pa and gang,

Thanks for all the birthday wishes. I got a bunch of letters from you guys just the day before and they sure did make me happy, but also very homesick. Wish I were home to taste my birthday cake made with that funny butter you keep telling me about. I'm sure you girls wouldn't have disappointed me!

So, a funny thing happened to me a couple of days ago. I jumped out of an airplane for the first time. Yep, I earned my paratroopers wings and the 'Screaming Eagle' regiment patch for my uniform. And now I can officially tuck my pants into the top of my jump boots, which I can tell you makes you pretty special in this man's army.

I know you probably think I'm crazy for becoming a paratrooper and I certainly didn't want you to have any more reason to worry, but I have to tell you that I feel like I'm doing something important. The paratroopers are an elite force of men and I think we're going to make a real difference when we finally see some action. I'm not ashamed to tell you I'm proud of myself, the training was brutal. I hope you're proud of me.

Let me tell you about it.

We took off in this crazy tin can of an airplane that they call a 'Gooney Bird' because it's so awkward looking. But it's actually a C-47, which is a converted commercial DC-3. There were 20 guys all crammed into it. They call that a 'stick,' don't ask me why. Well, we climb to 1,400 feet but you can't see anything because you're wearing so much gear you can't turn to look out the windows. Suddenly a green light comes on to tell us we're over the jump zone. So we all stand up and hook up our static lines — the thing that makes our chutes open when we jump out of the plane. And then just like robots, the jumpmaster says, "Jump!" So we jump! Right out of the airplane into the clouds.

Well, I closed my eyes at first and waited for four seconds to pass, the amount of time it's supposed to take for my parachute to open, and sure enough, right on schedule the canopy opens above me. But the damn thing didn't unfurl correctly because my lines were crossed. So here I am dropping like a rock with only a few seconds to fix the problem or then I have to try my reserve chute. If that didn't work I guess I would have been a grease spot on the Georgia countryside. But it was the darndest thing. The instructors told us to do a sort of movement with our legs like you were riding a bicycle if we found ourselves in this situation, so I did. One of you must have been praying for me at that moment because sure enough, the minute I started to ride that bicycle in mid air, my lines untangled and my canopy immediately filled with air. I tell you, it was the most beautiful thing I've ever seen. The rest of the ride down was uneventful and I even landed properly without breaking my ankles! One of my instructors came running over and I expected him to give me hell, but instead he told me I did a hell of a job for a first timer and even talked about it that night when we got together to be presented with our official jump wings.

Guess there ain't many guys who can say that's how they celebrated their 24th birthday!

That's about all the excitement from here, gang. I love and miss you all. I'm still at Fort Benning here in Georgia, honestly don't know where my next stop will be. I don't think it's going to be overseas anywhere because we still have training to do. I'll let you know as soon as I do. Say hi for me to everyone, please, and Pa, make sure you keep my sisters in line until the boys get home.

129

Has anyone heard from Jim? I know he's in North Africa in the thick of it. Bet old Bull is kicking some German butt. Please let me know if you've heard anything.

Hope you put up a Christmas tree. It will give me something to think about on Christmas day. Can't imagine not being with you for dinner. I can tell you it doesn't feel much like the holidays here.

Merry Christmas and love to you all,
Pfc. John Hughes — a Screaming Eagle!

*   *   *

To "Sergeant" Speck Hughes' surprise, his stay at McClellan Field only lasted a couple of weeks after his Doolittle adventure at the end of March. He was transferred back to Blythe Airfield in the southern California desert to his great disappointment instead of being shipped to a unit in the South Pacific. As usual, there was no explanation.

"I'm learning a lot that will come in handy after the war," he wrote to his father that summer. *"But it sure is frustrating turning a wrench all day when the whole world is exploding in the South Pacific. So far, with the exception of meeting Lt. Col. Doolittle, this experience has been pretty darned boring. And I am so lonesome and homesick I could cry."*

There was little Henry Hughes could do to console Speck, or Peachy for that matter, who was still trapped playing golf for the Jacksonville Naval Air Base instead of fighting the Japanese. John was itchy for action as well but Henry figured it was only a matter of time before that happened now that he was a paratrooper with the 506th regiment. All three of them took it hard when they learned that brother Jim was in the middle of the heavy fighting still being waged in North Africa.

Christmas 1942 was a miserable affair for the Hughes clan who were all desperate for information about Jim and full of anxiety about the next moves in store for their other siblings.

There were only 13 at the "grown-ups" table for Christmas dinner at Pa's that year, counting Vera Pignone, Ed Ames and Andy Anderson, and it was a somber affair made bearable only by the fun of the children opening a few presents. They were small toys that Pa had made with his own hands. At the end of the surprisingly tasty chicken dinner that the girls had whipped together despite the rationing limits, Pa ended Christmas Day with a toast to his boys wearing military uniforms. He stood in the living room next to the Blue Star Banner hanging proudly in the bay window and raised his glass to each of the four stars.

There was a catch in his voice as he spoke.

"This was not the day we hoped it would be," he began, "with all of our family gathered around the table, safe from harm and home where they belong. Truth be told, we don't know when that day will come, but it will, I know it in my heart, it will. I am proud of your brothers, each of them," he continued, gazing at the blue stars.

"But I am also proud of those of you who are here with us today, serving our country in a most critical way and helping to make it easier for Jim, John, Speck and Peachy until they march again through our front door."

He paused for a moment to collect himself, his emotions on the brink of taking over his tongue.

"We miss your dear mother today, as well, but take some solace from knowing that she does not have to

131

bear this awful burden. She above all would have suffered this intolerable separation from her boys and anxiety for all her family. But I know she is looking upon them, right now, and will guide them home to us.

"Until that day comes when we are once again reunited, let us all remain strong for each other, do our jobs, keep the children safe… and never stop praying."

A tear escaped his eye but he ignored it as it rolled down his wrinkled cheek.

"Wherever you may be today, my sons, we wish you a Merry Christmas and a New Year full of…" Henry lowered his glass slightly, unsure of what to say. There was an awkward silence until Ray slowly got to his feet and finished the sentence for his father.

"…and a New Year that will bring Peace to the world and our brothers safely home to us," he said.

Henry smiled and raised his glass.

"Thank you Ray," Pa nodded his head to his son.

"Merry Christmas, my children, I love you all. And let me finish with some words that my own dear Da would say to us at Christmas when I was just a boy."

He raised the glass to his chin.

"May the dreams you hold dearest be those which come true." He put the whiskey to his lips and drained the glass.

Beverly and Bobbie began to sob. Their daily visits to Sacred Heart Church and constant prayers seemed be to falling upon deaf ears. Both girls had held on to the hope that their brothers would be home by Christmas to the bitter end.

Henry Jr. was not about to let the day come to a close with tears. They all needed hope. He stood.

"Pa, forgive me, but I also would like to share an Irish toast that I think our brothers afar would enjoy as they celebrate Christmas on their own," he said.

A grin came to his father's face. "Just remember there are ladies in the room, Henry," he warned his namesake.

"Not to worry, old Da," he responded.

Henry cleared his throat and one by one looked each of his siblings in the eye as he spoke and winked at Bobbie and Beverly.

"May those who love us, love us," he said. "And those who do not love us, may God turn their hearts."

Henry looked around the room with his glass raised, a frown coming to his face for emphasis.

"And if he doesn't turn their hearts, may he turn their ankles..." he continued, then paused before growling out the punch line.

"So we'll know them by their limping!" he roared, raising his glass again.

The room was filled with laughter and hugs as Christmas 1942 came to a close for the Hughes family.

But in Blythe, California, Jacksonville, Florida and at Fort Benning, Georgia, Speck, Peachy and John spent Christmas day doing exactly the same thing: lying on their bunks, dreaming of going home. There was only one difference among them.

It was raining in the California dessert, a most rare occurrence, as Speck waited to be transferred to another assignment. This time he was going to Rice Army Airfield in Riverside County, a small base about 20 miles away near Rice, California. Like Blythe, Rice was part of the Army Air Force's Desert Training Center spread through the Mojave. The South Pacific assignment he wanted remained elusive.

That night, the 21-year old young man, struggling with homesickness, disenchantment with the military and his own impatience, wrote to Elvira to voice

133

his frustration. Before he realized it, his words to her led him to thinking about the future.

December 25, 1942

Dear Vera,

Merry Christmas, sweetheart! Wish I were with you. Pa told me he was going to invite you for dinner. I hope the gang didn't give you too much of a hard time. If they did, it's because they like you.

As I write this letter I'm sitting on my bunk, as I have been all day, waiting for transport to Rice Army Airfield in Riverside County, my next stop. It's late now so I don't think it's going to happen today. I'll probably just sleep in my uniform tonight because my blanket and sheets are packed away. To make it worse, it rained here all day. Can you imagine? It rained in the desert on Christmas day.

I can't tell you how lonely and frustrated I am, Vera and how much I want to be home with you. The Army is not for me, it's just one disappointment after another. I can't hardly believe I'm making much of a contribution to the war spending my days fixing broken cargo transports and old jeeps and trucks. I volunteered so I could fight and get this thing over with and get on with my life. My life with you, that is. But now I'm heading for Rice, which I hear is a bigger stink hole than Blythe. What's the use…

Eventually, I don't know exactly when, I'll probably get a furlough home for a few days, and when I do I want to talk to you about the future. I think you know what I mean. Sleep on that tonight; it's the only Christmas present I can offer. I hope you like it.

Got to turn out the lights now so I have to say goodbye.

I'll write from Rice as soon as I can and give you my new address.

Merry Christmas, sweetie.

Love,

Speck

*   *   *

On the other side of the world, 2nd Lt. James Hughes wasn't celebrating Christmas at all. In fact, he was oblivious to the holiday. He had far more important things to worry about.

Like surviving another day in North Africa.

After successfully taking the city of Oran following their harrowing amphibious landing and beach assault at the coast of Arzew, Jim Hughes and Combat Team 16 of the 1st infantry Division were taken off the line for rest and training in the desert terrain. Unexpectedly, in late December the unit was called upon by the British for assistance in holding the Algerian mountains of *Diebel el Ahmera* and *Diebel Rhar*, heights known as "Longstop Hill" that blocked the Allied attempt to secure the Tunisian capital of Tunis before the German infantry could reach it. Bordered by Libya and the Mediterranean, control of Tunisia was of great strategic importance to both the Allied and Axis powers as a supply port for the war in North Africa. However, the first British effort to secure the small country, a critical objective of *Operation Torch*, was ill fated.

On the night of December 23rd, the famed British Coldstream Guards, Britain's oldest and most experience infantry regiment captured the hills despite being undermanned and undersupplied, heavy German resistance and wind-whipped rains that made every foot of the climb treacherous. Almost immediately the Germans began efforts to retake the hills and the 1st Infantry Division's Combat Teams 16 and 18 were rushed forward to provide relief for the beleaguered British Troops. But by Christmas Day, German reinforcements arrived and the American troops were

135

overwhelmed. Exhausted and outnumbered, the 1st Infantry and the remaining Guards were forced to pull back.

Hughes and his platoon had been pinned down for more than 30 hours, desperately trying to hold the hills before getting the order to retreat.

"God dammit," he hollered when his radioman relayed the order. "I'm not about to give these SOB's one square yard of this hill, you understand me?" he responded, continuing to fire his M1 at the enemy even while arguing.

"Hell, Jim, if we don't give up this hill, we're going to be buried on it," First Sergeant Mike Pettig, Hughes' right hand yelled to him while also returning fire.

"Give it up Lieutenant, we live to fight another day. There's too many of them and not enough of us," Pettig argued.

"Shit," Hughes muttered under his breath while taking a bead on a German infantryman not more than 100 yards away. "Remind me to bust you to Private later," he responded, but knowing his loyal backstop was right.

"Pull back, pull back!" Hughes hollered to his men while Pettig began physically yanking the men from their positions. None of them wanted to give in.

"This is a one hell of a way to spend Christmas Day, Lieutenant," one of his men yelled to him. "We don't even get to say the good guys won."

Hughes laughed to himself despite their urgent situation. They were brave men who didn't deserve to be told to give up after all they'd been through.

""Pettig's right, live to fight another day, soldier. Pull back," he ordered again. "This piece of dirt isn't worth losing men over when we don't have the muscle to get the job done." Just as the words left his mouth, a German bullet grazed the left arm of his field jacket, piercing the sleeve but passing through. It was the second time he'd been hit without spilling a drop of his own blood since landing on the North African coast.

Hughes' Platoon D and 500 other survivors of Combat Team 16's Fox Company spent the night in troop transports racing over muddy, rut filled roads behind the lines to safety. They were exhausted and too tired to remember they hadn't eaten in a day and a half.

"You know, when this shit is over, I think I'm going to put up a hammock in my old man's back yard and sleep for a month," Pettig said to Hughes in the darkness of their truck.

"Hell, if we make it through this… I think I might lay down in the tall grass in front of the barn at my father's place, close my eyes and just listen. What I wouldn't give to hear my little sisters laughing or my Pa hammering away at some project. I used to take little things like that for granted. But you know what, Mike? Those are the sounds of peace. That's all I want. Just to hear that again," Jim replied. "If I get the chance, I'll listen a lot closer next time." He suddenly felt much older than his 32 years.

Pettig shook his head, a far away look in his eyes. "I hear ya, Bull."

Hughes pulled out a pack of cigarettes from the breast pocket of his filthy fatigues and lit up a couple of smokes. "Here," he said, passing one to Pettig. "This is as close to peace as we're going to get for a while. Enjoy it."

"I'll do that," Pettig said, taking the Lucky Strike. "Hey Bull, I almost forgot."

"What?" Hughes answered.

"Merry frigging Christmas, sir."

A grin came to Hughes' face.

"Yah, peace on earth, huh? Merry Christmas to you too, Mike. Guess it's one we won't forget."

Then the two men lapsed into silence in the darkness of the truck, each lost in memories of the worlds they knew back home. The glowing embers of their cigarettes slowly dimmed and they rode in quiet misery for several more hours back to Oran.

Jim Hughes abruptly remembered the bullet hole in his jacket and located it with his fingers. He toyed with the torn fabric for a moment contemplating how close the round had come to finding his arm. Then, remembering, he took his helmet off and traced the crease where a Vichy French bullet had almost blown his head off during the landing at Arzew.

He wondered how long his luck would hold out.

Thirteen

~~~ ൭ ~~~

"At the time I remember thinking how impossible it was that the Christmas holiday was worse than the year before. But it was. It really was," Ka continued, her voice breaking. "I said to myself it just can't get any worse." She shook her head, despairing at the memory.

"How wrong I was."

The night air had finally brought some relief to the unbearable heat. Now it was only sweltering. But the stars seemed exceptionally bright in the cloudless sky, a proper salute to the last minutes of another Fourth of July. My aunt's audience remained riveted, absolutely in awe of the story this 88-year-old woman was sharing with no signs of withering.

Reflecting on this night some years later, the thought occurred to me that Catherine's recollections were quite remarkable. One might think her performance was only the result of being blessed with a powerful ability to remember, that it was only a matter of recounting the history of a brief period of her long life.

It was more than that, much more, perhaps even heroic. Because she hung on to her memories out of love and respect for her family, despite her longing to forget.

The four years of which she spoke were so personally traumatic, so devastating an invasion of her own happiness and security, that she remembered every anxious moment shared with her family during the trauma in infinite detail. And every letter, every fear and tear shed while her brothers were off to war were scars burned into her soul that would never completely heal.

On the contrary, for all of us, her nieces and nephews and our own children who were old enough to understand, the vividness of her recollections and the secrets she was unveiling to us were more profoundly valuable than any Christmas gift imaginable.

None of us had ever heard this story before. And now, especially since their passing, we thirsted to know our fathers and grandfathers and uncles and who they were in the worst of their times.

They had gone off and done what had to be done, putting their own lives on hold and giving up all they cherished without question. The only certainty they had was uncertainty. They might survive the war or they might not. If they did, the memories of being homesick and lonely, of being afraid, of being wounded or maimed... would simply never go away.

For the first time I understood why my own father never cared to discuss the war, why he left that four-year gap in my knowledge of his life an empty space. He, like his brothers, wanted to bury his memories of those awful years in the deepest, darkest recess of his mind. But even hidden from the light, I'm certain they never completely faded. His only defense was simply not to talk about it.

"Of course, Jim was on everyone's mind, Ka continued. "About all we knew was that he was in North Africa where the fighting was bad. First he was in Algeria and then I remember he was part of the invasion of Tunisia. We heard from him only occasionally, he was rarely anywhere where the censors would let him write. I do remember him writing to us that he had just come through the Battle of Kasserine Pass. I think I remember that because of the name. 'Kasserine Pass.' It sounded like such an exotic place, almost romantic. But the way Jim described it later, it was anything but. We didn't do so well there, if I remember right and we lost thousands of boys in that one battle. I think that was in February of 1943 and there were many more battles that Jim was in before the Allies finally defeated the Germans in the spring. The only way we usually knew where he was at any time was the newspaper and radio reports. I'll tell you, we were all pretty jumpy then."

She paused for a moment, another thought coming to her.

"And Pa..." she said, and stopped again and let out a long sigh. "He wasn't doing so well. Ever since my mother died he'd been wrestling with the devil in that bottle and the stress of the boys being away was very hard on him. He was especially worried about Jim, and he had a right to be.

"My brothers and sisters worked it out so someone was with him most of the time. Dot and Flossie and Ray, Henry and Phil had him over for dinner all the time so he wouldn't be alone at night. My husband Andy worked nights so I came and cooked for him and sat with him a lot. We'd listen to the radio together. Jiggs

141

and Bev and Bobbie were still living home, so there was always someone around."

I looked around the table. There were a lot of tear filled eyes watching her. As a parent, I'd worried when my boys were five minutes late for curfew in their high school years. It was hard to fathom how anyone could deal with the stress of worrying about the fate of four sons, and usually not knowing where at least one or two of them even were. I felt my own eyes watering.

"Bobbie and Beverly used to tell me that when he wasn't in the barn working, he'd be standing in the living room at the picture window, staring at the Blue Star Banner hanging there. He lived in terror that a military car would pull up in front of the house. It got so that all of us would tense up at the sound of a car approaching the house. To this day, I hate to hear a car pull into my driveway if I'm not expecting anyone."

Around the table, my cousins with little ones had managed to coax them to sleep on their shoulder or had them sucking on a popsicle to keep them occupied. They weren't about to miss even a minute of this conversation, which would last as long as Ka could go on. She was mesmerizing.

"We all knew it was going to get worse, that the war was going to start hitting close to home. It was only a matter of time and we were right. That March, we got news that Cliff Lehman, a high school classmate of Speck's who had been reported as missing somewhere in the Pacific in June of 1942, had finally been declared killed in action. Charley Tourison, another friend of Peachy's was reported killed on a bombing raid in Germany and Gordon Hart, who was the grandson of Charles Hart, the founder of Hart Seed Company right here in town was killed in Europe somewhere." She looked down into her lap and stared at her long, thin hands. They were clasped together so tightly her fingers were white.

"I think that's when it really hit home that the war was real." She shook her head, shaking her slowly at the vision I imagined passing before her eyes.

"To see a Gold Star hanging in some family's window was truly devastating."

Ka looked up at the sky as it was suddenly filled with the colorful brilliance of one of the evening's final fireworks exploding over our heads. The sight conjured up another memory.

"Can you imagine what it was like for Jim when the mortar shells started raining down?" she said, lost in thought while the ember remnants of the rocket trickled down, glowing until they burned out and disappeared. "I suppose he was terrified. They all must have been terrified."

My son Jay, the spitting image of his grandfather, Speck, surprised us all with another perspective.

"I don't know Aunt Ka," he said, his eyes giving away how seriously he was thinking about her words. She turned and looked at him, puzzled.

"What do you mean, Jay?" she asked.

"Well, I think if it were me, I'd rather be fighting than waiting," he replied. "Somehow, being home and waiting for bad news would have been worse to me, more painful than watching those mortars coming my way. I don't think I would have slept for the entire war if I was a kid back then."

She smiled.

"It was terrible for my brothers, but it was no picnic home either, Jay, you're right."

"The anxiety must have been awful," he replied, "for all of you."

"It was, and it revealed itself in odd ways," Ka said, nodding her head.

"Such as?" Jay asked.

"Well, I don't know what went on behind closed doors in other families, but I can tell you that my younger sisters began acting very much out of character. In fact, I think the whole experience changed their outlook on life forever."

This was a twist I hadn't expected.

"You see, we all were affected by the absence of the boy's and worrying over their safety. But most of us were grown up and had other responsibilities to distract us from the war, at least a bit. We had husbands and wives, children... but Bobbie and Beverly, they were so young, only teenagers... they were just about overcome with worry. At first they turned to prayer, the two of them going to mass every day to pray for the boys to be home safely by Christmas of 1942. They were crushed when Christmas came and went and their prayers went unanswered. It was only a matter of time before one or both of them found some other release or got into some kind of mischief."

She left the question hanging in the air. I snatched it.

"Did they, Ka? I mean, I can't exactly envision my Aunt Bobbie as a hoodlum," I laughed.

She threw her head back and laughed out loud."

"No, she didn't take up a life of crime. Stealing cars or robbing banks wasn't in your aunt's nature," she said, still grinning.

She let ten seconds of silence go by then dropped a bomb.

"But she and Beverly did burn down a barn."

"What?" The question echoed around the table.

144

"Yes," Ka said without emotion, "caused a big ruckus, I can tell you."

The questions came fast.

"They burned down a barn?"

"Why?"

"Whose barn?"

Ka put a hand to her mouth, her eyes dancing with glee.

"Whoops, guess I let the cat out of the bag," she grinned, enjoying the shocked looks around the table.

"It belonged to the Country Club," she answered. "It was standing about a block away from our house and was in a terrible state. It was probably a hundred years old and it looked like it was about to fall down. The club hadn't used it for storage in years so it was just rotting away. And unfortunately, your Aunt Dot planted the idea in their minds one Sunday dinner."

"Dot? What did Dot have to do with it?" I asked.

"Well, I recall that Dot was cranky with worry about the boys and her own husband, Ed Ames who had a physical coming up with the Draft Board. She had gone out walking before dinner to clear her head and mentioned at the table that she'd passed by the barn and wondered how it was still standing. I think she called it a 'disgrace' and said that 'somebody ought to burn that thing down.'"

"So my mother and Aunt Beverly actually took her seriously?" Claudia said, her mouth slightly agape.

"Afraid so," Ka answered. "After dinner, the two of them marched over to the barn, went inside and waited until dark. Then they piled some old hay up against one wall, set it on fire and watched it burn for a while before running for home. It had been burning for quite awhile before anyone even noticed and called the Volunteer Fire Department. I think it was Pa who saw a

145

glow in the window and we all ran over to watch. By that time, the firemen were on their way.

"We'd all been sitting around listening to the radio and hadn't missed the two girls. Someone asked about them and I ran back home and went upstairs to see what they were up to. Well, I found the two of them in their pajamas and in their beds making believe they were sleeping. Trouble was they both reeked of smoke! I hustled them downstairs, told them to wait and went and fetched Pa. I didn't know what else to do. All I could think about was that my little sisters had committed a crime! They were arsonists!"

"What did my grandfather do?" Peter, my late Aunt Bobbie's youngest son asked, unsuccessfully hiding the amusement in his voice.

"I took him aside and whispered in his ear that the girls were in the living room and stunk to high heavens of smoke. He looked at me in disbelief, his eyes getting wider and wider and then just shook his head. He grabbed my hand and we walked back to the house. I couldn't tell if he was angry or just annoyed. He didn't say a word.

"We walked into the living room and there were Bobbie and looking all the world like a couple of cats who'd just shared a canary, all giggly like what they had done was funny. That stopped quickly when Pa went to take his belt off. But then he stopped, and other than ordering them to go bathe as best they could to get rid of the smell, he didn't say another word, just walked out of the house. The girls thought he wasn't mad and wanted to go and watch the fire, but I told them to hush up and do what he told them. Good thing, too."

"I can just see the two of them thinking they had gotten away with it," Beverly's son Steve said.

"Yah, they had those unmistakable grins whenever they were up to something," added his sister Mary.

Ka laughed out loud. "Pa knew what they had done was a crime even if it was a run down old barn but he wasn't about to let those girls get into any trouble. He walked back over to the burning barn and found the fire chief, a friend of his. Pa had just retired from the department about six months before so he knew all the guys who turned out.

"Hey Al, got a worker here, huh?" I remember Pa saying to him as the flames were leaping into the air. A slight breeze was kicking embers all over the sky, but there wasn't another house closer than Pa's so there was little danger of the fire spreading. The chief remarked that the wood was so dry on that old barn it hadn't taken much to get it roaring.

"But I wonder how it started?" he said to my father, who just shrugged his shoulders.

"I got an idea about that," Pa responded.

"Oh?"

"Yup," he said and proceeded to tell the fire chief the most bold faced lie I'd ever heard. I think it was the only time I ever heard my father tell an untruth.

"I seen a couple of odd looking fella's hanging around the barn this afternoon," Pa said.

"That a fact?" the Chief responded. "Let me get this put down, Henry and I'll come over and we can talk."

Ka stopped for a moment and took another sip of Limoncello.

"Bobbie, this is the sweetest little drink," she said to me, her eyes full of delight. I wondered how Henry had managed to keep his family in line. There was a wild streak in every one of his children.

147

Then she went right back to her story.

"Sure enough, about an hour later, the chief shows up at the door with the town constable and asked my father if he'd answer some questions.

"'Sure, sure,' he said, ignoring the hideous smell of smoke they both brought into the house. Upstairs, the freshly bathed girls were hiding in the attic!

"Well the constable says 'We were wondering if you could describe them fella's you say you saw hanging around earlier today. Sounds to me like they was a couple of drifters or draft dodgers."

Ka rolled her eyes.

"Pa looked them in the eye and said, 'Both of 'em needed a shave and a haircut, looked like they could use a meal, too. I felt sorry for them, to be honest, thought they might be looking to sleep in that old barn for the night. Cold out there. It was probably an accident. A cigarette or something.'"

She smirked at the memory of her father pulling it off.

"I tell you, Pa could have won an Academy Award for best actor for his performance. The constable and the chief left convinced that a couple of drifters had started the fire. My sisters got off with only having to deal with their father."

"And how bad was that?" my sister asked. "It seems Grandpa had a real soft spot for his two youngest daughters."

"Oh, yes he did, indeed. But I can tell you they didn't leave the house for a couple of weeks after the incident and their share of chores was about tripled to Jigg's delight," she chuckled. "But Pa never raised a hand to either of them. I think he understood what was going on with them. They were just acting out their fears about their brothers and they were angry about not being able to do anything about it. Pa wrote to the boys and told them what had happened and asked them to ride the girls a bit for their foolishness. He knew that would help, knowing the boys were getting a good laugh out of the whole thing."

She rested for a moment and I knew she was pleased when no one moved.

"Are you sure I'm not talking too much? It might be the Limoncello," she teased.

A chorus of "No's" rang out around the table.

"Please go on, Ka... you can't imagine how important this is to all of us," I said.

She gazed out over the sea of faces, reflections of her brothers and sisters staring back at her.

"Oh, I think I can," she whispered and patted my hand. Ka opened her small purse and rummaged around inside until she found a small handkerchief. She dabbed at her eyes with it.

"Where were we... oh, yes. I think that was in early March. I remember because the mailman surprised us within a couple of days of the 'barn burning' with a letter from Speck. It was addressed to Pa who ripped it open and let out a 'whoop!' you could hear clear into Rocky Hill. He was coming home on a furlough after being away a whole year! Jiggs told me that Pa's hands were actually shaking when he showed him the letter. He had him run and tell the girls and then go to the firehouse and use the telephone to call his brothers and sisters to tell them the good news. Speck was coming home for eight days."

That was the first time that night that Catherine actually cried at her memory. But they were tears of happiness.

"We all met him at the train station, every one of us and Vera, of course. We waited nearly an hour for that train in the cold, but no one complained. Finally, I remember seeing it pull around the bend and slowing down to enter Union Station. We all let out with hollering and crying the likes of which I bet you've never heard. And it wasn't just us. The train was packed with soldiers on leave and there were hundreds of families in the station all carrying on the same way. It was bedlam!

"The whole crowd began moving toward the oncoming train, everyone looking up at the open passenger windows, looking for a glimpse of their boy. Car after car went by and we didn't see Speck. I thought poor Vera was going to melt she was so teary. Then... all of a sudden, Ray yelled his name and pointed to his brother. He had seen him.

"Speck! It's Speck!" and sure enough it was. I thought my little brother was going to climb out of the window before the train stopped he was so excited to see everyone. It took forever, but finally the train came to a stop and we watched as he pushed his way forward and out the nearest exit. He just about jumped into Pa's arms and we all surrounded the two of them. Pa was crying and Speck couldn't stop grinning. I think I kissed him a hundred times. And then he saw Vera. I swear an electric current went through that little girl when she wrapped her arms around her boyfriend and he hugged her for all he was worth. That was the first time I was certain they would end up together."

She paused for a breath. "Oh, my, I really got carried away there, I'm sorry," she said to us. "But it was the first time I can remember feeling happy after such a long time. I will never forget that day so long as I live. It was one of the most precious moments of my life.

"Speck was home with us."

She dabbed at her eyes again, a bit overwhelmed by the moment.

"The celebration began at the train station and we partied for the entire time he was home. We would have big dinners, move the furniture out of Pa's living room, roll up the rug and dance until the morning hours. Neighbors would stop by with cakes and sweets they had made especially for Speck despite the rationing and they'd end up staying and having a drink and even joining in the dancing. I tell you, that homecoming were was just incredible."

I heard a few sniffles around the table and had to dry my own eyes. Her story had given me a vision of my mother and father in love, painfully separated during what should have been the most exciting and silly time in their lives! Two young people in love. The war took that joy away from them.

My Aunt turned to me again.

"The night before your father had to catch the train back to the West Coast, he proposed to your mother," she told me. "We hadn't planned anything that evening, figuring those two young people needed their time together. We were going to say our goodbyes again at the train station.

"I had stopped by with my husband to see Pa that night and all of a sudden Speck burst through the door pulling Vera by the hand behind him. He was wearing a smile from ear to ear... a Cheshire cat kind of grin. I don't think I'd ever seen him so happy. And Vera... well, she couldn't stop crying. Poor thing. The love of her life had just proposed and they were going to be separated again in the morning. Lord knows for how long this time.

"'We're engaged, Pa,' Speck said proudly to his father. Pa, who was a little bit in his cups because his son was leaving again, slapped his hands down on his thighs and said, "Well ain't that just wonderful!' and

151

hugged the two of them so hard I thought he was going to hurt Vera. He was so happy.

"I think, in a way, Speck getting engaged helped Pa with his leaving, because Vera was a sort of lifeline to us. She was like a rope that was going to pull him back to us safe and sound. Of course, it was all in his mind, but my father was desperate with worry over all the boys and he seized on anything that would help him believe we were all going to be together again when the war ended.

"Well the next thing you know, Pa had Jiggs go to the firehouse again to use the telephone and let everyone know. Wouldn't you know it, I think almost the entire family came home to congratulate them and we ended up partying again until well after midnight."

The smile on her face suddenly faded.

"But then morning was on us and we all trudged down to Union Station to see Speck off. It was like a funeral procession. We were all so sad, Pa was hung over and Vera was heartbroken again. It was terrible saying goodbye. Hugging him. I knew every one of us was thinking the same thing. Was this the last time we would ever see him? Touch him?"

She lowered her head and raised both her hands to cover her eyes, sobbing. The memory was so powerful, so painful. I heard her take a deep breath and she sighed.

"We all stood there and waved as the train pulled out of the station, right until it disappeared from sight. I still remember the sound in the station, whole families not speaking, but crying, sobbing. It was the exact opposite of what we had experienced eight days earlier.

"I think about it now and realize that in eight short days, our entire family experienced some of the happiest moments of our lives and one of the worst. It was so ironic. I put my arm around Vera, who was just so devastated, and walked her back to our car. She road home with Pa, Jiggs and I.

"I don't recall anyone saying a word the entire drive."

Fourteen

~~~ ❧ ~~~

Summer, 1943

Jim Hughes was sorely disappointed. After ten months of ferocious fighting with his unit of the 16th Combat Team, through the misery of Kasserine Pass where the Americans had been overrun by German Panzers only to rally and finally find victory in North Africa in May 1943, he thought he'd get a break. A letter from his younger brother Speck describing the joy of a furlough home had planted the idea in his mind and it took root.

But it wasn't his turn.

On July 4, the 16th Combat Team was back aboard a troop transport sailing towards southern Europe, this time to lead the invasion of Sicily in the Allied forces' *"Operation Husky."*

154

Hughes draped his six-foot-five inch frame over the ship's rail and thought how ironic it was that he was sad to leave Tunisia. Some of the worst moments of his life had been in North Africa, but after a month of catching his breath from the fighting the desert seemed like a swell place.

Not that he and his men had been lying around on the beaches enjoying the Mediterranean since the Germans had capitulated. He had been pushing them hard in training, sensing that the crack *Big Red One* wouldn't be idle very long. And that meant that Platoon B, Fox Company, 2nd Battalion, 16th Infantry would be leading the charge again in the amphibious landing of Sicily.

He knew that the invasion of the southernmost tip of Europe was vital for the Allies. Knocking the Axis powers out of Italy would be a huge blow to Hitler's strategy and would leave the door open for a full-scale assault on Europe. The day couldn't come fast enough for Hughes. Because then the 1st Infantry could take direct aim at Berlin, do their job, and finally go home. It was a day he dreamt of.

Jim shook off the twinge of elation that swept over him at the thought and reached into his pocket once more for months old letter from Speck.

March 13, 1943

Dear Jim,

I'll have you know I'm writing this letter from the comfort of my bedroom on Highland Street. Really. I can't believe it myself. I got an unexpected 14-day furlough after baking in the California desert for the last year and I'm trying to make the most of it. So you're not the last to know, Elvira and I are engaged. Hope you'll be home for the wedding, whenever that is.

I'm sorry to tease you about the desert, I know you've probably had your fill of the sand by now. From the reports by Edward R. Murrow's guys, it sounds like you've had it pretty rough these last months. I'm proud of you brother and wish I could get into the thick of it, too. I'm hoping my next assignment will be in the Pacific. Hitler and Tojo won't know what hit them when they see the likes of the Hughes brothers!

Things are fine here at home. I was pleasantly surprised to find the family coping well with the rationing and Pa is doing ok. Not great, but considering all he's been through and worrying about us, he's doing better than I expected.

We all miss you, Bull. Hope you catch a break from the action soon. Believe me, the party the gang will plan for you that will begin the minute you step off the train in Hartford will be one you'll not soon forget.

Be safe and keep your head down. I'm praying for you.

Speck

Hughes tucked the letter back into his pocket for safekeeping. Like all the others he'd received since leaving home, he would probably read it again a hundred times. There was nothing more satisfying or heartwarming than news from the family.

He sighed. Life would be peaceful for the next few days aboard ship, and then all hell would break loose again. There was another meeting scheduled later in the day to more fully brief combat officers on the mission. He'd feel better after knowing a little more about what was in store for he and his men.

In the early morning hours of July 10, Jim Hughes once again found himself hanging over the side of a Higgins boat retching into the Mediterranean as his 40-man platoon raced through the shallow surf towards

Gela, the first beach of Italy to be assaulted during Operation Husky.

Hughes knew that Gela had taken a pounding in the preceding days before the amphibious landing from Allied bombers and naval guns. The 505th Parachute Regimental Combat Team were dropped behind the beaches before midnight to take control of strategic villages and bridges before the *Big Red One* stormed ashore in the early hours of the following morning. If all had gone according to plan, he expected a soft landing for his guys. But the battle hardened soldier also knew there was plenty of room for things to go wrong.

And they did.

Unknown to the approaching invasion force, the 505th paratroopers had encountered heavy winds at altitude and their aircraft were blown off course. Consequently troops were scattered all over southeast Sicily between Gela and Syracuse and were unable to accomplish their mission. Hughes and thousands of troops from the 16th Infantry's Fox Company were sailing right into the gun sights of well-prepared and equipped Italian Army coastal units who met the invasion force with heavy machine gun and cannon fire. And once more, the Higgins boat drivers had to contend with unanticipated sand bars that made the landing that much more difficult. Hughes and his men found themselves again facing a long struggle to shore when their landing craft simply could not progress any further, stuck hundreds of yards from shore.

"Go, go, go!" Hughes screamed when the LCVP ramp dropped, the scene eerily reminiscent of his Platoon's assault on Arzew beach nearly a year before. It was at least 300 hundred yards to the beach and they were strafed with murderous machine gun fire as they waded slowly towards the beach without cover.

157

He took the first several strides toward the shore willing his powerful legs to keep moving in the waist deep water. The Italian infantry was visible high above the coastline, dug into elevated sand dunes and firing at will against the invaders. Hughes thought for a moment that they would be slaughtered before ever stepping foot on Sicilian soil, but suddenly he heard the ear splitting roar of big guns — artillery — behind him. When the invasion Command realized that the 505th's mission had been compromised — leaving the Italian troops free to defend the Gela beach — the destroyer USS *Shubrick* and the light cruiser USS *Boise* were directed to concentrate heavy artillery fire directly onto the Italian positions ahead of the incoming US troops. In seconds, dozens of 130-pound explosive projectiles were whistling over the heads of the struggling amphibious troops and pulverizing the Italian defensive effort.

Ahead of him, Hughes could hear the cheering of his men even above the roar of the incoming naval shells but machine gun fire continued to rake the surf.

"Keep your heads down, lay low for a few minutes, Hughes hollered, hoping the artillery fire would end or at least limit the firepower pouring down on them. The order slowed the advance of his troops toward the beach.

Then, as if his name was engraved on it, he heard rather than saw a shell that had been launched from the shore begin its whistling descent into the general area of where he hunkered in the surf, only his head visible above water. The mortar impacted 25 yards to his right with an ear-splitting roar. The ensuing concussion caused a huge geyser of seawater to propel him into the air and forward at least 50 feet. Hughes, deafened by the detonation and blinded by the water, hit the ocean surface head first, his helmeted head pushed below water until he was pile driven into the sandy bottom. The blow knocked him senseless and his crumpled and lifeless body rolled along the sandbar driven by the strong, shallow surf.

As he lay motionless three feet below the surface at the mercy of the ocean turbulence and unable to move his limbs, he had no idea if he had been wounded or was dead. Before he could worry about drowning, a black curtain descended over his eyes and he lost consciousness.

He felt nothing in this state. No fear, no sadness or pain. He heard nothing, despite the awful din of battle above the surface. The soldier had no sense of time or place, only that he was resting.

Suddenly, a vision came before his eyes. It was his mother again, urging him to wake up from his nap and dry off.

"*What do you mean, mother, why am I wet?*" he asked her.

"*Because you have fallen asleep under a tree in the backyard and it rained, Jimmy. Come in the house, I will dry you off in front of the fire and I have some fresh baked cookies for you... come along now...*" she said, smiling at him and wiping her hands on her apron. She looked so pretty. He smiled back at her, happy that she had come for him. She pushed the hair off his forehead and leaned over to kiss him.

"*But mother,*" he began..."*I don't think I am going to awaken...*" She disappeared before he could finish his sentence.

His eyes popped open and his body shook as he looked into the face of a medic who had broken a capsule of smelling salts beneath his nose to revive him. He tried to get up but only managed to roll to his side and he violently wretched bile and salt water from his

159

lungs and stomach. He coughed heavily, but his head began to clear. There was a loud ringing in his ears.

He looked around, desperately.

"Where's my mother?" he asked frantically. There was so much he wanted to say to her.

"You're mother?" the medic relied curiously. "You're mother's not here Lieutenant, trust me," he add, ducking his head at the sound of machine gun fire coming from the sand dunes above them. "I don't think you'd want the lady here right now." They were sprayed with sand from the bullets that had hit the beach yards in front of them.

"Lieutenant, I don't know how the hell you made it, but I can't find a damn thing wrong with you. You just got your bell rung," the young corpsman told him, still holding his wrist to check his pulse.

"But how...?" Hughes had gradually absorbed the smell of gunpowder and the sound of machine gun fire and loud explosions all around him. He reached down with his fingers and grabbed a handful of sand. He was on the beach at Gela.

"You landed right next to a guy making his way to shore and he pulled you out of the water, dropped you at my feet. That's all I know," the medic explained. "You must be a praying man, because I think you just met your guardian angel, sir."

"Hell, I haven't even seen the inside of a church since my mother..." Hughes stopped. He remembered her face again.

The 2nd Lieutenant looked around the beach.

"What's our situation?" he asked, back to business.

"We can thank those tin cans out there," he said nodding over his shoulder at the *Shubrick* and *Boise*, both ships continuing to fire supporting cover for the amphibious landing. "They saved the day. The beach is secure. We're headed to Ponte Olivo Airfield, last I heard, right according to General Patton's plan."

A familiar face slid into the sand next to Hughes.

"Hey Bull, you ok?" First Sergeant Mike Pettig inquired of his commanding officer. "Thought we had lost you, sir."

Hughes turned back to thank the medic. He was gone.

"What's the situation in Fox Company and the platoon, Mike?"

"Hell, while you were taking a nap, we just knocked the crap out of a whole division of Italian troops that should have been engaging the 505th. Those guys never made it last night and that's why we took such a pounding coming in," Pettig reported.

"Heavy casualties?" Hughes asked, already knowing the answer. His head was clearing fast.

"Don't know yet, but expected. The Italians here at Gela — we think they were the 429th Coastal Battalion — probably lost half their men. Fox Company completely overwhelmed them when they finally made it on to the beach, with a little help from the Navy. You should be proud of your guys, Bull."

Hughes nodded. He was proud but his silence told the story.

"Getting ready to move out now, sir. Don't know the number yet, but Fox Company probably had 100 casualties, at least five times that were wounded and will need to be evac'd. Platoon B is intact, Bull." He paused. "No letters…"

Hughes stared into the younger man's eyes. His relief was obvious. Pettig nodded, understanding.

"Got a smoke?"

The First Sergeant lit a couple of Lucky Strikes.

161

"Where are the men?"

"About 50 yards yonder," Pettig replied and pointed to his right. "Just taking a breather. Actually, praying that you were going to get up."

Hughes sat upright. He was dizzy but otherwise unharmed. A cheer went up from the men waiting for him.

"I'm fine. Let's move out," Hughes responded, beckoning them to follow him and determined not to show emotion. He'd learned that he couldn't get attached to his men. Life changed out here in a matter of seconds.

As Hughes and Pettig stood, B Platoon gathered together. Up and down the beach the troops of Fox Company could be seen getting ready to hit the road.

"We got word that there's a Panzer Division heading toward Gela. They'll probably arrive on Route 115, just over the rise. We may run into them if we don't get the hell out of here," Pettig reported. "We can't afford to be pinned down on the beach again if we're going to take that airfield before noon."

"Everyone informed?"

"Yes. And the Italians — the Liverno Infantry — are also known to have tanks that may try to blindside us on the way to Ponte Olivo."

"German or Italian tanks?" Hughes inquired. "Big difference."

"Dunno, Bull," Pettig replied.

"Shit," Hughes cursed. "Either way, so much for a cakewalk." He was still light headed from the pounding he had taken in the water. He wondered how he could have laid on the beach unconscious when the world was exploding around him.

"You're a lucky guy, Bull," Pettig said as he headed up the beach, the platoon falling in behind him. "So are we."

"Thanks for that, Mike. Stay sharp."

The big man was far shakier than any of his men knew. The concussion from the mortar round had really knocked his marbles loose and his legs felt like lead. He probably should be evacuated back to a field hospital to be treated for concussion trauma, but he wasn't about to show weakness to his men, especially after they had just taken their objective without his leadership. He was ashamed and proud at the same time.

They marched without resistance for about an hour and passed through the critical highway intersection of Route 115 and Piano Lupo, a major road that ran north to the hill towns of Casa Prioli and Niscemi. The strategic point, which overlooked the beach at Gela and had been fortified by the German and Italians with more than a dozen concrete pillboxes, had been secured by the remnants of the 505th Parachute Regiment the night before, one of the few planned objectives the unit had accomplished.

But shortly after, two Fox Company scouts in advance of the 1st Infantry Division marching on Ponte Olivo Airfield radioed that dozens of German Panzer tanks were rumbling toward them from Niscemi heading for Gela and would pass through Piano Lupo.

The Panzer III tanks, the most devastating weapon in the formidable German military arsenal with 75mm guns could devastate an exposed infantry force without slowing down. Immediately, the units of the *Big Red One* retreated back to Piano Lupo to reinforce the 505th and take a stand.

This was a battle for bigger guns than the infantry's small arms, however. Fox Company was overrun by the Panzers and the German tanks continued toward Gela unobstructed. It was only after the Panzers had reached within 1,000 meters of troops still coming ashore aboard landing craft that the Navy stepped in once again to turn the tide.

Still trolling several miles offshore to lend heavy artillery support, the *USS Subrick* and the *USS Boise* let loose an artillery barrage that knocked out a third of the Panzers force. Explosions, fire, smoke and mountains of sand blown into the air completely blocked view of the furious battle from thousands of troops approaching the shore in landing craft. But when the air cleared by early afternoon, Gela was secure again. Pulverized by the ferocious naval assault, the Germans were forced to retreat into the northern hills and left behind 16 burning Panzers, nearly a third of the division. The artillery onslaught was so intense that the amphibious landing of 1st Infantry Division troops was never interrupted by the counterattack.

At Piano Lupo, 2nd Lieutenant Jim Hughes stood amidst the carnage of the defensive block Fox Company had attempted to throw at the Panzers racing towards Gela. Nearly 40 dead, 70 wounded, nine missing. It was a heavy price to pay for a battle they'd had no business trying to win. The oily black smoke they could see rising over the Gela beach from the burning Panzers gave him only slight reason to cheer.

"Thank the man for those tin cans out there," he said to Pettig as word of the German defeat at Gela traveled to Piano Lupo.

"Yah, but not much to cheer about here, Bull," Pettig said. He lit a smoke. "I gotta round up the boys. We still need to take out Ponte Olivo and we are way late."

Hughes shook his head.

164

"We're going to have to kick some butt to get there," he said. "Got a bad feeling about this."

For the next 24 hours, Fox Company fought its way through skirmish after skirmish with Italian and German troops while advancing toward Ponte Olivo Airfield. The airfield was vital to the Allies' ability to supply the Sicily Invasion because it had the only runways near the coast. It was as strategically important to the Germans for the same reason.

A few miles north of the airfield, the Germans had occupied the town of Niscemi with a full battalion of troops and a Panzer division to be in position to defend Gela and the airfield. The counterattack on the amphibious landing at Gela had depleted the German's ability to defend Ponte Olivo. Nonetheless, the fighting would be fierce.

Fox Company engaged the last of the enemy blocking the road to the airfield at dusk on July 10. The *Big Red One* was already hours late in their objective of taking the field within four hours of the beach landing at Gela. Now they confronted another ambush: a fortified concrete bunker, unidentified on the Allied maps, that had been constructed by the Germans on a hillside at Guerra Mondiale overlooking Strata 117 which led directly to Ponte Olivo and Niscemi.

Machine gun fire erupted from the bunker as Fox Company marched unawares toward the airfield. The American troops were pinned down for more than two hours before they were able to take the bunker out with a Bangalore that Hughes' platoon had positioned and a half dozen well-thrown hand grenades.

"Grab a smoke," Hughes told his men as they inspected the remains of the bunker and its former occupants. It was as close as he could come to slapping them on the back. Two hundred yards south, with the airfield in sight, Fox Company encountered a modest village built on the outskirts. They had little time to reconnoiter the few streets lined with small houses, storefronts and apartments knowing that Panzers were probably racing toward them from Niscemi. Fox company platoons quickly fanned out among the village streets.

Hughes led B Platoon down a fairly wide two-lane road paved with ancient cobblestones. It appeared to be the main road in the village judging by the number of storefronts. It was clear that the village had already taken savage artillery fire as most of the brick and stone buildings had been reduced to rubble. The odor of smoke and gunpowder were heavy in the air. It was an acrid smell that reminded him of North Africa where he had fought his way through dozens of such small villages.

Now, as he gestured to his men to divide into two groups and advance down both sides of the street, staying close to any building that might give them cover, he scanned the rooftops and windows for snipers. Fox Company had no official intelligence that confirmed German presence in the village, but Hughes could feel it in his bones. It was hard earned instinct.

He saw shadows in a few windows and gestured to his men to clear out each building they passed. He heard the question, "Tedeschi?" the Italian word for "Germans" repeated loudly again and again to villagers who were being led out into the street by American troops.

Suddenly, a burst of gunfire somewhere ahead of them broke the relative quiet of B Platoon's advance. Hughes' men pushed the villagers back inside the nearest building that provided cover and bent low, scanning the path ahead for movement. Slowly, they

166

crept forward again, keeping a sharp lookout for snipers. They came to what appeared to be the center of the village, a large stone water fountain placed in the middle of a small rotary where the main street forked. Behind the fountain was the bombed out remains of a church, the heavy beams of its roof still burning. The crucifix mounted on the peak was missing its right crosspiece, completing the sacrilege of the violent destruction of the place of worship. On either side of the church, where Via Ponte Olivo split, were shops. Most them had sustained heavy damage and were wide open to the street. Shattered glass and smashed brick littered the road in huge piles.

Still they saw no German presence.

Hughes divided his men again at the fork but before they could split, a small, black-haired little boy, perhaps only six or seven-years-old, emerged from the doorway of what appeared to be the remains of a cobbler's storefront. The child was crying with tears visible on his olive-toned cheeks, but he did not speak. He began walking towards the fountain, then stopped, unsure of what to do.

Hughes raised his hand, a signal for his men to stop in place. "Don't move," he hollered and waved Pettig forward to join him. He whispered a few words to his First Sergeant.

"Why is this kid alone?" he said to Pettig as the boy continued to walk towards them. "I smell rats. Pass the word to defilade. I don't want us caught in a flanking fire. Hurry up and get right back here."

Pettig ran 20 feet to three men and gave them instructions to pass on. Within minutes, the platoon had virtually disappeared behind walls, doors or any barricade that would give them cover in the event that they had walked into a trap. Pettig scurried back to Hughes.

"I'm gonna get the kid to come to me so I can snatch him," Hughes said. "You guys lay down covering fire if we suddenly have company. Got it? Take a position in that doorway to the left and signal the guys. Then I'll get the kid."

The boy, choking on his tears, began speaking in Sicilian. Hughes sensed that he was terrified. He'd been around enough children in his life to know when they were genuinely afraid. There was nothing visible behind him, but Hughes knew someone was there. The soldier racked his brain, trying to come up with a scheme to save the boy. He waved at the child, trying to beckon him away from the fountain. Reluctantly, the boy took two steps forward, then stopped again, his big brown eyes wide with fear.

Pettig touched his index finger to his thumb to form a circle, the American signal for "ok." They were ready. Hughes nodded his head. Then he pulled a GI issue chocolate bar from his jacket pocket and waved it at the boy, now 50 feet away. The child studied him for a moment, uncertain. Then he grinned, understanding what the big man was offering him and began to walk forward again. Hughes waited until he got within 30 feet then jumped up and raced to him.

The child, alarmed by the giant soldier's sudden movement, turned and ran towards a building to his left. As Hughes watched in horror, the church doors suddenly flew open and two German soldiers manning a machine gun began spraying gunfire at him. He was forced to drop to the ground and return fire. Suddenly, shooting erupted from windows around the balcony of the church and from the doorway of the cobbler's shop from which the boy had come. Return fire from B

168

Platoon created an inescapable crossfire in the center of the village.

Pettig, seeing the child about to be caught in the deadly barrage dropped his weapon and sprinted from his hiding spot to the child. Without breaking stride he swooped the boy off his feet then turned back toward the safety of a demolished storefront, shattered bricks piled high in the street before it. He took no more than three steps before the German machine gunners caught him with at least three rounds to his lower body and he staggered, still clutching the child.

Despite the machine gun and sniper fire raking the ground all around him, Pettig got up on all fours and struggled to drag the boy towards the mound of debris and safety, only a few feet away. It was his only hope. B Platoon was furiously pouring return fire at the church and took out the machine gunners just as a sniper's round hit Pettig in the back. Blood spurted from the wound and he fell again. But somehow he lifted the child and thrust him over the pile of debris, protecting him from the gunfire. The Sergeant's body continued falling and his face hit the hard cobblestone with a sickening thud. His body jerked twice as snipers continued to find their target.

With the machine gun silenced, B Platoon fired hundreds of rounds into the church windows and the cobblers shop. Two men raced forward under the covering fire and ran through the front doors of the church. A minute later, hand grenades they tossed up onto the balcony finished off the snipers. The fierce covering fire continued until the two men inside signaled all was clear. For several minutes more, B Platoon took their fury out on the cobblers shop until the scant remains of the storefront literally fell into the street. Then the air went deadly silent.

Hughes rushed out to Pettig who was face down on the smooth cobblestones and screamed for a medic. The Sergeant had been hit at least a half dozen times, the most serious wound in his neck having severed his jugular vein. He was bleeding out as Hughes reached him, a spreading pool of blood gushing from the gaping neck wound. Hughes turned his face up, out of the blood.

Mike Pettig, a 22-year-old kid from New Hampshire could only ask with his eyes if the young child was safe. Jim Hughes glanced to his left and saw the little boy standing, shivering with fear, but otherwise unharmed.

"Yah, Mike, he's fine. You saved the little guy," Hughes said to him, looking deeply into his friend's eyes. Pettig could only grunt, but a barely perceptible smile came to his pale lips. He grabbed at Jim's arm and squeezed it as the life drained from his young body.

"Mike, hang on buddy, we got a medic coming..." He turned and screamed again for help and found himself surrounded by the men of his platoon. Most of them were staring at the ground or looking away from the horrific sight of watching a young man they all respected drift away.

Hughes felt a shudder through the grip on his arm and turned back to Pettig. He was shocked to see that his eyes were fixed and unseeing. He was gone.

"God dammit, Mike , no!" Hughes ordered, refusing to accept the shattering death of the only man he had allowed himself to befriend since they had faced the first moments of violence together on Arzew beach.

Someone touched him on the shoulder just as a medic arrived, a morphine syrette already in his hand. The medic searched for a pulse in Pettig's neck, but to his horror found only the gaping wound. He looked up at Hughes and shook his head. There was nothing to be done. Gently, he brushed the palm of his hand down the soldier's face, pulling his eyelids shut.

The finality of Mike Pettig's death hit Jim Hughes harder than any blow he had ever absorbed. It was like a punch to the solar plexus that drained every ounce of strength from his body. Not even his mother's death was quite as shocking.

He reached down and pulled the young boy's fingers from his field jacket, bloodstains marking the canvas material like claw marks where Pettig had frantically grasped his friend as life drained from his body. Hughes reverently removed the young man's helmet and slipped his dog tags up over his head. He tucked them into his jacket pocket.

How, he wondered, would he find the strength to write this letter? Tears filled his eyes from both grief and frustration. Never would he be able to capture the words that would adequately define the spirit of this young man, or what his friendship had meant to him.

When he finally, reluctantly stood, there was a commotion behind him. He turned to see villagers coming out of their hiding places and walking towards them. Several of the soldiers cocked their weapons, unsure of their intentions.

"Easy, guys..." Hughes struggled to speak.

Silently, one of the elderly women timidly approached Hughes. Her grey hair was matted and her clothes were torn and filthy. Deep lines of fear were etched into her smudged face. He wondered how long it had been since she had eaten or bathed or slept in peace. He was surprised when she took his hands and looked deeply into his eyes. Tenderly, she pulled his hands to her lips and kissed his fingers.

"Americano," she whispered. "Americano, t'amu Americano." She turned to the little boy, biting her lower lip as tears rolled down her cheeks. Then she looked back into Hughes' eyes.

"Grazie, Americano, grazie..." she said, kissing his fingers again.

Not a soldier present knew exactly what the old woman said, but all knew what she meant.

Several other women and two elderly men pushed through the crowd of soldiers and picked up Pettig's body. They carried him around the fountain and into the remains of the church, laying the dead soldier upon the altar.

Hughes' heart broke as he dug down and found the courage to move on. He had men to command. They had a mission to accomplish.

"Corporal Miller, front and center," he called.

Another young man, no older than Pettig emerged from the pack and stood at attention before Hughes.

"Yes, sir," he answered.

"Corporal Miller, " Hughes voice echoed over the demolished village. "You have just been promoted to First Sergeant of B Platoon. See to it that you conduct your responsibilities with the same dedication as Sergeant Pettig would have demanded. Am I clear?"

Miller dropped his head in respect to Pettig, then saluted Hughes. "Yes, sir," he responded, knowing that thanking the 2nd Lieutenant would be a mistake. No one on B Platoon wanted this field promotion to happen, least of all Miller himself.

"Round up the boys and let's move on that airfield. We are very late, gentlemen. We will return for Sergeant Pettig's body after we have secured Ponte Olivo with Fox Company. Move out," he ordered.

172

Miller stood motionless for a moment, then turned and began dividing the platoon into two units to cover both sides of the street. In the distance, they heard machine gun fire. Fox Company had found additional resistance.

"Stay low," Hughes ordered as his men began to advance again through the seemingly deserted village. "Look for shadows. Move and defilade, stay near cover."

He had to get his men moving again, before the shock of Pettig's death would spook them all into hiding. Hughes couldn't shake the thought from his mind that they were all just boys who only wanted to do their duty and go home. The somehow romantic notion of joining the military and going off to fight a war on foreign soil that had seduced them into volunteering for the infantry had disappeared in North Africa. Now, they just wanted to get the job done, come out of the experience in one piece, and go home.

Jim swore he was going to help them get there. Pettig's death had only hardened him to the job ahead.

After a long night of battling German and Italian infantry and the remainder of the Panzer division from Niscemi that ringed the Ponte Olivo Airfield, the *Big Red One* was nearly exhausted and running low on ammunition. Casualties were high. With sunup came the relief of artillery support from the Navy ships still cruising off the coast and within range of Ponte Olivo, as well as a division of M4 Sherman tanks that had finally made it ashore in the continuous amphibious landing of the 1st Infantry Division at Gela. The Sherman's were far inferior to the Panzers in both firepower and penetrability, but the sheer number of the American tanks that were able make it into battle overcame the disadvantages. The battle waged on all day on July 11

173

and into the early hours of the 12th when the Germans finally retreated into the hills. Ponte Olivio was secured much later than the Allied plan had called for, but nonetheless it was now ready to be home for the U.S. Army Air Corps 9th Air Force medium bombers and P-40 fighters that had been so instrumental in the Allied victory in the North Africa campaign.

Fox Company and Hughes' B Platoon had fought nearly 30 hours without relief. Newly landed 1st Infantry Division troops arrived to mop up the Ponte Olivo battle and move German and Italian POW's back to the beaches for internment. Fox Company was ordered to stand down for the next 12 hours and then to proceed north toward Niscemi.

Hughes left Miller with orders that every man in the platoon was to be fed and rested while he and two volunteers returned to the church at Via Ponte Olivo to retrieve Mike Pettig's body. There they found that the villagers had wrapped the young soldier's remains in clean sheets and were guarding the church. The child Pettig had saved sat at the base of the altar. He stood hesitantly as Hughes approached and handed him a crumpled piece of paper on which he had scrawled the words, "Americano, t'amu. Grazie," inside the outline of a crudely drawn heart shape. The boy had signed his name and someone had written his address below it.

Hughes felt a tug on his sleeve. He turned to find the same elderly woman who had thanked him after Pettig was killed.

"Americano," she began, "per favore, dare questo sua madre."

"I don't understand," Hughes answered, looking to his two men for help. They shrugged their shoulders.

The woman sensed they did not understand her or the boy's message.

174

She pointed to Pettig's body and then touched the paper in Hughes' hand.

"Madre. Sua madre," she repeated, and took the paper from his hands and held it to her heart.

"Dare a sua madre, per favore, Americanao…"

A smile broke through the big man's face.

"For his mother. Give this to his mother. Sua madre," he said.

The old lady beamed and pulled the child to her side, hugging him. Her eyes were wet with tears.

"Mio nipote," she replied, tousling his dark hair with her fingers. "I tedeschi uccisero la sua mamma e papà." She reached up with her hands and pulled her eyelids down. "Morto."

The Americans were silent for a moment.

"Lieutenant," one of the men broke the silence. It was Private Walter Bukowski. "I think she's trying to tell us the kid's her grandson and the murdering bastards killed his mother and father."

Hughes looked at the 23-year-old soldier of Polish-American descent.

"Think you're right, private." He nodded. "Pretty good. Not exactly your neighborhood." The soldier smiled.

"There's one of everything where I come from Lieutenant."

It was Hughes' turn to smile. He nodded at the soldier, knowingly. Wasn't that what they were fighting for? He hoped so, desperate to find meaning in Mike Pettig's death.

He took the paper from the white haired woman and gently touched her hands. "Grazie," he said and winked at the boy.

"Maybe someday, when you're old enough to understand why, you might look up Mike's parents in

175

New Hampshire," he said to the child, who just smiled. "I'll be sure to tell them about you."

With Pettig's body loaded on to the jeep, the three men departed Ponte Olivo, saluting the villagers as they departed.

"If there's one place I never want to see again in my life, this is it," Bukowski said. There was no response.

At the airfield, before he could sleep, Hughes sat down to write a letter to Pettig's parent's. Sleep would be impossible until he did. He would find it impossible for weeks to come, nonetheless. Then he wrote to his father.

July 12, 1943

Dear Pa,

By now you more than likely know that I'm in Sicily, having survived yet another treacherous amphibious landing. I want you to know that I am very tired but otherwise ok. Some day I'll tell you all about it. Believe me, I won't forget the details before I see you, if ever.

I also need to share with you that I lost my best friend yesterday, a young man by the name of Mike Pettig. Germans hiding in a church killed him in an ambush as he attempted to save a small boy who was in the line of fire. It happened in a tiny village near Ponte Olivo Airfield in southern Sicily, just a few miles from the beach at Gela where we landed.

Pa, I so wish I could sit with you in the living room at Highland Street and tell you about Mike. Trying to describe his humanity and courage in the letter I just wrote to his parents was so difficult, in fact I guess it was impossible. Maybe you could have helped me to find the right words that would make his parents understand why their 24-year-old son had to die. I tried, but I am already haunted by my failure.

176

I told them that I had never witnessed such an act of selflessness in my life and probably never will. He didn't hesitate to put himself in the sites of a German machine gun nest before running out to save the boy. The scene keeps going through my head, playing over and over. I keep seeing it happen, yet I can't bring myself to believe that it did. He died in my arms, Pa.

I tried my best to tell his mom and dad that Mike was the epitome of the bravest, most dedicated soldiers fighting here now — young men who volunteered to fight for all that we believe in. If I was a parent and heard such a thing, I would hope it would help me to bear the grief and incredible burden that comes with such a loss. Unfortunately, in my heart, I know it won't help a bit.

This is all so wrong, Pa. But I guess it is the price we must pay to eliminate the evil that would steal our peace and freedom. Sometimes I wonder how the enemy feels. You can tell just by the way they fight that not all of them believe in their cause like we do. I've seen them run and it helps me to believe that we will win this war, but we have a long way to go. Hitler throws men and equipment at each battle, no matter how wasteful and unnecessary. So I suspect it will take us longer than we want to reach Berlin. As sad as that makes me, I remain determined to see this through to the end. To give up would only desecrate the sacrifices of so many boys like Mike Pettig. I'm really sorry for weighing you down with my troubles, Pa. I know you have enough challenges of your own right now. But you are always the first person I think of when I am troubled.

I hope you and the gang are coping with the rationing and all. We appreciate your efforts over here, believe me. Tell everyone I'll write soon. With a little luck, we'll finish this Sicily campaign quickly and come off line for a while. I'd like the time to catch up with everyone.

Love you, Pa, be well.

Jim

177

Over the next two weeks, the 1st Infantry Division was engaged in constant, short but ferocious battles as it fought its way north across the tortuous hills and mountains of Sicily. The fighting was exhausting enough, but every inch they advanced sapped their physical limits that much more.

After taking the town of Niscemi on the night of July 12th, Mazzarino fell two days later. The *Big Red One* became a giant wave that mercilessly pushed the Germans back across the Island, town-by-town, village-by-village in vicious street fighting. After Mazzarino came Barrafranca, then Villa Rosa, Enna, Alimena, Boumpietro, Petralia, Gangi, Sperlinga, Nicosia, Mistreeta, Cerami, Gagliano, Pietraperzia and culminated in the desperate and deciding battle of Troina.

Here, the Germans waged a last ditch effort to stop the Allied surge, while providing cover for the withdrawal of military units to safety across the Straight of Messina to Italy. The 1st Infantry repelled 21 counterattacks by the Germans over six days of bitter fighting, but it was a frontal attack by the *Big Red One*'s 16th Infantry that finally sent the surviving enemy fleeing to the north. Fox Company's B Platoon was in the lead assault and miraculously survived without casualties.

It was August 6th when the American flag was raised over Troina. The *Big Red One* had fought continuously for 27 days. But the battle for Sicily was won and the Allies were a step closer to Berlin. The Division moved to Palma di Montechiaro for rest and to wait for new orders while the news of the victory was celebrated across America.

August 8, 1943

Dear Jim,

I've been elected to write to you on behalf of the whole gang who are gathered at Pa's to listen to the news of your amazing victory in Sicily and to toast our big brother. What a feat, Jim. The Big Red One is bringing this war closer to an end and you closer to home. There's not a one of us who doesn't dream of watching you march down Main Street in Old Wethersfield — our hero — when you finally get to come home after you and your boys do the same thing to Hitler that the Italians did to Mussolini!

I'm sure you'll be hearing from John, Speck and Peachy soon now that the mail can get through. It's really hard to go so long without hearing from you, without knowing that you're safe. But as they keep telling us over here, "Loose lips sink ships." We can get through anything if it helps keep you safe.

Things are going well here, nothing to worry about. We're managing the rationing so far. I miss my nylons, but that's not much of a sacrifice! Meat and sugar are becoming hard to get, but our Victory Gardens are certainly helping with fresh vegetables. Pa needs tires for his car and they are really hard to come by. He has to go before an appeals Board to make a request. I saw Walter Meals recently, and he told me that he could probably get the Board to approve some 'recaps', (whatever those are?) for Pa because of his job as a sheriff. He thought they would last him through the war. Walter told me to give you his regards and that sales of Plymouths are down since you left. He wants you to come work for him again as soon as you get home. I'll bet that old job looks a lot more attractive to you now. I promise, we'll all buy Plymouths if you come home safe and sound!

Did I tell you that Bobbie and Beverly burned down the old Country Club barn up the street a few months ago? Pa

179

was pretty upset. No harm done. We'll tell you all about it when you come home on leave. When do you think that will be? We've only seen Speck so far. Did he tell you that he and Elvira got engaged? Can you imagine? Your little brother is getting married?

That's about all the news from here, big brother. We do miss you terribly and I often look at the Blue Star Banner hanging in Pa's front window. There are four stars on it now. When I take walks around town I marvel at how may banners there are in the windows. I wonder how many Wethersfield boys are serving. It must be in the thousands.

Write soon, nothing makes the gang happier than to get letters from you boys.

All my love,
Ka

Several weeks later, it was raining in Palma di Montechiaro where 2nd Lieutenant Jim Hughes was temporarily waiting with the members of the 1st Infantry Division after their victory in Sicily. Palma di Montechiaro was a beautiful small town in the hills not far from where he had landed — and nearly died — at Gela on the coast. The rain was unusual, but did little to help him with the bad bout of homesickness he was struggling with. He sat on his cot and read and reread the letter from his sister Catherine. It was already mid-September and he was getting restless with the daily training and waiting for new orders.

'Plymouths,' he thought. What he wouldn't do to be selling cars again back home. His sister was right. The job he had found so wanting now looked very attractive after all the blood he had seen over the last ten months. He'd been away from home for a year and a half. It felt like a lifetime.

And although he could now imagine the end of the war, he knew that it would be at least another Christmas, perhaps two before he would see home again.

If ever.

Fifteen

~~~ ∽ ~~~

Fall, 1943

"We had no idea how bad things were for Jim," Catherine continued into the night. "He sure drew the short straw going into the infantry, but he was a master at keeping his terrible experiences a secret... except from his father. We only knew that from letters we found in Pa's belongings after he died. We didn't know about Jim's close calls until we found those letters. How he lived through North Africa and Sicily was really a miracle. But Normandy..."

I noticed her hands shake when she said the word.

"He was safe, that's all that mattered to us. Sometime in the fall they shipped him back to England where he waited for new orders. We all had a pretty good hunch about where he'd go next, but not when. Roosevelt and Eisenhower were itching to invade France and take on Hitler in Berlin, but they still had Italy to contend with. Thank God Jim avoided that. We were worried that John might see action in Italy, but somehow he was lucky, too.

"Where was John, Ka? He still hadn't seen any action yet?" my sister asked her.

"No..." Ka replied and thought for a moment. "No, we were all pretty upset when he volunteered to be a paratrooper. But as it turned out, there was so much training involved for the raw recruits in his unit, that he avoided the early battles in Europe, unlike Jim.

"I remember him writing that he had participated in some practice operation, I think they called it 'maneuvers,' in Tennessee and was jumping a lot, including at night. Can you believe that? Jumping out of an airplane in the pitch dark? I tell you, we all worried for John's sanity for a while.

"But then he got shipped to Fort Bragg in North Carolina and he was there the entire time Jim was fighting in Sicily. If I recall, John didn't get shipped overseas until sometime in the fall of 1943. I don't remember, but I think he went someplace in England."

"And my father and Peachy?" I asked.

"Peachy was stuck in Jacksonville. "That base commander wasn't about to let him go so long as there was a golf team. He was still furious," she said, laughing. "You're Dad had been shipped to another air base, I think it was Thermal in Rice, California. He was chomping at the bit to either come home and marry your mother or get shipped to the South Pacific. He was very unhappy and homesick. And he didn't like the desert heat. That's how Thermal got its name — from the super hot climate."

183

I imagined my father stuck on an Army Air Corp base in a California desert. He had never been the life of a party, but he liked people. Being stranded in an outdoor oven wouldn't have been his thing.

"Phil, Ray, Henry and Jiggs were still playing the waiting game with the Draft Board and none of them had been called up yet. My husband Eric, Dot's husband Ed and Flossie's Al were all in the same boat. But we knew it was just a matter of time for Phil, Jiggs, my sister's husbands and my own. Henry and Ray were the only unknowns."

She abruptly stopped, sighing deeply.

"You know I'm remembering all this and it just came to me that this was about the last time for a couple of years that we knew where everyone was. Things really began to escalate at the end of 1943. I keep saying it, but it's true. All we thought about was their safety."

The neighborhood had gone quiet. The Fourth of July was coming to a close. Every now and then we'd hear a distant crackle or boom as the kids used up the last of their firecrackers. The temperature was finally cooling too, and every so often we felt the slightest breath of a refreshing breeze cross the patio.

I kept waiting for Ka to signal she was done. My husband came out with a pot of iced coffee to audible appreciation from the adults around the table. Most of the kids were lying on the back lawn, picking out stars and sharing secrets. It wasn't often they were allowed to be up so late. It was a special night in every way.

"Things were getting more difficult at home," she continued after sipping her coffee for a few moments. "The air raid drills had us all spooked, but we had to go through them every Monday night at 9 p.m., just about the time the "Lux Radio Theater" came on. My husband Eric, Bobbie, Beverly and I would listen to it every week

184

with Pa, so I remember having to pull down the blackout shades Pa had in the living room and the kitchen before the show started. If we forgot, and the air raid siren went off before we pulled down the shades to block out the lights there would be a knock at the door from the Air Raid Wardens who walked the streets. I hated it. But the concern was real, I guess. We had Pratt & Whitney in our backyard and down in New London there was the submarine base, both big targets for the enemy. The blackouts made sense so that we wouldn't lead their bombers to those factories. But Lord, it was frightening.

"Rationing was becoming more severe as well. There wasn't much meat available, sugar was hard to find, too. But the most difficult items were gasoline and tires. We were only allowed three gallons of gas a week and we had to stretch that between Eric going to work and getting to Pa's. Tires were out of the question, although Pa and Eric managed to get some retreads through old Walter Meals, the guy that sold Plymouths. Jim worked for him. Even retreads had to be approved by a special board of appeals and most people were turned down. Anything to do with rubber was a real problem. So, the car became something only used if absolutely necessary."

"That's hard to imagine," my son Jay said, and I laughed. He liked nothing better than going cruising in his car with his friends. "I guess we all take our cars for granted now."

Ka smiled at him. "Don't beat yourself up, Jay. Before the war, there was nothing we liked more than jumping into Pa's old touring car and taking a ride to the shore, or driving through Old Wethersfield or even Hartford just for fun. We had to change our entire way of thinking once the government started handing out

185

ration books and stamps. We didn't know until after the war how much of a difference it made in the war effort.

"We even saved scrap metal of any kind including tin cans, if you can believe it. You would cut both ends off the can and then flatten it and the town would come around and collect the cans and anything else you had that was metal like old plows and rusty wire. I can remember putting cardboard in the soles of my shoes to make them last a little longer. Even newspaper and the tin foil from chewing gum and cigarettes were recycled, though I haven't the faintest idea why or what it was used for. But we saved everything."

There was a titter of laughter around the table at Ka's honesty. But most of us were amazed at her memory.

"There were a lot of things I didn't really understand back then. I was pretty young. For the life of me I never understood why we saved cooking grease."

"Cooking grease?" Claudia repeated.

"Yes, we would drain it into a big can and save it to be collected with the scrap metal. Someone told me once it was used in the making of explosives."

"I think they used the cooking grease and animal fats to make glycerin, which is highly explosive when mixed with other chemicals," Jack said. All eyes turned to my college student son. "What?" he said, looking hurt. "I took some chemistry classes."

Ka continued unperturbed by the interruption.

"We couldn't buy bobby pins or zippers. And matches were really hard to find. You could buy a certain number of cigarettes, but it was hard to find matches to light them! Nylons were nearly impossible to get, which I understood. The military needed silk and nylon for parachutes. But before the war, no lady would

186

ever be seen in public without nylons so it was a big adjustment. We fixed the problem by coating our legs with a tinted makeup that was like bottled liquid stockings and then we'd use an eyebrow pencil to draw in the back seam. From a distance, you couldn't tell the difference."

It was a subject only the ladies around the table could appreciate.

"Did I mention the War Bonds drive?" she asked. There was no response.

"Well, by 1943, the government had really revved up its propaganda selling War Bonds to finance the war. You paid $18.75 and in return got a $25 Bond that matured in ten years. They were a terrible investment if you looked at them that way. Actually, they were a loan to the government to pay for the war and a way for school children to get involved. Kids would bring 25 cents to school each week and get a Savings Stamp in return. They would put the stamp into a small book and when they filled the book it would total $18.75 and the student would receive a War Bond in return. It was very popular in the schools. And of course Roosevelt made sure employers ran programs to sell Bonds through payroll deduction. The campaign raised a ton of money for our boys, I'll tell you, even if it was about the worst investment you could make!" she laughed. "I remember your Uncle Jiggs was really involved in the War Bonds campaign when he was in high school and he had a lot of Bonds of his own. I think they help with a down payment on his first house when he got married some years later."

She looked around at each of us

"This probably sounds like I've made it all up," she said. "I admit it was a very surreal time. The news reports were hard to listen to, but they didn't make the war real to us. Every now and then something would happen that would shock us back into realizing a lot of our boys wouldn't be coming home. Like another new Gold Star banner somewhere in town." She dropped her head and stared at her hands, folded together in her lap.

"It was a tragedy for some poor family to have to deal with when it happened, but it was actually very hard on everyone. Pa really would go into a funk when some boy was lost, whether he knew the family or not. I remember the night we got word that Charlie Tourison from Wolcott Hill Road had been killed. He was 20-year-old boy who left his studies at Trinity College and volunteered for the Army Air Corps. I think it was in November, right before Thanksgiving when the news came that he had been shot down over Norway. Pa didn't know the family but he saw the announcement in the paper. It hit him hard. He had Jiggs walk with him to the boy's house and they stood out front for over an hour. Jiggs said Pa never took his eyes off the Gold Star in the window. Someone finally came out of the house, I guess it was Mr. Tourison and Pa walked right up and shook the man's hand and offered his condolences to the family. Then he walked back home with Jiggs, tears streaming down his face the whole way. He spent the night alone in the barn."

She looked so sad as the memory came back to her in all its horror.

"Just he and my mother's ghost... and that bottle."

Sixteen

~~~ ❧ ~~~

December, 1943

Private John Hughes rolled over and sat up on his canvas cot for the third time that night, reaching down to rub his left ankle. He had tweaked it in a training jump days before and was still sore. Of course the daily, non-stop regimen of training didn't help when it came to giving sore muscles time to heal. But it wasn't just the sore ankle that had him awake.

He'd just gotten a letter from Jim and understood how rough the war had been on his big brother. By comparison, it seemed all he had done since volunteering to train as a paratrooper, was just that: train.

He was homesick but also sick and tired of waiting to get into action. John Hughes wanted to go

189

home in the worst way but not before he finished the job he had volunteered to do.

As he tried to sleep on that cold, damp November night in the horse stall that had been converted into a bunkhouse for he and four other men in a village called Aldourne in Wiltshire County, his restless mind revisited the months since he had left the US with anticipation of going into combat immediately.

The 506th Parachute Infantry Regiment had "crossed the pond" with a limited naval escort on the SS *Samaria*, a 20,000-ton twin-screw passenger steamship built in 1922 and commandeered from the Cunard Line as a troop transport during the war. The 600-foot long ship had already seen her best days when Hughes boarded her with the other members of D Company, 2nd Battalion 506th Parachute Regiment. After having been stripped of anything remotely suggesting luxury accommodations, the old lady looked even more tired to the paratroopers.

Designed to be a cheaper alternative to the flagship passenger ships that plied the Atlantic prior to the war, *Samaria* was built with economy in mind and was capable of only 16 knots. That made her a sitting duck in the U-Boat infested North Atlantic, and the boys of the 506th were only too aware of their vulnerability during the sleepless crossing. On their third night out, in mid-Atlantic, Hughes remembered watching the phosphorescent entrails of a torpedo pass under the *Samaria* as he stood at the ships rail having a smoke. The ship had changed course immediately with the rest of the fleet, leaving behind a destroyer that spent considerable time dropping depth charges in pursuit of the U-boat. Hughes never did find out if they got the sub or not, but it was an experience that kept him from ever closing his eyes again for the remainder of the voyage.

SS Samaria docked in Liverpool on the 15th of September 1943 and the 506th was trucked to makeshift barracks in small villages like Aldbourne, Ramsbury and Foxfield, all in Wiltshire County. What lay ahead were weeks of training exercises that would soon turn into months as the successful invasions of Sicily and Italy, the first steps in the liberation of Europe took far longer than the Allied command had anticipated. While Jim Hughes was battling for his life in Sicily, John was doing more training for what would be the deciding invasion of the war.

December 20, 1943

Dear Gang,

Haven't heard from any of you recently, but then again, I suppose you have no way to reach me. I think the censors will let me get away with telling you that I have crossed the Atlantic and am participating in more training exercises.

It seems since I made the decision to become a paratrooper that's about all I've done. Poor brother Jim has been fighting for his life for more than a year, and all I've contributed is learning how to jump out of an airplane. But I will tell you this. When we finally do get into battle the 506th Parachute Regiment will be one formidable military unit.

I have been trained to do things I never imagined, like jumping out of airplanes in the middle of the night, becoming an expert marksman (I mean I can shoot the tail feathers off a turkey at 200 yards!) and am able to read a street map of a foreign village illuminated only by a cigarette lighter. Now those are some skills that will come in handy around the house when I come home, hey Pa?

Speaking of coming home, I wouldn't go planning any big party for me the way you did Speck. From what I can see,

191

the coming months will be full of more training and there won't be many furloughs back home unless it involves being on a stretcher. It breaks my heart to know that it will be another Christmas without you all, but we know the job that needs to get done. We'll have plenty of Christmas' to celebrate after we bury Hitler in Berlin.

I'm praying that all is well back home, and I'm excited for Speck and Elvira. What a great couple, but what a difficult way to begin a marriage. Hope they get a chance to get hitched before my little brother finds his way to a tropical paradise fighting the Japanese!

It's cold, always raining and damp as all hell here, but I shouldn't complain knowing that you're heading into another New England winter. But I gotta tell you, the sight of snow would make me cry with happiness. Stay warm and keep Jiggs busy chopping wood for the fireplace.

We'll have to see if my forwarding address survives the censors. If it does, I better see some letters!

Love you all, have a great Christmas. I'll save you some of my Spam.

John

John Hughes did his best to keep his spirits up, but failing that, he made sure he never let on to his family how homesick he was. He never dreamed the war would last so long and that he would be gone for years. But that's how it was shaping up.

*   *   *

Nearly 9,000 miles west, Sergeant Speck Hughes was enduring similar anxieties. He was tired of the desert and hated the climate, and desperately wanted to be shipped to the Pacific Theater. He, like hundreds of thousands of troops stationed or training stateside found the waiting for combat deployment almost unbearable.

For most, the work they performed or training schedule was a monotonous existence that was a far cry from what volunteers or draftees had anticipated. The truth was that the vast number of men inducted into the military had yet to see action and morale was low among stateside military personnel. Where Americans were fighting, the battles were savage. Where they were waiting or training, the boredom was insufferable.

But in the final month of the year, news reports and statements from world leaders made it clear that the coming year would be pivotal in the Allied efforts to win the war and a time of desperation for the Axis powers to stave off shattering defeat. It became clear to Americans that the momentum of the war had changed dramatically in sometimes chillingly graphic but encouraging news.

On December 1, President Roosevelt announced the *Cairo Declaration* after a summit with British Prime Minister Winston Churchill and China's President Chiang Kai-shek in which the Allies, for the first time, demanded Japan's unconditional surrender. But the silence from the Japanese that followed only reinforced confidence in the Allied strategy of "Island Hopping" to reach the Japanese mainland. The plan had begun on November 20 when US Marines stormed the island of Tarawa and raised the flag three days later after fanatical resistance by the Japanese. It was the first of dozens of vicious, bloody amphibious attacks by US infantry and Marines. It was clear that victory in the Pacific would cost America dearly.

Two days later, millions of Americans listened intently to celebrated war journalist Edward R. Murrow as he described a Royal Air Force nighttime bombing raid on Berlin. Murrow, who had been allowed to fly with the crew of a British Lancaster on the mission

193

summed up the intensity but turning tide of the war in his summary:

"Men die in the sky while others are roasted alive in their cellars," Murrow reported. "Berlin last night wasn't a pretty sight. In about 35 minutes it was hit with about three times the amount of stuff that ever came down on London in a night-long blitz."

On December 4, torpedoes from the USS *Sailfish* sank the Japanese carrier *Chuyo* off the coast of Truk with heavy loss of life. It was another crushing blow for the Japanese navy, which earlier in the year had lost its chief naval strategist and commander, Admiral Isoroku Yamamoto when American P-38's shot down his bomber transport over Bougainville Island in Papua New Guinea. The Japanese, which had dominated the naval war after its sneak attack on Pearl Harbor had devastated the US Pacific fleet, now had completely lost its dominance.

On December 22, the Nazi government announced that all boys aged 16 would be required to register for military duty.

On Christmas Eve, President Roosevelt, in a nationwide radio address announced that U.S. General Dwight D. Eisenhower had been appointed Supreme Allied Commander of the invasion of Europe that would be launched in 1944. Americans shuddered but cheered the news. If successful, the invasion would lead to Berlin and the end of the war in Europe.

And finally, on December 31st, both Hitler and British Deputy Prime Minister Clement Attlee addressed their nations with surprising candor about the days to come.

On New Year's Eve, Hitler admitted in a radio broadcast from the bombed out ruins of Berlin that

194

"1943 brought us our heaviest reverses," a statement that shocked the German people for its unusual candor.

"1944 will make heavy demands on all Germans," Hitler said. "This vast war will approach a crisis this year. We have every confidence that we will survive."

On the same day, the nation-wide radio address by Deputy Prime Minister Clementine Attlee warned the war weary British people of complacency.

"We do know that in the coming year, the war will blaze up into greater intensity than ever before, and that we must be prepared to face heavier casualties," Atlee said. "1944 may be the victory year; it will only be so if we continue to put forward our utmost efforts and if we allow nothing to divert us from our main purpose."

For Americans, the month-long blitz of strategic positioning by the Allied and Axis Powers led to only one conclusion. The tortuous path they had followed since December 7, 1941 was narrowing and the end was in sight. But the price to be paid in the months ahead would make the sacrifices already made pale by comparison.

Christmas 1943 was a time of reflection for hundreds of thousands of young men like the Hughes brothers who so desperately wanted peace but knew the worst was yet to come.

For families waiting at home, the agony of uncertainty and the growing number of Gold Star banners made Christmas less a time of giving and celebrating than of quiet, hopeful prayer.

Seventeen
~~~ ✑ ~~~

Christmas, 1943

It was Christmas morning on Highland Street and Henry Hughes was up early, rattling around the kitchen making coffee before Jiggs, Bobbie or Beverly got up or any of his other children came by. He poured a cup of steaming black coffee into a stained porcelain mug and added a jigger of Irish whiskey to sweeten it. He took a long drink, despite how hot it was. He'd need to be fortified to get through this day again and didn't hesitate to open the bottle and top off the mug again.

He closed his eyes and thought back to his favorite Christmas of all, the first with his only bride.

"Merry Christmas, Catherine, my love," he whispered and took another drink.

Henry wandered into the living room and sat in his chair, staring out the picture window as he always did in the morning. But now the view was always partially blocked by the red trimmed banner that hung in the window. This was no Christmas decoration. Sewn onto it were the four blue stars, one for each of his sons away in the military. He thought for a moment of Christmas past, when by this hour the house would be full of cheer, the laughter of excited children and the warm satisfaction of the nearness of loved ones. And, of course, his Catherine.

This morning, there was only silence and the sedating coffee to numb his aching heart.

He watched as the morning sun rose higher but his eyes never left the banner. His thoughts wandered to the boys. The coffee finally eased him into a foggy sleep.

Upstairs, while Beverly still slept, Bobbie had risen early as well. She thought about it being Christmas morning, but felt no joy. Her heart was filled with sadness as yet another Christmas had come and still her brothers had not come home.

She and Beverly still went to Mass everyday to pray for them. She wasn't so sure she could tolerate the church today, especially when it came time to sing the holy hymns written especially to celebrate the birth of the baby Jesus. She found the whole idea of celebrating almost blasphemous.

Bobbie knew that the one thing she needed to do on this day was help her father get through it with a minimum of pain. In a few minutes she would go down and wake Pa up in his chair, where she found him dozing most mornings. She would give him a bear hug and a kiss and wish him a very merry Christmas, despite her true feelings. Then she would make him breakfast before he fell asleep again.

Bur first, she needed to do something that would make this day worth remembering, something that she had been thinking about most of the night. She had to write to her brothers.

She quietly got out of bed and tiptoed over to her small desk, careful not to wake up Beverly. Her little sister had been suffering from nightmares for weeks. Sleep was precious. Bobbie began to write her letter, making a copy for each of her four brothers.

December 25, 1943

Merry Christmas, big brother! I hope you know how much I miss and love you and that I think about you all the time. I would do anything to make your Christmas day a little happier. Knowing that you were safe and at peace would be the most wonderful present!

Sometimes, in the very earliest part of the morning, while its still dark outside and the air is frigid cold and everyone is still asleep, I lay awake in bed and close my eyes, imagining that I can hear your voices in your bedrooms, downstairs in the kitchen or outside in the backyard. I hear you all roughhousing and laughing and fighting over who's going to win the foot race to school or have the first seat in the toboggan or some such silliness and the sound resonates through the walls and into my ears. It makes me so happy and I laugh out loud.

Then I remember that you're all off at war and it makes me want to cry. I'm afraid for you – and maybe, even though I know it's so selfish of me, I'm afraid for those of us waiting here at home for you. Because I know that our family will never recover if any one of you is hurt. For heaven's sake, we haven't even gotten over Mother's death, and that happened so long ago.

So know that I pray every night before I go to sleep and at the start of each day that you'll be safe and that soon you will come home again and fill this house with laughter and happiness again.

198

Please, please be careful and may God watch over you.
Your loving sister,
Bobbie

Eighteen
~~~ ❧ ~~~

Spring, 1944

Jim Hughes crouched lower in the hold of the landing craft as salt spray caught him with an unexpected cold shower. His stomach bounced up and down with the channel surf as he and his platoon neared the shoreline and he wished he hadn't downed a second helping of scrambled eggs at breakfast that morning. To ease his jitters, he forced himself to think about anything other than the live-fire training operation called *Exercise Tiger* that the *Big Red One* was about to participate in. Ultimately more then 30,000 troops would be involved in the mock amphibious landing.

He closed his eyes and thought back to the Church of Maria Santissima del Soccorso in the town of Augusta where he had visited months ago in the hours before he boarded a troop transport with his men, bound for the British Isles. Hughes remembered how troubled he had been as he knelt at the altar rail of the church. Now, as the shoreline loomed, he searched again for the peace he had found that morning in the solitude of the ancient place of worship. It was the first time he had been in a church since the ambush at Ponte Olivo where Mike Pettig had died, and the first time he had prayed in many years.

The date was October 23, 1943 and the *Big Red One* was sailing back to England to train for what he knew was going to be the decisive battle of the war. Hughes expected it would be the invasion of continental Europe, but when and where the *Big Red One* would strike was anyone's guess at this point. He only hoped that it would be soon. More than anything, he wanted to go home.

That morning in the privacy of the town church, the oldest son of the Hughes family offered his thanks to God. Not for a moment did he believe that some kind of divine intervention had gotten him this far in the war still in one piece. But he prayed anyway, just in case and for his brothers, wherever they were, and his family at home.

But that wasn't the reason he had slipped away from his men waiting at the dock and walked several miles to visit the church. Actually, he was deeply disturbed by the burden of his command and needed desperately to talk with his father, the only person he had ever allowed to see the real Jim Hughes. To his brothers and sisters he was "Bull," the big, tough, hard nose guy that swung first and thought about it later. Pa knew the truth about him; his lifelong struggle with self-confidence was their secret. Highland Street was a long way away. The church was his only option. In the little time he had to himself before shipping out, he had to find answers to questions that had been plaguing him for weeks.

As he knelt in the church that morning, he stared up at the hand-painted fresco that adorned the vaulted ceiling of the basilica, marveling that its beauty had withstood the centuries. The Mediterranean sun poured in through oversized stain glass windows that lined the church's nave, and brilliant colors danced across the smooth stone floors, polished by the footsteps of centuries of villagers who had worshipped there.

The vivid colors brought back memories of when he was a little boy and had sat upon his father's shoulders and watched WWI vets marching in a victory parade down Main Street in Hartford. He remembered the swirling red, white and blue American flags that people waved while they cheered and the radiant hues of the military regimental pennants carried by their color guards.

Little Jim Hughes also remembered the young men who awkwardly limped by on crutches or were missing a limb, and the scarred faces that surrounded eyes that were dulled by the horrors of war. The image of tears rolling down his father's cheeks was still clear in his minds eye. When he later asked him why he cried, Henry Hughes had explained that he knew many of the broken men.

Still, as a boy, Jim Hughes had played at back yard war like all little boys did, and there was always good guys and bad guys. He sighed at the memory. Playtime was over.

Over the last year he'd watched as thousands of young men — Americans, Brits, Canadians, French, German and Italians — fell on the beaches and in the villages and towns of North Africa and Sicily, their bodies shattered by bullets or bombs they never saw coming. He'd had to grit his teeth, step over their lifeless bodies and push on. Jim Hughes became steeled to death. He had learned how to kill and had felt the pain of losing men he cared for. It was the cost of doing his business: protecting the safety and freedom of those he loved.

That rationale made all the sense in the world when he laid down to rest — right up to the shocking moment when the eyes of the last man he had killed in battle appeared to him in his nightmares and woke him screaming from his sleep. It was then that the doubts began to dance in his head.

The letters he had written to the families of men in his platoon who were killed in action haunted him. No matter how hard he tried, no matter what words he wrote, the letters left him with an emptiness he couldn't accept. If he found them shallow and wanting, he could only imagine how poorly they were received. And what about those he had killed? Shouldn't he have written letters to their parents? Did they believe their sons were the bad guys? The questions filled him with anxiety because he was afraid of the answers.

He clasped his hands at the altar rail and begged God to help him live with the awful truth and the job he had been sent to do.

Still the conflicts raged within him.

He had witnessed the enemy callously use a little boy as bait for the opportunity to murder his men. Yet he had seen the same foe beg for his life and whimper for his mother at the end. Were these the same men? He turned the table. What act of violence or deceit was he capable of to win a battle — or to survive one? Would he cry for his mother if a bullet gave him only seconds to have a final thought?

He pondered these questions for as long as time allowed. Then he knew he had to put a stake in the ground or go mad.

There were only two conclusions he could come to, and ultimately he would have to live by them.

Good guy or bad guy? He knew it eventually made no difference. Jim Hughes wanted to believe that God was on his side in this war, that his was a righteous battle against an evil enemy. But in the end, he knew that God had nothing to do with war; it was the product of men who would have their way no matter how much bloodshed was required. His job was to ensure that his family was safe and to guarantee their freedom. To that end, he couldn't spend anymore time thinking about what the enemy's goal was. For it was a fact that given the opportunity, no German soldier would hesitate to kill him any more than Jim Hughes would if he had the chance to shoot first.

He also came to terms with the impossibility of justifying to grieving parents the death of their son, no matter the cause or circumstances. It was a blasphemous loss, undeniably cruel and insane. Sharing the last moments of their son's life might provide them with an image to hold on to, an account of his bravery, perhaps his last words to them, or the knowledge that he had not suffered at all. Conceivably the words would be helpful; he wasn't sure. Either way, he could not and would not shirk what he considered his duty. Jim Hughes would continue to write the letters so long as young men under his command died, and he would do so with words that reflected all the compassion and respect he could muster, even while knowing they might mean little to those who grieved.

The soldier made the sign of the cross, stood and genuflected then slowly walked out of the church and back to his waiting ship. If anything, the time spent in contemplation had helped him understand that his real dilemma was being caught in a time and place where reality forced him to ponder such impossible questions. He walked through the town streets back to his men at the loading dock, more at peace with his thoughts than he had been in a long time.

It was a long, difficult voyage back to England where the *Big Red One* arrived on November 5th, the specter of lurking U-Boats always present. Even so, sleep came more easily as his nightmares subsided. "Bull" Hughes was still alive and well, but a bit more certain of who and what he was and how he would manage the months of struggle ahead.

It was now April 27, 1943 and the final battle loomed ahead.

The sudden shout of the Coxswain of the Higgins Boat and the simultaneous drop of the landing gate into the shallow surf at Slapton Sands on the Devonshire coast of England snapped Hughes back to reality.

He didn't hesitate.

"Go, go, go," Hughes yelled to his platoon as they hit the water of the English Channel at morning's first light. "Stay low, stay low," he added as his men scrambled from the LCVP, even though the landing was hardly a new experience for his battle-hardened troops. Hughes listened for the sound of live rounds being fired over the heads of the incoming amphibious force, as he had been briefed to expect. Instead, without warning machine gun fire strafed the side of the boat and the water just ahead of them, flying splinters of wood and the staccato geysers of water telling him all he needed to know.

"What the hell?" Hughes yelled at the realization that the machine gun fire coming from the beach was painfully off target. They were being shot at with live ammunition. "Get down!" he screamed at his men. "Drop down to the waterline and stay in place! I repeat, stay in place, do not advance!"

*   *   *

Several miles inland, PFC John Hughes of the 506th Parachute Regiment had just completed a mock mission of capturing bridges after a midnight jump. The exercise had been a royal screw-up, he thought as he leaned against a tree having a smoke while waiting for orders to return to his barracks in Aldbourne in Wiltshire County. Poor communications had resulted in many of the paratroopers jumping at the wrong coordinates and only a fraction of the Regiment actually found their targets. Nonetheless, the mission was declared a success.

"If that was a success, I wonder what the brass would consider a failure," he thought to himself, fighting back a wave of anxiety. Thus far in training in the British countryside, he had experienced far too many similar instances of poor communications leading to mistakes that could take many lives. It left him wary of military officers who seemed too quick to label a training exercise "successful" when it was far from the truth.

Hughes had privately concluded that the mission he and the 506th were preparing for was the long awaited invasion of France. Like most GI's, the only real question he had was when and where it would happen. The exercise he had participated in today was slightly inland from Slapton Sands along the coast, an area he assumed had been chosen because of its similarity to where the actual invasion would take place.

He was relaxing with his cigarette, enjoying an unusual moment of inactivity, when he first heard the gunfire coming from the shoreline, miles away.

"Whoa," he said aloud to the men around him. "I imagine those are LCVP's coming in. Sure hope that's dummy ammo being fired at those guys."

Before anyone could comment, enormous explosions could be heard hitting the coastline. The sound was not unexpected. Naval bombardments would often be timed to soften up the beaches in the minutes before the amphibious troops came ashore.

"Hell's a poppin' on that beach," Hughes said. "Sometimes I think I made the right decision about joining this war from the air instead of swimming in from the beach."

He would hardly have been so cavalier about the action at Slapton Sands if knew that his own older brother was once again fighting for his life.

Ironically, in a training exercise.

*   *   *

In one of the war's most tragic events, *Exercise Tiger* was rapidly becoming a slaughter.

Jim Hughes' order to his platoon to stay in place and to minimize themselves as targets was spot on. No sooner than he had given the order the sky exploded with the smoky entrails of incoming naval artillery fired from British destroyers that had been ordered to shell the beach in advance of the Higgins Boats. But a miscommunication had delayed the timing of the shelling by an hour, a critical piece of information that offshore troopships had not received when launching the LCVP's. Consequently, the landing craft were making the Slapton Sands shore just as the British ships loosed their first salvos of artillery.

On the beach, US infantry playing the role of defenders were inexplicably firing live rounds directly at the incoming LCVP's, not over them as had been ordered. As men from the *Big Red One* leapt from their landing craft, they were mowed down by "friendly fire" to the horror of military observers who were unable to call for a ceasefire before hundreds of men had been killed either in the water or on the beach. More troops died as they raced across the sands in search of cover, caught by the naval shells that fell unmercifully for an hour.

By the time the exercise had been terminated, more than 450 men from the 1st Infantry had been killed.

Later than night, in a separate component of *Exercise Tiger* that involved landing thousands more troops and hundred of tanks on Slapton Sands in the darkness, tragedy struck again.

Nine E-Boats, the 115-foot-long German Naval variant of the US Navy PT boat patrolling the English Channel out of their base in Cherbourg, stumbled upon the training exercise and attacked the Allied flotilla of troop and tank laden LST's without warning. In the ensuing battle, another 750 American infantry and naval personnel were killed, two LST's were sunk and two heavily damaged.

Exercise Tiger had taken the lives of well over 1,000 US servicemen and given Supreme Allied Commander of the Expeditionary Force General Dwight D. Eisenhower reason for concerned pause. His worst nightmare in the final weeks leading up to the landing was coming true. It was undeniable that the Allied invasion force was nowhere near ready for the assault on continental Europe.

An impenetrable security net was dropped over the *Exercise Tiger* debacle and training efforts were substantially intensified even as military commanders scrambled to understand and correct their mistakes.

All Allied forces were quarantined to their bases spread widely over southern England and soldiers were drilled repeatedly for improvements in marksmanship, river crossings, long marches, street fighting, communication and physical conditioning. The 1st Infantry concentrated on assaulting pillboxes — heavily armed concrete fortresses that were expected to line the European coast. The 506th Parachute Regiment practiced jumping from the backs of moving trucks to simulate real parachute jumps and repeatedly attacked bridges that would be key strategic targets wherever they landed.

While thousands of Allied troops were essentially prisoners of the upcoming invasion, they were still encouraged to write home to keep up their spirits. What they weren't told was that none of their letters were delivered back home nor was any mail received given to them. Security was paramount. Eisenhower was taking no chances.

Only the few miles between their base camps separated Jim Hughes and his brother John. Each had hoped for a furlough home or even a weekend together in London. But it was not to be. Time was far too short, and every minute of every day found the men preparing in some way for an invasion they knew was coming. In the months they trained in the British Isles, their only contact was by letter. And now, even that connection was cut off. Still they wrote to each other and their family, every day expecting a reply. None would come until weeks after the invasion.

But where would it be? And when? They were itching to get on it with it, no matter the risk. The young men from America, Canada, Australia and New Zealand who were part of the invasion force were desperate to go home and the Europeans, among them the British, French, Belgians, Czech's, Greeks, Poles and Dutch were as eager to return to their homelands — free of Nazi occupation and persecution.

That they were preparing for a major invasion of Europe was hardly a guess by the troops of the 12 nations involved. But what none of them knew is that they were about to embark on the greatest military assault in recorded history. Nearly three million Allied troops were amassed in the south of England and a fleet of 4,000 ships and 1,200 airplanes waited to pounce on the last major obstacle to the destruction of the Nazi war machine: the invasion of continental Europe. *Operation Overlord* was the codename for the invasion of France. *Neptune* was the codename for the amphibious landing.

The location? Normandy on the southern coast of France. The date? Treacherous spring weather conditions made the exact date difficult to predict. But Eisenhower and his commanders were determined that the historical effort of the Allies to claw their way on to the beaches of France would take place as soon as possible.

Target: June, 1944.

Nineteen

~~~ ❧ ~~~

"It was as if someone had dropped a giant soundproof lid over the whole of England," Ka continued. "We were all trading letters with Jim and John in late 1943 and early 1944, but then as spring approached, the mailbox was empty. Day after day we waited for some news from them, but there was nothing. And we had no way of know if they were receiving our letters. It was horrible, especially for Pa."

I didn't know if it was the strong iced coffee she was sipping or just the adrenalin of the memories that were flooding back to her, but my 88-year-old aunt showed no signs of relinquishing her grip on the information starved audience in my backyard. She was as fresh as you might have expected a woman half her age to be after just waking up from a good night's sleep.

"Well, look at that," she said, abruptly pointing to the sky and every head turned upward. "It's a shooting star, did you see it?" she asked excitedly. Only a few actually had, but there was a consensus chorus of "Wow" from the table.

"Stars..." she began and paused before sharing her thoughts.

"I've had a certain fascination with them since those war days. After all, you couldn't look out of Pa's living room for nearly five years without seeing the Blue Star Banner, full of carefully embroidered stars hanging in the window. First, there were three stars, then four, then five, six and seven when Phil, Jigg's and Dot's husband Ed were drafted. Imagine that. Seven boys from the same family."

"Good Lord," I heard Claudia whisper. Her eyes were wet. "I can't imagine waking up every day not knowing if my children were safe. That banner must have been such a depressing reminder. I would have stopped looking out of the window."

"I know," Ka replied, her own eyes glistening. "That's about where my head was after more than two years of looking at it, even with only four stars. But for some strange reason that I've never understood, those blue stars gave my father something to hang on to. He would stare at that banner for hours at a time. And sometimes I'd find him running his fingers over each of the stars. They kept him connected, somehow. There was never a word of discussion about taking it down."

She sipped her coffee again.

"My nightmare — I guess one we all shared — was the thought of any of the blue stars being sewn over in gold. There were many Gold Stars in Wethersfield already, and more to come."

I shuddered and I know I wasn't alone.

"We all might have come undone when the letters stopped — if not for your father and Peachy," she said, turning to me.

"My father?" I asked, surprised. "And Peachy?"

"Yes," she said, nodding her head up and down. "He got another furlough and came home without telling us. Jiggs was the only one who knew because Speck wrote and asked him to pick him up at the train station and to keep it a secret. He wanted to surprise us all." She suddenly laughed out loud at the memory.

"Well Jiggs almost kept it a secret but he had a good reason for spilling the beans," she continued. "He shared the news with me, because he didn't want Pa to be alone when his boy suddenly appeared at the door. He was afraid he'd have a heart attack! So, I was there on the pretense of making him lunch when up rolled your father and Jiggs with someone sitting in the passenger seat. Pa was sitting on the front stoop and couldn't make out whom it was. And then the car door opened…"

She laughed again and I swear it was contagious.

"When Pa realized it was Speck he shot up from the steps like a rocket. He got dizzy from standing up so fast and he began to fall. Speck ran up the front walk and caught him in a bear hug. It was the most amazing scene. I ran to the door and saw that he was home and I swear I still didn't believe it. I wrapped my arms around the both of them and then Jiggs piled on and broke into tears.

This time she reached for her hankie and dabbed at her eyes.

"That's one of those memories you never forget," she said.

"Next thing you know, Speck grabbed the car keys from Jiggs and the two of them headed to Pratt &

Whitney where Elvira was working, to surprise her. And did he ever. He was in his uniform and walked in to the Pratt headquarters and explained who he was and why he was there. Some personnel guy took him right out on to the shop floor where Elvira was working. Your Dad snuck up behind and touched her on the shoulder. Well you can just imagine her reaction when she turned around and saw him! She put a hand over her mouth to keep from screaming but tears began rolling down her cheeks. Everyone around them broke into applause and then the personnel guy was kind enough to give her the rest of her shift off and they came home. Jiggs told me your father could hardly drive because Elvira kept hugging him.

"I remember the look on your mom's face when she walked in the door, Bobbie. She was radiant, just so happy. They were married on May 1 at St. Augustine's Church in Hartford. Jiggs was your Dad's best man and Elvira's sister Millie was the Maid of Honor. He looked so handsome in his uniform and your mother was just beautiful, an exquisite bride. She really was an Italian beauty. I think that was one of the happiest days of your father's life — and certainly Pa's. He was really heartbroken when your Dad had to return to California, but happy to know that Elvira was going to be with him. He figured at least his son wouldn't be so homesick."

"My mother went to California with Dad?" my brother Jeff asked.

"Yup, they lived in a small apartment in Riverside and your Dad would drive to the base every day like it was a regular job. He was so content after two years of being so lonely and unhappy."

"What about Peachy?" I asked.

"Well, wouldn't you know it but just a couple of weeks afterwards, Peachy came home for the first time

214

on furlough. He just missed being there for your father's wedding. Somehow he had convinced the base commander to give him a couple of weeks home even after all the trouble Peachy had given him about being on the golf team.

"We had so much fun with my two brothers, it was like a gift from heaven. Even today, my favorite month of the year is May, and Speck and Peachy coming home is just one of the reasons."

"What are the others, Ka?" my sister asked.

"I'm getting to that," she chuckled.

"Had you heard from Jim or John by then?" I inquired.

"No," she said, the lilting tone of her voice gone immediately. "But about a week after Peachy returned to Jacksonville, we understood why."

She hesitated for a moment, looking up at the sky in hope of finding another shooting star.

"It all became painfully clear about midday on June 6th, 1944.

My son Jack sucked in his breath.

"Oh..." he said, grimly.

"That was D-Day, the invasion of France."

Twenty

~~~ ໑ ~~~

Monday, June 5, 1944
D-Day Minus 1

Nearly 175,000 Allied troops amassed for *Operation Neptune*, the amphibious landing on the beaches of Normandy that was the first step in *Operation Overlord*, the invasion of continental Europe — were languishing on troop ships anchored in harbors in the south of England waiting for the word to go. They had already experienced one false start when Eisenhower gave the order to launch the fleet on June 4th, only to have to rescind it because of severe weather in the English Channel.

The weather was a serious concern to Eisenhower and his commanders, because the window of opportunity to launch the Normandy landing was fleeting. The Allied troops had been cooped up for days on the rocking troopships, horribly seasick and psychologically battered already from the anxiety of waiting. And every day that passed was one more the Germans had to continue fortifying the coast of France for an invasion they knew was coming. What the Allied troops didn't know was that the decision to launch the attack had been made before dawn that morning.

At 4 a.m. at Southwick House near Portsmouth where the Supreme Allied Commander of the Expeditionary Forces had been meeting continuously with his staff, Eisenhower had listened glumly to the weather forecast for the next 48 hours.

As the briefing went on, he was too keyed up to sit and preferred to pace the thick blue carpet in the large oak paneled conference room in which they met. It had once served as a magnificent library, but its now empty bookshelves were a constant reminder to him of the price for liberty.

Then, he heard the words he had been waiting for: a break in the weather should occur within the next 24 hours.

On the General's broad shoulders rode the burden of the fate of hundreds of thousands of Allied troops, the massive invasion fleet and the freedom of millions of Europeans being held captive by the Nazi's. No man had ever faced a more difficult decision and only he had the power to make it.

Finally, with his hands clasped behind his back, he stopped pacing and raised his chin off his chest.

"Gentlemen, ok... let 'er rip."

And with those words the invasion date was set for the next day, June 6, 1944. Troop ships would sail that night to be in place for a dawn amphibious landing, but paratroopers would be dropped as early as 2100 hours on the 5th to spend the night seizing strategic

217

targets in advance of the invasion from the Channel. Heavy naval artillery shelling would commence in the hours before the amphibious landing, targeting the German fortifications on the beaches. Allied bombers and fighters would pound key targets inland to pave the way for advancing troops. Timing of the operation was precise, with little room for error. But the success of the enormous operation, with uncertain weather conditions and so many unknowns would ultimately depend on the heroic actions of men who never dreamt of being heroes.

Within hours of the decision, a letter from Gen. Eisenhower was pressed into the hand of every soldier, sailor and airman who would lead the invasion. He had been working on the words since February in anticipation of this moment and knew he needed to inspire men to do the impossible.

Unaware of the decision to go, the men of the big *Big Red One* languished in the holds of dozens of ships that would eventually sail them across the English Channel to within sight of their target: Omaha Beach. Omaha was one of five code names given to the selected Allied landing sites. The others were Utah, Gold, Juno, and Sword Beaches.

Jim Hughes stood at the railing of the attack transport *USS Samuel Chase* late in the morning of June 5th, having spent another restless night in the stinking hold of the 500-foot long vessel. This was his fifth day on the ship, having boarded in Falmouth on the south coast of Cornwall, England on June 1. It was one of the most westerly embarkation harbors of the fleet and meant a long sail to rendezvous with the *Operation Neptune* armada. Most of the 500 men on board were seasick, having endured horrific weather conditions and high seas. He wondered if his men would have any strength left when the call to battle actually came.

The waiting was the worst of it, he thought. It was emotionally draining for guys who after months of battle and training were razor sharp to fight. They couldn't endure much more of this.

Someone tapped him on the shoulder and handed him a piece of paper. He looked down to see Eisenhower's message printed on the letterhead of the Supreme Headquarters, Allied Expeditionary Forces. Signed by Dwight D. Eisenhower, it was as if the General had heard his plea.

"Soldiers, Sailors and Airmen of the Allied Expeditionary Force!" the letter began.

"You are about to embark upon the Great Crusade toward which we have striven these many months. The eyes of the world are upon you. The hopes and prayers of liberty-loving people everywhere march with you. In company with our brave Allies and brothers-in-arms on other Fronts, you will bring about the destruction of the German war machine, the elimination of Nazi tyranny over the oppressed peoples of Europe, and security for ourselves in a free world.

"Your task will not be an easy one. Your enemy is well trained, well equipped and battle-hardened. He will fight savagely.

"But this is the year 1944! Much has happened since the Nazi triumphs of 1940-41. The United Nations have inflicted upon the Germans great defeats, in open battle, man-to-man. Our air offensive has seriously reduced their strength in the air and the capacity to wage war on the ground. Our Home Fronts have given us an overwhelming superiority in weapons and munitions of war, and placed at our disposal great reserves of trained fighting men. The tide has turned! The free men of the world are marching together to Victory!

"I have full confidence in your courage, devotion to duty and skills in battle. We will accept nothing less than full Victory!

219

"Good luck! And let us all beseech the blessing of Almighty God upon this great and noble undertaking."

Jim Hughes swallowed hard. He was moved, but hardboiled enough to know it was going to take a lot more than a spirited vote of encouragement from the top dog to accomplish their mission.

The one thing Eisenhower's letter did accomplish was to remind the soldier of the enormity of the battle ahead. There would be many sacrifices in the days to come. He folded the letter, put it in his breast pocket for safekeeping and went below decks to write his own letter home. He was certain that nothing he wrote would reach his family for sometime to come, but was cognizant of the fact that this could be his last message to those he loved.

June 5, 1944

Dear Gang,

I am currently sitting on my bunk below decks on the USS Samuel Chase trying to take my mind off the fact that at this time tomorrow, God willing, I'll be storming with the Big Red One through the countryside of France and headed for Paris. From there, it will be a hop, skip and a jump to Berlin where we can finally put an end to this Nazi madness. If only it were that easy.

But finally, after all these months away from home and all of you, and after all the fighting I've been part of I can see light at the end of a very long tunnel. I'm glad that tomorrow is the day that will launch the invasion. Much more of this waiting and I think I'll go mad.

Unfortunately, John and I never did have a chance to get together in the months we've been in England. That seems impossible, I'm sure, but everyday here has been packed with training and some form of preparation for the invasion and passes and furloughs are a thing of the past. I'm sure John will tell you the same thing.

But remember this: one way or another, I will find him in France and we will have a reunion like none you can imagine. Please, when you write him, tell him Bull will be looking out for him with every step I take towards Berlin.

I want you all to know that no matter how things go for me tomorrow, I will do you proud and that I am happy to fight for your peace and happiness. Hell, that's what big brothers are for!

Pa, you stay strong and look after all the youngsters until I get home and whip them all back into shape!

Know that I carry each of you in my heart and will love you forever.

Your son and brother,
Jim

Less than 50 miles away, John Hughes had just read Eisenhower's letter. He had been waiting on the tarmac of an airfield in the south of England for days, waiting for the same orders as Jim and was itching to get going. Surrounding him were thousands of paratroopers and hundreds of C47 aircraft, all emblazoned with the identical D-Day markings: four rows of alternating black and white stripes on the wings and tail. Like Jim, he followed the same instinct of his older brother to write home. He wrote several letters, including one to Speck, who he knew would probably be the next Hughes to join the fighting.

June 5, 1944

Dear Speck,

This is probably the last chance I'll get to write for a while. Just finished reading Eisenhower's letter to the invasion force. I'm sure you will have seen it by the time you read this. The landing is on, finally. We'll get the word to move out soon, I'm sure and I'll be glad when the waiting is

221

over. It's so damned nerve wracking, and you can't sleep with all the commotion. All I can think about is Pa and you and all the gang, wondering if I'm ever going to see everyone again.

It seems like just a little while ago that we were all playing baseball on Saturday afternoons out by the barn. Things were so innocent. I can almost smell those chocolate chip cookies Dot would bring us with a big pitcher of lemonade. And I think about lining up our cars after dark and shining the headlights on the golf course at the Country Club so we could sneak in a few holes. Oh, yah, I heard the girls finally burned down the Club's old barn. Crazy. They've been threatening to do it for years because it looked so bad. I'll bet Bobbie was the instigator. She's probably a real handful now. Hope they didn't get caught because if I know Pa he would have tanned their hides.

Sorry, I'm rambling on. I'm so homesick and I miss you all.

You ought to see it here, brother. I wish you could so that when your time comes to ship out you'll be ready for the emotions that will flood over you. Let me tell you about it.

It would be nice to describe for you how glorious it is as we wait for the order to board our C-47, that a late spring sun is baking the thousand of airplanes and gliders that line the runways of airfields all over the southern coast of England. Or that the warm yellow radiance of the dawn this morning exaggerated the brilliance of regimental colors and insignias which mark the dozens of Allied units in this massive gathering, with their deep blue, gold and crimson plumages that adorn each of their company flags. I'd like to tell you that it's better than any parade we ever saw back home as kids.

And I wish I could share with you how the morning smelled and tasted, how rich it was with the fragrances of war, the fuel and oil, guns and grease. And I'd like to be able to tell you how brave and heroic me and the guys all feel and how certain we are of courage and victory.

But it would all be a lie, Speck.

222

Because it's not romantic like that at all here. In fact, the morning was miserably cold and the skies are filled with great flocks of gray clouds and a bone chilling rain. How I wish it would stop raining! Seems like that's all it ever does here. June 5ᵗʰ dawned with the sky all mottled and wet, and cast a depressing pall over the entire airfield, sort of like the color of old Spam. Yah, the Spam we had for breakfast. I can't help but think that Spam is going to be my last supper.

The airfield stinks of toxic, nauseating exhaust fumes and burnt oil mixed with the stench of vomit that wretch from the guts of scared boys. Most of the guys are between 20 and 25 years old and like me have never really been away from home before and haven't yet seen any combat. All we've done is train. Train and train and train some more. It never seems to end. When the time comes, I wonder what the smells of war will really be like. I've heard from some of the guys who were at Anzio and Salerno that the smell of warm blood is rusty-like, but the worst is burnt flesh and shattered bone. They say you someday forget seeing it, but you never lose the smell. Guess I'll soon find out.

I haven't heard from big brother Jim, I don't know exactly where he is now here in England, but there's no doubt he'll be in one of the first waves when the Big Red One hits the beaches. I'll be one of the first in with the 506ᵗʰ Parachute Regiment (not sure now why I volunteered for the paratroopers!) hours ahead of him and miles inland before Jim hits the beach. So there's no telling when we'll catch up with each other. I only hope God lets us meet again. The two of us will have some celebrating to do in Berlin, if that's what's in the cards for us. Eisenhower is saying we'll all be home for Christmas. I hate to say it, but it will truly be a miracle if all of us survive this thing.

I gotta go, Speck, they're rousting us, maybe for a drill or this could be it. Give Pa and the girls my love when you write them and enjoy that tan you're getting in California while you can. Tell Elvira that I couldn't be happier for her

223

and that she's going to marry a great guy someday (if you two haven't tied the knot already!) I'm sure your unit will be heading out into the Pacific soon enough to mop them Japs up. We hear the Army Air Corps is kicking some butt as they get closer to Tokyo. I pray you don't have to go, little brother, but I know you won't hesitate if you get the chance. Keep them 'fly boys' in the air, Speck, you were the only one of us who could ever turn a wrench.

See ya around, little brother.
John

Within hours, the largest amphibious invasion force in history departed English harbors and began the long, torturous crossing of the Channel that separated the country from the coast of France. More than 4,000 naval vessels and 3,000 landing craft carrying 175,000 Allied troops aimed for the Normandy beaches in the foulest weather imaginable. Eisenhower was rolling the dice that his meteorologists were correct: the weather would break before dawn when the actual landings would begin.

Later that night, 822 Allied aircraft took to the sky for the two-hour flight that would bring 13,000 Allied paratroopers to drop zones several miles inside the Normandy beaches. Their mission was clear: pave the way for their brothers coming by sea.

For John Hughes of the 506th Parachute Regiment, the success of the paratroopers in their mission was not only a strategic necessity to the triumph of *Operation Neptune*.

It was a family affair.

*   *   *

Nearly 6,000 miles away, Speck Hughes was faced with breaking some bad news to his bride.

A week after the newlyweds had settled into an apartment in Riverside, California, Speck got new orders. In three days he was to ship out to Wheeler Air Field in Oahu, Hawaii, the airbase nearly completely repaired following the Japanese Attack in 1941. The orders were specific, however. His wife could not accompany him. The move was the final step in his training on assembly and repair of bombers and fighters before he would be shipped to the Pacific war theater.

The "Island Hopping" strategy that had been devised in 1942 was successfully moving the war ever closer to Japan and peace in the Pacific. But every island the combined US and Allied forces took from the enemy came at an abhorrent human cost. Roosevelt and his military commanders were determined to maximize the bloody successes by establishing air bases on the hard won islands that gave the Army Air Corps the ability to bomb Japan and its territories with merciless continuity. That effort not only required aircraft and trained flight crews, but an enormous support group as well. Sergeant Hughes was a prime candidate.

"Elvira," Speck told his weeping wife, "we knew this was a possibility. It's only been a matter of time before I end up out there, where the fighting is. And, truthfully, that's where I belong right now. It's what I signed up for."

She wouldn't have it.

"You belong with me. I'm sick of this war," she cried in anguish, only voicing the frustration of millions of young people.

"Elvira... try to understand," he pleaded.

She hugged him closer.

"Oh…" she lovingly punched him in the back as she pulled him closer.

"I do understand. It's just so unfair. We only got here…" She leaned her head against his chest and cried, harder now as the reality set in.

"They need me, sweetie…" he began.

"I need you!" she hollered back, pushing him away, then quickly returning to his arms. "How much longer can this go on…"

"No one wants it to end any faster than I do, Elvira. I want to go home and start a family with you and live quietly somewhere. But this is a lousy job that has to be finished." He kissed her softly on the lips.

They drove to San Francisco the next afternoon where Speck would embark on the *USS Republic*, a lightly armed, 33,000-ton troop transport that regularly ferried men and supplies from the mainland to Hawaii. The seven-day trip would be without escort and in total darkness at night. Japanese submarines were known to still be operating off the California coast. Speck didn't mention the hazards to his wife. Elvira bought train tickets to return to Hartford.

The next day Speck kissed his wife and held her a long time before letting go and boarding his ship. He went below and found his bunk, deposited his duffel bag and returned to the main deck. He wasn't surprised to see her still standing where they had parted. He waved and blew her a kiss as dockworkers threw off the *Republic*'s lines and the ship began to pull away.

"I love you," he silently mouthed and watched her lips repeat the words. They stared at each other until the ship was far out in the harbor. Broken hearted, Elvira took a cab to the train station and several hours later began the long trip back to the east, alone again. Days later she arrived at Union Station in Hartford and

226

to her surprise was met by her sister-in-law, Catherine. Speck had sent a telegram to her explaining the situation and asked his sister to meet his wife.

The two women met as Elvira got off the train and embraced.

"I've never been so happy to see a friendly face, Catherine," she said, breaking into tears again for at least the tenth time since she had kissed her husband goodbye. Catherine had no problem in joining her for a good cry.

"It will be over soon, sweetie," she consoled her sister-in-law, "And then he'll come home. I know it in my heart."

What she didn't say out loud were the last three words on the tip of her tongue.

"God be willing."

Speck arrived in Honolulu without incident a week after departing San Francisco. The date was June 6, 1944.

He was shaky from the trip, especially unnerved by sailing at night in darkness. He'd spent most of the voyage on the ship's main deck for fear of being caught below should it be torpedoed.

Immediately after docking, the several hundred airmen who had made the trip from San Francisco were assembled on the dock carrying their duffel bags. A captain of the Army Air Corps pulled up in a jeep and welcomed the group, but wasted no time in informing them of the latest major development in the war.

"Just an hour ago, we received news from the mainland that the invasion of Europe by Allied troops has begun on the Normandy coast of France," the captain began as he paced the dock, a grove of palm trees swaying behind him. The serenity of the Hawaiian paradise was bizarrely incongruous to his words. "At this time we have no further word on the status of our troops." Hughes and his fellow airmen shifted uneasily at the news. Were they about to be redeployed to the Atlantic war? The question was answered almost immediately.

"Understand this," he continued. "The war in Europe is progressing far faster than here in the Pacific. General Eisenhower, Supreme Allied Commander of the Expeditionary Force that has attacked Europe has promised his troops they will be home by Christmas. Six months from now, he expects the Nazi flag to fall in Berlin."

He paused and looked over the men assembled on the dock.

"I wouldn't bet against Ike, gentlemen. But there will be no going home by Christmas for us. The war against Japan has turned — there is no question we are pushing the enemy back where he came from — one engagement, one battle, one island at a time.

"But there are many more battles to be fought in the South Pacific and more islands to be captured before we will end this war with a victory over Japan. And that's where you all come in.

"Those islands out there..." he turned and pointed to the west, "are being won with the blood of American Marines. Each one that is captured becomes another airfield we can use to bomb the crap out of strategic targets in Japan. Getting aircraft to those islands and keeping them flying is our job, gentlemen. And if we do our job, maybe, just maybe we'll be home soon after our men in Europe.

"So, welcome to Wheeler Air Base. You'll like it here. The weather is indescribable and you'll find your quarters new and comfortable. But I warn you, don't allow yourself to get too cozy in Hawaii, because you are only going to be here for as long as it takes to complete your training as support mechanics on everything from P-38 fighters to B-29 bombers. Then you'll be shipping out again for wherever you're needed in the Pacific. And I can promise you that will be close — very close — to the fighting."

He paused again, looking for reaction.

"Any questions?"

After two years in the military, the airmen knew better than to ask.

"Then move out, gentlemen. And good luck."

Speck Hughes laughed to himself. Luck had nothing to do with any of this.

It was all about fate.

Twenty-One

~~~ ໑ ~~~

Tuesday, June 6, 1944
D-Day

The sun had long set when Pfc. John Hughes slid off the back of a troop transport onto a runway at Upottery Airfield in south England with 17 other members of his platoon. The C-47 that would fly them to drop zone C just west of the village of Sainte-Marie-du-Mont, a few miles inland of Utah Beach, sat fueled and ready to go a dozen yards away.

With few words between them, the paratroopers of D Company, 2nd Battalion 506th Parachute Regiment of the 101st Airborne began the task of putting on their heavy combat equipment: two parachutes, a half dozen hand grenades, a gas mask, an entrenching tool, M-1 Garand rifle broken down in a Griswold bag, musette bag with personal items including cigarettes, a bayonet, first aid pouch and a cartridge belt stuffed with ammunition. Some carried more. Their hands shook as they put on the gear, knowing this was no practice jump.

The group was commanded by Lt. Dan Mirrot, who quietly moved between the aircraft that would carry the sticks that made up D Company, checking their gear and offering last words of encouragement.

"How the hell am I supposed to get into the bird?" Hughes asked Mirrot, somewhat in jest. His equipment weighed almost as much as he did.

"You'll find a way, John," the demanding but admired platoon leader replied. "You won't be the only one who'll need a kick in the ass to get on board, trust me."

"You may have to save that kick for when we reach the drop zone, Lieutenant," Hughes responded with a look of worry on his face.

"I'm not concerned about that, John," Mirrot replied, patting him on the shoulder. "You'll do your job. I know you will." He put a finger to his forehead. "Just get yourself ready."

The Lieutenant moved on to his other men as Hughes watched.

"I've been ready for a long time," he said to himself. "Time to get this over, one way or another."

With letters mailed home, a $10,000 GI insurance policy signed over to his father and at peace with the righteousness of the job ahead, John Hughes was prepared as possible for what was to come. He managed to get aboard the C-47 with a shove from the man behind him and ended up being the sixth man in his stick.

Hughes looked at his watch and nervously tapped on the crystal. It was dark inside the aircraft, but in the slight bit of moonlight that snuck through the

231

small windows in the fuselage he could barely make out the time: 2330 hours. With luck, he thought they would be over the drop zone and on the ground by 0130 hours. He smiled at his own joke. "With luck."

Barely able to turn his head enough to look out a window, Hughes caught a glimpse of C-47's all over the runway begin to start their twin 1,200-horsepower Pratt & Whitney radial engines. A few seconds later, the cargo bay of the "Gooney Bird" in which he sat was filled with a deafening roar as its engines fired up. Several moments passed before he felt the airplane lurch as it began to maneuver into line for takeoff. It was more than 30 minutes before he heard the growl of the P&W engines pushed to their maximum RPM's and felt the airplane begin its rollout for takeoff. He leaned his head back against the fuselage and closed his eyes, willing himself to think through the mission assigned to Company D as the heavily loaded airplane lumbered into the air. He visualized the roadmaps and landmarks he had studied for hours in anticipation of this night. But gradually, his thoughts turned to home and of his father, brother and sisters and the old farmhouse on Highland Street.

A vision of his father came to him, sitting on the front steps of the house he had grown up in. He smiled when his mother unexpectedly walked up the path to the front door and sat beside Pa who reached for her hand. Hughes pushed away thoughts of her sickness and death, concentrating on the good times with his family. He might have actually dozed from the happy memories that filled him with calm despite the specter of violence he would face in the coming hours.

Even with the gale force winds that rocked the more than 800 airplanes pushing towards the Normandy coast, the flight across the English Channel was

232

uneventful. Hughes looked at his watch again, but couldn't make out the time. Suddenly, and far too soon it seemed, the red jump light on the cockpit bulkhead flashed on. It was nearly time. He looked out the window again and saw a huge fog bank ahead just as his aircraft crossed over the Cherbourg Peninsula. Below them was Normandy. Then all hell broke loose as the formation flew through the fog, the loss of vision causing some pilots to change course. They were suddenly in serious disarray.

Ignoring the ominous chaos that was developing in the skies around them, First Sergeant Nick Mascola stood up at the open jump door and began the process.

"Stand up," he ordered. Hook up!"

No amount of training could have prepared them for what happened next.

The antiaircraft fire began as the last words left the Sergeant's lips. In an instant, the sky was filled with shelling so heavy that pilots began taking evasive action to avoid being hit. In doing so, any chance of dropping the 506th anywhere near drop zone C vanished. Later analysis would show that only nine out of 81 planes carrying the 506th paratroopers found the drop zone. The rest were scattered as far as 20 miles away or shot down.

Without warning, Hughes' C-47 was rocked by an explosion and bathed in a flash of light. He looked out the window again and saw that a nearby aircraft still carrying its stick of men had exploded and was tumbling below them, completely out of control. The sky was rumbling with antiaircraft fire and another aircraft exploded next to them, raining flaming wreckage over the starboard wing of Hughes aircraft. He felt a shudder as shrapnel from an artillery shell found its mark in the forward fuselage. The airplane shook but flew on. Still the light on the bulkhead remained red. Not yet.

Then there was a deafening explosion near the aft wing and he felt the plane shake violently before it rolled to the left and into a steep dive. Mascola screamed, "Keep your feet, stand up!" But the gravitational pull of the steep dive threatened to send the entire stick careening into the cockpit bulkhead. Hughes looked out the jump door and saw the ground rushing up at them at a frightening rate. Somehow, at the last moment, the pilot managed to pull up the nose and the airplane began to climb again. Minutes later, the green light flashed. But they had already passed their intended drop zone. Worse, the airplane had only reached an altitude of 300 feet; the paratroopers were supposed to be dropped at 700. And they were flying much to fast to jump safely.

"Go!" Mascola screamed as the jump line moved forward and soldiers fell into space. Seconds later Hughes stepped out into the black sky that had turned into a cauldron of bursting antiaircraft shells, falling airplanes and burning wreckage. He was jolted by the 165 miles per hour air speed at which they had jumped instead of the 95 miles per hour for which they had trained. The shock alone was enough to kill a man. As it was, he was propelled backwards, miraculously avoiding the airplane's vertical stabilizer that would have cut him in half. From the corner of his eye, he saw a parachute line from one of the men who had jumped before him hanging from the tail. He glanced up just before his own chute deployed, and saw a paratrooper from another plane coming towards him in free fall, both he and his parachute entirely engulfed in flames. Hughes watched in horror as the man screamed in agony, writhing in an impossible attempt to free himself

234

from the flames. The blazing mass sped toward the ground.

The opening jolt of his parachute caught him by surprise and he was yanked up hard in his harness before the canvas mushroomed over his head and slowed his descent. But his stick had jumped at a far lower altitude than planned, and the ground rushed up at him at enormous speed. He braced for the impact of a hard landing just as his jump boots smashed into the ground.

Hughes waited for the pain of two broken legs to hit him but felt nothing but a mushy substance beneath his boots as his body absorbed the landing. By the grace of God he had come down in a marsh created when the Germans had flooded great areas of pastureland and tall grass. The soft surface had broken his fall.

Whipping storm winds caught his still inflated parachute and began dragging him through the wetlands. He reached into his breast pocket and pulled out the M2 switchblade all paratroopers carried for just such a situation and quickly cut the lines of his chute. The silk canopy released and was carried away by the wind gusts, leaving him kneeling in the swampy water. He sat on his heels for a moment just to catch his breath from the terrifying experience of the last few minutes and glanced at his watch for the time: 0125 hours. He looked up into the sky and was horrified at the number of aircraft trailing flames. Then he heard the sharp retort of gunfire erupting all around him and hurried to tear open his Griswold bag and assemble and load his M1 rifle. He scanned the darkness before moving, then, seeing no movement hurried towards a line of trees and a hedgerow less than 30 yards away.

It was only then that Hughes realized he was completely alone. He peered out into the watery field in which he had landed lit only by moonlight and waited. The roar of airplanes overhead slowly dissipated but on the ground there was gunfire coming from multiple directions. He decided to just sit and wait.

Ahead in the dimness of the moonlight, he thought he saw a glimpse of a helmet. Yes. There it was again… and several more. He hunkered down lower in the cover of the tree line. Friend or foe? There was only one-way to be sure. He reached into his breast pocket again and pulled out his cricket noisemaker, an Army version of the simple child's toy. Every man in the 506th had been issued one as a communication device. If you saw someone approaching, you clicked the cricket once, making an almost indistinguishable sound in the darkness of the country night. If the stranger clicked back, you had found a friend.

Hughes clicked once, and waited. There was no response. He waited a moment before trying again, but pulled a hand grenade off his gun belt to be on the safe side. He clicked again.

A cricket responded.

"Hey, Mac," a voice called out in a loud whisper. Identify yourself."

"Hughes, D Company, 506th. Your turn," Hughes responded.

"Hell, I'm from D Company, 506th, these other four guys are from the 82nd Airborne, about 20 miles off their drop zone."

"Come forward, under the trees," Hughes replied, carefully watching as the five men scrambled toward him.

"John Hughes," he introduced himself. The others called out their names. "And I'm Pete Miller, F Company, 506th."

"Any idea where we are?" Hughes asked.

"No, we're going to have to look for a landmark or a road sign. I don't think we're far from Sainte-Marie-du-Mont. Thought I caught a glimpse of it just before we jumped. But I doubt there's many of us in the right drop zone. With all the flak up there, a lot of planes got blown up or pushed off course. I think you and I are close to where we should be but we're gonna be the exceptions."

"Shit, I'm not sure we're even in the right country," one of the paratroopers from the 82nd Airborne quipped.

"Well, you guys stay with us for now," Miller said. Hughes caught the glint of gold lieutenant's bars on the soldier's jacket. At least there was someone in charge.

"Let's go," Miller said, moving out towards another hedgerow about 100 yards away. They crept quickly through the shallow marsh and saw nothing until they clustered again at the hedgerow. Then Hughes heard a cricket. He responded. From prone positions on the other side, a dozen men from various companies of the 506th rose up and hurried to join Miller's group. They moved out again, keeping low and staying in shadows as much as possible.

A dirt road was on the other side of the next hedgerow they reached by which time another 20 men from the 506th had joined the group. They came upon a farmhouse and took cover behind an old, tilting red barn that appeared to be near collapse. Then they heard it. Motorized vehicles approaching, fast. Miller gave the order to maintain position and to fire only on his command.

Minutes later, several platoons of German soldiers pulled up in front of the farmhouse and stopped. An officer stepped out of a military Kübelwagen, took a flashlight from his driver and spread a map over the hood of the Jeep-like vehicle. The officer had an edge to his voice as he addressed several subordinates. They appeared to be uncertain of their location.

Hughes and the 40 or so men with him shared their enemies' frustration, but at the moment were more intent on watching his next move. The German officer was angry and berated his driver, then suddenly stopped. One of the hidden paratroopers had moved, causing just enough noise to interrupt the German conversation. Miller and his men watched as the commanding officer held up his hand for quiet, then listened. Slowly, he reached down to remove a holstered Luger strapped to his waist. The German troops quietly stepped from their vehicles, weapons trained on the barn where Miller and his rag-tag group hid, unaware their every movement was squarely in the sights of an M1 or Thompson submachine gun. The Germans began to advance towards the Americans. That was a mistake.

Miller gave the order.

"Fire."

A barrage of gunfire exploded in the night, catching the enemy completely by surprise. More than half the German unit fell to the ground before firing a shot. All John Hughes could remember afterwards was the deafening noise of gunfire and how brief the encounter actually was. Bullets flew back and forth over the 75 feet between the enemies until abruptly it ended. There were no more German soldiers standing. The air was quiet again.

Hughes heard a groan and turned to find the man behind him with a wound to the chest. He fell on him, placing his hands over the gushing blood, pressing down to stem the flow.

"Medic!" he called as men rushed to help him. Miller pulled out his first aid kit, tore open the soldier's jacket and stuck him with a syrette of morphine.

"We got any medics here?" Hughes pleaded continuing to apply pressure to the wound. The soldier began to bleed from the mouth and grabbed Hughes' arm as he fought to stay alive. But there was nothing to be done. The soldier drowned in his own blood, his eyes clouding over as he stopped struggling. They were fixed on John Hughes as he died.

"Jesus…" he said, still pushing on the man's chest.

Miller backed away.

"Give it up John, he's gone. Not even a medic could have helped him," the Lieutenant said. He reached up and closed the soldier's eyes then pulled his dog tags from around his neck.

Hughes bowed his head and sucked in a breath of air. In less than an hour, he had jumped from a mortally wounded airplane, had nearly been killed by a soldier engulfed in flames and survived a hard landing and a firefight with a German military unit. He had used up a lot of luck in a very short period of time.

Miller put the dog tags into his jacket pocket.

"Let's go," he ordered. "We've got bridges to take and a town to liberate before the 4th Army lands at Utah. There aren't many of us, but we've still got to get the job done."

He walked away and the group followed him, Hughes taking the point without being asked. He turned and asked over his shoulder.

"What was his name, Lieutenant?"

"Robinson. PFC William T. Robinson, 506th, B Company,' Miller replied.

"Kid wasn't 20 years old," Hughes observed.

239

"You think that's the last boy you'll see die here, Hughes? We've only begun the killing."

Miller turned and faced his men, walking backwards, checking the look on their faces as they passed him. Each of them had just had their first taste of blood and of losing one of their own. They walked by him, heads down, their eyes avoiding his own. The dog tags felt hot in Miller's pocket. Robinson was the first man he had lost. He wouldn't be the last. He felt his stomach turn, but pushed down the bile.

"Move out," he repeated. He checked his watch. It was already 0330. There were objectives they had to accomplish before the beach landings began in the next three hours.

"Where to, Lieutenant?" Hughes asked.

"Foucarville. About four klicks from here," he replied. "We're late already. That probably means the Germans will have had a chance to beef up their defenses in the village. We've got to clear it out quickly and get to Sainte-Marie-du-Mont and the bridges before the boats start coming in."

John Hughes sighed. Eisenhower's prediction that they'd all be home before Christmas came to mind.

Yah, for sure.

The question was: what year?

*   *   *

At 0315 hours, the attack transport USS *Samuel Chase* dropped anchor some 12 miles off the coast of Normandy near Colleville-sur-Mer, carrying more than 500 troops from the *Big Red One*. The waters were roiling and nearly every man on board was deathly seasick as they waited for the order to launch the ship's landing craft toward the beach.

Jim Hughes huddled with his men at the rails of the *Chase*, anxious to climb down the rope nets into the LCVP's that bobbed like corks on the heavy seas. Anything was better than another minute aboard the *Chase*, which had been their prison for nearly six days in the foul weather. They were already wet, cold, sick and exhausted. The stench of vomit was overpowering.

To keep his men busy, Hughes had them check and recheck their equipment, making sure that every man had at least 20 clips of ammunition for his M-1 and that the rifles, at least for the moment, were in firing order.

Finally, at about 0400 hours the ship's bullhorn blared the order to board the landing craft. Hughes and his men, burdened by as much as 200 pounds of weapons and other equipment, slowly lowered themselves down the rope nets one slippery foothold at a time. Above them bullhorns screamed, "Keep in line, keep in line!" adding to the stress of their struggle not to skid off the wet ropes. More than one man met his end in the darkness, falling from the ladders and drowning under the weight of their equipment.

As the boats filled they pulled away from the *Chase* and slowly motored to a staging area where they would circle for the next hour or so until all the landing craft were assembled and ready for the advance to Omaha Beach. The seas continued their merciless assault on the physical condition of the troops as the small LCVP's battled six-foot waves even so far off shore.

At 0530 they were ready, and the helmsman steered the Higgins boats carrying Jim Hughes and his platoon toward the beach. Almost immediately, a Naval artillery barrage began as planned to "soften up" the significant defenses the German had constructed along the coast. The US battleships *Arkansas* and *Texas* were

241

joined by American destroyers *Emmons* and *Satterlee* and the British *HMS Tallybont* in launching a massive bombardment of Omaha Beach, specifically targeting eight huge reinforced concrete gun casements, 35 pillboxes and more then 85 machine gun nests the enemy had built along the entire length of the Omaha shoreline.

The ear-splitting cacophony of noise descended on them just as dawn broke and shocked the anxious troops slowly advancing toward the beach. Artillery shells the size of small cars were flying over their heads in the Navy's non-stop shelling for the next 30 minutes. Even before it stopped, the air was filled with the roar of 448 Army Air Corps B-24 Liberators that had flown across the channel to bomb the landing areas and inland defenses. From their perspective on the water in the bobbing LCVP's, it appeared the Navy and Air Corps bombardment could hardly have left the approaching troops with a sliver of dry land upon which to begin the long awaited assault on the continent.

Unfortunately, they would have little time to realize how little damage the combined bombardments had inflicted upon the enemy because the men in the boats were struggling to stay alive while they were still miles from the shore.

Below the terrifying aerial bombardment, approaching LCVP's were filling with frigid water from the enormous waves that grew as they approached the coast. Frantically, troops used their helmets to bail water from the boats before they swamped. Jim Hughes scanned the water around him and watched helplessly as several Higgins boats capsized, tossing heavily weighed down soldiers into the churning seas. They had no hope of survival. He urged his men to bail faster as their own boat took on more and more water, slowing their approach to the beach. But they kept on. There was no choice but to keep moving.

Hughes' boat also passed men struggling to stay afloat in life preservers or rafts, having abandoned their "Donald Duck" Sherman tanks that had sunk in the high seas almost immediately after being launched from their specially built landing craft. The nickname came from the duplex drive system that should have enabled the tanks to "swim" to shore under propulsion of a propeller system and with the assistance of a flotation collar. The DD Tanks performed well in flat seas or a minimum swell, but were completely overwhelmed by the storm conditions on June 6th. Only two out of more than 80 tanks in the *Big Red One* force made it to shore in the first wave.

Suddenly, small arms and machine gunfire began to rake the boats and mortar and artillery shelling erupted from the beach. Hughes dared to raise his head again and look forward. He swallowed hard at the vision that rose up out of the mist and smoke that had settled on the shoreline.

Rising out of the surf before the 3,000 men who were in the first wave to attack Omaha Beach were a terrifying mass of crossed steel girders, a nearly impenetrable man-made fence of hedgehogs and metal obstacles that ran the entire coast line about 150 yards into the water's edge. And lashed to the miles of steel devices protecting France from just the sort of invasion the Allies were attempting were more than six million land mines that Hitler had installed using slave labor. At that moment, Hughes realized he and his men were going to have to abandon their Higgins Boat far sooner than intended in deep water. They were still more than a half-mile from shore. But even if they were lucky enough to run the landing craft right up on to the beach, they would be forced to sprint across several hundred yards of open beach before finding the first shelter from German machine guns that were already strafing them without mercy.

It soon became apparent that the Naval and Army Air Corps bombardment had failed. In fact, the Naval shells had fallen with amazing precision on their targets, but the Germans had done an equally amazing job of fortifying the pillboxes and gun casements that were hardly dented by the massive explosives unleashed upon them. The bombardment had only succeeded in dazing the crews inside the concrete bunkers. The Air assault too, had failed. High winds had caused the B-24's to overshoot targets and drop their bomb loads far inland. Very few bombs actually found their targets. Consequently the shoreline defenses were still intact and even worse, unbeknownst to the Allied High Command, an entire division of combat experienced German troops had arrived at Omaha Beach just the day before for practice maneuvers.

The battle-hardened men of the 1st Army Infantry and it's vast armada had literally sailed into a trap comprised of a vast number of enemy troops supported by extensive firepower including tanks, artillery, machine guns, rockets, mortars and flamethrowers, and millions of booby-trapped coastal impediments. The Allies had no place to go but forward into this hell storm.

Hughes turned to warn his platoon. He didn't have too. Fear was lined on their faces and he could smell the panic setting in. Now they were about 200 yards from shore.

"Stay low!" he screamed to them as machine gun fire whipped over their heads. The landing craft had taken on more water as the bailing had stopped and was riding dangerously low in the water. By the time another twenty yards passed they were in real danger of sinking. Hughes had to do something. He gave the order to abandon ship and motioned to the helmsman to drop the gate.

"Ok, we're ok guys," he yelled. "Inflate your vests, the water's going to be…"

Before he could finish, the landing craft took a direct hit from an artillery shell almost dead center in the boat. Hughes felt the spray of warm blood as a number of men were killed instantly. He saw more die as they stepped off the gate and disappeared into the water. Others were caught by murderous German machine gun fire as they stood up. Hughes dove forward into the water and was hit by a wave generated by the concussion that washed across the LCVP, finally swamping it. The surge pushed him down several feet and the weight of his equipment held him under. He dropped his M-1, tore off his backpack and struggled to the surface. His head broke the surface in a frenzy of men screaming for help as they struggled not to drown. There were wounded everywhere and soldiers floating face down in the water. Next to him was a man who was thrashing about, screaming in agony. One of his arms was missing. Hughes grabbed him by the back of his jacket and began dragging the severely wounded soldier towards the shore. At six-foot-five, his head was just above the surface as he walked across the sandy bottom.

And then things got really bad.

Still dragging the wounded man as they made it to the waters edge, he was abruptly forced to drop to his stomach when machine gun bullets kicked up spits of water all around him. He felt the man he was holding shudder and turned to look back. Two rounds had pierced his helmet and the back of his head was gone. He was dead. Hughes never knew his name. He cursed at having to leave the dead man floating face down in the shallows only feet from the shore.

The 2nd lieutenant knew he was a sitting duck and forced himself to get up and sprint forward a few yards before dropping again to a sandbar. He took deep breaths, fighting to calm himself and took in the scene.

Behind him a half dozen LCVP's were in flames and dozens of bodies lay at the shoreline. The ocean water was red with blood where it lapped the sands. The Germans had turned the beach into a shooting range, randomly spraying it with machine gun and artillery fire. Dead and wounded were everywhere. Body parts were strewn across the strand. Desperate men missing limbs hopelessly dragged themselves forward, only to be shot dead by snipers.

Jim Hughes thought if there was a hell on earth, this was it.

Those few men from the *Chase's* LCVP's that had managed to survive the landing were taking cover behind the hedgehogs. Watching in dread, Hughes saw a man from his platoon that had hidden behind a hedgehog disintegrate as a German sniper's bullet detonated a land mine attached to the metal structure. The soldier's body parts rained down in a red mist over the beach.

Horrified, Hughes jumped up again and raced toward a four-foot-high sea wall 150 yards away. Immediately, machine gun fire began dancing at his feet and he threw himself back to the ground, taking cover behind the body of a dead GI. He took the man's rifle and got up to run again.

Almost immediately, more machine gun bullets whizzed by him and kicked up a spray of sand only inches from his boots. Hughes hurled himself to the ground again, knowing that a German machine gunner was following him in his sights. The game of cat and mouse could only end badly for the soldier unless the gunner was distracted. He waited for long minutes, hoping the enemy would think he was dead. About 50 feet away, Hughes saw several men racing toward the wall when the machine gunner began firing in their direction. Bullets cut them down in their tracks but the shooter wasn't satisfied. He savagely continued to pour fire into their prone bodies for what seemed like minutes.

Hughes forced himself to look away from the carnage, then swallowed hard, jumped to his feet and sprinted the rest of the way to the sea wall carrying the M-1 he had picked up. Just as he reached the wall an artillery shell flew over his head, detonating not 20 feet from where he'd just been. He ducked his head and burrowed into the base of the wall. Shrapnel pinged off his helmet and swooshed over him. He looked back at the crater in the sand, wondering at his luck, but saw four men lying dead just beyond it. They had been running for the same protection the sea wall had provided him.

Rage boiled in Hughes' veins and he raised his head slightly over the top of the sea wall, straining to find the machine gunner or an artillery placement. His eyes locked on two Germans firing from a nest about 100 yards up the hillside.

He was almost blind with vengeance but he focused on stopping the snipers. The slaughter would continue unless he did something.

Cautiously, he raised the M-1 he'd found on the beach and rested the stock on the revetment of loose rock and chunks of concrete that made up the barrier that had saved his life. The top was firm enough to allow him to use it as a sort of tripod for his weapon to steady his shot. He took careful aim at the German firing the machine gun who was oblivious to the American that had fooled him into thinking he was dead. With the hatred of a man who had watched his own men butchered before they could even step onto French soil, Hughes pulled the trigger several times rapidly and watched as the machine gunner absorbed at least two rounds to the face. He slumped over, dead. His accomplice looked down at his partner and then back in the direction the shots came from. A look of disbelief came over his face. No matter. Hughes turned his weapon on the German who had been feeding the gun's cartridge belt and squeezed the trigger twice more. The results were the same.

Immediately, he scanned the hillside above for the gun casement from which the artillery shell had been fired. Just as he looked up, the gun fired again at a Sherman tank just reaching the water's edge and scored a direct hit. The shell hit the gun turret but the hatch flew open and the American crew inside began scrambling out as the tank caught fire. Machine gun fire from a pillbox several hundred yards away cut them down one by one as they spilled out of the tank. The last man out was engulfed in flames and writhing in pain and panic as he tried to escape the fire. A German bullet ended his struggle.

Hughes screamed to a half dozen men behind him, still taking cover behind hedgehogs.

"Get off the beach! Run to me! Stay there and you'll die," he hollered.

Somehow, men frozen in fear found their legs and raced toward the sea wall as commanded. Snipers blanketed the beach with bullets but Hughes stood and

248

laid down covering fire. Miraculously, all six men made it to the revetment.

The 2nd Lieutenant wasted no time as he scanned the beach from which they had come. Men were still being mowed down as they stepped out of LCVP's more than 100 yards from shore or were cut down as they raced across the beach for shelter. Unless the *Big Red One* eliminated the artillery casements and machine gun nests, Omaha Beach was lost.

At that moment, the struggling troops were startled by the unexpected roar of a squadron of Army Air Corp P-47 Thunderbolt fighters that dove towards the hillside, each of their six .50 caliber Browning machine guns blazing. Behind them were a squadron of British Spitfire's fully loaded with machine guns, cannons and rockets. The British pilots, too, dove their aircraft at the Omaha Beach hillside and raised havoc with exposed German machine gun nests and troops who were dug into trenches.

The hills erupted with multiple explosions and dense smoke rose from the fighter strikes. The heavy machine gun fire was stilled for the moment. But Hughes was able to see that the artillery encasement had escaped damage and was still firing at troops on the beach.

"We need to get that gun... the son of a bitch has a clear line of fire right into the landing zone," he said. "Any of you packing TNT? And we're going to need a Bangalore to get through the barbed wire surrounding the casement..." He looked at their faces. Each man was from other platoons and companies of the 16th Regimental Combat Team of the 1st Infantry. He wondered if there were any survivors of his own platoon.

"I've got TNT," one of the men replied. "And there's a Bangalore with a couple of guys who got nailed by that machine gun nest... think they're about 50 yards from us. Poor bastards..."

"Nothing we can do about them. Let's get that torpedo. Volunteers?" Hughes asked. Two men nodded immediately.

"Ok. We'll shoot while you scoot. On my mark, we lay down covering fire just below that gun encasement. I think that's where the nest is. The air boys missed that encasement, so the machine guns are probably still hot, just laying low for the moment," Hughes said.

He looked at the faces of the small group of men. There wasn't one of them older than 22, he guessed.

"Ready?" he said.

"Let's get the bastards," one of them replied.

"Ok," he nodded, looking them in the eye.

"Go!"

With his order the two volunteers ran back down the beach toward the location of the Bangalore while the remaining five stood and fired continuously at the spot they expected to find a machine gun nest. As he expected, the second the men ran from the sea wall, the machine gun opened fire, but gave their position away as well.

"There, my 11 o'clock. Take him," Hughes ordered. They each emptied a full flip into the hillside. The machine gun went silent.

He turned and saw his men furiously gathering up the four sections of pipe that made up the 50 foot Bangalore and the rocket that thrust through it. A sniper continued to fire on them as they worked and Hughes trained his eyes on the hill trying to follow his firing path. He saw a lone German firing, taking aim at the two men.

"I got the bastard," he said, training his weapon on the enemy soldier. He raised his M-1 and squeezed the trigger twice. The sniper fell, but not before one of his men had been hit.

"I'm going for him," Hughes hollered. "Covering fire," he ordered racing off before anyone else could object.

The 50-foot run felt like miles. At any moment he expected to feel the hot burning sensation of a bullet piercing his back or the blackness that would instantly follow the top of his head off being blown off. He was there in less than ten seconds, weaving his way at a full sprint. Hughes slid in the sand next to the soldier who had taken a round in his left leg. He was bleeding profusely.

"Medic!' he screamed and pressed down on the wound. Incredibly, a soldier with a red cross painted on his helmet slid in beside them.

"I got this sir," he said, already holding a tourniquet in his teeth. He stuck the wounded soldier with a morphine syrette and inspected the wound. He shook his head. Hughes knew the man would lose the leg.

"Go, I got this," the medic said, and Hughes squeezed his shoulder in thanks.

"You'll be ok, pal. We'll stick this Bangalore up 'Fritz's butt for you," he said to the wounded man. See you back in England."

"Let's go," he said to the other man, ready to retrace his run with two lengths of pipe and the Bangalore torpedo. "Grab those other two sections." He began to get to his feet and then stopped. Hughes reached over and pulled the dog tags off the two men

251

who had been slaughtered racing for cover. The machine gunner had decapitated one; the other had bled out when his leg was shot off.

He looked up at the hill. "You will pay for this," he mouthed, then signaled the men at the sea wall that they were coming back.

The two men, carrying the heavy pipe lengths sprinted back to the cover of the sea wall despite machine gun bullets from another hidden nest dancing at their boots.

"Boy, those guys are really starting to piss me off," someone said.

Hughes wasted no time. The *Big Red One* was still being butchered on the beach.

"Let's go have a party with our friends," Hughes said and issued instructions to the group. Minutes later, two men scrambled over the sea wall carrying the Bangalore and ran to a heavy mass of barbed wire blocking access to the artillery gun casement. The big gun was continuously raining shells on the helpless troops coming in on LCVP's.

In less than five minutes, Hughes saw one of the men wave, the signal for "'fire in the hole." Almost immediately, there was a loud explosion and the barbed wire was penetrated. The two soldiers ran through the break and towards the encasement. Hughes and his men jumped over the sea wall and ran toward the gun, drawing the attention of the German gun crew but giving the two soldiers time to set up TNT charges at the base of the encasement. They waved again and fell down to the ground, covering their ears. The TNT exploded but the reinforced concrete was barely damaged.

"Shit," Hughes swore but watched as the two soldiers got up and tossed hand grenades into the concrete bunker. Smoke billowed out as they detonated and they threw more grenades inside. Finally the gun was suppressed. By this time Hughes and his men had climbed to the top of the casement and were waiting for any crew left alive to straggle out. They shot three men who staggered out of the upper hatch.

Below, amidst the carnage, men cheered at the sight of the artillery gun being silenced. Up and down Omaha Beach similar engagements were gradually knocking out the German's fortified artillery and machine gun nests. Entrenched German troops were pulling back up the hillside.

The *Big Red One* had carved out a fragile toehold on the blood soaked sands of Omaha Beach that would grow into a firm grasp of the coast so vital to the launch of *Operation Overlord*.

But it was not the brilliance of the Allied invasion plan that brought success.

It was, as Eisenhower had privately predicted, the result of the heroic actions of men who never dreamt of being heroes.

Twenty-Two

~~~ ❧ ~~~

"The news of the Normandy invasion came in the middle of the night," Ka recalled. "It had already been underway for hours before the radio broadcast General Eisenhower's letter to the troops. We all knew it was coming, but still, when it happened it was shocking.

"I had just gotten out of bed to make Eric's breakfast and drive him to work and turned on the radio as I always did. And there it was."

Ka's backyard audience was spellbound again.

"I woke Eric up and made the poor man go to work without breakfast," she continued. "You see, I was so worried about Pa... we knew John and Jim were in England. I drove to Highland Street as soon as I could." She paused. "It's a good thing, too."

Ka dabbed at her eyes again with her handkerchief. Her memory was quite amazing, but I was even more impressed by her stamina.

"Jiggs, Bobbie and Beverly had all gone off to school after breakfast with Pa and they were unaware of what was happening. Then my father sat in the living room to listen to the news as he did each morning and was stunned to hear the invasion had begun.

"When I got there, he was sitting alone staring at the stars on the banner in the window, the radio blaring in the background. He didn't even hear me come in, he was so lost in his thoughts. The poor man was ashen with worry. I didn't say anything, just sat on the arm of his chair and held his hand. Jiggs and the girls came home about an hour later. They'd just skipped out of school after catching up with the news and hurried home.

"It was really all to much for Pa. He was becoming ill with worry as it was and was drinking heavily. Just the week before, Dot's husband Ed had been called up to report in August and Phil had been notified that he would probably be drafted in the fall. They both had kids! " She turned to me. "And your father was shipped to Hawaii in preparation for being sent to the South Pacific where the war was getting bloodier by the day. I met your mother at the train station after she had come all the way back from California alone when he shipped out. She was heart broken and we were all so apprehensive at what was happening.

"Truly, it felt like our family was being torn apart. But it wasn't only us. Families everywhere were being touched by the war. The demand for new recruits was so high that both teenagers and men with families were being drafted. We knew it was only a matter of time before Jiggs got his notice; he was graduating from high school in a couple of weeks. And I waited every day for a letter from the Draft Board for my Andy. I knew it would come."

She shook her head and took in a deep breath. Her eyes wandered over to the pool again, moonlight rippling over the water. Some of the kids had stretched out on towels around the decking and were asleep.

"So then comes the news of the invasion of France and Pa just knew that John and Jim were in the thick of it. It's a wonder he didn't suffer a stroke or have a heart attack that day, I tell you. It was just awful."

"You hadn't heard from either of them before the invasion, Ka?" my sister asked.

"Not a word. The military had put a blanket over everything trying to keep it a secret. And God bless, it worked, but it was so hard on the families, not knowing."

"I can't imagine that..." I said, "I mean, not knowing..." I couldn't bring myself to finish the sentence.

"We all went to church and prayed," Ka continued "Even Pa, who wasn't much of a church goer. I remember the papers were full of pictures the next day of churches all over the country packed with people. I guess everyone had the same idea. We all filled the void of not knowing with prayers."

The fireworks had ended save for a random cherry bomb somewhere in the distance. The patio lapsed into silence as my Aunt stopped again. Ka's story was more than any of us had ever imagined.

"But you know of course... that it got worse... much worse," she went on.

"The news reports began to suggest that the casualties, at first described as minimal, were far worse. In fact, a little town in Virginia... Bedford, I think it was... lost 19 of its boys in the first 15 minutes of fighting."

Someone gasped.

"As it turned out, at Omaha Beach, where your Uncle Jim landed, at least 2,000 young men were killed on the first day of fighting. When all was said and done, more than 50,000 Americans died in the invasion of Europe, the battle that ultimately won the war against the Germans. Probably 20 percent of those killed in action during the entire European war died on D-Day. More than 10,000 American boys in a single day."

Eyes widened all around the table.

"Within the week, another Wethersfield family, the Hall's, were notified that their son William had been killed in the first wave of the D-Day invasion. And the Army Air Corps confirmed that Warren Mason, one of four brothers from town who were serving in Europe had been killed in a bombing raid over Germany in May. Our little town had two more Gold Stars to mourn."

"Oh, dear God," my sister whispered.

"And then, as if everyone wasn't anxious enough, a rumor began circulating through town about a local mother who had done something unspeakable... to prevent the Army from drafting another one of her sons."

"The pressure on parents must have been immense," my brother said. "I can imagine they would have done anything to..."

"No, Jeff, this was far worse..." she interrupted him. "The family had already lost a son in the war. I think he was killed in action sometime in 1943.

"They were a very prominent family, and I don't really want to mention the name because the children still live here in town... in fact, I know the younger brother."

No one protested.

"You see, his mother shot him in the leg so that he couldn't be drafted... so that the Army couldn't take away another one of her sons. Unfortunately, she nearly killed him herself. They had to amputate the boys leg to save him."

I think I gasped with everyone else at the story. It was so horrible that it was inconceivable that Ka would have told us unless it was true.

So I asked her.

"Ka... you said it was a rumor. She nodded. "It wasn't a rumor, was it..."

"No," she shook her head, then hesitated for a moment.

"Before you ask... nothing ever came of it. Pa wouldn't let it. Remember that he was the Town Constable then. As awful a thing as it was, he couldn't let that mother be punished for wanting to save her son. He had so much empathy for her. It was decided that the shooting was accidental.

"That poor woman was never the same afterwards, even though I know for a fact that her son forgave her and loved her till the day she died. I remember going to her funeral some years later and I'll never forget what the pastor said about her.

"'She was not as we once knew her,' he told the congregation. You could have heard a pin drop in that church."

I wiped a tear from my own eyes. I don't think I was alone. And then my wise and so elegant elderly aunt said something that I think of every time I read or hear a news story about an American soldier being killed in some far off battle.

"You, know I've always found it ironic after living through those years, when so many boys died, to hear someone say to a parent, 'You should be proud of the sacrifice your son made for his country.'" She shook her ahead and widened her eyes in mock confusion.

"Proud?" she went on. "The Gold Star mothers weren't proud. They were angry and heartbroken. I remember talking to one of them after the war and she blamed herself for her son's death. This mother had brought her son up to be an Eagle Scout, and he was proud to be an American and so he felt he needed to fight for his country.

"'I killed my son,' she said to me. And I know she believed that. It was so sad. But she didn't kill her son. That mother just raised him to be a good man, never dreaming that the pride she instilled in him would someday play a role in his death."

The tone of her voice changed. It was harsh, unlike I had ever heard her speak before.

"I find it so ironic that the men who make war still haven't figured out that when soldiers shoot at each other, someone usually dies. And that someone is typically a young person… who had a mother and a father and maybe some brother and sisters."

I watched as she swallowed hard.

"I guess that's just the crazy notion of an old woman," she said. "But I dearly wish that chest beating old men would stop sending young people to fight wars they start!"

She startled us all with her passion. That was the first time I understood that she was angry, too. They had been hard years for her and the sad memories were still fresh.

My aunt was quiet for a few moments then, leaning back in her chair, composing herself and staring up at the stars.

"So many stars tonight. I'm always taken with them." And then she added a thought that I believe she had carried with her for more than 50 years.

"We had so many stars in our window."

She considered that for a moment, drank from her coffee and continued the story that changed my family forever.

Twenty-Three

~~~ ತ ~~~

Summer, 1944

On Omaha Beach, the *Big Red One* had stormed the heavily fortified bluffs and found holes through the heavy German defenses. Despite the 1st Infantry Division's appalling losses the survivors headed inland toward the village of Colleville-Sur-Mer.

Hughes and his men and other units of the 16th Combat Regiment found heavy resistance and engaged in constant firefights all the way to the village. The Germans were well trained and outnumbered the badly depleted Americans. But the resolute infantryman had not fought their way off the massacre at Omaha Beach to be pushed back.

By nightfall they had reached the outskirts of Colleville-Sur-Mer, pausing their advance to take

261

advantage of a naval shelling of the village. Early on the morning of June 7th, Hughes and the 16th Combat Regiment engaged in house-to-house clearing of the village, rooting out dug in German infantry and snipers. It was not until nightfall of the next day that Colleville-Sur-Mer was secure. After more than nearly 72 hours of battle, the *Big Red One* was ordered to stand down for the night.

Before allowing himself the luxury of a dinner of K rations and a bedroll, Jim Hughes wrote a letter home, uncertain of what to share with his family. He could only imagine their fears and despite wanting to share his own, he didn't want to burden them more. His hand was shaky as he scribbled under the dim glow afforded by a lit cigarette.

June 8th, 1944

Dear Gang,

I can only imagine the headlines and Edward R. Murrow's reports coming in over the radio from Europe. No matter what you've read or heard, I'm sure it understates the facts. But most importantly, I want you all to know that I'm ok. Not even a scratch. I'm tired as all hell and cranky as a son of a bitch, but you already know that!

I came ashore at a place called Omaha Beach near the village of Colleville-Sur-Mer in the first wave of landing craft at dawn on the 6th. Before the shooting started, the channel was stormy but the sun was just rising as we neared the coastline. It appeared that more than a week of the most God-awful weather was ending.

Afterwards, I couldn't begin to tell you what the weather has been like for the last three days. I haven't had a moment to think about it.

I pray that John is okay, I'm sure he jumped sometime the night before, probably just a few miles from me. If he and

*his unit took as heavy resistance as we did on Omaha, then he
had a helluva time. Please tell me what you hear from him.*

*I can't really describe how bad it was at Omaha, I
don't think you would believe me.*

*We hit the beach at daybreak and a lot of my guys were
shot before they ever made the beach. It was horrible for a
while and heartbreaking to see so many young lives destroyed
before they had even had the chance to fight back.*

*Most of the LCVP's coming in to unload dropped their
troops in water too deep and some guys just couldn't swim
wearing all that heavy equipment. Jerry had put up a lot of
barricades – barbed wire, concrete and steel crosses and mines
– to block us and they were spraying us with machine gun fire
even before the shoreline, sometimes nailing guys as they put a
foot in the water. It was a real bloodbath. I saw men on either
side of me get hit in the head, there'd just be this puff and
spray of blood and their bodies would drop like a stone. They
were killed within seconds of stepping off their boat.*

*I was luckier and managed to crawl ashore and take
cover behind a sea wall that runs the length of Omaha Beach. I
guess the Germans had a hunch we might try to land here and
God help us they were ready. It was horrifying to watch all
those guys get hit. Christ, most of them were just kids. What
a mess.*

*We were stuck on the beach for quite a while doing
little more than returning fire, but we eventually pushed
forward. If we had stayed on the beach we would have died. So
we sucked up our guts and wiped out some machine gun nests
and heavy artillery gun encasements on the bluffs overlooking
Omaha and got a toehold. That stopped some of the sniper fire
and shelling of the landing craft still coming in. But we had to
climb a 100-foot high bluff to get to the Colleville-Sur-Mer
plateu and safety and it was a fight the whole way up. I ran
out of hand grenades and my M-1 was hot by the time we
reached the summit but we left a lot of dead Germans behind
us. It took a bunch of killing but I don't think about it much.*

263

After all, they would have blown my head off if they'd had an open shot at me.

We fought for the next two days into the village of Colleville-Sur-Mer and had to clean out the houses one by one. But now that it's secure we are standing down for rest for the next 24 hours. I can barely keep my eyes open, I'm so tired. It's going to be a long battle to Berlin. But I promise you: I'll still be coming home to tell the tale when the job is done. Count on it.

I appreciate your prayers and want you to know that I pray for each of you, too. We're going to win this thing, although it may take a bit longer than we had hoped. But the day will come when I'll be calling one of you for a ride home from the train station.

I love you all,

Jim

P.S. Please let me know should you get any word about John. I'll be looking for him wherever the road leads.

*   *   *

By the afternoon of June 6th, most of the second battalion of the 506th Parachute Regiment, which had ben dropped near the village of Sainte-Mère-Église, more than 20 miles from their target, had reassembled near Foucarville. As confused as the situation was, the 506th was intent on achieving its objectives of clearing the way so the incoming 4th Infantry Division would be unopposed while moving further inland after landing at Utah Beach. That would require knocking out secondary German defenses above the landing area and capturing the four causeway bridges between the villages of Sainte-Martin-de-Varreville and Pouppeville. The 506th was also tasked with seizing the la Barquette lock and destroying a bridge near the town of Carenten while also taking control of two other bridges that crossed the Douve River near the town. As the sun set on June 6th, the 506th had taken the beach bridges but was unable to seize the crossings over the Douve because of heavy German resistance.

The 506th had to dig in outside the village of Sainte-Côme-du-Mont for the night, fighting off one attack after another through the following day. The Regiment took heavy losses but was ordered to move on to Carenten to secure the bridges over the Douve.

After three days of intense combat, the paratroopers were successful in securing the bridge at Carenten, and engaged in house-to-house fighting on the night of June 11th and all day on the 12th until the Germans retreated from the town. John Hughes' D Company was assigned to help with the "mop up" of German snipers still in Carenten and began a tedious process of checking every building in the town. Shots rang out intermittently as stragglers were found.

Hughes and two buddies from D Company entered what looked to be the remains of a vintner's shop. It had been heavily damaged in artillery shelling and appeared to be empty. The smell of wine from smashed bottles and cordite from the shelling lingered in the air, at once pungent and smoky. The men gave the shop a quick once over, and then finding it apparently empty, went to leave. Suddenly, from behind an overturned counter, a lone German soldier who had been hiding raised his MP40 submachine gun and screamed, "Halt, Amerikaner!"

Hughes turned instinctively, bringing up his M-1 to defend himself, but the German fired first and hit the American with a single shot from an errant burst. The enemy was dropped a split second later by the other GI's. Hughes fell to the ground, a bullet lodged in his left shoulder, just above the sternum and dangerously close to his heart. Blood was pouring from the wound when his buddies got to him. One worked to stop the bleeding while the other ran to fetch a medic.

John Hughes was awake but rapidly going into shock when the medic got to him and plunged a syrette of morphine into his arm. He was calm, but had lost a lot of blood and was shivering with cold.

"We gotta get him out of here, quickly," the medic said to the soldiers. "Help me carry him." The three men carried the limp John Hughes about two blocks where they were able to commandeer a jeep to race the wounded soldier back behind the lines to a field hospital.

"Good luck, John, you 'll be ok buddy," one of the soldiers said to him as the Jeep pulled away, the medic at the wheel. The other squeezed his hand and Hughes managed a grin.

"Knock the hell outta these bastards, will ya?" he said. "Let's get this over by Christmas, fellas."

The soldier passed out in the Jeep and only reawakened after being treated in a temporary field hospital set up in a tent near Sainte-Côme-du-Mont, ironically a battleground he had already safely escaped.

He dropped in and out of consciousness for several hours, morphine keeping him from clearing his head. He thought he heard doctors near him explaining that he needed surgery, that the bullet was lodged too close to his heart and that he was being evacuated to England.

He tried to speak, but could not form the sounds despite trying several times. There were only a few people in the world that would have understood him, anyway.

What he was desperately trying to say was, "No... Highland Street."

Twenty-Four
~~~ ❦ ~~~

"The car pulled up in front of the house late in the afternoon a few days later when Pa was working out in the barn," Ka recalled. "He never heard them coming. It was Bobbie who saw them first. A man in a starched military uniform and one of the priests from Sacred Heart Church got out of the car and came knocking at the front door. My sister saw who it was and was afraid to open it and ran out the back to get my father. She was hysterical as she ran to the barn and kept screaming for him.

"Pa came out of the barn after hearing Bobbie's panicked call and it was only then that he saw the two men.

"'What's the problem...' he began to ask but then he realized who the men were. He looked at them in silence. His worst nightmare was standing in front of him, the one he envisioned while he stared at the stars in

268

our window for hours at a time. He stopped dead in his tracks and held out his arms for Bobbie, who was so frightened. He held her for a moment and then was overcome by the grief he knew was to come and dropped to his knees."

Ka stopped then, looking around the table at our faces. I think she wanted to be sure we understood the horror of that moment for all of them.

"The priest ran to Pa and dropped to his own knees to support him from falling over. He was a nice young man who had the unfortunate duty of sharing dreadful news with his parishioners. The military officer hurried to them. Bobbie told me that he was nervous and sweaty and hadn't yet opened the telegram.

"'Mr. Hughes, I have a Western Union telegram addressed to you from the Secretary of the Army,' he said. 'I don't know…'

"Pa reached up and took the telegram from his hand and gave it to the priest. He asked him to read it. The priest stammered his sympathy before opening it, and Pa lost his temper.

"'Just read it, God damn it,' he said.

"I guess the poor young man tore open the letter expecting to read the worst. As Bobbie told it, his eyes widened because it wasn't what he expected." She paused.

"No, it sure wasn't.

"I remember the words in that telegram, not only because thy were so shocking, but surprisingly, because they gave us hope." She closed her eyes, reciting the words from memory.

"'I regret to inform you that your son, PFC. John Hughes was wounded in combat on June 12 in Normandy, France while fighting for his country. He has been evacuated to England for treatment.'"

269

Ka rocked in her chair as she said the words, her eyes locked shut. Her hands were clasped so tightly her fingers turned white. "There were more words about the Army keeping us informed of his condition and thanking us for his sacrifice. But Pa wasn't listening. He hadn't heard a word after 'wounded.'

"He wasn't dead. And that's exactly what Pa said as he got to his feet.

"'He's not dead. Only wounded,' he insisted. 'There is hope for your brother, Bobbie,' he said to my sister.

"Now keep in mind that we had no idea how seriously he was hurt or if he was still alive, where he was in England... there were so many questions we didn't have answers to. But it didn't matter. All Pa knew was that his son had just been in the greatest battle in American history and that he was still alive. He told Bobbie to go and fetch Jiggs and to make sure everyone in the family knew that John had been wounded, but was alive."

"What did you do, Aunt Ka?" my son Jay asked. "I would have gone crazy not knowing."

"Well, I had gone to pick up Eric at work and didn't even know about it until we came by to make dinner for Pa and the kids about an hour later. I found my father in the living room, standing and staring at that those stars in the window. Bobbie said he hadn't moved from there since the men left. He was holding a bottle that was half empty in one hand, the crumpled telegram in the other. Eric helped him to his chair and sat with him and the girls while Jiggs and I went to the Red Cross office in Hartford to see if they could get any information for us. They were nice enough, certainly sympathetic, but told us that it could be days or weeks before they could reach him or find out his condition. I told them I would check in with them every day."

"How long was it before you heard anything," I asked.

Ka sighed. "It was so frustrating," she replied. "It was only a few days before the Red Cross confirmed he was in England, but they couldn't get any information other than that he had been seriously wounded. They couldn't tell us where he was or give us an address to write to. We couldn't get answers to where he had been injured or what 'seriously' meant. I mean, we were left to conjure up the worst scenarios... had he lost a leg or an arm? Could he walk? Had he been disfigured? Did he have a brain injury? You can't conceive the horrors the human mind can summon when there is a void of information. I tell you, knowing he was alive was such a relief. But not knowing his situation was torture."

She stopped again and took a sip from her coffee. Her eyes were moist but emotionally she was in better shape than her audience. I think we were all pretty shaken. But she wasn't done yet.

"Then one day, weeks later, the mailman came."

There were more than a few gasps around the table, including my own.

"He brought a letter." She shook her head up and down, remembering, a slight grin coming to her face.

"It was from my brother, John, dated July 4th, 1944."

Twenty-Five

~~~ ⚮ ~~~

July 1944

July 4, 1944

Dear Gang,

Since I haven't heard from any of you, I can only suppose that neither the Army nor the Red Cross has been keeping you informed of my whereabouts and recovery. I'm sure I've caused you a lot of anxiety the last few weeks, but please forgive me. I'm only now able to write again after having my left shoulder immobilized since I took a German bullet in a little town called Carenten in France. Now I am recovering and getting stronger everyday in a Station Hospital here in Cheltenham, just on the outskirts of Cotswolds in Gloucestershire, England. I'm told it's actually a lovely place, but this hospital is so busy caring for GI's wounded in France there's no one who has the time to take guys like me for a tour.

272

Anyway, I'm sure I scared the dickens out of all of you and I don't mean to treat what happened to me so lightly. Truthfully, there is nothing to worry about. I had a close call, but other than a nasty scar, there'll be nothing but some lousy memories and a Purple Heart from my commanding officer to remind me it ever happened. So I'm here, family, alive and kicking and it's going to take a helluva lot more than a German bullet to take me away from you.

It was my own stupid fault. My unit had been in the thick of the fighting since we parachuted in over France early in the morning of June 6th, hours before Jim's 1st Infantry was to hit the beach by landing craft. I haven't heard from him or know anything about his experience coming in, but the Red Cross has told me he's ok and scheduled to be taken off line sometime soon for a rest. Who knows... I may even see him here in England. It sure isn't the place I'd choose to celebrate the Fourth of July, but it would be the best day of my life if I got to see him.

I'm sure you're anxious to know what happened so I'll try to tell you what I remember, at least.

Two buddies of mine from D Company and I were going house-to-house in Carenten, trying to rid this little town of German infantry snipers and stragglers. I got a little careless, I guess because I had come through some tough scrapes over the last six days. So we didn't do a very thorough job of cleaning out this bombed out storefront, a wine shop of all places, because one of the bastards surprised us and put one in my shoulder.

The doctors were worried because the bullet was lodged just above my heart so they got me back to a field hospital in Sainte-Côme-du-Mont, a village we had just liberated, and then on to a troop ship back across the Channel to England for surgery. I don't remember much of the trip being all doped up on morphine. Needless to say, the surgery went ok, and here I am, mending quickly and nearly fit for duty again.

273

I was only in battle for six days, but I can tell you it was exciting, to say the least.   We flew in a C-47 from an airbase in the south of England across the Channel to the Cherbourg Peninsula in really rough weather. It was hell for our pilots to stay on course and then we ran into antiaircraft fire so thick I swear you could step out and walk on it. It ended up that our pilot missed the drop zone completely and we came down miles from where we were supposed to be. The jump was unimaginable. I hope to God that some day I will forget all the horrible details of it.

Within hours of hitting the ground, a bunch of us had organized into something resembling a company and we went about trying to fulfill our objectives. We were supposed to fight for three days and then get relieved and sent back to England for rest. It didn't happen.

As it was, I was in constant combat for more than six days before I got hit with no hope of relief or reinforcements. The rest of the 506th spent 33 days fighting the Germans before being relieved. They'll be coming to England soon for a well-deserved break. I'll join up with them as soon as they release me from the hospital.

I'd like to tell you that I was a model of courage throughout this whole experience, but that would be a lie. I was terrified. The fear was more gripping and deeper than anything I've ever felt before. And I know I wasn't alone in those feelings. As we waited for the jump, I swear I watched young men take on the appearance of old men right before my eyes.

And I'd like to tell you that I was so mentally prepared for this fight that all I focused on was the mission ahead or in contemplating the exhilaration of meeting the enemy and butchering him like I'd been so well trained. The truth is, in the days before I landed here, and especially during the flight across the Channel on the night of the invasion, I didn't think much about the enemy at all.

274

What filled my heart and mind were thoughts of all those that I loved, of all of you, thousands of miles away, safe on Highland Street and in your homes and away from the carnage we knew was coming.

The wrinkled and cracked photographs of you that I've been carrying with me since I left home nearly three years ago stirred my memories. The pictures were never farther away from my grasp than my rifle. I protected my most precious possessions from the rain, mud and blood of war in the pockets of my heavy fatigues and in the lining of my helmet.

I'd like to tell you how brave I was in those six days that I was fighting in France, but that too would be a lie, too. I just did my job, without question or hesitation. Mostly, I fought away the constant fear burning in the pit of my stomach as I moved with my buddies from village to village, house to house, slowly but steadily extinguishing the enemy on soil that he had taken, but had not earned. I felt no overwhelming sense of patriotism or righteousness, only numb resignation that I had a job to do, and when it was done, God willing, I could go home. But always in my mind was the fear of the bullet with my name on it. Well, one did find me, but I'm still here. So much for that fear.

The painful truth is that I'm very lucky. Many of my friends, men who jumped with me over Sainte-Mère-Église, who I fought next to at Sainte-Côme-du-Mont and Caranten weren't so fortunate. Many died. And in the villages, where the French people greeted us so warmly as heroes, there is the stench of death and destruction everywhere. It is unconscionable what has happened to the French and all the European people who have suffered at the hands of that Nazi madmen and his war machine. Their countries are destroyed, nothing but rubble, but at least they are liberated. What irony. They've lost everything, but they are overjoyed that Americans are there for them. Now I really know what freedom tastes like. But what a price...

275

I hope you are all well. Please know that I think of each of you everyday and dream about coming home to Highland Street. Keep me in your prayers and as the song says, tonight, 'I'll be looking at your moon, but I'll be seeing you.'

Please let me know if you hear from Jim.
Love you all,
John

Twenty-Six

~~~ ౪ ~~~

Fall, 1944

Jim Hughes and the *Big Red One*'s 2nd Battalion 16th Infantry never saw the respite from combat in England they had expected. Still smarting from the brutal Omaha Beach landing and the beating they had taken at Colleville-Sur-Mer, the 16th barely took a deep breath before pushing 23 miles over the next week to take the village of Caumont in savage fighting. By mid July, the *Big Red One*, although exhausted and depleted, took the heavily fortified German stronghold of St. Lo with the assistance of massive Allied carpet-bombing. The St. Lo breakout led to the successful capture of the town of Marigny on July 27, essentially breaking the back of the initial German defense of Normandy and the Cherbourg Peninsula.

277

Over the next month, The Allied forces moved through France with speed that overwhelmed the German military, now in full retreat. The 4th Infantry Division liberated Paris at the end of August. But while Parisians celebrated, it was a long way still to Berlin. The 1st Infantry juggernaut continued to crush any resistance in its path, leading the Division to the doorstep of Germany on September 11. The Nazi menace was within reach. Maybe Eisenhower was right after all, many GI's thought. "Home by Christmas."

Jim Hughes, exhausted and living in a state of constant depression brought on by the deaths of innumerable men killed in action while under his command, was sick of war. Despite chronic fatigue and an almost irrepressible urge to lay down his rifle, find his brother John and make their way home, he fought on, telling himself the only way to the end was to finish the job. But he prayed for a break from the endless combat.

September 11, 1944

Dear John,

I finally received word that you are alive and well despite being wounded. I can't express my relief at knowing you are ok but in the same breath my frustration in learning that you weren't sent home. I knew you were a tough little bastard, but being strong enough to face more of what the German's have to offer is almost superhuman. I have no idea where the 101st Airborne is right now, but I hope wherever you are you're pulling guard duty in a town or village that has seen the last of the Germans!

You'll be happy to know that the 1st Infantry has moved with lighting speed through Belgium, most recently in driving the enemy from Liege. We are now on the outskirts of Aachen, the first major city in Germany and I anticipate the battle for control of it will commence within days if not hours.

Actually, I'm so tired and hungry I'd just as soon get back into the fight. Every foot we take in this hellhole, every town and village that we kick the German out of means I'm that much closer to a hot shower, a warm meal and a week in a soft bed. Sometimes I think if I have to spend one more night in a dirt foxhole after a dinner of cold K rations I'll go mad. What I wouldn't do for dinner with Pa and the gang at Highland Street and the bed in my old bedroom on Highland Street.

You take care, John, I'll keep my eye out for you because we have some serious drinking to do!

Love you brother,
Jim

Within hours of penning the note to his brother, Jim Hughes was moving forward again to battle the Germans in Aachen. For the next ten days, the *Big Red One* fought to take the heavily fortified city in vicious house-to-house fighting that often saw hand-to-hand combat with fixed bayonets. American casualties were deplorable; German losses were even more horrific.

On October 21, the 1st Infantry raised the Stars and Stripes over the once beautiful city destroyed by artillery fire and the destruction wrought by the German SS. The entire city was in ruins. Not a single building stood undamaged. Streets were impassable, water and sewer lines were all breached and the stench of rotting animal carcasses enveloped the city. The *Big Red One* had gutted the enemy's efforts to push back the Allied surge but the price had been steep. Still, surviving residents cheered for the American victors, having suffered under the control of the German military since the outbreak of war. There were miles to go, but suddenly Berlin was within reach.

The 1st Infantry then moved east and joined the Battle of Hurtgen Forest on the Belgium-German border, where the Nazi's were intent on halting the Allied penetration aimed at Berlin. The fierce battle lasted over six weeks and resulted in more than 33,000 American killed or wounded. The Americans were painfully unaware of the vast German resources invested in the strategic battle as well as the construction of extraordinary fortifications that blocked American tanks. As well, the steamrolling Allied advance from the Normandy beaches had been so swift, it was now slowing because supply lines to the front couldn't keep up with the pace.

The *Big Red One* had retaliated for it's terrible losses at Omaha Beach with vengeance. But the Division's luck couldn't hold forever. The 1st Infantry took it on the chin at the village of Langerwehe-Merode on November 29th. Jim Hughes's platoon was among the two Companies that initially took the village, but were crushed in the early morning hours of the 30th in a determined German counter-attack. Hughes saw nearly half of his platoon cut down in the battle.

Finally, after six brutal months of constant combat, the *Big Red One* was depleted and exhausted. The Division was pulled off the line and moved to a rear area for a long deserved rest in early December.

On that first night of relief from combat, Hughes was despondent as he wrote to the parents of the 19 men in his platoon that had been killed in Langerwehe-Merode. He had never allowed himself to get close to any of them. Yet by the light of a candle in his tent, he could see each of their faces as he held up the dog tags he had taken from their lifeless bodies. He had become inured to this task, and despite his emotional state worked through the night to find the words he

280

desperately sought to bring comfort to the grieving families of his men. But as dawn broke, he knew that once again he had failed.

There were no words that could possibly fill the void of a young son slaughtered in the name of peace. The entire concept was a contradiction in terms.

He had planned to write to his father with hope that he would find comfort in sharing his struggle with someone he loved.

But as he blew out the candle and lay his head down on the thin pillow of his canvas cot, Jim Hughes knew he was just plain out of explanations.

*   *   *

While John Hughes recovered, the 101st Airborne, including the 506th Parachute Regiment, spent the summer licking its own wounds and pulled back to Cherbourg for rest then moved on to England to resupply. The unit had suffered heavy casualties in Normandy and was in desperate need of replacement troops and equipment before it would be ready for its next mission.

While his brother Jim was engaged in the Allied offensive at Aachen, John returned to his unit in late August, combat fit once again. As it turned out, the call to action for the 506th came within days of his reinsertion. After daybreak on the morning of September 17 the battle hardened regiment of the 101st Airborne once again found itself the target of heavy antiaircraft fire as the paratroopers prepared to jump from C-47's over the village of Sint-Oedenrode in the Netherlands. As usual, the 506th had been chosen to lead the next Allied offensive against Germany: *Operation Market Garden.*

Hughes' second combat jump was considerably less dramatic than his first over the Cherbourg Peninsula four months earlier. This time, despite heavy antiaircraft fire, pilots of the jump planes held formation as they approached the pre-designated landing zones and the paratroopers were delivered on target. The 506th dropped near the town of Son with two missions: take the Beatrix bridge over the Wilhelmina Canal and then move south to secure the village of Eindhoven and four other bridges. It was the first phase of an operation designed to seize an opening between Eindhoven and Arnhem in the Netherlands, through which Allied troops could eventually cross the Rhine River and into the Ruhr valley, the industrial heart of Germany. If successful, the European war would be over by Christmas. The only way for the plan to succeed was if the paratroopers could maintain control of the roads and bridges that allowed movement around the innumerable dikes, canals and rivers of the countryside.

It wasn't to be.

Moving quickly toward Son, the 101st Airborne came under heavy attack by the Germans but managed to clear the town of the enemy. John Hughes took more fire in the first few hours of *Operation Market Garden* than he had in all of his time in Normandy. Taking the bridge at Son appeared to be imminent, but as the paratroopers approached the target, confidently marching down the main road, German 88 millimeter guns positioned at the bridge opened up on the exposed and unsuspecting 101st Airborne. Chaos ensued as huge artillery shells rained down on the paratroopers who hadn't anticipated the need to find cover. The casualties were appalling.

The 506th had been on the point and immediately took direct hits. Hughes and dozens of men dove for shelter and rolled down an embankment into a drainage ditch that followed the main road. All around him he saw men butchered with a fury that could only be rendered by large explosives detonating among troops in close quarter ranks. He froze in position, digging into the soft soil of the ditch trying to hide from the horrific scene that unexpectedly resurrected memories of D-Day and his own close encounter with death.

Hughes had managed to suppress the battle-induced anxiety that drove many men nearly mad as they recovered from their wounds, knowing they were faced with returning to the front lines. Even as he stepped from the C-47 into the exploding skies over Sint-Oedenrode he oddly felt no apprehension. He jumped without hesitation and fearlessly engaged the enemy almost immediately after hitting the ground. He felt good to be back with his unit in the thick of it, pushing towards Berlin so he could go home.

But when the big German guns began dropping shells on the 506th, John Hughes was suddenly gripped with a viselike fear unlike anything he had ever known. He felt a cold sweat under his uniform and his vision blurred. He forced himself to raise his weapon and return fire at the German gun crews manning the heavy artillery that guarded the bridge, but his legs had turned to lead. He was unable to move. His hands shook as he fired his weapon. A shell landed directly to his right, rendering him momentarily deaf.

Hughes dropped his carbine and clasped his hands over his ears, trying in vain to shut out the terrifying roar of the incoming artillery and the blood curdling screams of paratroopers cut to shreds by the explosions and spray of shrapnel. Something heavy bounced off his neck and fell beside him leaving the back of his neck and uniform wet. Instinctively he reached behind him to wipe off the dampness and found it sticky. He stared at his fingers and shuddered. They were covered in blood. Panicking, he frantically searched the ground for what had hit him then froze in horror when he located the macabre object. It was a human leg, torn off at the hip, a paratrooper's boot still laced tightly to the foot. Screaming in revulsion, he forced himself to crawl forward in the ditch to get away from the hideous remains.

All around him men were going down with appalling wounds as the barrage of artillery shells from the German 88's continued to rain down upon the exposed 506th for what seemed like hours but was actually only a few minutes. Somehow, a platoon managed to flank the guns positioned at the bridge and took out the half dozen enemy troops manning them. But the few German soldiers had inflicted mortal damage on the 506th.

The tragedy continued when moments later, the Germans, who had taken advantage of the time they had successfully held off the Americans to wire the bridge with explosives, detonated the charges. Just as troops from the 506th stepped upon the decking of their hard won prize, the steel structure erupted in a series of blasts that ripped it from its piers and into the sky, reducing the village lifeline to twisted metal and rubble that fell into the Wilhelmina canal at Son with a roar. Paratroopers scampered off the apron of the structure just as it disappeared into the water. The loss of more than a hundred men from the 506th Parachute Regiment of the 101st Airborne had all been for nothing.

John Hughes, still shaking from the hellacious enemy shelling, burrowed deeper into the shallow cover of the drainage ditch as debris from the bridge showered over him and hundreds of other troops shattered by the attack. For long minutes, none of them moved until officers began barking orders in an attempt to rile the 506th back into action. They were surprised by the slow reaction from men who were used to reacting to any order without hesitation.

The shocked survivors began struggling to their feet. They hesitated to leave the little bit of cover they had found, and instead were nearly hypnotized by the slaughter they saw on the roadway. Those who watched were all unwilling spectators at the most grotesque theater of the absurd imaginable. While they had not been injured, they had been invisibly wounded, forever.

Medics moved quickly through the hundreds of casualties, treating some, marking others as hopelessly wounded and giving them morphine. A lone chaplain moved from body to body, praying with boys who gripped their hands in fear, administering the Last Rites to the dying and dead. Stretcher-bearers carrying men who desperately needed surgery ran in every direction to jeeps and trucks that began arriving. Platoon leaders knelt beside their dead or wounded men, offering a comforting word or pulling dog tags from around their necks.

John Hughes struggled to his feet, then dropped down to one knee, leaning on his weapon to keep from falling. He was hardly in any shape to go on. Dazed, his eyes darted from one broken corpse to another, the bodies of young men lying grotesquely where they had fallen in the road. He felt someone place a hand on his shoulder and turned to find the face of a buddy.

""Hey John... you alright?" It was Al Lipton, one of the men he had trained with at Camp Toccoa, a lifetime ago. "Bite down, Currahee," Lipton said, referring to the motto the paratrooper trainees had embraced, the Cherokee word meaning, "We stand alone together."

285

Hughes shook his head, trying to get his emotions back in check.

"Yah, Al. What the fuck happened?" he asked, still shaking.

"Dunno," Lipton answered. "I got a feeling the brass wasn't exactly expecting that reception. This place is crawling with Krauts. " He reached inside his jacket pocket and pulled out a worn leather encased flask.

"Here. It was a gift from my old man. Said it would come in handy at times just like this. Trust me, it has. Take a swig." Lipton handed it to Hughes, who put the flask to his mouth without question. He took a long pull from the whiskey, and then another. Almost immediately he felt the shaking in his hands begin to abate.

"Thanks Al," he nodded to his friend. "Don't know what's come over me. Hands are shaking..."

"You're not alone, buddy. Here," he handed Hughes the flask again. "There's plenty more. I got a couple of bottles in my pack. It helps me get through this shit," Lipton said. "Don't be afraid to ask." John Hughes didn't argue and drank deeply again.

While a team of engineers worked to build a footbridge across the canal, the 506th was ordered to dig in just south of Son. They would spend the night there in foxholes, cross the canal, march on Eindhoven the next day and hope for better luck with the other bridges. John Hughes purposefully dug his foxhole near his friend Lipton and the two men spent the night secretly sharing a bottle of cheap whiskey. They drank in silence, each wide-eyed in the darkness, their nerves frayed to the point of breaking. By midnight, when the Germans launched a major counterattack, the two were stinking drunk. But they were fortified enough by alcohol to fight with the reckless ferocity of young men who had no regard for danger or the worst possible consequences.

For John Hughes, the tranquilizing effects of the whiskey had unexpectedly but profoundly influenced his ability to deal with the demons that had risen up to stalk him. Although he had survived his Normandy wounds and miraculously escaped injury at Son, the brutal incidents had left him "shell shocked" and severed the last vestiges of his youth and gentle nature. For many men, the experiences would have ended their role in the war, their spirits shattered to the point where they were no longer able to function. But alcohol, for which he had never before had a liking, had mercifully numbed John Hughes' abrupt separation from his naiveté and the sudden cognition that he was mortal.

He was now the perfect soldier: inured and oblivious to his own danger and callous to inflicting the most cold-blooded of mayhem upon the enemy.

When the German counter attack was finally repelled, Hughes and Lipton looked with disinterest over the pile of enemy bodies in front of the foxhole they shared. They were each out of ammunition, having used up every clip between them and the last few charging Germans had been bayonetted The two soldiers were lauded for their courage by officers and fellow soldiers and there was even talk of a medal.

But all Hughes wanted was another drink.

And for the next 70 days of combat that the 506th would endure in their punishing and prolonged defeat in the Netherlands, John Hughes had three objectives: stay alive, kill Germans and remain sedated by any drink he could pilfer in the ruins of bombed out towns and villages along the German border. He became withdrawn, sullen and reclusive, stopped writing home to his family and deliberately ignored their letters.

In late November the 101st Airborne, including the 506th Parachute Regiment, moved to the city of Mourmelon in the north east of France for rest and resupply. It was a bittersweet time of relief for the troops who had seen the opportunity to end the war before Christmas disappear with the Allied defeat in the Netherlands. A victory celebration in Berlin seemed a very long ways away now for the weary paratroopers.

Filthy, desperately in need of a hot meal and warm bed, John Hughes drank from his own flask on the truck ride to Mourmelon as he contemplated his chances of surviving the war. He scanned the back of the truck and saw more than a dozen mirror images of himself: men who had long ago lost their sense of humanity and endlessly struggled to keep their nerve for one more day. They were sunken-eyed and listless, mostly silent and hair-triggered at the first sign of danger. Too many of their Currahee brothers had been left behind in temporary military cemeteries for them to continue to embrace the esprit of a fighting force with a noble objective. Now, although they still had the will to fight on, it was more a defensive state of mind than courage or patriotism that kept them going. The unrelenting exposure to death, the bottomless spigot of blood and the pure weariness of life in a foxhole had turned them into soulless warriors.

Hughes shook his head at the inescapable truth. He unscrewed the cap of his flask and took a long pull from the brandy he had pilfered in the bombed out Dutch city of Nijmegan just before pulling out. For a moment he recalled the ruins of the 2,000-year old city, once a center of art and culture. The German occupation and Allied bombing had indiscriminately reduced it to a pile of rubble.

He thought of the small shop he had entered on patrol just the night before and the Germans he'd surprised who were probably doing the same thing he was. Looking for something, anything to drink. He'd survived the encounter only because he was the one who had done the surprising. He raised the flask to his lips and drank, silently toasting the enemy he had killed.

Just before passing out, his thoughts turned to Highland Street. That world was fast becoming a distant memory. Perhaps that was a good thing, he considered. First, because the odds of his making it home were getting narrower with every day. The other alternative was more alarming.

What if he made it home?

John Hughes knew the people he loved would know longer recognize the man he had been. Their son and brother had died sometime ago.

And he was sure they wouldn't like the new guy.

Twenty-Seven

~~~ ❧ ~~~

"And just like that, my little brother John disappeared again," Ka said, wringing her hands.

"We didn't know what to think. He hadn't written in months and we had no idea if he was getting our letters. Jim, Speck and Peachy all tried contacting him, too, but there was no response. We kept expecting that god awful telegram..."

She shook her head with frustration that had obviously never been satisfied.

"It was so bizarre and unlike him. We were sure something had happened," she continued. "Pa would take the trolley to the Red Cross in Hartford nearly every day trying to get some news about him, but they couldn't help. All we knew was that John was somewhere in Holland and had not been reported as missing, wounded or..." She hesitated, as if her mouth

290

wouldn't allow her to say the unspeakable. It was obvious that even after all these years she still agonized over the memory.

"Or killed," she said, finally finishing the sentence as she looked down at her hands, now clasped tightly together. "It wasn't until late November that we got news from the Red Cross that his entire unit had been taken off the front lines and shipped back to England for rest. His name was on the list. We kept writing to him, desperate for any kind of reply, but heard nothing."

She leaned back in the patio chair and raised her head to the sky, once again searching out the stars. A deep sigh escaped from her trembling lips and I was sure that she was exhausted. Once again, she surprised us all.

"For Americans, the war lasted three years and eight months, finally ending when the Japanese surrendered in August 1945. But the war in Europe ended much sooner. It was in May, after Hitler committed suicide. And I can tell you, those last six months of the fighting in Europe were the most excruciating of all for my family.

"Jim and John were in the middle of the worst of it all and we were waiting every day for a letter from Speck telling us he was shipping out to the Pacific. Phil and Dot's husband Ed Ames had been drafted but they were pretty safe for the time being. Phil was at Camp Kilmer in New Jersey working in Army administration. I think he was helping to process troops going off to Europe. And Ed was involved in training at Fort Bragg in South Carolina. Jiggs was the last to be called, into the Navy, just a few days after Christmas 1944.

"Those of us who were left saw them all off at Union Station, and even though we knew they were safe for the moment, there was no telling what the future would hold for them. We'd gotten beaten up very badly by the Germans in Holland and now the country was full of insecurity about when the war would end.

"Everyone had been so hopeful it would all be over, at least in Europe, by Christmas. But that didn't happen. In fact, some of the worst fighting was yet to come. And of course, the war against the Japanese was still undecided and everyone was terrorized by the idea of having to invade Japan. Americans in general had a lot of confidence that we'd win both wars, but how long it would take was anyone's guess. In fact, I think most people thought it was going to take years longer. It was a dreadfully depressing time."

"So all the boys were gone by January, 1945?" my sister asked.

"Not all. Henry and Ray both had deferments because of their jobs. And my husband Eric somehow missed the call. I guess we were blessed."

"Maybe it was a gift, Aunt Ka," Claudia said. "Because you had done so much to hold the family together all those years."

The corners of Ka's mouth turned up ever so slightly. The thought pleased her.

"Perhaps, Claudia. It's nice of you to think so," she replied. "After my mother died, taking care of my family filled the hole she left in my heart. But I never dreamed life would scatter so many people I loved all over the world, and put them in such terrible danger."

She dabbed at her eyes with her handkerchief. I thought she was on the verge of a real cry. But I underestimated her backbone, even now at her fragile age.

"The hardest part of it all was the uncertainty. Not knowing where some of his boys were or if they were safe, not being able to talk to them, not knowing when it would be over. There was just no end in sight. It was hard on all of us, but particularly Pa. When John stopped communicating, I thought that would finally break his heart. I really did expect to lose him at any moment. He was drinking hard, never got more than a few hours of sleep at night and other than going to pester the Red Cross, nearly never left the house for fear he'd miss the postman… or a telegram."

I saw her hands shake at the mention of the word "telegram." It had brought back another very sad memory.

"You see, there were a lot of them… the telegrams, I mean… being delivered in town," she said, an unexpected and startling twist.

"You mean, news of boys from Wethersfield who'd been killed?" Jack asked.

"Yes, exactly," she said, bowing her head. "Nine Wethersfield families received those hideous telegrams from the Secretary of War during the fall and early part of the winter of 1944. Nine. I tell you the whole town was reeling from the shock of it.

"Some of these boys had died of wounds they received on D-Day, but most in the fighting in France and Germany that followed. I think some were killed in Italy where they were still fighting. We seemed to lose another boy every week for several months. I remember some of the families. It was a smaller town then, everyone knew everyone and the prayer services and funerals masses would be packed with neighbors."

"Do you remember them, were any of them friends of Pa?" Claudia asked.

"Oh, yes," Ka answered, nodding her head slowly. "Sometimes I wish I could forget." She brought a finger to her lips. "I remember young Dick Elrick was killed, his father Bill was a great friend of my father's.

293

And there was Bart Hanusovsky, a guard at the Wethersfield Prison before he enlisted. He was sweet on my sister Flossie for a while. Larry McCrann, Al Parkes, Clayton Jones, Bill Waymouth, Joe Normandin... goodness, he was a handsome boy, lived on Brimfield Road..."

She closed her eyes, digging deeply into her memory. I was astonished at what she recalled.

"This is terrible, I'm having trouble... oh, of course. Doug Gilbert and John Wheeler, they were both lost in the Pacific just before Christmas. More than 30 boys from Wethersfield died before it was all over."

"My God... how horrible," someone whispered. Ka heard the comment.

"Horrible? You can't imagine. Especially when seven of your own family..." She didn't finish her thought. She didn't have to.

"I guess you can see why we were so anxious and why Pa was such a mess. It's a wonder we all didn't go a little crazy."

I shook my own head in wonder. For so many years, I, like my siblings and cousins had looked at Ka, my father and the rest of the Hughes family as a close-knit, mostly reserved but somewhat offbeat cast of a real life sitcom. Each of them had their own unique personality and an odd trait or two, but it didn't take much scratching below the surface to find a strong family identity and bond. I'd often wondered how such a large family could manage to stay close for so many years. Now, the truth sent shivers through me. The struggles they had survived, as a family, was actually the glue that held them together. The agonizing death of their mother at such a young age, my grandfather's depression and alcoholism and the years of anxiety and cruel separation during the war taught them to circle the wagons when any one of them was threatened. Instead of driving them apart, life's punishing challenges had pushed them closer.

It was after ten o'clock now and finally the neighborhood had gone silent. All of the younger children were asleep in front of the television in the family room, curled up on the lawn furniture or lying on beach towels spread out by the pool. Even the cicada's had packed it in for the night. A slight breeze had come in from the west and the air had turned quite comfortable. The sky was as clear as I had ever seen, ablaze with millions of stars. But for those of us sitting around the patio table, there were only seven stars that interested us. And the elegant, elderly lady who was the center of our attention had all the answers to the mysteries of each one.

"On New Years Eve, those of us who remained gathered at Pa's on Highland Street," she continued, "and we all sat together and wrote letters to each of the boys. We had no way of knowing if they would ever get them. But it was the only way we could convey how we felt, how much we loved and missed them. Pa was in no condition to write, but he signed his name to each of the letters as we finished them. It took us hours, but it was perhaps the most joyous thing we did together during the entire war. Writing the letters made us feel like a family again. At midnight, Ray surprised us with a bottle of champagne and offered a toast to his brothers and brother-in-law. I remember it was quite moving."

Ray's son Henry laughed at the thought.

"My Dad always had the reputation of being a tough guy. Quick with his fists."

"Yah," his older brother Gary chuckled. "Hard to envision him being so eloquent. God bless him. Hitler was lucky he never met Ray Hughes."

295

"I'll say," Ka agreed. "The next day, Pa took down the banner with four stars that had hung in the front window for so long and replaced it with a new one he'd had made. This one had seven stars on it. Can you believe it? Seven blue stars.

"To this day I can see it hanging in the window, " she said, "so big now it was nearly a tapestry. But what I remember most was my father staring at it for hours at a time.

"In his mind, those blue stars somehow connected him to his boys. And I swear, secretly he believed if he gazed at it long and hard enough, he could wish them home safely."

She stopped and looked up at the sky again, remembering.

"I tell you, there were a good many nights when Bobbie, Beverly and I would join him in the living room, staring at the banner, each of us praying that his dream would come true."

Twenty-Eight

~~~ ❧ ~~~

January 1945
Bastogne, Belgium

It was the cold that was so exhausting.

Not the gnawing hunger, the constant rain of mortar shells from an enemy hidden just hundreds of yards away, it wasn't even the snow. The goddamned snow that just wouldn't stop. No. It was the absolute, bone-chilling cold that penetrated every joint in a man's body, made it impossible for him to sleep, robbed him of his energy and worst of all, his will to fight on.

The 101st Airborne, just young boys who had bravely fought their way from the skies over St. Marie Eglais, Fourcarville, Sainte-Marie-du-Mont, Colleville-sur-Mer and through hundreds of towns and villages on

297

the Cherbourg Peninsula of France, had suffered grievous casualties in the last eight days. And now they were nearly done in, overrun by a desperate German counter-attack in the Ardennes Forest in Belgium that had begun ten days earlier on December 16. It was the enemies list ditch effort to stop the Allied advance toward Berlin.

As John Hughes and his fellow paratroopers shivered in their foxholes on the day after Christmas, the only protection they had from the freezing cold and endless mortar, rocket, artillery and sniper fire, most of them thought their time had come.

They were literally freezing to death without winter uniforms in sub-zero temperatures, snow fell constantly, there was little food and the field hospital had been captured so there was scarce medical help. Perhaps most threatening was that the men who were able to fight on were down to their last several rounds of ammunition. The Currahee's were nearly beaten, and they were the Allies last chance to hold the Germans back, all that separated the enemy from launching a major assault on the Third Army led by General George Patton that was racing to save them. Would Patton arrive in time? Or would he find the 506thth wiped out and his own assault force facing the mother of all ambushes?

As he unconsciously felt for the empty flask in his jacket pocket again, hoping for a touch of the magic elixir that would warm his body and soul one more time, he was certain he knew the answer.

He wasn't going home.

Ever.

When the Germans had launched the major offensive at dawn on December 16, 1945, the 101st Airborne, including the 506th Parachute Regiment, was asleep in only the second week of its long overdue relief from combat. But after only a short rest and refitting at Camp Mourmelon in France, the 101st Airborne was once again called upon to lead the charge as it had done in so many pivotal battles before. But this would be a defensive mission for which the 101st was woefully unprepared. Its battalions were in urgent need of replacements, winter clothing for the harsh winter and precious provisions, including food, medical supplies and ammunition.

Nonetheless, the remaining 12,000 men of the 101st were squeezed into trucks and rushed overnight to the strategic town of Bastogne, situated on a ridge in the province of Luxembourg in the Ardennes. Bastogne was the key to the German success because of its vitally important crossroads. The confrontation soon became known as the "Battle of the Bulge."

A circular perimeter of defense was established around the town of Bastogne immediately, but the 101st's inadequate manpower left it with innumerable soft spots that were often tested by the Germans. By the 19th of December, the entire 101st Airborne, including Hughes' 506th PR was surrounded by enemy troops and isolated on the outskirts of Bastogne in the Ardennes forest.

The Germans wasted no time in launching the first of countless savage attacks on the Americans, inflicting heavy casualties on the undermanned, outgunned division. As many as 15 different German divisions, including four crack armored units attacked repeatedly. Within a week, the 101st had suffered more than 1,700 wounded, nearly 350 killed in action and 516 were missing. The ranks of the division were so depleted it was almost incapable of defending the Bastogne ridge. Allied efforts to resupply the troops with critical provisions by airdrops were unsuccessful because of the brutal weather. Most of the provisions inadvertently landed in German hands.

"Merry Christmas, Al. What I wouldn't give for a drink," Hughes said to his buddy Al Lipton with whom he shared a foxhole they had dug in the Bois Jacques Woods outside Bastogne. The sun was just rising and they had to keep a constant vigil for the enemy. The trees in the Ardennes were planted in rows, so visibility was good in one direction but a blank wall of trees hid the other. He raised his rifle and peered over the edge of the snow encrusted dirt hole that had become their home.

"Christmas was yesterday," Lipton responded through chattering teeth, "but..."

He never finished the thought.

As the last word fell off his frozen lips, a sharp crack rang out in the woods less than a hundred yards ahead. Nearly simultaneously, Lipton's helmet flew off and his body slumped to the bottom of the dugout.

"Al?" Hughes screamed as he scanned the woods for the sniper. "Where are you, bastard," he cussed finding no sign of the lone shooter as he scanned the woods. He dropped his rifle and turned to Lipton. Only the makeshift scarf he had wound tightly around his mouth muffled his scream. A bullet had pierced his friend's forehead, just below his helmet. Lipton's eyes were open but unseeing. Blood trickled from the perfect circle of the entrance wound but was pouring out the back of his head.

"Medic!" Hughes screamed for help while he held his Lipton in his arms. "Medic? Medic!" His frantic voice echoed through the forest. Hughes heard the sound of boots racing toward them and a man dove into the foxhole beside him. It was the only medic left in the 506th, Theo Morton.

"Let me have him, John," Morton yelled. "Give me the morphine you have in your first aid kit," he ordered. Each man's personal morphine issue was all that was left in the unit. Hughes dug for it in his jacket, wrestling the case out with frozen fingers. Morton suddenly raised a hand, stopping him.

"Never mind, John. He's gone. It was instant," the young medic said, hopelessly. "There's nothing to be done. I'm sorry."

"Fuck, no!" Hughes hollered back at him, grabbing Lipton by the shoulders and shaking him.

"Wake up, Al, wake up, dammit!" he ordered his friend. "Jesus Christ, please wake up," he sobbed.

"He's gone John..." Morton said, putting a hand on Hughes' shoulder. "Not your fault..."

John Hughes fell back heavily into the snow pack lining the foxhole. He had a momentary urge to put the end of his rifle in his mouth and use one of his last rounds on himself. He buried his face in his filthy hands, shaking off the nightmare. Morton covered Lipton's body with a tarp.

"I gotta go, John. We got more wounded. Hold it together, man." He leapt over the edge of the foxhole and was gone to the next hopeless situation.

For more than an hour, Hughes burrowed against the body of his friend for warmth. He didn't think he could make it through another night, especially without his buddy to help him. Suddenly he remembered Lipton's backpack. He knew there was a bottle of French cognac hidden inside, a present for his father back home that he had bought in Mourmelon before pulling out for Bastogne.

301

Frantically, Hughes ripped open the backpack and found the bottle. His hands were so frozen he could not pull out the cork with his fingers and had to use his teeth. His cracked and torn lips bloodied from the effort, but finally he raised the bottle to his mouth and drank, deeply. His throat burned as the copper colored liquor trickled down his throat. Tears came to his eyes as his mind went silent, his only focus being to drain the bottle.

He drank until it was finished. Somewhere nearby, shots rang out. It made no difference, he thought, as he faded into sleep, the numbing effect of the alcohol hitting him quickly on an empty stomach. The falling snow quickly covering his exposed face.

He had no idea how long he had been unconscious when John Hughes felt strong hands pulling him out of the foxhole and placing him on a stretcher. He passed out again and awoke hours later in a Third Army field hospital several miles back from the front. The 101st had held off the Germans long enough for Patton's forces to reach them.

Like the thousands of other 101st Airborne survivors who were rescued from the Ardennes forest, after a hot meal he was wrapped in blankets inside an insulated tent and allowed to sleep for several days. Then he was resupplied, issued warm clothing and sent back out with his unit with orders to resume the battle.

Hughes, and most of the men he served with, were shadows of the soldiers they had been just weeks before. But with victory now in sight, they drew on their incredible reservoir of courage and stamina and followed orders.

While Patton's Third Army continued to steamroll toward Berlin, the 506th was ordered to attack north and recapture the villages of Recogne, the Bois des Corbeaux and Foy. Each had been lost to the Germans while the 101st Airborne was encircled in Bastogne. While terrified villagers hid in cellars of their bombed out homes and shops, American troops fought house by house against stubborn resistance, emptying one building at a time.

After an area was cleared of the enemy, John Hughes was assigned with several other members of the 506th's Fox Company to search for weapons left behind. It gave him the perfect opportunity to pilfer homes and stores of wine and alcohol, the fuel that was keeping him going.

On January 15th, the 101st Airborne launched an attempt to recover the town of Noville, a bitter mission for the exhausted men and especially the 506th. The occupation of Noville had been bloodily contested in the opening rounds of the Battle of the Bulge and American forces had finally taken the town at a heavy price. The Germans had retaken it shortly after when the 101st had become bottlenecked in Bastogne. The paratroopers wanted to finish the job, once and for all.

The 506th's Easy, Fox and Dog companies marched on Noville the day after taking Foy. Men with hair-triggered instincts spread out cautiously through the bombed out rubble of what had once been a beautiful, historic Belgian landmark. The Allied and German bombing of the town a month earlier had virtually destroyed it. There would be nothing left after this engagement.

John Hughes crouched low inside the shell of a church in the main village square of Noville, scanning the surrounding area from its blown out stain glass windows for snipers or hidden armored vehicles.

"There... my 11," Hughes whispered, pointing to the shadow of a man in a third floor window roughly 50 yards away. The sniper had a clear shot at the group huddled in the church. Hughes wondered why the rifleman hadn't already targeted them. He reached inside his jacket pocket for the flask he had taken from his Lipton and took a long pull. The liquor had a bite going down but warmth filled his belly. A second later, he felt the numbing sensation that always followed. It felt good in the frigid cold. But what was more gratifying was the instant shot of courage that flowed through his veins. He took action without a second thought.

"Cover me," he said to the three men with him in the church as he ran boldly out into the street. The sniper fired once, missing the sprinting, weaving Hughes, then pulled back into his hiding place. He was a smart one, John Hughes thought as he threw himself over a pile of broken bricks on the other side of the street for cover. A second shot would have given away the shooter's location. Covering fire rang out from the church as the 506th reacted but only succeeded in doing more damage to the destroyed building.

Hughes quickly got to his feet and advanced toward the sniper, hugging storefronts and ducking below piles of shattered wood and broken bricks and mortar. He made his way to the building in which he had seen the sniper, squeezed through a partially blocked door and dropped to his knees. Raising his rifle he quickly scanned the room that appeared to be the remains of some sort of market. A few canned goods and bottles of wine were all that remained on the shelves. He reached for the flask again, calming his nerves then slowly crept to a staircase he spied at the back of the shop. He stopped and listened. Small arms fire from the 506th continued to hit the upper floor of the building. He climbed to the second floor and stopped at a window, signaling to the Americans to ceasefire by slashing his

304

fingers across his throat. Then he resumed climbing, slowly, one step at a time.

The stairs creaked slightly as he moved up, and he hesitated at each step, listening. Suddenly, there was a rush of heavy footsteps and the German appeared at the top of the staircase, his rifle aimed directly at the defenseless Hughes. He fired but the bullet went wide, missing his target by inches. Broken plaster blew out of the wall. The American's return shot was on target and the enemy fell forward down the stairs, brushing Hughes as he fell with a thud to the second floor landing.

He walked slowly back down the stairs, keeping his weapon trained on the German and thought about shooting him again. Something held him back. Instead, he reached down and picked up the German's rifle and holstered Lugar, throwing them both out the window at which he had signaled the 506th a few minutes earlier. Then he exposed himself at the window and a cheer went up from inside the church.

When the members of his platoon arrived at the church a few minutes later, Hughes was sitting on the first floor with two bottles of wine. One had already been drained, more than half of the other was gone. He raised the bottle in mock salute to his buddies and then put it to his lips and finished it off.

"Hughes, you are one crazy bastard," someone said.

"Yah," he replied. "Should have saved the second bottle for later. Let's see if there's any more."

That night, the 506th was transferred to Haguenau in France to retake the city from the Germans. The vicious, house-to-house fighting of which the unit had become accustomed continued until February 23, when the paratroopers were finally pulled off the line for rest.

The fire in John Hughes' soul was nearly cold by then and his dependence on drink was all that kept him going. Only once did he think of writing home, but quickly dismissed the idea. He had become a complete fatalist and was certain he would not see the end of the war. The thought of writing to his family was so painful he could not bear to even attempt it. Instead, he kept himself plied with whatever liquor he could find and stumbled from one combat encounter to the next, always waiting for the bullet with his name engraved on it.

*   *   *

Less than ten days after being pulled off the line at Langerwehe-Merode in Belgium for rest and resupply, the *Big Red One* was rousted back into action with the surprise German offensive at Bastogne on December 16. Second Lieutenant Jim Hughes had just finished writing a letter home when the news came.

December 16, 1944

Dear Gang,

Well, we did our best, but it seems it wasn't quite enough to get us home by Christmas. I'm still in a rest camp in Belgium miles from the front and hopefully will be here for some time. The Big Red One is one tired fighting machine.

I know you're all disappointed, but don't think for a moment the tempo of the war has changed. We've got the Germans backpedaling home and fully intend to chase the bastards until they crawl back into their hole in Berlin. I promise you, next Christmas will be different. I'm really looking forward to a helluva big turkey, Ka, so be prepared.

I haven't heard from John yet, have you? I check with the Red Cross here whenever possible and he is still listed as active with the 101st Airborne, 506th Parachute Regiment who

306

are currently off line at Camp Mourmelon in France. I'll keep trying. I know in my heart there's an explanation for his silence and that he's ok.

Keep the home fires burning gang, and I'll see you soon.

Love you with all my heart and Merry Christmas,
Bull

Jim Hughes hung his head in despair after finishing the letter. He wasn't so sure about his brother John's situation. Sometimes it took a while before men were added to the missing in action list. It just made no sense that his little brother would stop communicating unless he was wounded or worse.

As well, Jim was keenly aware that despite the fact that the war in Europe would probably be over soon, they had a ways to go to finish off the Germans. And then there was the 800-pound gorilla in the room that no one wanted to talk about: Japan. He was certain the *Big Red One* and most American units would be shipped to the Pacific war soon after they finished their business in Europe. And from everything he heard, the fighting was going a lot slower against the Japanese than the government was letting on. He laughed to himself about Christmas, knowing the truth. It might be years before he saw Highland Street again.

If ever.

An hour after he posted the letter, word came that the entire 1st Infantry Division was being shipped to the Ardennes. The Germans had counterattacked and launched a major offensive designed to split the Allied forces from advancing towards their homeland and to seize the port of Antwerp, a strategic supply depot for the Americans and British. Division officers were briefed that they would pull out in two hours and would be

307

trucked to Butgenbach — a small village in the province
of Leige. Situated on the north shoulder of the
Ardennes, it was a weak point in the American lines that
the Germans would most probably attempt to ram
through.

Driving all night in trucks jam-packed with still
tired, shivering troops, the *Big Red One* arrived just
before 0900 hours. The men in Hughes platoon couldn't
help but grouse about their abbreviated relief from
combat during the long, cold drive in sub-zero
temperatures.

"Pipe down," Hughes said reassuringly. "We're
almost there. Let's get this job done and go home."

Within the hour, hundreds of German Tiger
tanks were wreaking havoc with the American
infantryman who had quickly dug in outside the village
to prevent the German advance. The 60-ton enemy tanks
emerged from fog and a wind driven snowstorm that
enshrouded the ridge and limited visibility. But their
blazing machine guns left no question that they had
arrived.

"Bazookas!" Hughes called to his men, who
were, as usual, on the front line. "Aim for the tracks and
then be ready for the crews to bail out."

German infantry appeared behind the tanks
oblivious to the waiting Americans. They were instantly
dropped by machine gun and rifle fire by the entrenched
1st Infantry. The German foot soldiers never did break
through the American lines but several tanks did.
Hughes and his men fell back in pursuit. The snow-
covered battlefield was littered with burning tanks and
glistened red with blood from the broken bodies of both
armies.

Grabbing a bazooka, Hughes aimed at the rear of
one of the tanks that had gotten through and fired. He

scored a direct hit on the undercarriage of the mammoth tank, but it continued on for a few yards. Suddenly, it careened off the road, driving over and crushing an abandoned jeep before crashing into the burned out hulk of another Tiger.

Immediately, smoke billowed from the gun ports of the wrecked Tiger and the hatch flew open. Hughes' men picked off the crew as they emerged, the last two Germans writhing in agony from the flames that enveloped them before being shot.

Hughes' platoon gave chase to another Tiger that had broached the line and was racing unchallenged through the main road of Butgenbach. The German crew must have spotted them in pursuit because the tank abruptly stopped and swung its gun turret 180 degrees, aiming directly at the pursuing Americans.

"Get down!" Hughes ordered as the tank unleashed the first of several 88mm cannon shells at them. The first whizzed by Hughes' head, exploding less then 25 yards away from where he crouched. The concussion threw him to the ground and knocked him unconscious. The tank gunner managed to fire off two more rounds before one of the infantrymen climbed aboard and pushed a thermite grenade into the turret. The ensuing explosion and fire turned the otherwise invincible mechanical beast into a smoking hulk. Two of the German crew died instantly. Two others escaped the tank but with severe burns.

Hughes awoke several hours later in a field hospital a couple of miles from the battle where he been evacuated after the close call with the German artillery shell. He had a headache and probably a concussion but otherwise was still fit for duty. He donned his helmet, grabbed his rifle and left without speaking to anyone. Outside, he hitched a ride from a passing jeep that slowly wound its way back to Butgenbach on roads nearly impassable with wreckage.

Jim Hughes shook his head in disgust at the near complete destruction of the village, a simple place like his own hometown where people had once lived in peace. He had seen the same sad outcome dozens of times since going to war. For a moment he felt the pang of guilt. The 1st Infantry Division had contributed to the destruction. "Was there an alternative?" he asked silently. He thought not. The Allied Powers were executing the only strategy that could possibly reduce Hitler's grandiose plans for the Third Reich to ashes: the same blunt, merciless force with which Hitler had overrun Europe. If the enemy so much as burped, the American response with firepower was shockingly fast and overwhelming. The German military was getting a taste of its own, much feared "Blitzkrieg" strategy that had overwhelmed Poland and France in the early days of the war and nearly defeated England. Soon the social, political and economic doctrines of Nazism would be reduced to ashes. Unfortunately, so would most of Germany and much of continental Europe. The price of victory was simply staggering, especially the human toll.

He sighed, turning his thoughts back to the job that wasn't finished yet. His men had done good work today and survived against stacked odds. The American line had held. They were another mile closer to Berlin.

For the next month, the *Big Red One* turned back innumerable counterattacks by the desperate Germans. The brutal weather made the fighting that much worse, but Allied air support and a steady stream of air drops kept the 1st Infantry well provisioned, unlike the 101st Airborne on the other side of the Ardennes bulge. Jim Hughes had no idea his younger brother was so close and in a desperate fight for survival.

On January 15th, simultaneous to the breakout of the 101st Airborne from Bastogne and their subsequent victories in Foy and Noville, the 1st Infantry Division pulled out of Butgenbach and attacked and overran the Siegfried Line once more. Then they raced to occupy the Remagen Bridge over the Rhine River — the long sought path into the heart of Germany, and victory. On March 16, the exhausted but inspired 1st Infantry broke out of the bridgehead and then assisted in the Ruhr Pocket encirclement where over 400,000 German soldiers surrendered. Then the men of the *Big Red One* lit out with fire in their eyes to attack one of the final enemy strongholds, the city of Paderborn.

It was April 1 — Easter Sunday — when the *Big Red One* pulled up outside of Paderborn, a city north of the Rhine that traced its ancient roots to the first century and Charlemagne. Although the division was heavily depleted and desperate for replacements after taking heavy losses over the last month, it was bristling with new weapons and artillery, ammunition, rations and medical supplies. The men were tired but well fed and were driven by the prospect of ending the war. After completely defeating the Germans at the Ruhr Pocket, it was only a matter of days before the war in Europe could be won.

Coming off a brief rest in Haguena, the 101st Airborne also participated in the Ruhr Pocket encirclement and then received new orders: support the 3rd Armored Division and the 1st Infantry Division in retaking the heavily fortified city of Paderborn. The 506th Parachute Regiment pulled in alongside the *Big Red One* just hours before the attack was launched. The 3rd Armored Division was already waiting and raring to go.

Unaware of the arrival of the 101st Airborne, Jim Hughes sat quietly at a hastily arranged briefing for 1st

Infantry officers, skeptical of what he was hearing. The plan to take Paderborn depended heavily on the division's ability to surround the city from its south, southwestern and southeastern gates and slowly crush the remaining German resistance with sheer firepower. It wasn't having enough guns that worried him. It was the lack of manpower.

"And now with the support of the 101st Airborne, we should be able to throw a giant lasso over Paderborn and pull it tight," said Major General Clift Andrus, commanding officer of the *Big Red One*.

Hughes blinked, startled by what he thought he had heard. Unthinking, he jumped to his feet.

"Sir, does that include the 506th Parachute Regiment?" he interrupted. Nothing else in the world mattered to Jim Hughes at that moment except the next words Andrus would speak.

The General restrained himself from reacting to the unusual outburst. Jim Hughes was one of the finest men in the division, a proven leader and one tough soldier.

"Why yes, 2nd Lieutenant, it would include the 506th... some tough SOB's. Glad to have have 'em with us," he answered and expected Hughes to respond. But the officer simply replied, "Thank you, sir, thank you," and sat back down, a huge grin on his face. Andrus stared curiously at him, but went on with the briefing.

"As I way saying..." the general continued, but Jim Hughes struggled to concentrate. In his mind he rattled off the mail address he knew by heart that he used when he wrote to his brother John: D Company, 2nd Battalion, 506th Parachute Regiment.

It was his brother's unit that had joined them outside of Paderborn. No one in the family had heard from him since his last letter home from England where

312

he was recuperating from being wounded. That was last July. For nine months letters from his brother and sisters, including his own, had gone unanswered. It was as if his younger brother has just disappeared. Yet the Red Cross continued to insist he was active with the 506th. One way or another, he was about to find out. There was not enough time to search for him before the assault began. That meant he had to survive one more assault, take one more city before he could find his brother. It was all the motivation he needed.

"I don't know about you guys," Jim Hughes said to his platoon just before the assault, "but I'm damn sick and tired of carrying this rifle and eating out of a tin can. It's time to go home, boys. Let's turn on the lights in Paderborn again. We'll be that much closer to turning them off in Berlin."

There was a spontaneous cheer among the anxious young men who'd seen more than their fare share of battle. Only a handful of the unit with which he had fought in North Africa was still among them. So many dead, so many wounded, he thought. He prayed he'd have no more letters to write when this was over.

"So keep your head down and follow me," he barked. "Got it?"

"Yes, sir," they growled back to the man they'd all grown to respect.

"Then let's hit it," ordered 2nd Lieutenant "Bull" Hughes.

At the first light of dawn, the *Big Red One*, the 101st Infantry and the 3rd Armored Division pounced on Paderborn with a fury and urgency nearly unparalleled in the European war campaign. It wasn't because the city was that strategically important or victory that critical. It was simply that the American soldiers had tired of war and blood and just wanted to go home. No army in

313

history would have stood a chance against them that day.

It was over within 24 hours. The Americans threw everything they had and a little more at the enemy in an effort to take the city quickly. The German resistance was remarkably determined given the state of the war, but more than 200 American tanks, 30,000 men, flamethrowers, and non-stop artillery and rocket fire combined to pulverize the enemy into surrender. When it was over, more than 85 percent of the ancient city lay in ruins, only the skeletons of centuries old buildings left standing.

Jim Hughes wasted no time celebrating the victory. He knew full well that the *Big Red One* was too valuable to sit around Paderborn for long and would be getting orders to move out again quickly. Within an hour of debriefing his platoon, he was standing in front of Major General Andrus with a request.

"You say you haven't heard from him in nine months?" Andrus repeated, incredulous.

"And you're sure he's alive?"

"The Red Cross insists he is, sir and my family has had no message from the War Department to inform us otherwise," Hughes answered. "I know he's out there."

Andrus looked over Bull Hughes. He'd been fighting since North Africa and never even asked for so much as a pass.

"Then what the hell are you waiting for, soldier?" he said as he scribbled a note and signed it.

"Here, this will get you by any SOB who thinks he's big enough to challenge Bull Hughes on a mission and permission to take a jeep," Andrus said.

He handed the note to the anxious officer.

314

"Sir, thank you sir," Hughes replied and saluted the General.

Andrus stood.

"No, Bull, thank you, and good luck." He snapped off his own crisp salute to Hughes. "You've got 48 hours until we pull out of here. We're going to be crossing the Weser River into Czechoslovakia. Be here. Got it?"

"Wouldn't miss it, sir, " Hughes promised and hurried out of the command post.

He quickly found a jeep and began winding his way through the outskirts of the ruins of Paderborn, keeping a sharp eye out for snipers hidden in the rubble. He knew the 506th had driven through the southwestern gate of the city but the drive was slow. The roads were almost impassable with wreckage and debris. Finally he drove up to a checkpoint manned by several paratroopers who had their rifles aimed at his head as he brought the jeep to a halt. Tensions were running high. Hughes fished the note Andrus had given him out of his jacket pocket.

"I'm looking for the 506th, D Company, Second Battalion," he told the solder barring his entrance.

The soldier eyed the gold bars on Hughes uniform and answered with respect for his rank.

"Can't say for sure where you'll find D Company, sir, but ask ahead and I'm sure they can point the way," the paratrooper replied.

"Would you know a John Hughes, private?" Jim asked.

"Can't say that I do sir, but it's a big outfit."

He drove the jeep slowly through the thousands of troops of the 101st Airborne who were mostly smoking, eating or cleaning their weapons. They were a sorry looking bunch, tired and dirty yet too wired to

315

sleep. He knew the signs of men who'd been fighting a long time. These guys were quiet and didn't look fondly on strangers. They looked him over with suspicion. His own men would react the same way. He stopped the jeep by a group of men who were standing around a kerosene drum, warming themselves by a fire. It was almost spring but the winter cold was in no hurry to give way to warmer days.

"Hey, fellas... anyone know where I can find D Company... I'm looking for a guy named John Hughes," he asked. "He's my brother."

A couple of them looked up at the mention of "brother." There was a moment of silence and then someone said, "This is Easy Company. I don't know him but you can check just over there," he said pointing, then looked away.

"I think you'll find what's left of D Company," said. "Good luck."

"Thanks," Hughes said, somewhat unnerved by the reply. He stepped out of the jeep figuring he'd draw less attention if he were on foot. As he walked in the general direction of where D Company was supposed to be he casually asked about his brother. The answer was "no" each time. He went on, undeterred.

Finally, he came upon another group of paratroopers gathered around a fire and asked again.

"Yah, sure," a lanky young man with a south Boston accent responded. "This is D Company. I just saw John right down what's left of that street, Lieutenant. Can't miss him. He's the one sitting on the fountain. Got a couple of bottles of wine or something for company. He don't like to talk much these days."

Jim Hughes' heart began to pound. He nodded his head in thanks for the information and set off toward a stone village fountain he saw in the distance. He could

316

just barely make out the image of a man sitting at the base of it. He quickened his pace, then broke into a run toward the lone soldier, unable to wait any longer. He stopped just a few feet in front of him.

He stared at the soldier who was drinking from a bottle of cognac with one hand and holding a Colt 45 pistol aimed at Jim's head in the other.

Neither said a word. The wisp of a man sitting with his legs splayed and his back to the fountain startled Jim Hughes, he looked that beaten. He couldn't be sure if the emaciated, sunken-eyed little guy who looked much older than he should was his brother.

"Hey buddy, I'm looking for John Hughes," he said, hesitatingly.

There was no response while the soldier took another swig from the bottle.

"Who wants to know," he said, cocking the hammer on the 45. The words came out as a snarl.

"Easy little guy. I'm his big brother, Bull," he said with hope.

"'Bull?' That's a helluva name," he said, dead serious. "Where you from, big fella?"

"Wethersfield. Highland Street."

"That so…"

He said no more but took his time studying the big man in front of him and took another hit from the bottle. Then his eyes softened and a broad grin broke through his chapped lips.

"I'm John Hughes, ya big lunk," he said, his voice cracking. "Where ya been hiding, big brother?"

*   *   *

317

April 3, 1945

Dear Gang,

I hope you received my telegram from the Red Cross and can breath a little easier now. Yes, I found brother John and he is alive. He's pretty worn out, to be honest and I got him into a field hospital for treatment. But the good news is that he is safe and still with us.

I guess it was fate that finally connected the two of us. The 1ˢᵗ Army, 3ʳᵈ Armored Division and the 101st Airborne Division, of which John is a member of its 506ᵗʰ Parachute Regiment all joined to assault a city called Paderborn north of the Rhine on Easter Sunday. Suffice it to say that we annihilated what's left of the German Army and took the city within 24 hours. I went looking for John immediately after. It took some searching, but sure enough, my instincts were right.

I spied this little guy sitting under a stone fountain in the village from about a half-mile away, and Christ when I got closer to him, I found a pitiful wreck of a man. The poor bastard was just so beat up, a cut over his right eye oozing blood and you couldn't even tell the color of his skin from the dirt and grime dug into his face. I'd swear if I had breathed hard on the guy it would have knocked him over. I honest to God didn't know it was John. But I underestimated him.

He was drinking from a big bottle of schnapps and was wasting no time in sucking it dry, but even so, I heard him chamber a round into his service revolver as I approached with the ease that comes when a man has used it a helluva lot of times. And I could tell he wasn't afraid to put a couple in my head if he didn't think my intentions were good. I mean it was pretty clear that the guy had been fighting for his life for a long time. But all I wanted to do was ask him a question.

I knew John's unit had been in the thick of the fighting since even before the Normandy invasion, and I wasn't even sure he was still alive. But I figured if I spotted him I'd sure as hell recognize my own brother right off the bat. John's always

318

had the whitest teeth and the clearest eyes of any of us and he was even a bit dapper with the slickum in his hair and all.

I finally found his unit and asked some guys about him and right away they pointed off in the distance. My heart about jumped because they knew him and that meant that he was alive, son of a bitch. But as I got closer all I saw was this really miserable, wretched looking guy all beat to shit sitting under this fountain. Now you know I'm no shrinking violet myself so I walked right up to the guy and just asked, 'Hey Mac, you know where I can find John Hughes?'

"Well, this feller looks up at me and stares me right down even though I probably had 12 inches and a full 50 pounds on him. I'll be damned if he didn't say, 'Who wants to know,' all pissed off like, so it came out as a growl. Christ, I'll never forget that moment, or the feeling that came over me when he finally dropped the tough guy act and showed me his pearly white teeth in a big smile and said, 'I'm John Hughes, ya big lunk.' And by God it was him, my little brother John, and I set to bawling and just reached down and yanked him to his feet and hugged him till I damn near broke his back. Christ, I'll never forget the feeling, but I could barely tell it was him, he was so worn out and broken down and drunk. I couldn't stop hugging him.

I told him how worried everyone was and that set him off. He must have cried for an hour. Now, I'll tell you that I've seen some things these past few years that I'll never forget. But it's pretty clear to me that John has been to the gates of hell and back. His mind is a mess.

He told me he couldn't bear to write to you all or even to read your letters because he was sure that he was not going to make it, that he would never come home alive. He's just been a machine these last nine months, fighting everyday without a soul or any hope. There is no doubt in my mind that he is suffering from severe shell shock.

I spent hours with him by that fountain in Paderborn trying to help him understand that he was going to make it, and that we were going to go home. Anything that would give him hope for the future. We drank and talked all night. I got him to thinking about what could be if we all make it home alive. I told him about the GI Bill that Roosevelt signed last fall that could give all of us who were in the war a chance to start over and to forget the stuff we've seen. That got him excited. He actually said, 'Maybe we could start a business together.'

I don't know if it did any good, gang, but at least brother John knows we're all there for him. Write some letters to him, please, he promised to write to you real soon.

Ya know, John's even got me thinking about the future. We just have to finish this thing here and then beat the crap out of the Japs.

I have to go now, my unit is pulling out again. We're almost to Berlin. Pray for us.

I love you all and if it's God's will maybe we'll have Easter Dinner together next year.

Love,

Bull

P.S. Hey Pa, I remember there was a piece of property for sale at the corner of Jordan Lane and Silas Deane when I left home. Wonder if you could see if it's still available. I was thinking it would be a great place to build a garage, maybe where a bunch of brothers could build a business…

Twenty-Nine

~~~ ❧ ~~~

"When we got the Red Cross telegram from Jim on April 3rd telling us he had found John alive, I think the family was more excited than the day Germany finally surrendered," Ka said. "I mean, on VE day, May 8, 1945, people were literally dancing in the streets in New York. But when that telegram came to us a month earlier, we rolled up the rug in Pa's living room on Highland Street and danced all night. My God... I remember even Pa was doing a jig. What a night!"

Her eyes were glistening as she remembered the joy of Jim's telegram. It was a simple message that breathed new life and hope into the family.

"All it said was, 'Have found John. Safe,'" she recalled, closing her eyes and remembering the single most important scrap of paper she had probably ever held in her hands.

"I mean, just imagine if you can how important those four words were to us. And it was signed by Jim after some of the heaviest fighting of the war. So we knew they were both safe and the conflict in Europe was almost over.

"I tell you, after nine months of holding our breath, it was like getting a message from Heaven. "

"And that's why your favorite 'holiday' is 'The Telegram Day," Jack said. "April 3rd." The pieces fit. She smiled at his understanding.

I could appreciate just from watching how animated she became in telling us about the telegram how much relief they all must have felt when Jim's news arrived. But the look of elation just as quickly disappeared when she told us about her older brother's detailed letter.

"But a few weeks later, just before the war officially ended, Jim's letter arrived explaining how he had found his brother. I think I cried for a week after reading it. Bobbie, Beverly and I went to the Red Cross and to the Institute of the Living in Hartford to find out all we could about what Jim called "shell shock" and it was very depressing to know our brother had been so affected by what he had experienced in the war.

"You see, John had always been the gentlest of souls, probably the last man on earth you could imagine holding a gun. The war did terrible things to him that he would struggle with for many years to come. But just like Jim getting him to a field hospital before he had to move on again, we all took care of John, however he needed us for the rest of his life."

She dabbed at her eyes. So did the rest of us.

"I never dreamt of spending all this time with you tonight telling this story. But I'm so glad that you gave this old woman the chance. Maybe it might help you understand why we were always so close."

Suddenly she reached for her pocketbook.

"You know how some people carry around something very special in their wallet or purse because it is so important to them? I guess for most people it's a photograph. But not me. Mine is a letter, one that we received from John a few days after we heard from Jim, which I saved. It was just a few words from my little brother, but they were so important to me that I've carried his letter with me ever since."

To our amazement, she took her wallet from the purse and reached into a small seam in the leather. Carefully, as if it was a scrap of cloth from the Shroud of Turin, she removed a piece of paper that had been folded hundreds of times. She gently unfolded it, so yellowed, worn and tattered it had holes in the corners.

She slid her glasses down to the end of her nose and moved the paper back and forth until the letters came into focus.

"I won't read it all, just the part that touched me so much," she said.

The world seemed to stop as she began to read.

April 10, 1945

Dear Gang,

I wish I could be there to tell you all face to face how sorry I am that I've hurt you with my silence. It may take me some time to understand why I could not write or even read your letters. In the meantime, I beg you to forgive me.

But most of all what I want to share with you is the one single moment, that few exquisite seconds when it finally came to me that it was really over, that I had survived and I

323

really might be going home, that I actually might live to see you all again.

It came in the time it took me to raise my head and look up from where I lay under a stone fountain, bloodied, exhausted, filthy and just drunk enough to kill the pain in my heart. It was in that instant, when I looked up to see those familiar big brown eyes and a huge ham-hock of a hand reaching down to yank me up and embrace me, that it hit me.

I wish you had been there to hear the "whoop!" of happiness that came out of my throat when I realized it was my big brother, Jim. I'd like to say that our tears together were sweet and filled with joy, but they weren't. They were salty and bitter, tasting of all we had been through but also full of relief that we were simply alive and together again. We were speechless, he and I, only able to hug and embrace and all Jim and I could do was jump up and down together in absolute relief. The guys in my unit must have thought I'd gone nuts. But I didn't care, I just didn't want to let him go. And when finally we were able to find words, we talked about what we might do if we really did survive the war, that we might find something to do with our lives, together, far from the terror and horrible noise that has become our world. I think the notion of all of us being together again is the only thing that is bringing back my sanity...

Silently and so carefully, Ka refolded her paper treasure and placed it back in her wallet.

"That was how John explained it too us... he was in such bad shape it's a wonder he was even able to write at all," Ka concluded.

No one said a word. I think we were all too stunned to speak, and I for one was on the verge of a major cry. Even 50 years after it all happened the story was hard to hear. I couldn't imagine having actually lived it.

But the crowd asked for more.

324

"After the war in Europe ended, did Jim, John and my father all come home?" my sister Kathy asked.

"No, the war in Europe may have ended, but not in the Pacific. The troops in Europe were held in place and began training for the Japanese invasion. The only boys who could come home were those who had enough 'points' based on time in the military, months overseas, battles... it was very complicated. Only Jim had enough to qualify to come home right away but he wouldn't have it. Not with John still in Europe and the Japanese war not ended. He was going to stay in until he thought the job was finished.

"So from the second week in May until September, when the Japanese finally surrendered, all our boys were stuck. But they were safe. Jim was in Czechoslovakia, John had been pulled back to France and Speck was still in Hawaii." She looked at me. "Your Dad was probably only days away from getting his orders to go to the Pacific when Truman ordered the second Atomic Bomb on Nagasaki and everything came to a halt. Peachy, Phil, Jiggs and Ed Ames were stuck on their bases waiting to be released.

"But it was over. They were all safe. There would be no Japan to worry about. A miracle had happened." She paused again, and raised her head to the evening sky once more. It was ablaze with stars on this clear, moonlit night.

"We still had seven Blue Stars hanging in our window," she said, a single sob finally escaping her.

"I remember they came home one by one, except for Jim and John who walked up the steps to Pa's house together. They looked so much older, especially John. As each of them came home, the rest of the family and our neighbors would all line up in front of the house and welcome them home. It was always a mass hug! We

325

never said very much; words just got in the way. All we wanted to do was touch them, hold on to them. It was all so amazing." She swallowed hard.

"When Speck finally came home — he was the last — he had Vera on his arm, and as usual she was crying. But if any girl ever deserved to cry it was Vera. Pa had the whole family over for dinner to celebrate. And afterwards, he assembled us all in the living room where we gathered in front of the picture window. Hanging there, for the entire world to see, was the Blue Star Banner that he had stared at for nearly four years, willing his boys to come home safely.

"Without saying a word, he took it down and gently kissed each one of the stars," she said. "Then with tears streaming down his face, he carried it to his bedroom."

There wasn't a dry eye in the house.

"He never shared it with anyone again."

Epilogue

~~~ ৩ ~~~

My beloved Aunt Ka finally succumbed to a stroke at age 90, several years after our fictitious Fourth of July family gathering where this story takes place. While much of the Hughes family history is reiterated on these pages, Ka took with her an immense treasure chest of memories that only a family of 13 children could fill. She had lived life to the fullest, and loved and buried two husbands, 8 brothers, three sisters and her revered father, leaving only her younger sister Beverly as a survivor.

Although she never had children of her own, she was adored by dozens of nieces and nephews and "Grands" who found her personality as endearing as I did.

When my father and his brothers returned to Wethersfield from their assignments in the war, they did indeed take advantage of the G.I. Bill, that small token of appreciation that Congress had approved in late 1944 that made such a difference for so many veterans. For some, it made possible a college education or a new home. For others, it meant the opportunity to own and operate a business. And that's exactly what the brothers Jim, John, Speck, Peachy, Phil and Jigg's Hughes did with the low interest $2,000 loan each of them could borrow from the government. With that combined $12,000, Hughes Brothers Garage was built and opened at the corner of Jordan Lane and the Silas Deane Highway in 1946 where it prospered for more than 50 years.

That garage was my father's world where he and Jim could forget about war, and where my Uncle John could take refuge from the demons that haunted him until the day he died.

To this day, when I drive by the spot where Hughes Brothers stood, my heart breaks a little at its demise. My father loved it so. The same goes for the house on Highland Street, that little farmhouse now occupied by my darling Aunt Joan, the widow of my late Uncle Jiggs. It's hard to fathom that 15 people lived in that small house with the big barn at one time, but out of it came a family who knew nothing but devotion and commitment to each other. I knew and loved them all as a child, and cherish my own memories of each of the Hughes of Wethersfield. While the family has dispersed as the years go on, on those rare occasions when we gather, there remains an invisible connection and pride in our heritage.

I will always be proud to be my father's daughter, and to share his love of life, family and his hometown.

Bobbie Hughes Granato
January 17, 2018

Acknowledgements

Every writer sees words as treasures, but I have come to see it a little differently: perhaps it is the treasures in one's life that inspire the words. If the latter is true, my cup runneth over.

And so, to my treasures...

I know that I would never have written a word without the support and encouragement of my wife, Bobbie. She has owned my heart for more than 50 years and continues to fill it with inspiration I could not find alone. But the icing on the cake is the family she made possible — one that defines the truest sense of the word. Our love is unconditional, unwavering in its care and loyalty and we never miss a birthday together. To my sons Jack and Jay, of who I am infinitely proud, you give me reason to swagger. But that's not your style, so I admire you as quietly as this old curmudgeon is capable. Andrea, my beautiful daughter-in-law thank you for giving me my pals Charlie and Jackson and my new granddaughter Ella who fill me with joy that is beyond words.

When I began writing so many years ago, I was blessed to have the encouragement of four old friends who have sadly passed on. To Bob, Cathy and Ag King and Eileen McCarthy, I will forever miss your love and friendship and I hope you are raising hell together wherever the party is. And to my great furry pal, Groban, I miss you, faithful friend. You'll be happy to know that Hogan is slowly figuring things out.

To my Grandfather, William J. McGrath, a man who epitomized love and humility, instilled in me a passion for history and filled my imagination, thank you for being there for me. The older I get the more I think of our time together. I hope to see you again.

Special thanks also to my friend Lisa Orchen, whose insights, logic and perspective have made me a stronger writer; to Joyce Rossignol, who taught me to love the art of writing and especially for sharing with me her personal recollections; to Julie Follett, who opened my eyes; and to my age old friends Bill and Debbie Bartlett, Genevieve Allen Hall, Steve Bazzano, Diane and Ray Lord, Steve Zerio, Carol Russo, Jan Smith, Gail Donahue, Carla Unwin, Michael Jordan-Reilly, Peter Larkin, Cheryl Zajack Barlow, Sharon Tomany Marone, Lisa Rivero Jankowski, Patty Curcio, Earl Flowers, Ann and Lou Hock, Keyne Reid and David Kelly, Captain (Ret.) Timothy J. Kelliher and Frank Droney of the Hartford Fire Department; Hartford Hospital Fire Marshall and Chief of the Rocky Hill CT Volunteer Fire Department Michael Garrahy; Michelle Royer of the Lucy Robbins Welles Library; and Sandy and Marshall Rulnick, my everlasting thanks for your friendship and endless support.

And finally, my condolences to the family of Beverly Hughes Kaminsky, the last child of Henry Thomas and Catherine Hughes who died just recently. My thanks to the many members of the Hughes family who provided me with an endless supply of anecdotes about their most amazing family.

F. Mark Granato, January 2018

About The Author

F. Mark Granato's long career as a writer, journalist, novelist and communication executive in a US based, multi-national Fortune 50 corporation has provided him with extensive international experience on nearly every continent. Today he is finally fulfilling a lifetime desire to write and especially enjoying the adventures of historical fiction. In addition to *Stars In Our Window*, he has published *This Boy*, a love story set in the tumultuous 1960's, *UNLEASHED*, the story of one man's fight against a ruthless corporation, *Out Of Reach: The Day Hartford Hospital Burned*, an historical fiction account of the tragic 1961 fire, the acclaimed novel *Finding David*, a love story chronicling the anguish of Vietnam era PTSD victims and their families, *The Barn Find*, chronicling the saga of a Connecticut family brought to its knees by tragedy that fights to find redemption, *Of Winds and Rage,* a suspense novel based on the 1938 Great New England Hurricane, *Beneath His Wings: The Plot to Murder Lindbergh,* and *Titanic: The Final Voyage*. Readers are encouraged to visit with Mark on his Facebook page at Author F. Mark Granato, e-mail at fmgranato@aol.com his website, Fmarkgranato.com.

331

Made in the USA
Middletown, DE
01 February 2018